Praise for Kia Abdullah

'Terrific and hugely thought-provoking'
Ian Rankin

'One of my ten best reads of the year. Easy five stars'
Lisa Jewell

'Intelligent, clever, poignant, sharp, and thought-provoking, right through to the perfect final line. Another sure hit for Kia Abdullah, I loved it and can't wait to see what comes next'
Andrea Mara, *Sunday Times* **bestselling author of** *All Her Fault*

'Brilliantly pacey and wonderfully written with a lovely big twist. Highly recommended'
Neil Lancaster, *Dead Man's Grave*

'A stunning, thought-provoking and morally challenging read . . . It was so vivid and will make readers question their own values and viewpoints all in the context of a world-class story'
Graham Bartlett, author of *Bad For Good*

'[A] searing, twisty thriller'
Woman's Own

'Gripping'
Woman's Weekly

'A deeply profound and thought-provoking read'
Heat

Also by Kia Abdullah

Take It Back
Next of Kin
Truth Be Told
Those People Next Door

Kia Abdullah is a bestselling author and travel writer. Her novels include *Take It Back*, a *Guardian* and *Telegraph* thriller of the year; *Truth Be Told*, which was shortlisted for the Diverse Book Awards; and *Next of Kin*, which won the Adult Fiction Diverse Book Award, and was longlisted for the CWA Gold Dagger Award. *Those People Next Door* was a Waterstones Thriller of the Month pick, and Kia has also been selected for *The Times* Crime Club.

Kia has written for *The New York Times*, the *Guardian*, the *Financial Times*, *The Times* and the BBC, and is the founder of Asian Booklist, a non-profit that advocates for diversity in publishing and helps readers discover new books by British Asian authors.

For more information about Kia and her writing, visit her website at kiaabdullah.com, or follow her at @KiaAbdullah on Instagram and X.

KIA ABDULLAH

WHAT HAPPENS IN THE DARK

ONE PLACE. MANY STORIES

HQ
An imprint of HarperCollins*Publishers* Ltd
1 London Bridge Street
London SE1 9GF

www.harpercollins.co.uk

HarperCollins*Publishers*
Macken House, 39/40 Mayor Street Upper
Dublin 1, D01 C9W8, Ireland

This edition 2025

1
First published in Great Britain by HQ,
an imprint of HarperCollins*Publishers* Ltd 2025

Copyright © Kia Abdullah 2025

Kia Abdullah asserts the moral right to be identified as the author of this work.
A catalogue record for this book is available from the British Library.

ISBN: HB: 978-0-00-857002-6
TPB: 978-0-00-857003-3

Set in Sabon LT Pro by HarperCollins*Publishers* India

This novel is entirely a work of fiction. The names, characters and incidents portrayed in it are the work of the author's imagination. Any resemblance to actual persons, living or dead, events or localities is entirely coincidental.

All rights reserved. No part of this publication may be reproduced, stored in a retrieval system, or transmitted, in any form or by any means, electronic, mechanical, photocopying, recording or otherwise, without the prior written permission of the publishers.

Without limiting the author's and publisher's exclusive rights, any unauthorised use of this publication to train generative artificial intelligence (AI) technologies is expressly prohibited. HarperCollins also exercise their rights under Article 4(3) of the Digital Single Market Directive 2019/790 and expressly reserve this publication from the text and data mining exception.

Printed and bound in the UK using 100%
Renewable Electricity by CPI Group (UK) Ltd

For more information visit: www.harpercollins.co.uk/green

*For my big sis, Jay,
who taught me to be tough*

PART I

Chapter 1

Safa Saleem hadn't come far in life, literally or otherwise. Her office above a shabby Ladbrokes was a mere five minutes from her childhood home and not much further from where she lived now. She tried not to think about this fact as she walked up Mile End Road, dodging the greasy remnants of someone's kebab from the night before. The wind was fierce and blew grit into her eyes so that anyone passing the other way might think that she was teary. They would be wrong, of course, because Safa Saleem did not cry.

She paused at a heavy black door next to the Ladbrokes and let herself into a narrow stairwell that smelled of stale beer and smoke. She took the stairs two by two, keen for the heat of other bodies, but it was barely any warmer inside the newsroom. The whole of East London, it seemed, was nervously watching their heating bill. She took off her coat, a long unstylish thing that crackled with static when she hung it. The air felt dry and electric, the sort that harboured colds and dried out her sinuses. She burrowed her face into her scarf and wrapped her hands around her flask of coffee. Her desk was near a draughty window that overlooked Mile End Road, the artery that connected grubby East London to better parts of the city. It was a far cry from her sleek former offices in St James's Park. *This* in comparison barely felt like a newsroom, the pace too sluggish and the space too sparse to indicate real import.

She sipped her coffee, black and scalding, and scrolled through an influx of emails. She deleted a dozen press releases that had nothing to do with her beat and then scanned anything loosely related: the reduction of fly-tipping in Tower Hamlets, the community graffiti clean-up. She reminded herself – as she did daily – that *these* were the crimes that affected normal people. It couldn't all be multi-national exposés and high-profile trials; sometimes, the small, incremental wins had the deepest impact. But, still, for an investigative reporter, being booted to the *East London Echo* was like a drawn-out death – slow and exhausting.

She cleared her inbox just as a new email landed. She felt a click of anxiety when she saw the name of the sender: Nick Rosenberg, general counsel at *The Clarion*, the UK's most respected broadsheet and Safa's former employer. It was a cease and desist letter – markedly less polite than the last. If Safa didn't stop harassing their employees, it said, they would refer the matter to the police. Anger flared in her chest, but one thing she had learned in this game was that she wasn't allowed a temper. She remembered the things they had called her: *frantic, neurotic, deluded*. They had taken the things that made her a good reporter – her persistence, her attention to detail, her ability to see the bigger picture – and turned them into embarrassing adjectives.

She re-read the email and spent a few minutes trying to word a suitable answer, but knew better than to do so in anger. She pushed away from her desk and reached into the bottom drawer. Like a compulsion, she pulled out a dark green binder. There was barely anything inside but Safa had backed it all up regardless and kept two copies at home. *That* was a lesson she had learned the hard way.

'Hey, Safa,' said a voice over her shoulder.

She covered the green folder and turned to find Tim by her desk. Tim O'Leary was a reedy new graduate, fresh from City University, Safa's alma mater. He was unlike the other grads that swanned through here on their way to better internships at *The*

Times or *The Clarion*. Tim, in comparison, lacked what one might call 'cultural polish', that subtle blend of accent, confidence, taste and etiquette that Safa could only now – in her thirties – pull off with any conviction. She had become Tim's mentor of sorts during his tenure here.

'Do you have five minutes?' he asked, awkwardly pulling up a chair next to her.

'Sure. What's up?'

'So, um, Kevin asked me to come up with a headline for this article. It's about some local musicians suing an AI website for using their back catalogue without permission.' Tim dolefully offered her a printout. 'So far, I have "local musicians sue RhythmAI for copyright infringement".'

Safa was careful not to smile, wary of knocking his confidence. She scanned the first paragraph, then angled her head in thought. 'How about "Algorithm & Blues"?' she said after a moment.

Tim's face lit up in awe. 'How do you do that so quickly?'

'Years of practice,' she told him.

'Thank you, Safa! You've saved my skin.'

'I'm glad I could help.' She handed back the printout and sent him off with a wave. Warmth pitched inside her, but it was easy to look good on a local paper where most of her peers were a decade younger. She shouldn't even *be* here, but that's what happened when your career was derailed with hardly any warning.

Safa flipped open the green binder again and looked through the scant material. She had rebuilt what she could from memory: a meagre list of witnesses and snatches of descriptions. She had lost contact with the only witness who might have agreed to speak, and it made her ache with guilt. The crime in question was so heinous, so taboo, that all other victims refused to even acknowledge it.

Safa paused on a well-thumbed page and read a list of traits: a lean but athletic frame, a coarse and scratchy beard, cold and veiny hands. It was these specific details – sensory ones she could *feel* – that she remembered clearly. She also knew that he might have brown skin but, beyond that, the details had been lost, curtly denied to her by the latest email from Nick Rosenberg. His blunt refusal maddened her.

She drafted a two-word reply. *Fuck. You.*

Then, she selected the text and pressed delete. Safa was not going to cease or desist, but she knew what it was to use the wrong words. They had upended her life twice already and she had learnt through years of rage never to use them carelessly.

*

Lily Astor caught the driver's eye from behind her shades and flashed him a bright smile. She always felt anxious before going on air and dialled up her cheer to hide it. Smoke and mirrors and makeup were the only three things you really needed to succeed in TV.

Chris, her designated driver, parked in her usual spot. Lily thanked him and sleekly exited. She strode into Broadcasting House, tossing her long blonde hair in a movie-star gesture. Inside, the doorman swept her towards the security gates as if she might not know the way.

'Good morning, Ms Astor,' he said in his deep, warm baritone.

She smiled. 'Good morning, Brian. How's the cough?'

He patted his chest. 'Better, Ms Astor.'

She nodded graciously and slipped through the barriers, catching the lift in time. When she had started at the channel ten years ago, she had made a point to learn the names of anyone that wasn't 'talent': the doormen, the cleaners, the dinner ladies. Others did the same but always in the smarmy way of life coaches and politicians. Lily, in comparison, knew what it was like to be invisible. As a child, she had accompanied her mother, Gabby, on early morning cleaning shifts in an office block in Canary Wharf. She saw how people barely moved their legs when she vacuumed beneath their desks, or dropped plastic cups still full of liquid straight into the bin. Sometimes, Lily had to finish the job when her mother wasn't fit to, and not once did someone question what a child was doing there.

Of course, her life now was exhausting in a different way. This – the softly curled hair, the demurely full lips and bright white smile – wasn't natural, literally or figuratively. In fact, Lily had come upon it all by accident.

It started at the *Sunday Times Magazine* where she had secured two weeks of work experience along with her then best friend, also an aspiring journalist. Lily was keen to make an impression. Over lunch one day, she overheard two of the senior journalists talking about a voiceover for a radio advert. The child actor they had booked had cancelled and they were desperate to find an alternative.

Lily, remembering her favourite teacher's advice that journalism was mostly about confidence, worked up the courage to say, 'I'll do it.' She had fully expected them to gasp in relief and whisk her off to the studio, but instead she was met with blank stares.

'Do what?' asked Peter, the taller of the two.

'Oh, sorry,' she stammered. 'I heard you needed a child for the voiceover. I'm fourteen so I could do it if you wanted me to?' The two men shifted awkwardly and she looked from one to the other. That's when Amelia Ranger, the editor at the time, stalked up to them.

'What are you doing?' she snapped. The two men parted to reveal Lily in the middle. Amelia gave all three a withering look. 'Well?'

'Um, this young lady suggested herself for the voiceover?'

Amelia looked at Lily and then laughed – a cruel tinkling sound.

'Don't be stupid,' she said. 'She sounds like fucking Dick Van Dyke.' She marched the two men away and Lily was left staring at their wake. She didn't understand what had happened until, back at her desk, she looked up Dick Van Dyke and realised that Amelia had been talking about her accent. She burned with humiliation and spent the afternoon convinced that everyone was staring at her. For the remainder of the week, she avoided talking to anyone. She dove from corridors into empty rooms whenever she saw someone she recognised. In the end, the voiceover was assigned to another student on work experience: a young blonde posh girl – plummy but bubbly with the cutest dimples you ever saw. Lily watched her and thought, *I want to be that girl*. And, now, she *was*. Lily-Ann Baker was now Lily Astor and that was worth remembering when the act got tiring.

The lift stopped and two security guards got in.

'Morning, Steven, Ashley.' She flashed her teeth.

'Morning, Ms Astor,' they said in unison.

She could feel the slight tension in the lift. It was always the same whenever there was a celebrity inside it. Not that she ever called herself a celebrity. More a *public figure*. As co-host of *Arise*, the BBC's flagship breakfast show, Lily was often recognised both inside the building and out on the street. Her persona gave people licence to approach her at all moments of the day. It was made worse by the fact that she had spoken openly about a childhood bout of disordered eating. People believed that she had taken them into her confidences and were all so eager to reciprocate. Women and girls would bustle up to her in queues and stations, desperate to share their stories. Lily would want to close her eyes and dig her nails into her thigh – what made them think that she *wanted* to hear their stories of trauma? Did they not think that this might add to her own? But all she could do was *smile, smile,* then *puppy-dog eyes.*

The lift pinged to a stop on the sixth floor and Lily touched the arm of one the guards.

'Have a lovely day, Steven.' She smiled at the other. 'And you, Ash.' They beamed at her and called out thanks. She made her way to makeup, a boxy room at the top of the corridor. It was overly warm, and heavy with the smell of coffee.

Jenna, a manic pixie makeup artist with pink tights and green hair, pushed a warm mug into Lily's hands.

'You're an angel,' said Lily. Plummy but friendly. She sat in a padded white chair, her shades still on – a fixture at 7 a.m. *Arise* began at nine after the more serious news programme, so Lily had plenty of time. She took a sip of coffee, then casually took off her shades.

Jenna balked when she saw it. 'Jesus, Lily, what the hell happened to you?'

Lily had made no effort to cover the bruise, knowing that *that* would look more suspicious. She had practised her answer in the mirror that morning, first trying sheepish admission (I can be so clumsy), then distracted avoidance (sorry, I just need to reply to this email) and finally cool denial (it's nothing).

She met Jenna's gaze in the mirror. 'Ugh, I'm sorry,' she said with a casual flick of the wrist. 'It was a tennis accident.'

Jenna bent towards her and Lily could smell the cloying scent of her perfume mixed with a hint of sweat that suggested she had worn that top one too many times before putting it in the wash. 'It looks really nasty, Lily. Did you get it checked out?'

Lily angled it towards the light. It was dark and livid, and covered her left eye socket. 'Oh, gosh, it looks worse than I thought.'

'When did it happen?'

Lily studied the bruise as if annoyed with herself. 'Saturday. Richard and I were playing tennis at Ropemakers. We're both stupidly competitive and . . .' She did a little wave as if to say *voila*.

'Richard did that?'

Lily clucked impatiently. 'Well, don't say it like *that*. It was an accident.'

Jenna smoothed her frown. 'Okay, well, we better cover it up or the tabloids will be abuzz.'

'"Richard Astor gives wife a shiner",' said Lily with a laugh. She caught the harsh trill of it and tried not to grimace, knowing that Jenna would see it.

The girl pumped moisturiser onto her pixie fingers and rubbed it into Lily's skin. The bruise didn't hurt anymore, not really, but the thought of the tender flesh being pressed made Lily want to recoil.

Jenna carefully added layers of makeup: primer, foundation, concealer, powder and then setting spray. Lily was lucky, she supposed, that she worked in a job that called for so much makeup. When Jenna was finished, the bruise was barely noticeable – just the faintest patch. She eyed it critically.

'Do you want me to do another layer?' asked Jenna.

Lily turned her head from side to side. 'No, I think it's okay. People get bruises all the time, right?'

There was a beat before Jenna spoke. 'Right.'

'Great.' Lily rose from the chair, then paused at the threshold. 'Please don't mention this to anyone, Jenna.' She held her gaze. 'You're the only one who knows.' She pitched it in a friendly way, but the subtext was clear: if this gets out, I'll know it was you. 'We joke about the tabloids, but you know that's exactly what they would do.'

Jenna nodded vigorously. 'Of course, Lily. You can trust me.'

'Great. Thank you.' She flashed her warmest smile then walked out onto set.

*

Safa finished her news piece about the council's new Hate Crime Strategy, then read and reread it. She doubted that even ten people would read it, but Safa had what she called the 'fitted sheet problem'. Years ago, she had come across a facetious tweet that read, "Folding a fitted sheet is really easy if you don't care." The problem was that Safa *did* care and how she did anything was how she did everything: to the best of her ability.

She pressed publish on the piece just as her desk phone began to ring. She snatched it up.

'Got a minute?' asked Kevin, her editor.

'Yep,' she said and hung up. There was a shorthand between them, hewn over the last ten months. She grabbed her pen and notebook, a simple spiral Pukka Pad in lieu of the many Moleskines that people gave her as gifts. She locked her laptop and headed to Kevin's office, the only one with walls in the open-plan newsroom.

Kevin Giles was the reason that Safa didn't feel like a complete failure here. The loud, proud Scot was an old-school newspaperman. He had exacting standards and a bloodhound's nose for a story. He was a brilliant editor, which is why Safa had been surprised to learn that he had originally wanted to work in fashion. Unlike journalism, however, where you could hide in the corners of local papers, there was no equivalent periphery in fashion – not unless you wanted to work in a factory – and so he was here instead, in his cufflinks and braces, making Safa believe that this wasn't just a local rag stuffed above a betting shop.

He motioned at a chair. 'Safa, you know Lily Astor, right?'

'The presenter?' she asked, buying time.

'Yes, the presenter.'

'A little, yes.'

Kevin scratched his beard with a pen. 'Why did I think you were friends?'

'I guess we were, once.'

'And now?'

Safa shrugged. 'We drifted apart. As people do.'

Kevin eyed her curiously. 'Lily came into work with a black eye this morning. Social media is ablaze and I thought you could get her to give us a comment.'

Safa tensed. 'We don't have that sort of relationship.'

He angled his head. 'Why? Did things end badly?'

'No, but they ended.'

'Could you try?'

Safa hated to refuse. When she started out in journalism, her first editor gave her one piece of advice: *say yes a lot*. He told her about the time he said yes to a press junket about the launch of a new class of seat for an Austrian airline. He was struggling to make rent at the time and went along for the free food. There, he happened to meet the frontman of the Red Hot Chili Peppers and ended up on a three-day bender in LA with the band. He wrote a feature about it in *GQ*, which went on to win him a Whitney – the most coveted award in journalism – all because he said yes to a junket.

Safa traced the rungs of her notebook. 'Yes,' she told Kevin. 'But since when were we happy to run celebrity gossip?' She immediately regretted the jibe for it was clear that it genuinely troubled him. *The Echo* was often dismissed as a local rag – not least by Safa herself – but the calibre of stories and the quality of writing held their own against the nationals. One of Kevin's best achievements as editor over the past two decades had been resisting the ad-ridden clickbait of other news sites and papers. Lately, however, he had made concessions on their more popular stories. Safa knew that he hated the auto-loading video ads, but they brought in valuable income.

She raised a hand in apology. 'I'm on it.' She sprang to her feet and headed back to her desk. There, she Googled Lily's name.

There were stories in several tabloids and thousands of posts on social media. Safa zoomed in and studied the photos. Only then could she see the faint greenish bruise. It was almost certainly innocent, but there were stories in the *Sun*, the *Daily Mail* and, Safa noted wryly, on the front page of *The Clarion*. Last year, she had pitched a feature to her section editor there: a deep dive into the case of Farah Ali, a fifty-two-year-old British-Pakistani woman from East London. Farah had sought help at her local police station, but she couldn't speak English and they had no interpreters available and so they sent her home. Two weeks later, Farah was dead – killed by her abusive husband. Safa remembered the sick feeling on hearing the story. How many women would die because they could not, or would not, speak for themselves? Safa had wanted to cover Farah's story as part of a wider piece on violence against women and girls.

But it's not really news, her editor, Francesca, had told her. Safa had had to bite her tongue. Francesca was a wealthy, privately educated woman with a strong network of support. It wasn't news to her, but it *was* newsworthy to the thousands of women who couldn't escape abuse. Their reasons were manifold – lack of language, lack of money, lack of control – and Francesca could relate to none. Now that *Lily* was the victim, it qualified as news. Like Francesca, Lily was rich, white and pretty – and ostensibly from money, although Safa, of course, knew otherwise. If someone had told her in their youth that Lily would be on TV, Safa wouldn't have believed it, but there she was: beautiful, blonde and bubbly, playing down her natural smarts to make herself more appealing. Safa would find it insulting if she didn't know how hard she had worked; how far she had travelled from Globe Road and the council estate of their childhood. She could hardly blame Lily for leaving it all behind – including, eventually, Safa herself.

She thumbed through her phone and found Lily's number. She

wasn't even sure that it worked anymore. First, she dialled from a private number, but it rang through to voicemail. Sure enough, here was Lily's voice asking the caller to leave a message. Safa hung up and tried again, this time with her own number.

'Safa?' Lily sounded out of breath.

'Lily, hi!' Safa was caught off guard. She hadn't expected her to answer.

'Is everything okay?'

'Yes. I know this is out of the blue. I'm sorry not to have been in touch lately.' They both knew that this was a courtesy. Safa's last four texts to Lily had gone unanswered. 'Do you have time for a chat?'

A pause. 'Yes.'

'I can meet you at the BBC?'

'Oh. I thought you meant now, on the phone.'

Safa coloured. Why had things got so hard between them? 'Okay, sure, if that's easier.' Another thing that she had learnt early in her career was to always try to meet face to face. Email interviews allowed people to curate their answers and the phone wasn't great for rapport – but she also knew to take her chance while she had it. 'It's about the bruise.'

Silence.

'Lily?'

'Yes.'

'I'm sorry to just call you and ask like this.'

Lily let out a one-note laugh. 'God, not *you* too.'

'I thought you might want to set the record straight.'

'Come on, Safa.' Her tone was arch and patronising. 'You're better than that.'

'Well, I'm sorry to have to stoop so low, but not everyone landed at the BBC.'

'That's not my fault,' Lily said tersely.

Safa didn't respond. Lily was right, of course. It *wasn't* her fault that Safa's career had lagged, but an old, juvenile instinct made her lash out. 'I'm sorry,' she said after another silence. 'It's just . . . so bloody hard. I'm at the shitty *East London Echo*.' It hurt her to denigrate her paper this way. 'I just need *one* scoop to get my name back out there.' Then – and this really hurt – she added, 'Please.'

'For fuck's sake,' snapped Lily.

Rather than upset her, the words made Safa smile. They were a hint of the friend she used to know, one who was sarky and cutting and fun and cool; not the sweet, sanitised version that had won the nation's heart. 'Thank you! Can I put you on speaker?'

'Fine, but I'm only giving you a quote. That's it. No questions.'

'That's all I need.' Safa opened the Audacity app on her laptop to record Lily's words. After what had happened last year, she was wary of publishing anything without evidence to back up her notes. 'Okay, go.'

'I'm very heartened by the nation's concern over my bruise. I was playing a rather overzealous game of tennis with my husband, Richard, on Saturday and a stray ball caught my temple. It's a good lesson to take to the future: we are not, and neither should we pretend to be, one of the Williams sisters.'

Safa waited. 'Anything else?'

Lily thought for a moment. 'Can you add, "I do want to take this opportunity, however, to remind the powers-that-be that, in England and Wales, *two* women are killed by their domestic partners every week. The strength and support of the media could do a lot of good for the women who need it most."'

Safa noted this down. 'Was anyone else at the tennis game?'

'You've got your quote, Safa.'

'Okay. I'm taking you off speaker.' She held the phone to her ear. 'Is that really what happened?' A tinkle of laughter that she knew was fake.

'Come on, Safa. You know me. Do you really think I'd let myself become a *battered* woman?'

Safa grimaced. 'Yes, I do know you.' A pause. 'Some days, I think I'm the only one who does.'

Lily tutted. 'It's not like you to be melodramatic.' She didn't wait for Safa's reply. 'Anyway, I've got to go. You'll take care, won't you?'

'Yes, I will.'

Lily hung up without saying goodbye.

Safa should be grateful, she supposed, that her old friend hadn't insulted her with platitudes: *let's do coffee! We'll get together!* The truth was that their lives had gone separate ways, now too far apart to intersect. Safa still didn't understand how a friendship more than two decades old could wither to almost nothing.

The two of them had met when they were eleven years old where many great friendships are forged: in the school canteen. It was the first week of secondary school and Safa had made a tentative friendship group. While she waited for them at a table, she unwrapped her sandwiches – two cleanly cut slices of white bread stuffed with *aloo bhazi*, a deliciously spicy potato mix that her dad had made for dinner the night before.

It had been a nerve-wracking first few days. The halls felt too wide and the ceilings too high compared with her intimate primary school. She took a bite of the sandwich, comforted by the salt and spice.

She had her back to them, but something alerted her to their attention. She felt it at the base of her neck, the weight of it making her hunch.

God, that stinks, said a girl's voice – a whisper, but wilfully indiscreet.

And it looks like diarrhoea, said another.

Her shock was like a burn: hot and sudden. Safa didn't

turn but knew that they were talking about her food. She was mortified, for it had never occurred to her that others might find it offensive. In primary school, she had been eligible for free school meals and so ate platefuls of mash and soggy cheese flan like the rest of the pupils. She held the sandwich aloft, not wanting to take another bite but fearing the jeers should she put it down. She squirmed with indecision as the noise in the room grew louder: the clang of metal on metal, the screech of chairs on flooring.

There was movement over her right shoulder and she flinched by instinct. A girl – skinny, with stringy blonde hair and gaps between her teeth – walked round and sat down opposite her.

'What's that?' she asked, lifting her chin at the sandwich.

Safa eyed her with suspicion. The girl's voice was studiedly friendly, the sort a bully would use before snatching an object of interest. 'A sandwich,' said Safa – slow and pre-emptively curt.

'I'm not an idiot. I mean what's in it?'

'Potato,' Safa said tersely.

'Can I try it? I'll swap you.' The girl pushed forward one half of her sandwich. Before Safa could say no, she picked up the other half of Safa's one and took a massive bite. Her eyes rounded in genuine surprise. 'Wow, that's actually really good,' she said through her mouthful. She finished it with relish, then looked pointedly at the other table. 'It's much better than the pig that *pigs* like to eat.'

A burst of shocked laughter rose behind Safa and she turned instinctively. One of the girls swiftly set down her bacon sandwich. Her fair skin grew pink and her jaw was hard with malice.

Safa spun back around. 'Do you know her?' she asked with awe.

'No, but I know girls like her.'

'I can't believe you just did that.' Safa felt a rush of admiration. The casual pitch of her voice, the razor sting of her insult, was something to behold. 'What's your name?' she asked her strange new ally.

'Lily-Ann, but call me Lily.' She angled her head. 'You?'

'Safa.'

'Suffer?'

'It's spelt S-A-F-A, but, yeah, it's pronounced like suffer.'

Lily considered this. 'Cool,' she said, and took another bite of the *aloo bhazi* sandwich. When Safa bit into Lily's, she found that it had only butter in it. She frowned but didn't remark on it.

The next day, Lily found her again in the canteen and sat down opposite. Wordlessly, Safa pushed half of her sandwich across the table, and Lily did the same. Through that small ritual, they became good friends and then best friends. Lily taught Safa to stand up for herself and she taught Lily that doing well in school didn't make her a nerd. She taught her to think beyond their council estate, to read widely, to write, to *reach*. Over the next seven years, they charted a future as famous writers. Together, they did work experience at the *Sunday Times Magazine* and went to sixth form and studied the same A Levels. Safa had thought that they would go to university together, but Lily had other, better plans.

These days, when her jealousy surfaced, Safa reminded herself that she had never wanted to be a broadcaster. She had always imagined herself as a reporter on a national paper or perhaps a political magazine. Working in print gave her the space and time to cover issues she cared about. Instead of standing in a studio speaking from a script, her job was to give voice to the vulnerable. Safa had told the stories of women like Halema Begum who had been denied an epidural during a traumatic birth. Safa's research had led her to the awful discovery that British-Bangladeshi women were 24 per cent less likely than white women to receive an epidural. There was also the story of Kellie Johnson, a fifteen-year-old girl who was strip-searched in school. Safa came to learn that Black girls were three times more likely to undergo invasive strip-searches by the Met Police.

Safa was proud of this work, but her envy persisted, rearing its head when Lily went to the BAFTAs, fashion awards, charity galas, and dinner parties with celebrity journalists and not just the *rah* variety but good, honest journalists that Safa truly respected. She had seen Lily with all of them – the BBC like a cabal. Lily had it made it. And Safa? Safa had not.

She had had one chance: two years at *Clarion Content* – the paper's commercial arm which ran sponsored articles – followed by a dream role on Special Projects. Safa couldn't believe that she had landed one of the most coveted jobs in investigative reporting. After a mere four months, however, things went catastrophically wrong. And now here she was at *The Echo*, begging her old friend for a bone.

*

Lily's driver, Chris, parked by her house on Narrow Street. It was tucked behind black iron gates with five others like it, all with a view of the Thames. Her neighbours were eclectic on the face of it – a teacher who had inherited the house from his grandmother, a celebrity chef, an auditor, a film director and an events planner – but they all shared a common thread. Like Lily, they were left-leaning liberals who were too ethical to send their kids to private school. Instead, they had congregated here, in this East End enclave, conveniently located in the catchment area of one of the best state schools in London. *Privilege without the stink,* as Lily would describe it.

She paused by the gates and pretended to search for her keys. She wanted to take a moment before she went inside. She glanced up at her house. It was 4 p.m. but the lights were already on. The ivy that crept up all three floors seemed to reach for the windows, craving the light inside. Lily thought about what she had said to Safa and felt a lurch of shame. *Do you really think I'd let myself become a battered woman?* The glibness of it, and the blame implied by the word "let", was deeply callous, she knew. But, importantly, it was exactly what Safa would expect her to say if it was the truth.

She walked through the iron gates and let herself into the house. She sensed movement inside and tried to map its source. Harry upstairs or Richard on this floor? The mood hung in the air, dark and expectant, lifting her onto her tiptoes as she walked to the living room. It was so easy to pity a meek woman, especially one who purports to be strong. She remembered how Hillary Clinton was described as a feminist, and thinking *what sort of feminist stays with a cheating husband?* Lily's friends would say that it takes real strength to save a marriage – but no, what took real strength was to leave.

'Lily?'

She spun to find Richard in the doorway. 'Gosh, you scared me!' She saw the tension in his shoulders and flashed her sunbeam smile. *How was your day?* she almost asked but pulled it back from the tip of her tongue. Richard had lost his job during the Covid pandemic and his freelance work as a science journalist had largely dried up, so asking about his day would only make him bristle.

He came closer and studied the bruise on her brow. 'Does it hurt?'

'No,' she replied quickly.

'What did you tell them?'

'That it happened at tennis.'

Colour rose in Richard's face. 'They believed you?'

'Yes.'

He let out a strangled sound. 'God, I'm sorry, Lily.' He pulled her into his arms.

She relaxed into him, too fatigued to resist.

'I love you,' he said.

'I love you too.' Her words were muffled in his chest. His jumper smelled of mothballs and leather, the smell of a man much older but she found it comforting. It was so far from the smells of her childhood: cigarettes, cheap alcohol. She had come so far from that and couldn't let it fall apart.

When she had met Richard at Oxford, he was everything that she was not: worldly, cultured, confident. She had been hovering outside the dining hall on her very first day when he had walked by and noticed her.

'Hi,' Richard had said as if he already knew her.

Lily had shifted uneasily. 'Hi.'

'Would you like to join me for lunch?' Seeing her uncertainty, he'd quickly added, 'I could do with the company.'

She had smiled – a pure, guileless smile, freshly out of her braces – and that was that. They spent the next years together and his culture quickly rubbed off on her. Gently, he would remind her that it was poor manners to cut the nose off the brie or to butter her bread in one go or to hold her flute by the bowl. She hewed her accent to be more like his and though her working-class roots occasionally shot through, Richard lent her a shield of respectability. Their love was easy and effortless. While others were playing games – counting hours before they replied to a text – Lily didn't care. She threw herself into their romance and, later, their marriage, knowing that this one love was all she would ever need. Life was good. Until it wasn't.

Richard kissed her hair, bringing her back to the present. 'I'm making tacos,' he said.

Lily feigned gratitude. Tacos were Richard's healing food; his attempt at the sort of fun, light family that cheerily gathered in adverts. These fictional families, however, only served as a contrast. Instead of messy fillings dripping over edges, there was a strained, formal quality to these evenings.

She pulled away and looked up at him. 'Should I go up and talk to Harry?'

Richard frowned. 'No, Lily, we've been through this. He doesn't need your glare on him.'

'He would have seen the headlines. We can't just ignore it.' She waited for Richard to cede. It wasn't lost on her that she was seeking permission from her husband to talk to her own son. 'I'll be quick,' she said, desperate to appease him. 'We'll be down in a minute.' She peeled off before he decided to object more roundly. Upstairs, she knocked on Harry's bedroom door. When he didn't answer, she knocked again and called his name. He snatched open the door and looked at her expectantly.

'Your dad's making tacos,' she said with an apologetic wince.

Harry's features tightened. 'Well, that should fix everything.'

Lily looked into the room tentatively. 'Can I come in?'

He huffed but stepped back to let her in. She rarely came in here anymore, fully aware that Harry didn't like it. The last markers of his childhood – the thin Spiderman curtains, the row of action figures – made her heart ache. At thirteen, her boy was slipping away from her, replaced by this surly teen who had somehow grown as tall as her.

She tried not to react to the smell in there, tried not to say *open the window, change your sheets, air your smelly trainers*. She sat in his desk chair and looked across at him.

'Do you want to talk about it?'

'About what?' He puckered his lips stubbornly.

'The headlines.'

He lifted a shoulder.

'Did anyone at school say anything?'

He scoffed with teenage boredom. 'Believe it or not, Mum, the boys at St Anne's don't spend all day talking about our *national treasure* Lily Astor.'

Lily knew that this meanness was a defence mechanism, but it hurt nonetheless. She reached for something funny; to maybe spark a repartee, but her humour failed her. She wanted to go to him, to sit by his side and wrap him in her arms, but she couldn't face his rejection right now. 'Dinner must be almost ready,' she said.

'I'm not hungry.'

Lily smiled indulgingly. Mothers flattened so much of themselves — their bite, their sting, their verve — to make space for patience. 'Please, Harry. Your father wants you to.'

'Does he?' he asked acidly.

'Yes, he does. I know we're going through a difficult time but he loves you. Please don't ever think otherwise.' Harry closed his eyes and there was something so helpless in it, it made Lily want to cry. She let the moment pass, then stood and dusted off her slacks with a sense of industry. 'What do you say?' she asked, her jolliness ringing false.

'Fine,' he said with a stagey sigh. He followed her downstairs, his tread heavy and sullen behind her. She prayed that his mood would lift, so that Richard wouldn't try to goad him from it.

In the dining room, she hovered by her chair until Harry sat in his. Richard placed a large serving dish of Mexican three-bean chilli in the centre of the table. He followed with heaps of cheese, salsa, salad and his special spice mix, then sat down opposite Harry.

'How was school?'

'Fine,' said Harry.

Richard jauntily filled up a taco in lieu of a follow-up question. He and Harry hadn't always had a strained relationship. They used to go fishing together, play rugby and practise cricket, but emotionally there had always been distance. Richard had been raised with a stiff upper lip and simple things like telling his son 'I love you' had never come naturally.

Lily reached for a taco. 'Guess who I talked to today,' she said to fill the lull at the table. 'Safa Saleem.'

Harry looked up quickly. 'Aunt Saffie?'

It hurt to hear the lift in his voice. He and Safa used to be close before Lily ceased contact. Safa had a way of rooting out the truth and Lily couldn't risk that. Her old friend would see through her lies and find the darkness in her perfect life.

'How come?' Harry asked.

Lily realised that she had led them right back to the elephant in the room. 'Oh, just a catch-up.'

'Can I see her?'

Lily was surprised. It was the first thing he'd asked for in such a long time and she hated to deny him outright. 'I could try to arrange something.'

Harry almost smiled. 'I'd like that.'

Lily was warmed by this glimpse of her son as she used to know him: sweet, hopeful, sincere, with none of his teenage armour.

Richard cut in. 'I think it's best we stay away from reporters.'

Lily's expression was studiedly neutral. 'It was just an idea. But either way, Safa would never write about us without my permission.'

'She's a reporter.'

'She's my friend.'

'Is she?' he asked coolly. 'When was the last time you saw her?'

Lily was chastened. 'Fine,' she said quietly. 'If that's what you think.' She shot Harry a look of apology, but he ignored it. It was clear that he had lost respect for her. Could bringing Safa back into their lives help her win it back?

Lily still felt guilty about the way that their friendship had ended. Had it really been three years since she'd seen her last? A snatched coffee in bitter January just before the third lockdown? Safa had been struggling with freelance life, but Lily didn't have the bandwidth to counsel her friend through the doldrums. She remembered checking her watch halfway, and the look on Safa's face when she noticed. Lily cringed at the memory. Safa had always been someone who turned up when you needed her. When Lily's mother died in their first year at uni, it was Safa who had made the arrangements.

In uncharitable moments, Lily would think that it was easy for her because she didn't have a child to raise, a marriage to save, a high-pressure career, but it had been true of Safa even in their youth. Lily remembered one particular day at school – in Year 8, just after Lily had turned thirteen. It was a sweltering June and the air was muggy with the smell of thirty pupils crammed into a classroom. When the bell rang to signal the end of the day, Safa and Lily hurried out with the rest of the pupils. Lily was in high spirits; the weather was warm, which meant she could spend the weekend outside instead of cooped up in the flat.

'Hey, can I ask you something?' asked Safa.

Lily looked at her side-on, wary of her tone. 'Yeah,' she said carefully.

'Earlier, when we were leaving class, I saw you checking your skirt.' A pause. 'I've seen you do that a lot.'

Lily tensed. It was *just* like Safa to notice something that she had tried to hide. 'So?'

'So, I've also seen that you leak sometimes.'

Lily's cheeks were hot. 'So?' she said, overly aggressive. 'It happens.' Since she had started her period earlier in the year, it had happened to her a few times but she had always been able to hide it – except from Safa, of course.

'Not as much as it happens to you,' said Safa.

Lily felt a lump in her throat. 'You're being weird,' she said, changing her pitch to non-committal.

'Hey.' Safa touched her arm, forcing her to stop. 'What's going on?'

Lily puckered her lips and shook her head, dismissing her own pain. 'Nothing.'

'Tell me.'

Lily looked out to the distance, bouncing on her toes. 'Mum doesn't buy us sanitary towels, all right?'

Safa let her breath out slowly. 'So, what are you using instead?'

Lily shrugged.

'Lily?' Safa said gently.

'Tissue from the school toilets,' she admitted, blinking rapidly.

Safa's face creased with compassion. 'Oh, Lily.'

'It's not a big deal.' The wads of paper-thin tissue that she rolled into her underwear clearly didn't work.

'Lily,' Safa repeated.

'It's fine. Honestly.' Lily stepped backwards. 'Anyway, I've got to get home. Mum'll go ballistic.' Lily turned and marched up the street, Safa trailing behind, struggling to keep up. At home, Lily locked herself in the bathroom and cried hot, glassy tears of shame.

The next morning, Safa handed her a green and white plastic bag. Inside, was a pack of twenty-six sanitary towels. 'Let's not make this weird, okay?' she said. 'You can't keep using tissue.'

Lily swallowed hard, clearing the choke in her voice. 'Okay.' She placed them in her bag. 'Thank you.' For the next five years, Safa gave her a pack a month. At some point in adulthood, Lily had half-joked that she should pay her back. The truth was, of course, that there was no way she could repay Safa for everything she had done.

*

Safa unlocked the door and gave it a shove to get it open. She felt the heavy brocade curtain give way and fall to one side. Her dad, Jahangir, had strung it across the door to keep out the draught. Last year, the council had replaced the flimsy plastic door but the new one sat poorly in its fitting, letting in the chill. The house was better than the tiny flat of her childhood, but it was still squat and charmless.

She pushed the door closed with force and took off her shoes. She noticed that the hallway carpet was speckled with dirt. Her dad was normally house proud but his arthritis had flared up so Safa usually whizzed round with the Hoover when she came round to visit.

She stripped off her long down coat and hung it on the banister. The house had the steamy feel of recent cooking, so she headed to the kitchen. She found her dad at the cooker and kissed him on the cheek.

'*Asalam alaikum.*'

'*Walikum asalam.*' He stirred the buttery chicken curry. 'Give me five minutes? This is the last one.'

She peered into the pan and felt her mouth water. Her father was an excellent cook. It hadn't always been this way, but he had been forced to learn. 'Where's your new one?' she asked.

He gestured towards the back of the house. 'I shut her away because she's nervous around strangers.'

'Can I go and see her?'

'Yes, but be careful. I don't think she likes women, so speak in a low voice and don't make any sudden movements.'

Safa headed down the corridor. Tentatively, she opened the door to the storeroom and heard a little yip. 'Hey sweetheart,' she said gently as she stepped into the low light. Her father had had a dimmer installed to make the dogs more comfortable. Safa approached the skinny cocker spaniel, whose tag read 'Millie'.

Safa knelt down and held out her palm. Millie sniffed it, then quickly retreated. She took a moment to gather her courage, then ventured forward again and licked Safa's palm.

Safa noticed the new toys scattered around Millie's bed. She tutted gently. 'He's a big softie, isn't he?' she said. 'Just a stupid big softie.'

Safa's dad had become a foster carer for dogs after retiring from his job as a bus mechanic. He was a natural nurturer and cared for the dogs as if it were his one true purpose. Sometimes Safa thought that he gave them all the love that had nowhere else to go. Other bereaved fathers had pent-up emotion too – grief, anger, depression – but with him, it had always been love. Pent-up love. Some days she thought that it hurt the worst.

Safa cleared her throat and sent Millie bolting to a corner. The dog crouched beneath the sewing machine that had lain unused for years. It had belonged to Safa's mother, which meant they would never sell it. It wasn't the big, heavy memories that hit Safa the hardest – she at eight years old, in her father's arms, receiving the news that her mother was 'in a better place now'. She was vigilant about avoiding those. Rather, it was small, mundane things like the first time her father had tied her ponytail. It had been too tight, pinching at her scalp, and Safa had cried. She had always felt guilty for that. In a sea of inadequacy, she had made her dad feel worse.

After that, she had tried to be tough with all her might, never realising that what he needed was softness. Perhaps this was why he filled his house with food and dogs and toys – an ongoing effort to build a home worth living in.

Millie ventured out again and, after some cajoling, let Safa pet her.

'You're very lucky,' she told the dog. She swallowed hard. '*We're very lucky.*' She scratched Millie's ears, then stood and dusted off her jeans.

Back in the kitchen, she peered into the three pans on the table, then whooped when she saw her favourite Bengali dish, a light, sour fish stew cooked with green tomatoes.

'You made *tenga shira*,' she said.

'Yes. It's your mother's recipe.' Out of respect, her dad never called her mum by her name, as was custom in British-Bangladeshi families. Relatives and neighbours would refer to her as 'Safa's mum', mapping her forever to her daughter. No one ever spoke to Jahangir about 'your wife', which Safa found quietly tragic. Even language had left him bereaved.

Safa noticed that he was struggling with the knife and took over chopping the salad.

He leaned on the counter. 'So, what exciting stories are you working on?'

Safa's grip tightened on the knife. The thing that hurt most was disappointing her father. He had been so proud when she got a job at *The Clarion*. The daughter of a mechanic at the most hallowed paper in the country. He told her frequently that he was proud of her work at *The Echo*, but the two did not compare.

'Nothing huge at the moment,' she said. 'I did write something about Lily Astor this week. Or Lily-Ann Baker as we used to know her.'

Her dad made a pensive sound. 'I liked that version a lot more.'

Safa pictured teenage Lily's bad teeth, grubby joggers and lank ponytail. 'You might be the only one.'

'I don't think I am,' he said pointedly.

Safa carried on chopping. 'Maybe,' she conceded. 'But you can't blame her for changing, Dad. People like us have to, to make it in the media.'

'You didn't change.'

'And maybe that was my problem.'

He frowned. 'You don't believe that.'

Safa shrugged. Sometimes, she *did* wonder if things would have been different if she had tried a little harder to fit in with her peers in the media; if, like Lily, she had changed her East London accent and spent all her money on clothes and shoes – but Safa had never wanted to. She was *proud* of who she was. To be anything else would be an insult to her father who had raised her with such care. Yes, there'd been days at *The Clarion* when she had keenly felt her roots – a colleague aping her glottal stop, another correcting the way she said *coup de grâce* – but on most days, she was proud. Sometimes when she felt low, she told herself that Lily – white, Oxbridge and married to wealth – was always going to find it easier to outrun their roots, but Safa had seen the truth up close: there was no substitute for a parent's love.

Lily's father had left when she was three years old and her mother's addiction to alcohol left little to give elsewhere. Lily's childhood home was a barren, loveless place, made with literal scraps: the piecemeal lino in the hallway, patches of mismatched curtains, the foam that hung like a tongue from the sofa. Safa remembered visiting it one winter in the lead-up to exams. Usually, she and Lily studied at Safa's home, but the heating was broken there and they agreed to meet at Lily's. When Safa walked up to the fifth floor, she found the front door wide open – Lily's mum did that sometimes on her way out of the flat. Safa closed it and walked along the hall towards the voices in the kitchen.

'Do you have any money?' Lily was saying. 'Safa's coming over and there's nothing in.'

'Yeah, I'll just pull that out of our lottery winnings, shall I?' replied her sister, Natalie.

Safa heard the slam of cupboards and drawers, the seal of the fridge pulled open.

'There's got to be something.' Lily was clearly agitated.

Safa paused, almost at the threshold. She considered going back out and knocking on the door, but the lino creaked beneath her foot, giving her away.

Lily spun and nearly jumped out of her skin. 'Safa! Who let you in?'

Safa gestured solemnly. 'The door was open.' She scanned the kitchen, the bare shelves and empty fridge. 'Are you all right?'

Lily pushed shut the fridge. 'Yeah, fine.' She ran a hand across her forehead, sweaty with effort. 'Um, Mum hasn't had a chance to do the shopping so we don't have a lot in.' It was a pointless lie. Safa knew that Lily and Natalie rationed their food, so that their mother could stay drunk. In that moment, however, they needed a bit of dignity – and Safa let them have it.

'It's okay.' She patted her stomach, awkwardly formal. 'I ate before I came. I'm kind of stuffed to be honest.'

That evening, Safa asked her dad if they could host the girls for Christmas dinner. She remembered Lily's delight at the spread that they prepared: thick gravy, buttery potatoes, tender meat and stuffing. The girls had third helpings, followed by Christmas pudding. Safa never told Lily that her dad had never made a Christmas dinner before. He had borrowed *Delia Smith's Christmas* from their local library and together they spent a week trying out the recipes.

Safa looked up at him now. 'You did a good thing, Dad, helping me with her.'

He gave her a plaintive smile. 'I was glad to do it. But, Safa, please be careful about getting close to her again. You did a lot for her and it wasn't nice that she dropped you.'

Safa grimaced. She didn't like to dwell on her friendship with Lily because it so often left her low. It brought on a strange melancholy, which Lily didn't merit. Safa would much rather pretend that the end was mutual. 'People drift apart,' she told her dad.

'Yes, and some do it on purpose when they no longer have use for people.'

'Well, she was decent enough to give me an exclusive quote,' she said breezily, setting down the knife. 'You're just a worrier.'

'I'm not a worrier. I'm a realist.'

Safa's laughter was bright. 'You are many things, Dad, but you are *not* a realist.' She kissed his cheek, then handed him the salad, still chuckling with affection.

Chapter 2

Safa pushed through the doors into Bethnal Green Police Station. It smelled stale inside, like clunky old radiators left on too long. She took barely two steps towards the front desk when the officer there – a burly man in his mid-thirties – held up a hand in genuine alarm.

'Oh no, you don't.' He pointed at her. 'You get the hell out of here.'

Safa cracked a grin. 'Billy, have you fallen out of love with me already?' She placed a coffee on his desk, which he eyed suspiciously. 'Cinnamon with extra-frothy milk from the wood-oven place you like.'

His voice dropped to a fierce whisper. 'Do you have any idea how much trouble you got me in last time? Sarge tore me a new one.'

'Come on, Billy. Talk to me.'

'Nuh-uh.' His gaze flicked to the coffee. 'Imran was right. "Safa by name. *Suffer* by nature."'

She made a face. Her name had given Imran, her on-off ex-boyfriend, much material for humour. She slid the coffee towards Billy and said his name in a singsong lilt.

He looked at it with longing. After a second, he snatched it up and held it to his chest protectively. 'I've got nothing,' he told her.

'There's always something.' It had been a slow news week and she was working her contacts for potential stories. Last time, Billy had revealed some details about an ongoing case and though Safa hadn't named her source, the trail had led to him. Before she could pester him further, she heard a voice behind her.

'Safa?'

She scrunched her eyes shut in guilt. After a beat, she turned, her face now smooth and neutral. 'Imran. Hi.'

'What are you doing here? Did you get my text?'

She squirmed. 'Yes. I'm sorry. I've been busy.'

His eyes flicked to Billy.

'Look—' she and Imran spoke at the same time.

'You go first,' she told him.

'Can we go somewhere to talk?'

She hesitated. 'I don't have a huge amount of time.'

'It's important,' he insisted.

She watched the light-brown flecks in his eyes and felt a familiar yearning. 'Okay, sure.'

Imran spoke to Billy briefly and then escorted Safa out. Bethnal Green Road was especially dreary in the first week of April. The kerb was lined with litter and each passing vehicle spat up spurts of gutter water. Imran steered Safa to the inside as a bus motored past them. It speckled his coat with mud and he wiped it absent-mindedly, only spreading it further. Safa tried not to smile. Signs of thawing would only encourage him.

Together, they walked to the Green Cab Café, a small and shabby building stuck on the corner of Pott Street. The tables, walls and floor were all grey, and the sickly yellow lighting did nothing for Safa's complexion. Imran motioned her to a corner table and brought over two mugs of tea.

Safa wrapped her hands around her mug. 'How are you?' she asked, intentionally casual. He was kneading the back of his neck and winced as he hit a knot. Safa flashed onto a memory: her massaging him, the strong muscles of his back rippling beneath her touch.

'I'm okay,' he replied.

'I'm sorry I haven't been in touch. I know you wanted to talk. It's just—'

'That's not why I asked you here,' Imran cut in. He traced the peeling trim of the Formica table. 'He's back, Safa.'

It took her moment to switch gears. 'The Glassman?' she asked, barely daring to say it.

'Yes.'

Safa's grip tightened on her mug. 'How do you know?'

'Whispers.'

'From who? Where?'

He shook his head.

'Imran, you have to tell me more.'

'There is no more, Safa, you know that. It's voices on the wind, rumour and myth.'

'I can't fucking believe this.' Rage reached up inside her, looking for an outlet. She took a deep, controlled breath, then slowly let it out. The only way to help was to do what she could do. 'There must be something else. A name? A neighbourhood?'

'All I've been given is White Horse Road. That's it.'

'A door number?'

'No.'

Mentally, Safa mapped the length of White Horse Road. It was roughly half a mile of mainly terraced houses with one block of flats, not the Glassman's usual hunting ground. Safa remembered that detail from her old case files, the ones she was fighting *The Clarion* for. It was likely that she had the most comprehensive file on the guy, certainly more than the police.

The Glassman was a serial rapist in East London – but was barely more than myth. As Safa understood it, he was male, thirty-something, possibly Asian, possibly mixed race, and was able to remove perfect squares of windowpanes without making a sound. His victims fit a very specific demographic: elderly, widowed, Asian women who lived by themselves. The first time Safa heard of him, her enquiries had led nowhere. But then it came up a second time and she dug a little deeper. There were no official police reports and Safa understood why the Glassman targeted these women specifically.

He knew that they would be too ashamed to report it. In many cases, even to their own families. These women were first-generation Bangladeshi immigrants, governed by modesty, piety and sobriety. To admit any indecency, even as a victim, would cause unspeakable shame. And so they didn't speak.

The two cases that reached Safa had slipped through the web of silence. Since then, she had heard of another two victims. The last was an eighty-two-year-old woman. It was one of the grimmest things that Safa had heard in all her years of reporting, but the police were doing nothing. Only Imran, a Detective Sergeant at the London Met, had spent any time investigating over the last year and a half. He, like Safa, was also from the Bangladeshi community and knew how deep the shame ran. The older generation in Tower Hamlets lived in an enclave of sorts and the harder they tried to preserve their heritage, the more it curdled. Their values had turned into a form of moral tyranny. *If you're good and pious and modest,* it said, *nothing bad will happen to you.* And while it was never put so coarsely, the implication was that if something bad *did* happen, then you must have in some way deserved it. Both Safa and Imran understood that violence and abuse or anything that broke their community's strict morality was likely to be buried.

For Safa, the case became a compulsion, the thing she went back to in periods of down time. She collected every scrap of evidence and diligently filed it in *The Clarion*'s Google Drive. She hadn't thought it necessary to keep personal copies. *The Clarion*'s systems, after all, were some of the most robust in the world. She hadn't predicted that her departure would be so swift and sudden, and her access revoked in seconds.

'Imran, you need to get your bosses to look into it.'

'You know I've tried, Safa, but we can't investigate a report that doesn't exist.'

She felt a familiar guilt. She was furious with herself for being careless with her data. In her last weeks at *The Clarion*, she had made contact with one of the victim's daughters who said she would try to persuade her mother to speak. Before Safa could suggest a date and time, she was shut off from *The Clarion*'s email systems. Safa had an eye for detail and had tried to recreate the daughter's email address from memory but every permutation failed. She hadn't forgiven herself for forgetting it. Her naivety had come at such a high cost.

'There must be something more we can do,' Safa insisted.

'I'm trying,' said Imran.

'Is it worth going door to door on White Horse Road?'

'And saying what? "*Assalamu alaikum, auntiji*. We heard that you might have been raped"?'

Safa flinched. These isolated elderly women were some of the most vulnerable in society and it tortured her that the system had failed them. 'Maybe,' she said defiantly.

Imran angled his head. 'Come on, Safa.'

'I've got to do something, Imran.'

'But what are the chances that you'll find the right woman?'

'Zero if I don't try.'

Imran was pensive. 'If you're serious, then I'll come with you.'

'No. They won't talk if a man's there. It has to be me.'

'You're going to do it regardless of what I say, aren't you?'

'Yes.'

He sighed. 'Okay, but promise me you'll be careful.'

'I always am.' She took a gulp of her now tepid tea.

They fell into an awkward silence and Imran broke it haltingly. 'Now that we're here, can we talk for a minute?'

She tensed imperceptibly. 'Imran.'

'I'm not asking you to *marry* me, Safa. I'm asking for a conversation.'

She arched a brow. 'Well, now that you've set the mood for romance.'

'Safa,' he said, softly chiding.

She set down her mug. 'Okay,' she said. 'Let's talk about us.'

*

Lily liked the way she could hush a set. Any woman could draw noise and attention – a wolf whistle, a come-on, a drive-by obscenity – but it took something special to silence a room. Of course, she also had to defuse it: to smile, to be warm, to put others at ease. It was one of the reasons that people loved her. At any one time, she was attuned to everyone else in the room. Whenever someone told her that she was destined to be on screen, Lily would think *if only you knew*. They hadn't seen teenage Lily with her bad teeth and awful clothes. In truth, she had had to fight like a savage to get to where she was. She would have killed for it – and not just metaphorically. When she fell pregnant with Harry in her final year at university, she had tried to abort him. Unplanned motherhood happened to girls on Globe Road; not to girls at Oxford. She and Richard agreed that it was the logical thing to do. He paid for the abortion privately and went with her to the clinic. There was no groundswell of guilt as she filled in the forms. She took the pill unceremoniously and she and Richard headed back to halls.

A week later, Lily was told that her pregnancy was one of the 1 per cent that continue after the abortion pill. On learning this, a pendulum swung in her brain, muffling logical thought. Her baby – and it *was* a baby now – had clung on to life; had survived her attempt to kill it. The knowledge made her sodden with emotion and no matter what Richard tried, she knew she was going to keep it.

She put off her career to look after Harry and vowed to love him fiercely. Her love was big and showy, and sometimes she worried that he would smell the reek of penance on it. On those days, she tried to be less desperate, less crowding, but she always feared that Harry could tell. That he inherently *knew* what she had tried to do to him.

When he went full-time at nursery, Lily finally started work, as a runner at the BBC. She relished her new milieu and threw herself into the role. Ten years later, she was sitting on Britain's most famous sofa, here on the set of *Arise*.

'Lily, can you bend your legs a bit more and put one ankle on top of the other?' called Jack, the producer.

Lily did as he asked. She knew that her ankles were tubby and this was a good angle for them. It mattered less when she wore trousers but today she wore a white knee-length dress beneath a green cardigan. The opening credits ran and she and Stevie fixed on their smiles, their energy ramped up twofold.

'Hello! I'm Lily Astor.'

'And I'm Stevie Paul,' said her male co-presenter.

'Welcome to *Arise*!' Lily read the autocue, which promised a mix of cookery, entertainment and their standard 'real life' segment. Today, it would feature a woman addicted to plastic surgery pitted against a belligerent columnist. Some days, it was ridiculous like the hairdresser who had married her dog or the self-styled model who had the biggest breasts in the world but other days they looked at serious topics like influencer culture and mental health.

They cut to a montage of the upcoming show and Lily took the opportunity to take a quick swig of coffee. As she drank, Stevie knocked her arm, spilling coffee all the way down the front of her cardigan.

'Oh no!' he gasped. 'Lily, I'm so sorry!'

Jack cut in. 'We have fifteen seconds until you're back on screen, Lily. You'll have to take off the cardigan.'

Lily stared at the stain, dismayed. 'It's not that bad,' she said.

'It is, Lily. Quick.'

'No. It's cold in here.'

Jack looked at her in bafflement. Lily was usually a pro. 'We'll get you another one.' He clicked his fingers. 'Jenna, can you grab it please? Quickly.'

Jenna, the makeup artist, ran on set and grabbed at Lily's cardigan.

'Wait,' said Lily, but Jenna tugged it off her shoulder. She gasped and the two of them locked eyes. A look passed between them, lightning fast, and Jenna pulled the cardigan back up, then scurried out of frame just in time.

Lily was shaken, but stepped right back into her role, flicking her hair to the front to obscure the stain as much as possible. After the first segment, she was bundled off set and hurriedly given a different green cardigan. The rest of the show ran smoothly and Lily saw no sign that anyone other than Jenna had seen it. She apologised to Jack, made some light comment about acting like a diva, then hurried to her dressing room. Soon after, Jenna looked in.

'Lily, can we talk?' She took a tentative step inside. The kindness in her eyes awoke something inside Lily – something tender and needy – but she tamped it down. She had to keep on her game face. Jenna perched on a chair. 'Do you want to tell me what's happening?'

'First of all, it's not what you think.'

'Then what is it?'

It took her a moment to land on the reason. 'It was a riding accident.'

Jenna tipped her head to the right. 'Do you expect me to buy that?'

Lily was surprised by her tone. 'You don't have to.' An edge crept into her own.

'So, what do I do instead?' Jenna leaned towards her. 'Lily, I've seen this sort of thing before.'

'It really isn't what you think.'

'It's just you and me here. Please tell me what's going on.'

Lily had spent so long building the perfect life and wasn't about to tarnish it now. To admit that something was wrong was to face the masses, the judgement, the advice and, worst of all, the pity. She simply couldn't bear it. 'I appreciate the concern, I really do.' She ran her fingers through her hair, leaving it casually tousled. 'But come on, Jenna. You *know* me. Do you really think I'd let myself become a battered woman?'

Jenna looked sad. 'I think that many women – brave, powerful, *strong* women – do illogical things for the men they love.'

Lily rolled her eyes. 'That's not what's going on here.' She tossed her hair to one side. 'Honestly.'

'It looked really bad, Lily.'

'It's fine.' Lily could feel the bruise even now, covering her upper arm in moody blue and purple. 'I'm fine.'

'But it's the second time in two weeks.'

Lily gestured wryly. 'Yes, I'm aware of the unfortunate timing.'

Jenna smoothed a crease in her lap. 'Lily. If a woman like you can be silenced, who among us *can't*?'

Lily looked at her like she was the sweetest, stupidest thing in the world; she did it on purpose to make Jenna with her candy-striped tights feel callow. 'You Gen Zs are always looking for a fight, but there is no *cause* here, Jenna. The reason I was so keen to hide the bruises is because I'd have to do exactly what I'm doing right now: explain myself for the comfort of others.' Lily's face twitched with irritation. 'It was an accident and honestly I'd like both of us to just move on.'

Jenna, made aware of their power differential, switched to a lighter tone. 'Okay, but I'm gonna be watching your skin like an incel.'

Lily's laugh was full and indulgent. 'I would expect nothing less.' She stood and took her coat off the rail, cueing Jenna to leave. She waited until the girl was gone before she let her smile drop.

*

Safa squirmed beneath Imran's gaze. The very first time she had met him, over a year ago now, she had been struck by that stare. She had been in court that day reporting on a case when Imran and a colleague escorted in a defendant. Safa noticed him immediately: 5'11" – crucially, not too tall for Safa's 5'4" – with jet black hair and those light brown flecks in his eyes. He wore a stab-proof vest and the way that it fit his frame made something stir inside her. Imran caught her looking and she quickly turned away. She felt his eyes on her, but told herself not to read anything into it. She knew she had redeeming features thanks to her Bengali heritage – high cheekbones and feline eyes – but she couldn't dress for shit and her hair was always drab in a ponytail or bun. That's what you get, she supposed, when you grew up with no women in your life.

Later that day, she saw Imran in the court canteen. He paused by her table and motioned at the seat opposite her.

'Do you mind if I join you? Everywhere else is full.'

Safa looked around at the deserted canteen, then smiled despite herself. 'Sure,' she said with a shot of sarcasm. Imran had an easy confidence and Safa was glad to let him lead. She had never been much good at flirting. Her colleagues said that she didn't know how to be playful and men never knew where they stood. Safa was indeed a little formal at first, but Imran was bullish that way, forging ahead with the confidence of a seasoned flirt.

Now, sitting in the Green Cab Café with his tepid tea, he seemed less sure-footed.

'I'm tired, Safa,' he said.

She sipped her tea and waited.

'And I wanted to talk to you to tell you that I'm giving up.'

Safa's face revealed only the slightest uncertainty.

'It's been a year and I'm tired of this late-night booty-call bullshit. I'm thirty-five and it's time I grew the fuck up. If you're not into it – and it's clear that you're not – then we need to end things once and for all. Cleanly.'

Safa nodded, carefully aloof. 'Okay,' she agreed.

He flexed his fingers, gathering resolve. He clearly had something prepared and was determined to deliver it. 'I should tell you that I think I might have met someone.'

The words fell like an anvil, making her vision hum. Every selfish part of her wanted to reach for him. *Don't do it,* she wanted to say. *Don't end this.* Instead, she sipped her tea in a show of nonchalance. 'What's her name?' she asked.

'Amina.'

'She sounds nice and traditional.'

'She is.' If he caught the edge in her tone, he didn't show it.

'That's great. It's what you need.'

'What do you mean by that?'

She half shrugged. 'Men like you think you want a woman like me – a woman who is "modern", who'll tell you to fuck off when you need to hear it – but when it comes down to it, you all want an Amina to stay at home and cook and clean.'

He blinked. 'That's a shitty thing to say.'

'*Is* it?' she asked, reflexively mean.

'Why do you do this, Safa? Every time there's a chance that you might feel something, you hit back. You hit hard.' He leaned in, desperate to make her understand. 'I don't want *a woman like you*. I want *you*. I don't think I've ever given you a sign otherwise, but every time I try, you push me away, insist I want something else, someone else.'

'And now you do.'

'Well, I can't wait forever, Safa. I thought I could – I thought I *would* – but I can't.'

'That's fine. I never asked you to.'

'Yes,' he said sardonically. 'As if Safa Saleem could ever show *need*.'

Safa forced herself to stay in her seat, trying for maturity. In the past, she had always run, but Imran had asked for a clean break and she owed him that at least. She pictured this woman, Amina: a pretty pharmacist, or glossy-haired dermatologist, who was all too ready to give up her career to start their family. The depth of Safa's bitterness made her ashamed of herself, but it hurt to think of Imran with someone else. Who would he be with Amina? The lighter, happier version of himself that Safa had slowly sobered? He deserved a woman like that. He deserved that life.

She swallowed her bitterness, forced herself to sit up straight. 'I want you to be happy, Imran.'

A muscle tensed in his jaw. 'Okay, Safa.'

The quiet way in which he said it made her understand that he really was giving up. She drained her tea, slow and deliberate, keeping a lid on her pain. 'I have to go now, but I'll let you know how it goes on White Horse Road.'

He sighed softly. 'Fine.'

'Thanks for the tea.' She stood and left the café and didn't stop or look back until she was halfway down Globe Road, almost back at *The Echo*. Regret hit her like a bullet, hot and corrosive. She wished she could have asked him to stay, to wait, but the past two decades hadn't fixed her and she knew that two more would not.

*

Lily parked her car and checked herself in the rearview mirror to make sure she looked okay. She had piled her blonde hair beneath a brunette wig and swapped her expensive clothes for ripped jeans, an oversized hoodie and chunky Timberland boots that she had bought specifically. She wore bottle-top glasses and her face was free of makeup. She hadn't practised a different accent; she could simply revert to her natural one. It was always there, beneath the surface of her cut-glass vowels, threatening to emerge given the slightest chance. Sliding into Lily-Ann Baker was the easiest thing in the world.

Outside, she checked her Google Maps, then walked into a draughty hall. It was part of a council building and smelled of damp plaster. There were posters everywhere spelling out threats to beleaguered women – DV, VAWG, EBD, CPA, SSA – most of which Lily didn't recognise. She scoured them with interest – this esoteric language which she had to learn.

She checked her wig in a windowpane and ventured further inside. Timidly, she took a seat in the circle and fixed her gaze on the floor. The group met on Wednesday evenings, led by Meena, a large woman with frizzy brown hair. She smiled at Lily kindly and let the others settle before starting with her own story.

'It began three years ago when I put on weight.' Meena pinched her brown T-shirt which hung tent-like over her body. 'I was laid off from work and money got tight. Sam blamed me for it, as if I had done something to make them sack me. I began to comfort eat, but that began a vicious cycle. He would catch me in the kitchen and it started out as teasing: "wobbly", "flabby", "pudgy", "roly-poly" – childish words that sounded harmless, but then it became "lardy" and "chunky" and I asked him to stop. I *told* him to stop, but it became "lard-arse" and "whale". He even called me "unfuckable", can you believe?' Meena's voice was neutral but the tension in the room grew thick.

'He called me all sorts of things, but it was always verbal – nothing physical – and I thought it would be okay once I lost weight. I tried to diet but he would scoff at me, which sent me back to the fridge. I didn't recognise myself anymore, but I couldn't stop eating. He told me he was embarrassed of me. He didn't want to be seen in public with me. One time, he was on his way to a five-a-side match with his mates and he forgot his kit bag. I dropped it off at the pitch, thinking he'd be pleased. That night was the first time he hit me. He said, "Do you know how fucking embarrassing it is for my mates to see you?" I was stunned. He had never been violent. Mean, often, but never violent.'

Meena gathered her hands in her lap. 'I never understood what changed him. Was it purely the fact that I was fat? Or that we didn't have money? Did he really hate me so much that he had to hit me? I tried to talk to him, to get him to talk to me. I told him again and again that I loved him, but it was like I wasn't a person anymore let alone someone he could love back.'

'What happened?' asked Lily.

Meena nodded patiently. Clearly, Lily wasn't the first person to rush her towards the end of her story; to grasp at the hope that might be waiting. 'It carried on for three years.' Meena patted her own knee in a soothing gesture. 'Three years of hiding bruises, three years of keeping silent.'

'How often did he hit you?' Lily knew she was being insensitive but she needed something to anchor to.

Meena was stiff, as if braced. 'Daily.' The word had a chilling effect.

'What happened after three years?'

There was flint in Meena's eyes; a resolute composure. 'As soon as he could afford to, he moved out.'

'And that was it?'

'That was it,' she said softly. 'And I haven't seen him since.'

Lily felt an awful sense of hollowness. It wasn't lost on her that *he* had been the one to leave. Meena had simply endured it. She felt a raging sense of injustice that women were so often bound like this.

'Would you like to share your story?' Meena asked.

Lily's face was hot. She had come here, finally, to talk, but now that seven women were staring at her, she felt mute and clumsy. They waited patiently and Lily groped for courage.

'My name's Ann,' she said, picking up the flattened vowels of her childhood. She steadied her nerves and began. 'For me, it started three years ago. Like Meena, I don't know why it started but I do know when: in Jan 2021 halfway through the lockdown. One thing I always loved about us is that we always talked. My friends used to say they were jealous 'cause we could talk for hours – something they never could. We'd do the crossword together, can you believe? We'd laugh about all sorts of silly things. We just never ran out of things to say. But when Covid happened, it was like he became a different person. He was always on his phone or prowling around like a cat – and that was fair enough. We were in lockdown and there wasn't anything to do, but then he started to lose his temper over nothing. He started by hitting things. When he couldn't do something simple – like open a jar, or get his charger out of the socket – he would punch a cushion or slam a drawer. He'd always been calm by nature, so I didn't talk to him about it. I just thought he'd be all right once we came out of lockdown.'

Lily laced her fingers, gripping her knuckles tight. 'The first time he actually hit me, we were sat in the garden on this sunny day in April. I was feeling good because there were signs of things getting back to normal. Schools were open again. You could meet outdoors. Shops and salons were open. I was feeling hopeful and, because of that, I guess I got careless. We were doing the crossword and he said a word wrong. I can't even remember what it was, but I laughed and corrected him and that's when he switched.

'He grabbed my hand and dug his nails into the back of it. He said, "Don't fucking laugh at me." Our neighbours were in their garden and I was so embarrassed in case they heard. I snatched my hand away and told him, "Don't *ever* do that again." Do you know what he did? He laughed. He laughed and strolled back into the house.'

Lily paused to steady her accent. In times of stress, she reached for her Astor vowels; her shield against the world. 'One day, the three of us were eating dinner: me, Harry – that's my son – and Richard, my husband.' Lily used their real names to keep her story straight. 'I'd made his favourite meal – slow roasted lamb – and it'd taken me hours but he just sat there on his phone. I asked him to put it away while we ate.' Lily drew in a jagged breath. 'He threw it at my head. It hit the wall behind me and I just sat there, stunned. There'd been no warning. It's not like we'd argued beforehand. One second, he was on his phone, the next, he was throwing it at me. Harry was just as stunned as I was. He was only eleven then and sat like a deer in headlights, waiting for me to do something. I told him to go upstairs. He said no and I snapped at him. I was terrified of what might happen. Richard had never hit him before but we all know how quickly men can get aggressive.'

Lily cleared her throat. 'I told myself not to overreact; that it wouldn't happen again, but it got worse. Only *I* know how bad. Mostly, I've coped on my own, but I'm starting to lose control.' She looked around at the women, her voice shaking. 'And I need help.'

Meena's face was full of compassion. 'Have you sought help for him, Ann?'

'We've been to therapy,' she lied. 'When I get him on a good day, he apologises, but on bad days, he can't be reasoned with.'

'You said that you're starting to lose control. Do you want to talk about that?'

Lily leaned forward in a protective slouch. 'When I was younger, I had a bit of a funny relationship with food. Sometimes, there wasn't enough in the house so, when there *was*, I would sometimes overeat.' Lily touched her cheek to cool the burning. 'I keep wanting that again. When he hurts me, it's like my body needs that security blanket from my childhood. I think he knows as well. He's seen me get tense around food and I think he likes to watch.'

She met Meena's eye and they shared an understanding. How did men know to target women's bodies? At what age did they learn to hate the folds and curves that nourished them as children? Was it instinctive or did they acquire it?

'I don't know what to do,' said Lily. After three long years, she was on the cusp of breakdown. The bruises were beginning to show and the jibes about her diet were taking hold. She couldn't metabolise the pain anymore. She couldn't keep the peace. One of these days, Richard would surely hit Harry – and Lily could no longer protect him. She needed help from women who understood what she was going through.

'You're here,' soothed Meena. 'And that's a start.'

'But what can I do?' Lily pleaded.

'The very first step is to put a safety plan in place. How will you get out of the house if you need to? Carry a list of numbers you would need to call. Ensure you have access to a phone. Keep cash on you in case you need to use a bus, taxi or train, keep a spare set of house and car keys in a safe place.'

Lily brought her palms together. 'I don't need a safety plan. I need to know how to fix him.'

Meena gave her a quick, sympathetic smile. 'Ann, if he's physically abusive, it's a good idea to have a safety plan even if you never have to use it.'

'But how can I make him stop?'

'That's what we're here to discuss and we'll do a deep dive but for now, I can share some techniques.' Meena told her to write a list of reasonable and unreasonable behaviour as a reminder to herself. This would act as an objective set of boundaries when emotion got in the way. She told her to use 'I' statements such as 'I expect', 'I need you to,' and 'I will/will not' instead of 'you'. She spoke about 'de-escalation' and 'reconciliation gestures' and other opaque labels that seemed feeble in the face of violence.

'Have you ever hit him back?' asked a voice to her right. It was a small, bird-like woman with fine hair and delicate wrists.

Lily blinked. 'No. Of course not.'

'It helped *me*,' said the woman. 'I whacked the little fucker with my iron.'

Lily stared, open mouthed. 'I don't think violence is the answer,' she said, wincing as her Astor accent surfaced.

'Sometimes, they need to be shown that you're willing to fight back.'

Meena cut in quickly to stress the importance of nonviolence.

Lily listened and nodded along when the other women shared their stories, but all the while she was thinking how powerless they were, how cowed by male strength, how weakened by their own emotions. With this knowledge came a familiar question: *Do you really think I'd let myself become a battered woman?* It was cruel and mocking, and as she looked around the room, it made her hate herself.

Chapter 3

When Safa was younger, East London's hidden pockets of wealth and beauty used to delight her: the neat row of townhouses in Tredegar Square, the bone-white yachts of Limehouse Marina, the green beacon of Canary Wharf promising Gatsby-esque riches. As an adult, however, she grew to resent them for she knew that they were closed to her. It made it all the more bittersweet that Lily had ended up in a Thames-side townhouse on Narrow Street. When Lily and Richard had first bought it, Safa had searched online for houses for sale nearby. The only one available was marked with 'POA' – price on application. She had checked sold house prices and landed on a figure of a million and a half.

She looked at the house now, bathed in evening light – a storybook picture brought to life. She walked through the black gates that she had only ever seen open. *Privileged but not divided,* she thought wryly. She passed a Bentley and a Maserati and thought of her one-bed flat in a faceless new build in Stepney Green. Her living room, dining room and kitchen were all in one space and she had only a Juliet balcony.

She cut across the gravel towards the row of houses. They had a laidback class, nothing too self-conscious. The Maserati had streaks of mud across the body, screaming everyday use. The greenery was rakishly overgrown, shrubs and flowers spilling onto gravel. Here, they wore their money lightly.

She counted down the door numbers and paused outside Lily's house. Safa had planned to go to White Horse Road to follow the lead from Imran, but Kevin had sent her here. Rumour had it that an *Arise* crewmember had seen Lily with bruises on set yesterday after a mishap with her cardigan. Kevin's thinking was that the initial flurry of journalists would have dispersed, leaving Safa a clear route to her friend.

She rang the bell and listened for movement. She counted thirty seconds and rang again. When there was no answer, she walked to the left of the house and peeked into the side passage. It was clear except for three bikes – coloured red, white and blue – and a hosepipe slung around a brass tap. The sight of the child-sized helmet slung over a handlebar made her heart contract. It had been so very long since she had seen Harry. Safa wasn't maternal and her early contact with him had felt somewhat unnatural – Safa too bony and jerky to offer his tiny body real comfort. As he grew older, however, Safa became enamoured. Harry was a happy, soulful child, quick to laughter but also quick to concern. Safa remembered walking in on him as he watched a nature documentary one day. Three penguin chicks were dying on screen and though Harry was only three, his face was ripe with heartbreak. It was clear that he somehow understood the finality of death. Safa had scooped him up into her arms and he had wept into her neck – hot, quiet tears that seeped into her T-shirt.

The memory made her breath catch. She stepped back, needing physical distance. The shift of gravel beneath her feet brought her back to the present. She made a low, soft *woo* sound and retreated back to the door. She rang the bell a third time. Then, she bent and looked through the letterbox. She startled when the door was yanked open. Richard Astor eyed her with suspicion.

'Can I help you?' he asked tersely.

She had forgotten how plain he was: mouse-brown hair, sunken eyes and a forgettable Englishman's face. 'Richard, hi. It's been a while.' She saw no sign of recognition. 'It's Safa. Safa Saleem.'

He tensed with irritation.

'We haven't seen each other in a while. A few years in fact.'

'How may I help you?' he asked.

Safa was thrown by his formal manner. She and Richard had never spent much time together, but surely he remembered her. 'I was hoping to talk to Lily. I've been trying to get a hold of her since yesterday and—'

'Lily's unwell.'

'Oh, I'm sorry to hear that. Do you think I could pop in and say hi?'

'She's unwell,' he repeated.

'I really won't be long. I just want a quick chat.'

'Why?'

Safa worded her answer carefully. 'I'm sure you know that there's been a lot of interest in Lily's bruises. I thought that maybe she'd like to address them through someone she knows and trusts.'

He angled his head. 'And that would *be you*?'

'Yes.' Safa frowned. 'You *do* remember me, right?'

A muscle twitched in his temple. 'Lily doesn't want to see you.'

Safa's own tone cooled. 'Can she tell me that herself?' Safa had known plenty of men like Richard at *The Clarion*: well-heeled, well-educated, with a baronet or two in the family tree. She knew that their respectable pedigree hid a multitude of vices – a coke habit, workplace bullying, chronic infidelity – but she hadn't believed until now that Richard could be hurting Lily.

'I think you should go.' Richard flexed his fingers wide, then curled them inwards.

Safa instinctively held the door open. 'Is she hurt?'

He fixed his coal-black stare on her. 'This is none of your business.'

'I think it *is* my business, Richard.' She pushed the door just enough so that he could feel its tension. He stepped out through the doorway. At 6'1", he towered over Safa and though she didn't retreat, she felt herself begin to sweat.

He brought his face close to hers. 'You need to get off my property.'

'Are you hurting her, Richard?'

'I said: get the *fuck* off my property.' His hot breath hit Safa's skin, making her recoil.

'I want to see Lily,' she insisted.

'And *I* want you to get off my property.' He placed a finger on her chest with the barest pressure. 'Please.'

It took Safa a second to absorb that he was touching her, his forefinger digging in just above her breasts. Her stomach gave a single churn as she shoved his hand away. 'What the hell are you doing?'

He bared his teeth – a smile but not a smile. 'Has it ever occurred to you that you're just a cheap hack, Safa? Yes, I remember you. I also remember Lily saying how embarrassing it was that you won't let her friendship go, how you clung on like a leech, desperate for a job at the BBC. She won't tell you straight, so I'll tell you instead. Leave. Her. Alone.' With that, he slammed the door in her face.

Safa slid off the stairs, smarting at his words. Could Lily really have said those things? It was true that Safa had persisted through several unanswered texts, certain that Lily had meant to reply; that it had just slipped her mind. She cringed now at the breezy tone of the text she had sent after the last time they had met: *Hey, I forgot to ask: I don't suppose there are any jobs going in your team atm? No worries if not! I'm just getting a bit tired of freelance life!*

Safa had always been mindful not to ask Lily for favours. As her success grew, more and more people asked her for things and Safa didn't want to add to the noise. Sometimes, she sensed that even finding time for dinner put too much pressure on Lily. It's why she had couched her request so lightly. *I'm just getting a bit tired of freelance life!* In truth, she had barely been able pay her bills amid post-pandemic budget cuts.

Safa landed at *The Clarion* not long after, but Lily never replied to that text, or the several after. Perhaps it was inevitable. When childhood friends achieved such different levels of success, it was naive to think that they could stay close. In asking for that favour, Safa had only confirmed the difference in status between them. To learn now that Lily had griped about it to Richard humiliated her. Safa had spent so much of her career being made to feel small or callow. For Lily to do it now made her burn with shame.

She backed away from the steps, her nerves still jangling from the confrontation. She looked up at the house and saw a shadow retreat from a window. She waited and watched for Lily, but nothing else stirred. Safa's pride bristled. If Lily truly didn't want her around, then Safa would stop trying. Her intuition, however, told her not to be so childish. If there was something darker happening here, then Safa couldn't just let it be.

*

Lily stood by the window and watched Safa go. Seeing her after all this time made her yearn for contact. Meena at the therapy group had spoken about building a community, of letting aggressors know that you do not stand alone. Safa had always been there for her. In a constant and quiet way, over the course of *years*, she had made sure that Lily was safe and fed. Seeing her now made Lily want to cry out for help.

She heard Richard's tread on the stairs and pulled back from the window. She felt exhausted at the thought of another fight. She didn't want to face him; knew how weak she must appear to him, how different to the girl he married.

She hid in the ensuite bathroom and checked her nose in the mirror. Delicately, she touched the sore spot and felt a pulse of pain. The bleeding had stopped but her nose was red and bloated. She heard the bedroom door open and quickly wiped her tears.

His footsteps advanced across the room. A knock on the bathroom door.

'Lily.' Richard's voice. 'Come out, will you?'

She took a moment to steady herself. 'I just need a minute.'

'Come out.'

'Richard, please.'

She heard a soft thud and knew that his fist was poised on the door, knuckles white with anger. If she didn't open it, she knew what would happen next. Sure enough, as she finished cleaning her face, she heard him go upstairs and rattle the handle to Harry's bedroom.

'Harry, turn down that music.' He pounded on the door. 'Harry! Turn off the fucking music!'

Lily willed her son not to unlock the door. At thirteen, he was already stronger than her, but he was still a child. If he dared to face up to Richard, he would end up with far worse than a bloody nose. The thought brought her out of her paralysis. She darted out of the room, driven by the powerful, primitive need to shield her only child. The music was skull-crushingly loud and made it hard to think.

'Richard, leave him alone. Please.' She grabbed at his sleeve.

He jerked away from her. 'I swear to god I'm going to smash down this door if he doesn't open it.' Inside the room, the music grew louder. 'Harry! Open the fucking door!' Richard's face was unrecognisable. His eyes were round and bug-like, and his skin was pink with impotence. He looked around the landing, caught in a sort of mania. He spotted the heavy brass lamp and Lily knew instantly what he intended to do. She sprang in front of him and held up her palms. She didn't think that the lamp was heavy enough to break through Harry's door but she couldn't take that chance. If he reached Harry, he wouldn't hold back. She reached frantically for Meena's advice. *Use 'I' statements. I expect, I need you to, I will not.*

'Richard.' Her voice was too loud in its bid for authority. 'I need you to come downstairs with me,' she tried again more calmly. The keen control in her voice gave him a second's pause. It seemed to vent just enough of his anger before it hit a roiling boil. Lily spoke again. 'I need you to listen to what I'm saying. I need you to come downstairs with me.' Richard looked at her through the fog and, in that moment, she glimpsed the man she used to know. The smart, confident, worldly man who felt at ease in any room. The man she loved before this toxic violence took over their lives.

She didn't beg or plead; simply turned and walked downstairs, praying that Richard would follow. She didn't hear his footsteps over the thumping music but when she reached the living room, she turned and found him there. She slackened, and he came to her instinctively. She let him hold her and kiss her hair and promise that things would change. She didn't believe him, but she was weak with relief for another disaster averted.

*

Safa waited outside the BBC building and sipped her Starbucks coffee. It was weak and tepid but kept off the April chill. She checked the time: 12.30 p.m., half an hour after *Arise* came off air. Every time a blonde woman left the building, Safa felt a spike of nerves, not unlike butterflies. It had been three years since she and Lily had last seen each other. Turning up unannounced felt a little crass, but there had been something in Richard's demeanour that had forced Safa here today. She drained her cup and dropped it into a bin, jittery from the caffeine.

She caught a flash of blonde at the edge of her vision and looked up towards it. Their eyes met in the same instant. For a dreadful moment, Safa thought that she would walk on, but her entire body changed, like a weight had lifted off – her spine, no longer rigid, her shoulders, no longer taut. Her face creased with emotion as she drew closer. To Safa's surprise, Lily threw her arms around her with a strange, strangled sound. Everything about the moment – the scent of Lily's perfume, the ferocity of her hug, that strange, childlike cry – filled Safa with nostalgia. They stood locked in a hug and Safa closed her eyes. After a long moment, she gently pulled back.

'Hey,' she said softly. 'How the fuck have you been?'

Lily laughed – a harsh, emotional sound. 'If it isn't Safa Saleem.'

'In the flesh.' She assessed her old friend. 'How have you been?' she repeated.

'Oh, you know.' Lily batted the question away. 'How are *you*? What are you doing here?'

'Actually, I came to see you.' Safa chose to be direct. 'I don't suppose you have time for a coffee?'

Lily tensed but it was barely perceptible. 'Uh, okay.' She clenched her fist and Safa knew it was an effort not to check her watch.

'Just a quick catch-up?' Safa added.

'Yeah, sure,' but she didn't sound sure at all.

Safa had scoped out the local cafes and chosen a nearby eatery that was quiet enough for them to talk, but not so small that others could eavesdrop. She led Lily there, thankful that the streets were too busy to allow for awkward small talk. She ordered them a black coffee and a green tea, and sat opposite Lily.

'I came by your house yesterday,' she said.

'Yes, Richard told me.' Lily played with her teabag, avoiding Safa's gaze.

'Were you home?'

'I was sleeping.'

Safa studied her. Usually, she could tell when someone was lying but Lily hid it well. 'Were you really?'

Lily set down her spoon. 'What are you really asking?'

'I want to see if you're okay.'

'Of course I'm okay.'

Safa didn't believe her. 'Lily, you've always been tough and god knows you've had to be, but it's *me* you're talking to. Safa, your friend; not Safa, the reporter.'

Lily rolled her eyes. 'God, this whole thing has blown way out of proportion. There is nothing going on.'

Safa watched her carefully. 'Promise me.'

'Christ, I see you're as dogged as ever.'

'Lily. Promise me.'

Lily fixed her grey eyes on her. 'I promise,' she said.

Safa shifted uneasily. 'So why do I feel like there's something going on?'

Lily's laugh was warm. 'Safa, come on. Save your efforts for someone who needs it. I'm *fine*.'

'Then why was Richard so hostile to me?'

Lily gestured dismissively. 'I'm sorry if he was. We had reporters at our door all day and I guess he didn't make the distinction between you and them.'

'But he *knows* me. I know it's been a while since we saw each other, but still.'

Lily angled her head in apology. 'Honestly? I think he thought you were using our friendship to get a story.'

Safa drew back. 'You know that's not why I'm here, right?'

'I know, but either way, you don't need to worry about me.'

Safa narrowed her eyes. 'It really was just a game of tennis?'

'It really was just a game of tennis.'

Safa exhaled upwards, slack with relief. 'Jesus. I really thought I'd come to rescue you.'

Lily grew sombre. 'You did, Safa. Every time I needed you.'

Safa realised how much she missed Lily – and how much it hurt that she had left her behind. There had, of course, been early signs that it would always happen.

Safa and Lily had sat their A level exams and applied to university together. They had filled in their UCAS forms and dreamt of the fun they would have – but then their plans went awry. Safa still remembered that day with crystal clarity. Lily had bounded over in the college refectory, brimming with her news.

'I got in!' she shouted jubilantly, all teeth and braces. 'Safa, you won't believe this! I got into Oxford!'

Safa felt a jolt of shock. 'You what?'

'I got into Oxford!' Lily saw the look on Safa's face and clutched the sheet to her chest. 'Sorry I didn't say anything about applying.'

Safa stared at her. 'Why didn't you tell me?'

'I didn't think they'd let me in so saved myself the embarrassment. I only told Ms Allen because I needed help with the funding.'

Safa's face was hot. 'But if I'd known, I would have applied too.'

Lily frowned. 'Safa, you know you wouldn't leave your dad.'

'Maybe I *would* have for Oxford!' Safa felt choked with betrayal.

Lily faltered. 'I didn't know that you would have applied too.'

'Of course I would have! We always spoke about going to uni together!'

'Yeah, but I didn't know.'

Safa was overcome with emotion – anger, frustration, indignation – but forced herself to swallow them all; to smile tightly and say, 'Okay, wow. Well, I'm happy for you.' And she *was*, eventually, but those feelings never went away fully. They were always there, like a fishbone caught in her throat. Lily could sense it no doubt, and resented being made to feel guilty.

Safa remembered what Richard had said yesterday: that Lily found it embarrassing that Safa wouldn't let their friendship end. *You clung on like a leech, desperate for a job at the BBC.*

Safa wanted to ask about it now – *how come you stopped replying to me?* – but was afraid to hear the truth. *Because I didn't want my unemployed friend from childhood embarrassing me at the BBC.*

'Anyway.' Lily checked her watch. 'I better get on.'

'Okay, sure. Thanks for the chat. It was nice to catch up.' Safa waited, but Lily didn't offer to make other plans. 'I'll see you soon?' said Safa, regretting the slight inflection that turned it into a question.

Lily smiled with kindness. 'See you soon, Safa.' She kissed her cheek and gave her shoulder a little squeeze. Safa watched her go and felt a sense of finality, like this might be the last chapter closing on her oldest friendship. If Safa was honest, Lily might have been ready to let it go all the way back in Oxford. All the way back to the day of the funeral.

It had been a small affair: Lily, Natalie, Safa and her dad, Jahangir, and four or five of their neighbours. Lily's mother had died from liver failure and though she was only forty-five years old, there was a sense of inevitability. It seemed the consensus that after fifteen years of alcoholism, death would finally bring her peace. There were lots of platitudes but very few tears. In fact, the only person who cried was a neighbour from Withy House.

Lily approached the funeral with a calm pragmatism; a duty she had to do before returning to exams. She didn't want to stay at Withy House so was heading back to Oxford that very same evening. Safa, who was insured on her father's car, offered to drive her up.

'Is this where you live?' she cried as they approached Lady Margaret Hall, Lily's college at Oxford.

Lily waved casually. 'It's not even one of the nicer ones.'

Safa looked up at grand portico and felt a burst of regret that she herself had never applied. She wanted to explore the grounds but couldn't ask that of Lily right now. 'Can I come in and use the loo? I know you have to revise so I won't hang around for long.'

They were halfway across the lawn when they heard Lily's name behind them. Safa turned and saw a young man with dark brown curls and a blandly pleasant face.

Lily startled with surprise. 'Richard!' she trilled. 'What are you doing here?'

Safa glanced at Lily, surprised by the change in her accent.

'Hi, darling. I wanted to be with you.' He pulled Lily into a hug. 'You didn't let me come to the funeral so I wanted to see you.'

'I didn't want to disrupt your exams, Richard. It's your final year.'

Safa stared at Lily. At first, she thought that the accent was a joke, but Richard didn't find it funny.

He looked at Safa curiously. 'Who's this?'

'This is a childhood friend of mine: Safa Saleem. Safa, this is Richard Astor.'

Richard reached out his hand. 'How do you do.'

Safa shook it. 'I'm well. How are you?' She sensed Lily tense next to her.

'Were you close to Gabrielle?' he asked.

It took Safa a second to realise that he was talking about Gabby, Lily's mother. 'Somewhat,' she said. 'I've known her since we were children.'

'I'm sorry for your loss.' He sighed sadly. 'Cancer is *such* a scourge. It took my uncle and the entire thing was just awful.' He rubbed Lily's shoulders. 'But this one has been such a trooper.'

Safa saw the colour in Lily's cheeks. She waited to catch her eye, but Lily didn't look at her.

'Safa here needs a quick rest stop before she heads back.' Lily gripped Safa's elbow. 'Can you give us a few minutes?' She ferried Safa into the building. 'The bathroom's just there,' she said, her accent back to normal.

Safa arched her brows. 'Cancer?'

Lily's eyes flashed with venom. 'You wouldn't understand.'

'You told Richard your mum died from cancer?'

Lily grew impatient. 'Look, Safa. I like Richard and he likes me.'

'So why lie to him?'

'I couldn't tell him that my mother's a fucking alcoholic, okay? You don't understand people like Richard's family. If they knew, I swear they'd be able to smell the booze on *me*.'

'That's fucked up, Lily. And what's with your accent?'

Lily huffed. 'I *knew* you'd be like this.'

'Like what? I don't understand what's going on.'

'You don't get it, Safa. You've always had your dad, but I had no one. Richard is my first chance at something proper, so shoot me if I've told a few white lies to fit in with his family.'

'Saying your mother died from cancer is more than a white lie.'

'Says who?' Lily's shoulders jerked defensively. 'Why does it even matter? It's not like he's going to order her *death* certificate.'

Safa was at a loss. She couldn't untangle Lily's reasoning, but knew that it was wrong. 'I think if you tell him the truth, he will love you for who you are.'

Lily gave her a wistful smile. 'Safa, you are so young sometimes.'

The words made Safa flinch. In that moment, she felt like she understood very little about the world. It was that day perhaps that the chasm between them began to open, leading up to this very moment when the dust on their friendship finally settled.

Safa wondered now if she had shoehorned herself into Lily's

life. She had carved out time to see Lily and Harry, suggested dates and outings, persisted with rescheduling. She thought she was being a good friend, picking up the slack while Lily was busy with motherhood – but had it been one sided?

Safa was certain, at least, that her bond with Harry had been real. She remembered taking him swimming as a child, as Lily hated the water. Safa would hold his pudgy body in her hands and watch him squeal with delight. Afterwards, she would wrap him up in his fluffy blue towel, his lashes still thick with water. The memory raised a tang of pain: bright and sudden, like an open sore touched by mistake. Safa had never reckoned with how much it had hurt to be cut off from Harry. There was something almost uncouth about it. Safa had no formal claim to him. She wasn't his aunt or godmother – that honour had been given to one of Richard's cousins – and it didn't feel socially acceptable to miss a child you weren't related to. In this moment, however, Safa felt the absence so keenly, it made her throat contract. She flashed a plaintive smile at the empty chair where Lily had sat. *It's okay. I don't mind.*

She tried hard to believe it. Really, she ought to be grateful for the time that she *had* been given. The softness and joy that he'd brought to her life was more than she'd ever expected. More than she deserved.

*

Kevin Giles stood at the front of the newsroom. Darkness had fallen in the windows but the mood inside was loose and cheery. These Friday evening meetings were a chance to let off steam after the paper was published. There was an easy camaraderie among the team who lay strewn about the newsroom in various states of productivity – some with a foot already out the door, others bedding in.

'The site stats are in for the week. The most shared piece on social was . . .' Kevin glanced at his iPad. '"Algorithm & Blues" by Tim O'Leary.' He arched his brows, impressed. 'Nice headline,' he said, finding Tim in the newsroom. A chorus of praise went up around him.

Tim blushed. He instinctively looked over at Safa who gave him the slightest nod. 'Thank you, sir,' he said quickly.

'How would you feel about working on the Robert Knox story?'

Tim did a double take. 'I would love that, sir. I—'

'It's yours.'

Tim lit up. Robert Knox was a controversial influencer who peddled toxic masculinity to his millions of followers on TikTok. Firmly in Knox's audience demographic of fifteen to twenty-five-year-old men, Tim was well placed to examine his appeal.

Kevin moved on. 'Our most read story was the exclusive quote from Lily Astor, courtesy of Safa Saleem.'

Her colleagues called out praise and Safa nodded graciously.

'How did you get on with your follow-up?' Kevin asked Safa.

'I spoke to Lily. She insists the bruises are innocent.'

'Do you believe her?'

Safa recalled the ease in Lily's manner, the lightness in her tone. 'Yes.'

'You're sure?'

'Yes.'

'Ok, what do you have for next week?'

Safa listed a number of local stories: a hit-and-run in Shadwell, an illegal dog-fight in Canning Town. 'There's another story I'm looking into, but I don't have anything concrete yet.'

'What is it?'

Safa hesitated. She wanted a chance to find the witness on White Horse Road before she said anything more. 'Can I see if there's something there first?'

'How long do you need?'

'Two weeks to start off with?'

'Fine,' said Kevin.

He moved on with the agenda and Safa relaxed. This was the benefit of working on a small paper; she had a level of freedom – but she didn't want to get stuck there. She recalled Richard's insult. *Has it ever occurred to you that you're just a cheap hack?* The words still stung a whole day later. Of *course* it had occurred to her. It was why she was intent on clawing her way back to a national paper.

In idle moments, Safa dreamt of winning a Whitney, and this rarely happened to a writer on a local rag. If Safa managed it, she would have her *pick* of roles in journalism. She would have the power to decide what *was* and *wasn't* news. Some of her well-heeled colleagues in the press would only ever see her as a mechanic's daughter, but a Whitney would prove something – to them and to herself. It would prove that if you worked long enough, if you cared about your subjects deeply enough, and fought for them hard enough, you could make it in this merciless industry without selling your soul.

*

Safa let herself into her dad's house and felt the tension leave her body. Friday evenings were their quality time and allowed no scope for work.

'Dad?' she called, looking into the living room. She headed to the kitchen and heaved two bags of groceries onto the counter. She noticed that the fibreboard edge around the sink had grown brown and rotten and made a mental note to chase the council again. She spotted her dad in the garden, bent over his tomato plant, which was struggling at this time of year. She felt a sense of melancholy when she saw his hand on his hip and the crooked angle at which he stood to ease the ache of his arthritis. He wasn't a big man but had always been tough and strong. To see him finally yield to old age filled her with sorrow. She looked away, feeling guilty for intruding on a moment of privacy. She focused on the groceries. As she unpacked the first bag, she heard footsteps in the machine room – not a dog but human. She stopped moving and listened. There it was again. A shuffling lope. Gently, she closed the fridge door and ventured into the hall. She heard the shuffling again.

'Hello?' she called out unsurely. The machine room door opened and Safa did a double take. 'What are *you* doing here?'

Imran seemed surprised to see her. 'Your dad called me. He wanted the Diamond betel nut that they sell round my way in Poplar.'

She scowled. 'So, he called *you?*'

He lifted a shoulder. 'He always calls when he runs out.' A pause. 'I didn't know you'd be here.'

'Yeah, but *he* did.' Safa was reluctant to tell her father that she and Imran were properly over. They had met by accident, early last year when she and Imran had first started dating. Imran had been helping to move her dad's bed downstairs in preparation for his knee surgery. Her dad was supposed to be out walking his dog but came home early to find them lugging the bed downstairs.

'So this is the fella that's put a spring in her step,' he quipped from the doorway. He forced Imran to stay for dinner. All the while, Safa tried to put distance between them, but failed to separate house and fire. The two of them became friends. They went to the cricket at Lords, shared barbecue duties at gatherings and taste-tested each other's experimental recipes. Safa had worried about how swiftly her dad had taken to him, how aggressive their bond. She couldn't help but think that Imran took the place of the son that her dad had so desperately wanted.

'Do you want me to leave?' he asked.

'He won't let you go without eating,' said Safa.

Imran shifted unsurely. 'I can say I got a call from work and have to go.'

She dismissed this with a wave. 'It's fine. We're both grownups. We can have one meal together.' She turned and headed back to the kitchen.

Imran followed and together they unpacked the groceries. She watched him out of the corner of her eye. His ease in this kitchen unlocked a certain tenderness. How long would it be until she found another man who could own the space like this?

He glanced at her and caught the wistful look on her face. 'You okay?'

'Yeah,' she said quickly. 'I'm fine.'

She heard the garden door and turned to greet her dad, not wanting him to witness this picture of domesticity. She kissed his cheek and set about laying the table, which was tucked into one corner of the kitchen.

She listened to them joke and spar, and tamped down all her emotion. How easy it would be to let him stay in their lives. She and Imran were right for each other in so many ways, not just in culture and background but also mood and humour – Safa, dark, and Imran, light, each rebalancing the other. But there was one obstacle they couldn't clear: Imran wanted children and Safa did not.

They had cycled through several iterations. First, Imran telling her that she would change her mind. Next, Imran deciding that he didn't want kids after all. For a while, Safa had tried to believe him but she saw his silly, goofy side and his wholesome, traditional side and she knew that a man like him would never be satisfied with anything less than 2.4 children. Last, they had tried the 'late-night booty call bullshit' as Imran put it, but he had wanted them to give it a proper try. Safa knew that the longer she let it go on, the harder it would be for them both, and so she pushed him away.

Safa wished that she *did* want children – not just for Imran's sake but her father's too. After all, isn't that what a family *was*? Children and their tiny shoes, tickles and giggles, *Spot the Dog* and *The Very Hungry Caterpillar.* Instead, they had Safa – tough, sedate and emotionally guarded. She lacked the soft edges and vulnerability that a man like Imran wanted. He was right to move on, but as she watched him with her father, that tough centre that she worked so hard on wasn't quite tough enough to let him go.

Chapter 4

Safa zipped up her coat as she walked down White Horse Road. After leaving her dad's last night, she had stayed up late in her flat and charted out this route. She had to be methodical to make sure that she didn't miss the crucial door. White Horse Road was a long street of mainly residential houses. There was one large block of flats, squat and plastic, like the worst of Le Corbusier made to fit East London budgets. Safa had decided to leave the block till last. As far as she knew, the Glassman didn't target flats. He preferred the easy access of back yards and ground-floor windows. With that in mind, Safa started at the northern end of the road, nearest St Dunstan's Churchyard. This was the most isolated part and would provide most cover for a break-in.

Safa rang the doorbell and checked her reflection in a pane of glass. Rain was in the air and had frizzed her hair at the temples. She smoothed it impatiently and glanced at her watch. She knew that 11 a.m. on a Saturday wasn't the most polite time to doorstep a source, but it *was* a good time to catch most people at home. She heard movement inside and a woman opened the door. She was trim, white and had silvery hair clipped in a bun so tight, it showed fine slivers of her pink scalp.

Safa smiled warmly. 'Good morning, I'm Safa Saleem from the *East London Echo*. I'm looking into a local story and wondered if you had a moment to talk?'

The woman cocked her head with interest. 'You're from the paper? Might you do something about the bin collection? Those men simply lift the lid and if it's not yet full, they leave it until it is. I live alone and it takes me an age to fill it, so it lies there rotting for weeks.' The woman spoke in a cut-glass accent and Safa noted once again how money and poverty lived cheek by jowl in this part of London.

'I can certainly ask my colleague who covers local government to look into this,' said Safa sympathetically. 'I personally focus on crime and was wondering if you had heard anything about a break-in nearby.'

The woman didn't seem to hear any of this. 'When I complained about the litter, they sent one of those vehicles with the whiskery things, but that was six months ago and I've never seen them again.'

Safa hid her grimace. 'It's not very pleasant, is it?' she said. 'For the moment though, I was wondering about the break-in. Have you heard anything recently?'

The woman grew irritated. 'No. I'm afraid I can't help you there.'

'Have you seen a repair van anywhere here in the last few weeks? Perhaps a specialist in glass replacement?'

'I'm afraid not. Most of it's social housing around here so it would likely be the housing association that fixes it; not an external company.'

'Are their vans usually branded?' Safa knew that Newlon Housing Trust looked after the local area.

'I've never seen one.'

'Okay, thank you. Can I leave you my number? If you see a repair van in the area, can you tell me which house they visit?' Safa handed her a card and thanked her for her time.

It began to rain and Safa drew up her hood, then thought better of it. People would be more likely to open the door if her face wasn't obscured. At the next house, she found a young family who also hadn't heard about a break-in. This theme repeated itself over the next hour as Safa moved slowly down the long straight road. The houses became a little shabbier and Safa had a hunch that she was getting closer. The Glassman would choose a house unlikely to have an alarm. She arrived at a house with a red door. This one was perfectly positioned: end of terrace with a narrow passage leading to the backyard. Safa knocked and scanned the windows. No one answered, but she saw a curtain twitch. A wizened face quickly retreated when it saw that Safa was watching. Safa rang the bell again, then knocked gently on the window.

'*Sasi,*' she swapped to Sylheti. '*Dorza kulbayni. Afnareh ekhta zikaytam,*' she asked her to open the door. She could make out the shape of a woman, hunched with hesitation. '*Boht zoruri,*' said Safa, insisting that it was important. It took an age but the woman finally opened the door, blocking the gap with her body. She was in her seventies and wore a loose scarf around her lined face.

Safa's senses bristled. Some lizard instinct told her that this might be the crucial door. She had to persuade this woman to let her inside her home. There was no hope of candour out here on the doorstep.

'My father lives nearby,' said Safa in Sylheti. 'Jahangir, the widower?' The community's collective sympathy meant that few people in the area hadn't heard of her father.

'You're his daughter?' asked the woman.

'Yes, my name is Safa. Can I come in for a minute?'

'What's this about?'

Safa indicated the rain with a stagey grimace. 'Can I come in? I'm getting wet out here.'

The woman hesitated, but her Bengali manners won out. She led Safa inside, along a short corridor and into a living room. It was small and cramped, filled with trinkets and paisley upholstery. It smelled musty and yet it was somehow draughty.

'Will you have some tea?' asked the woman.

'Yes please, but can I help?' In their culture, you wouldn't let an elder serve you like this without offering to help.

'No, no,' the woman said firmly. 'I'll bring it right in.'

Safa sat and noted several things. There was a prayer mat folded up on the arm of the sofa, a string of prayer beads known as *tasbih* on the coffee table, and the calendar on the wall had a picture of the *kaaba*, the iconic black structure in Mecca. The woman was clearly devout and although this was hardly surprising given her generation, it made Safa worry. In her experience, religion was yet another layer in a woman's shame.

There were footsteps in the hall and Safa hid the look on her face. 'You have a lovely home,' she said sweetly as the woman set down a tea tray. Safa took her cup with thanks and made small talk for a while as was Bengali custom. Casually, she asked, 'Does anyone else live here, auntie?' The woman's name was Rukshana but Safa addressed her as auntie as a sign of respect.

'No, only me.' Her hands shook a little as she set down her cup.

Safa nodded evenly. Rukshana lived alone – like the Glassman's other victims. 'Auntie, I grew up here so I know the Sylheti community well.' Safa knew that she would have to tread extraordinarily carefully. 'We have all worked so hard to make a life here and I'm so proud to be part of this community.' She paused. 'But as I'm sure you know there are also problems within it. We don't face things head on, we never say what we mean, we accommodate others to our own detriment, and rightly or wrongly we put *izzat* above all else.'

Izzat was a word from the subcontinent that meant dignity or honour. So often – *too* often – it was pegged to a woman's chastity. Men tasked their wives and daughters with upholding the family's honour. *Izzat* was as thick as a noose and yet flimsy as a thread, easily torn by a mere word or glance deemed to be immodest.

Rukshana neatened the folds of her sari. 'Well, what is there without *izzat*?' she said.

Safa's cheeks flushed. She had so much to say to that, but she needed to restrain herself. She could not lecture a woman of Rukshana's generation out of her views. 'It depends who decides what *izzat* is,' she said, studiedly measured. 'So often it's our fathers and husbands when really it should only be God.' Rukshana nodded and Safa was glad for this small bit of rapport.

Rukshana's mind was elsewhere for a moment, but then her eyes refocused. She set down her cup. 'What is it that you want to talk to me about?'

Safa knew that the word *journalist* or *reporter* would be a bombshell, so instead she said, 'Auntie, I work for *The Echo* and my job is to investigate crimes in the community.' She paused for resistance, but Rukshana let her continue. 'I heard recently that something bad happened in this area and I'm trying to find some details.' A shadow passed over Rukshana's features. Safa tensed, certain that her host knew *something*. 'I'm looking into this because a friend of mine lives nearby and said that several women have been hurt.' She didn't say that her friend was a policeman.

Rukshana's eyes grew hard. 'I don't know anything about that.'

'That's all right, auntie, but I'd like to ask a few questions nonetheless.'

Rukshana took a careful sip of her tea.

'Have you heard anything about a break-in on this street?'

'No.' She didn't pause to think.

'What about the surrounding streets? Anything in the last six months or so?'

'No.'

Safa watched her intently. 'I've heard that someone has been targeting elders in his area.' Safa used the word *murubi* – 'respectable elder' – on purpose. She hoped it showed that the victims were indeed respected. 'Have you heard anything like this?'

'No. If the Bengalis haven't heard about it, then it probably isn't true.' Rukshana's smile was eerily wide.

Safa didn't laugh. 'Auntie, have you ever heard the name "Glassman"?'

Rukshana's cup clattered onto its saucer, spilling tea everywhere. She leapt up, clasping her wet sari. 'Oh goodness! Please excuse me.' She hoicked up the folds and hurried out of the room.

Safa watched in alarm. Was it likely that Rukshana had heard the moniker? Had she spilled the tea in fright, or was it merely unlucky timing? Safa listened to the tap running. It felt rude to sit there impassively, so she stood and went to the kitchen. It was deathly cold in there but Safa saw from the boiler in the corner that the heating was off.

'Auntie, can I help?' she asked, hovering in the doorway.

'No, no, that's okay.' Rukshana spoke quickly. 'Please go and sit. I'll be just a minute.' Her gaze flicked to a spot beside the door.

Instinctively, Safa glanced in the same direction. Her heart seized when she saw the window. In the centre of the glass was a man-sized hole. It was hastily taped over with a cardboard box, but the shape and size was unmistakable. Safa whirled towards Rukshana and caught her look of sickly alarm.

'Auntie,' she said breathlessly.

Rukshana turned off the tap. 'Please go.'

Safa was flooded with horror. It was like liquid in her gullet, rising to her throat. In a tightly controlled tone, she asked, 'Auntie, can we go back to the living room?'

Rukshana didn't meet her gaze. 'Please go,' she repeated.

Safa fought the instinct to pray, beg, genuflect, to make Rukshana talk. 'Auntie, please. Can we just sit down for a minute?'

Rukshana turned her back on her and began to wipe down the countertops. There was vigour in her movements; a jerky determination. She ignored Safa and scrubbed at a spot of limescale. She flinched when Safa came nearer, but didn't stop cleaning. It was only when Safa laid a gentle hand on hers that Rukshana grew still. Safa felt it tremble beneath hers and added the slightest pressure. Rukshana's breath was rapid and shallow. Her shoulders curled in, bowed by her shame.

'You're not the only one,' said Safa.

Rukshana swallowed audibly. When she blinked, a tear landed in the sink, lost among the water. Safa waited, her hand still on Rukshana's. She felt it clench as Rukshana's whole body tensed with effort. Her features were strained and desperate as if she were trying to berate herself out of her silence. Safa held her breath, but Rukshana slackened. She shook her head, her eyes still wet, and slid her hand from Safa's.

'Auntie,' Safa repeated. *'Please.'*

Rukshana slung a tea towel over her shoulder. 'I have so much work to do.' Her voice wobbled beneath her casual tone. 'And it's almost time for prayer. I really must get on.'

Safa had to stop herself from physically protesting. She wanted to grip her wrists and beg her to talk. *You won't be the last*, she wanted to say, but couldn't add guilt to the shame. 'Auntie, it's happened to other women. To *murubis* like you.'

Colour rose in Rukshana's cheeks. 'I need you to go now.'

'If you can just give me five more minutes, I—'

'I need you to go.' There was steel in her voice now and her chest rose and fell in her effort to stay calm.

'Auntie, this is important.'

Rukshana gripped Safa's elbow with surprising strength and steered her out of the kitchen. 'Thank you for your visit.' Her shoulders were rigid with dignity.

Safa tried to pull out of her grip but found that she could not. Sorrow welled up inside her. This woman had had something horrific done to her body, but clung onto her poise. It was only in the doorway that it slipped.

'Don't come here ever again,' she said in a savage whisper. She released Safa into the rain with a little shove.

Safa saw the anguish on her face. 'Auntie, please don't shut me out.'

Rukshana closed the door.

Safa stared at it, dismayed. Rukshana was proof that the Glassman was real. The thought made Safa fold over, hands on her knees, the jump of bile in her throat. None of her experience, her persistence, her grit had actually prepared her for this. The idea of the Glassman creeping into Rukshana's home, clamping a hand over her mouth, knowing that he would silence her for long after the act, filled Safa with tar-black sorrow.

She stayed there, hunched, for a moment, daunted by the weight of duty. Someone would have to speak for these women when they were finally ready. Someone would have to distil their cawing horror into something decipherable. And who would do it but Safa?

She covered her face and allowed herself one true moment of fury, her teeth bared behind her palms. She let it burn, for she knew that if she persisted, she would have to do it with extreme delicacy. The Glassman had woven an intricate web of shame and Safa would have to unpick it one tripwire strand at a time, leaving no room for fire or fury.

*

Safa rounded the corner of White Horse Road and came face to face with Oliver Witherow, an old colleague from *The Clarion*.

'Well, well, well. If it isn't Safa Saleem, East London's intrepid investigator.' Oliver's voice was honeyed and plummy – fattened by a private education and the sort of quiet nepotism that passes as merit. He arched a brow at Safa's long down coat. 'A *stunning* Outfit of the Day. I hope you shared that to your socials?' he said. In contrast to Safa, Oliver looked expensive with his perfectly coiffed hair, bright white blazer and shiny tassel loafers. Safa pitied the fool who wore white to this part of London where fumes lined your cuffs and collars with a soot-like grime.

'What are you doing here?' she asked.

His gaze flicked to a spot behind her.

Safa was hit with a sick realisation. 'Oliver, don't.'

'Don't what?' he asked innocently.

'Don't do this.'

'Do what?'

'Go knocking on those doors.' Oliver was in no way equipped to talk to Rukshana.

'Why not? I received a tip and I'm following up, as any good journo would do.'

A vein tensed in her wrist. 'Oliver, this is my story and you know it.'

'I think you'll find – as per your contract – that it's *The Clarion*'s story,' he said tartly.

Safa stepped hard on her anger so that she could focus. 'Listen, can we stop with the territorial bullshit for a minute? These women are vulnerable. Perhaps the most vulnerable in society. They won't speak to you. All you'll do is spook them.'

Oliver rolled his eyes. 'Here you go again with your "Safa from the block" shtick. They might have lapped it up at *The Clarion* but my god I find it dull.'

Safa reddened for she knew that Oliver had a point. Maybe it was true that she had a chip on her shoulder about her working-class roots, but this case wasn't about that. Oliver was about to jeopardise Safa's only witness, a woman who had already been immeasurably hurt. 'Don't do this, Oliver. This isn't just a story for me. This is my community.'

He smirked. 'Well, then maybe you shouldn't have fucked up so royally.'

'What happened last year was *your* fault and you know it.'

'That's not what the report says,' he said with a half shrug. He side-stepped her smoothly and headed up White Horse Road.

Safa was careful of herself, holding back her bite. 'Oliver, don't do this. Please.' She filed through her options. Tail him down the road? Warn Rukshana that he was coming? But that would just spook her further – and it would alert Oliver that Rukshana was somehow important. Anger flared in her chest, fuelled by her impotence.

She marched after Oliver. 'Hey!' He turned and the snide look on his face cut the cord on her self-restraint. She grabbed the lapels of his blazer and shoved him against a wall. 'If you do this, I will tell everyone what you did.'

Oliver's shock was clear and satisfying. 'No one will listen,' he said, his nostrils curled in a snarl.

Safa brought her face close to his. 'I will call Rookwood myself and tell him I got fired from *The Clarion* because daddy pulled strings for his son. How do you think that will play out?'

Oliver scoffed. 'As if he'd take your call.'

'You know what they say.' Safa smiled coldly. 'My enemy's enemy is my friend.' Rookwood was a right-wing blogger who loved scoring points against left-leaning media. Safa found him deeply distasteful but knew he could serve a purpose.

'No one will care,' said Oliver.

'Really? The editor of *The Clarion* fires a woman of colour to save his nepo-baby son? You really don't think that will inspire *discourse?* Shit, maybe I should do it anyway. Who gives a fuck if I never work in news again? It might be worth it just for shits and giggles.'

'You wouldn't.'

Safa pressed closer to Oliver, their noses almost touching. 'Try me,' she said coolly. She waited, not blinking. When it became clear that he had nothing else to say, she released him with disgust. 'Go home, Oliver.'

He righted his blazer and Safa was pleased to see that crumbs of brick now dusted the shoulders. 'Your editor will hear about this,' he said primly.

'Ah. *Your* daddy can't help so you'll run to *mine*?'

'Fuck you.'

Safa laughed sardonically. 'But, Oliver, you've already done that so well.'

He smirked. 'You can have this shitty story about the so-called Glassman.' He wriggled his fingers like a ghost when he said the name. 'Even if he *is* real, half these people don't speak English. How do they expect to get justice?'

'They don't,' said Safa. 'That's the point.'

Oliver didn't understand, but clearly didn't care. 'Well, I hope you have fun. You've saved me from having to come back to this backwater shithole.'

'You're welcome, Oliver,' said Safa, icily polite.

He turned on his heel and marched up the road.

Safa slackened with relief. Oliver had no idea how close he had come to a real-life witness. She watched as he crossed the road and headed towards Limehouse station. It made her cringe to think that she had tried to impress him when they'd first met at the paper. They had been placed together on the Special Projects team. Oliver wasn't a trained journalist, but his father – the editor – had pulled some strings and secured him a role in the paper's most coveted news team. Safa and Oliver had worked alongside each other and she – fully aware of who he was – had performed for him the way she might perform for her boss. She was always the first to arrive on the desk and often the last to leave. Once, she quoted Latin at him as if that might win his respect – a memory that made her squirm. Meanwhile, he regarded her as a curious, sexless thing; a novelty paperweight that had *some* utility and aesthetic value but not enough of each.

Safa tried to prove her worth by stepping in to help him. It's not that he was stupid. In fact, he was objectively smart – and charming when he wanted to be – but he wasn't used to working hard. His deadlines often piled up and affected Safa's own. In the lead-up to an exposé on the justice system, Oliver told their desk editor that he couldn't analyse all the raw data in time. A chunk of his workload was reassigned to Safa even though they had started with an even split. The pressure meant that they had to take shortcuts, like writing up profiles without listening to entire interviews. One of the people that Oliver had interviewed was a young magistrate who had strong views on the broken justice system. The magistrate talked for an hour about her own forced marriage and how the system had failed her.

When Oliver sent the audio file to Safa, his only instruction was 'don't go into the forced marriage stuff'. Given that the magistrate had spent so long talking about it, Safa assumed that 'don't go into' meant 'don't go into the gory details' rather than 'don't say anything about it at all'. In the resulting profile, she mentioned briefly that the magistrate had first-hand experience of forced marriage. Oliver was meant to check everything that Safa wrote on his behalf before it went to print – but he didn't.

When the profile was published, they received a horrified email from the magistrate, followed by a letter from her lawyer suing them for damages. The piece, which didn't have a byline, was traced back to Safa and she got fired. As it turned out, the original recording did indeed have the magistrate asking that they don't mention her marriage. Safa hadn't listened to the whole recording – she couldn't deny that – but she had written the piece as a favour for Oliver and had sent him the text to check. Nevertheless, *she* was the author of the profile and *she* was the one who got fired. Inaccurate language had failed her for the second time in her life.

Safa had turned to her union but they told her she was better off moving on. She knew that trying to expose *The Clarion* would leave her exposed as well, so she left quietly with her tail between her legs. The experience was traumatic. All she had ever wanted was to be a reporter. She had come up against so much, worked so hard for so long: five long years at *Asian Bride* magazine followed by another five in the hinterland of freelance life. She had got her big break at *Clarion Content* before finally landing at Special Projects. Meanwhile, Oliver had swanned in with his music degree and not a day of training. Safa had refused to be po-faced about it. Instead, she threw herself into the work, intent on proving her worth. The fact that *she* was dumped instead of Oliver was still a festering wound. He had taken so much from her, she couldn't let him take this too. There was too much at stake. If Safa failed, the Glassman might carry on for *years*, quietly amassing victims under a cloak of silence.

*

Lily checked her reflection in the bathroom mirror. She tucked a loose strand of hair into her backcombed ponytail and straightened the twisted strap of her dress, a shimmery knee-length design in deep midnight blue. She dabbed a piece of tissue on the shiny patch on her forehead and cursed herself for leaving her makeup upstairs.

Laughter rose in the living room above the muted music.

Richard's book, *Left-Handed DNA: What Culture Gets Wrong About Science*, had been published earlier in the week. Richard's mid-sized publisher said they couldn't fund a launch party, so Lily was hosting one at home. Despite what people thought, she had never enjoyed entertaining. She spent so much of her life on camera, she didn't want to perform at home. She was thankful that Richard had agreed to a 'Garden Party' theme. It was a little premature for April, but it gave her an excuse to host it during the day and have everyone clear off by eight p.m. – seven if she was lucky, especially given Richard's mood. Based on early sales, *Left-Handed DNA* wasn't likely to be a bestseller like his last book and that had put him on edge. He had lost his job at *Nature* magazine during the pandemic and this book was meant to put him back on course. To the casual observer, he was just as happy and charming as ever but Lily knew him well enough to see the subtle signs: the erratic beat of his fingers along the seam of his trousers, the stiffness in his smile. Lily had assured him that it would hit the list next week, that no one would think any less of him, that he was and always would be one of the best science journalists in the media, but Richard remained tense and that had raised her own hackles. She had gone to so much effort to make sure that the party was perfect. She had hired Grape & Fig for a lavish grazing table, bought champagne by the caseload and ordered a custom cake, but it clearly wasn't enough. Lily worried that she might snap at him if he didn't shake off his mood and so she kept her distance from him. She hoped that talking to others would loosen him up, but she sensed that it was having the opposite effect. Without Lily close by to vent to, Richard was steaming up – but she was allowed one night off. Tonight, Richard could deal with his anger alone.

Lily discarded the greasy tissue and headed back to the party. A group of her colleagues had pooled in one corner of the living room and she slid into the circle. Ben, her Australian cameraman, stood next to her. She felt his presence like a drumbeat. Lily had never cheated on Richard. She knew that he loved her but also that he would not persevere. He would be too hurt, his pride too wounded, to try to save their marriage. She dare not risk the life she had – but if she *did*, then it would be with Ben. She had felt his sexual energy the first time they had met. It practically hummed between them. He was a man's man: confident, outspoken, direct. He was a far cry from Richard who, while endlessly charming, had that uptight air of Englishmen.

Lily lightly touched Ben's arm when she spoke. She wanted just one night to remember who she was. Not a wife, not a mother, not a victim – but a woman who was interesting and desirable, one who men strove to be close to. The thought of it was a balm and Lily let herself embrace it. She flirted with Ben, tipping her head back in laughter, exposing her elegant neck.

'Oh, you've got a piece of hair,' said Ben, lifting his hand to her face but not touching it.

She could feel the strand on her lashes but couldn't find it. 'Would you mind?' she asked, closing her eyes.

'Of course not.' Ben's fingers were hot on her skin as he tried once, then twice to pull the strand away.

'That's better,' she said, gazing up at him. In the next second, she felt a presence by her side and then a grip on her upper arm.

'Excuse me, may I borrow my wife?' said Richard. He didn't wait for a response. He steered her through the party and into the kitchen. 'What are you doing?' he demanded.

She picked up a glass of wine, intentionally sloppy, and took a sip. She wanted to show him that *she* at least was enjoying herself. 'What?' she asked combatively.

He steadied his gaze on her. 'You said you wouldn't drink too much.'

Lily scowled. 'It's just my second glass.'

'I count third.' His voice was brittle, ready to snap.

'Really, Richard? *This* is what you're doing?'

He closed his hand around her wineglass and lifted it out of hers. 'You know what happens when you drink.'

'Jesus Christ, I'm not allowed to relax for *one night*?'

A vein pulsed in his temple. 'Not if it means draping yourself over another man.'

'So *that's* what this is about.'

'You know I don't like that guy,' he said in a low snarl. 'He clearly wants to get in your knickers.'

'Don't be so crass.'

'The way you're all over him. No wonder he has ideas.'

Lily sighed. 'Give it a rest, Richard.'

'No, *you* give it a rest.' He set the glass on the table, clenching his fist so not to slam it. 'I don't think you should drink any more tonight.'

'You're not my fucking father.'

'Yeah, if only you had one,' he snapped.

Lily flinched, fazed by his cruelty. Richard knew that her father had abandoned her when she was three years old; old enough to have formed a bond.

Richard saw the look on her face. Hit with guilt, he reached for her. 'Lily, I'm sorry.'

She jerked away from him and stalked out of the kitchen, nearly running straight into Talia, one of Richard's friends from university. The woman blushed, clearly embarrassed to have been caught listening.

Lily gave a tight shake of the head. 'Just a lover's tiff,' she said airily and moved down the hallway. She was angry with Richard for piercing her mood. She had wanted just one night to forget. Instead, she had spent most of the party hyper-aware of his distance from her. She stopped halfway down the hall, not knowing where to go; a stranger in her own home. She wanted their guests to leave. She wanted to go upstairs and curl into her sweats and read a book in bed on her own. For a mad moment, she was tempted to actually do it. The strain of the past few weeks, *years*, was crushing her. She was exhausted from measuring her words, actions, gestures, to minimise the threat of violence. Here, in the safety of company, she thought she could relax for just one night.

A peal of laughter brought her to her senses. She fixed on a smile and returned to the party. She scanned the crystal flutes to make sure they were full, then turned her back to Ben and joined Richard's colleagues instead.

*

The last two guests, Talia and Edward, hovered in the hallway. They were Richard's friends from Oxford and Lily had never liked them. Talia had always flirted with Richard even back then. At parties and gatherings, she would contrive ways to bring up old in-jokes to which Lily had never been privy. She watched now as Talia touched Richard's elbow and then creased in laughter. Richard laughed too and Lily wondered if he was hamming it up to punish her for Ben.

'We *must* get together, just the four of us,' said Lily.

'Oh no!' cried Talia. 'We would just bore you with all our old war stories.'

Lily held onto her smile. 'We've known each other for fifteen years, Talia. I've heard all your war stories.'

Talia looked knowingly at the men. 'Oh, trust me. There's one or two we've kept close to our chests.' She turned to Edward. 'You remember that night at Tarantino's?' She gasped in disbelief, as if whatever shock had happened there still echoed through the ages.

Edward bundled an arm around her, bear-like in his affection. 'We can reminisce another time. Let these two get some rest.'

The twinkle dimmed in Talia's eyes. Clearly, she hadn't got the reaction she'd been angling for. 'Well, my darlings.' She planted a kiss on Richard's cheek and gave Lily a hug. 'This was a triumph. Do say hello to Harry.'

Lily nodded. 'I'm sorry he didn't say hi. You know what teenagers are like.'

Talia laughed lightly. 'Not really. I've managed to escape that fate.'

'Ah, well.' Lily was running out of steam. 'Lucky you.' A few banalities later, they were finally out the door. Lily sagged with relief. She looked to Richard for acknowledgement, but he walked off without a word. She knew that he was mad at her for not coddling him all evening. She rolled her eyes at his back, then went into the living room. She gathered the empty glasses and cake knife.

'Leave that for tomorrow,' said Richard, watching from the door.

'Oh, I won't be able to sleep knowing that this mess is here.'

'I'll help you in the morning. I'm too tired for it now.'

'You don't have to help,' Lily carried on.

'I'm not going to have you clean up after *my* party.'

She sighed heavily. 'I don't mind doing it. Richard. Please, just go upstairs. I don't know why you're so wound up about it.'

'Just leave it,' he said, but she didn't listen. 'Lily. I said, *leave it.*'

'Fine.' She dropped the knife with a clatter. 'Then you clean it *all* tomorrow.'

'For fuck's sake, why are you being like this?' His features creased with hostility.

Before Lily could answer, she heard a creak on the stairs. She gestured at Richard to be quiet. She didn't want Harry to see them fighting. It was important to put on a united front.

'Hi, honey,' she said as Harry ambled in. 'Are you all right?'

'Has everyone gone?'

'Yes.'

He set his phone down on the sideboard. 'Is there any food left?'

Lily felt a rush of maternal warmth. Harry asked so little of her now and she missed how much he used to need her. She yearned for her young son and the solid heft of him. These days, he didn't let her get near him, his body too large and unwieldy.

'I'll fix you a plate,' said Lily.

Harry looked at the spread, picked over by dozens of guests. He wrinkled his nose at the greasy film on the cheese and the stale sourdough bread. 'Is there anything hot?'

Lily lowered the plate in her hands. 'Not right this minute but I can fix you something. We have—'

'It's okay,' Harry cut in. 'I'll get some chips.'

'Chips?'

He motioned at the front door. 'Stephen texted me. He has the new *Grand Theft Auto* and said I could go round.'

'Now?' Lily checked her watch. 'It's coming up to nine, Harry. You can't go round now.'

'But Stephen said I could. Anyway, I've stayed at his house way later than nine.'

'That's not the same as getting there at this hour. It's not polite.'

'But it's Saturday,' he whined.

'I'm sorry, Harry, but no.'

He squirmed with frustration. 'It's not fair! I've been stuck in my room all day!'

'That was your choice, Harry. We're allowed to have our friends over to celebrate an important occasion.'

'It wasn't my choice,' Harry snapped. 'Dad told me to stay in my room!'

'No, he didn't. He . . .' Lily turned towards Richard and caught the look on his face. 'Richard, you didn't.'

He squared his shoulders. 'I didn't want him sulking around the party.'

She was dismayed by the thought of Harry stuck in his room for hours. Here she was again at that familiar junction: keep the peace or prepare for battle. She bit back her anger and fixed on a breezy smile. 'I could call Stephen's mum and see if she'd be okay with it?' She aimed the question into the space between them, unsure from whom she was seeking permission.

'Lily.' Richard's voice was hard. 'He's not going to his friend's house at nine o'clock in the evening just because he wants to.'

She clung onto her smile. 'Stephen's parents are a lot less strict about bedtimes. I don't think they'd mind.'

Richard ignored her and spoke to Harry instead. 'Go to your room.'

'No,' said Harry, clear and firm.

Richard's skin began to pink. 'No?'

Harry lifted his chin. 'No.'

'Harry. I said, go upstairs.'

'No. You told me to stay out of your way and I did, but now I want to go out. You can't force me to stay inside!'

'Guess what? You're thirteen years old, so I can.'

Anxiety moved in Lily's gut. She had to find the path of least violence or this would become a full-blown conflict. 'Let him go, Richard.'

He looked at her, baffled. 'Are you serious?'

'Yes.'

'Lily. I'm not going to let him do whatever he wants.'

'It's Saturday and he's been cooped up in his room all day.'

'No.' He ordered Harry back to his room.

'You can't tell me what to do.' Harry's voice climbed to a girlish register.

'Like hell I can't.'

Lily was gripped by panic. The touch paper was about to catch. She moved to intervene, but was cut off by Harry.

'Fuck you!' he screamed. Overwhelmed by teenage rage, he swiped at the table, sending food and cutlery everywhere.

'You little bastard.' Richard bolted towards him.

Lily grabbed his sleeve, lightning quick, but barely arrested him. She watched the scene in slow motion: the inevitable finally happening. Richard was going for Harry, as she always knew he would. 'Go!' she shouted at her son.

Harry didn't move, caught in fright and shock.

'Go!' she screamed, jolting him into action. Harry tore out of the room and Lily held onto Richard.

He wrenched out of her grip and chased after Harry. Lily expected her son to cry out – fingers on his collar at the very last second – but she heard his footsteps on the gravel outside, charting his escape. She keeled with relief. Harry had got away. For now, he was safe.

In the hall, Richard was quiet. Lily's stomach knotted at the sound of his cold, neat footsteps coming back to the living room. Calmly, he paused in the doorway.

'Lily.' He gestured at the mess: the heirloom rug drenched in sauce, the sofa splattered in chilli oil, the heaps and puddles of food and grease. 'Why did you let him do this?'

Lily's gaze seemed to hum. There was no way to keep the peace now.

He shook his head in a reprimand. 'Sometimes, Lily, I think you bring this on yourself.' He watched her for a moment, then took a step towards her.

Lily squared her shoulders and, quick as a flash, he closed the distance between them.

*

Safa took a swig of coffee and grimaced as she swallowed. It was cold and tasted ashy. She tried to decide between making herself another one and packing up for home. She had no obligation to be here so late on a Saturday but she found the newsroom more comforting than the thirty-two-square-metre hole in the sky that passed for a flat in London. She preferred it here with the gentle hum of sleeping machines and distant blink of lights, letting her know there was life nearby. Her flat, in comparison, felt hermetically sealed even with the windows open.

She pushed back from her desk and headed to the kitchen with her mug. She was halfway across the newsroom when her landline rang. She checked her watch. It was past 9.00 p.m., but one thing she had learned as a reporter was that you always answered the phone. She jogged back and saw that it was an internal number.

'In my office. Now,' said Kevin's voice on the line.

She winced, knowing that his tone spelled trouble. She replaced the receiver, grabbed her notebook and headed to his office in the corner.

Kevin took off his glasses and pinched the bridge of his nose. 'Sit,' he instructed. He waited a beat, then asked, 'Did you see an Oliver Witherow this morning?'

Safa's shoulders rose at the mention of his name. 'Yes.'

'Who is he to you?'

He's the wanker that cost me my job. 'He's a former colleague.'

'What happened?'

'Nothing. Why?'

'Did you *assault* him?'

Safa scoffed in disbelief. 'Did he call you to *tattle tale*?'

'Actually, Hugh Witherow called me.' Safa stiffened. Hugh was, of course, Oliver's father and the editor of *The Clarion*. The decision to fire Safa for the forced marriage debacle had ultimately come from him. 'He said that their lawyer would be in touch.'

Safa felt a jab of anxiety. 'I barely touched him.'

'He's threatening to press charges.'

'He wouldn't.'

'What happened between you?'

Safa fell quiet. When she had told Kevin why she had been discharged from *The Clarion*, she had given him the simplest explanation. She'd told him that she had missed something in a transcript and promised it would never happen again. The intricacy of the error, and Oliver's role in it, would have got lost in translation and made Safa look petty. In this game, you owned your mistakes and rolled with the punches. Whininess and disloyalty were sure to get you blackballed and so she had taken responsibility. To backtrack now was pointless.

'Talk to me,' said Kevin.

Safa sighed. 'We got into a bit of a thing and I might have *brushed* him.'

'"Brushed" him?'

'That's all I'll say, Kevin. I don't want them to fucking *court martial* you.'

Kevin laced his hands on the desk. 'Is there anything else I should know?'

Before Safa could answer, her phone pinged with a message. She clicked it onto silent mode but automatically read the preview. It was from a source of hers at the Met Police – not Imran for he was far too strait-laced for leaks.

Emergency call to Lily Astor's house at 9.15 p.m. Ambulance and police.

She frowned and re-read it.

'What is it?' Kevin sensed that it was important.

'Something's going down at Lily Astor's house.'

Kevin, an old pro, told her to *go*.

Chapter 5

Lily's hands were slick and sticky. The room smelled of copper and she nearly retched from the way it filled her sinuses. The towel was now a dark scarlet and the knife lay nearby. She watched the blood seep through the towel but didn't fetch another. Her brain was in panic mode, fire in its circuitry. A kernel of logic insisted that if his blood was still flowing, it meant that his heart was pumping.

'Lily, Lily, are you still there?' The woman on the phone spoke to her calmly.

'Yes.' Lily's own voice sounded far away and she actually looked at one corner of the ceiling to see if it was coming from there.

'Is he still breathing?' asked the woman.

Lily tried to think through the heat in her head. 'Yes, I think so.'

'Okay, the paramedics will be there soon. Will you be able to let them in?'

'If I move my hands, he might bleed out.'

'Okay, I'll communicate that to the police and they can find their own way in. Would that be okay?'

'Yes.' Lily swallowed the glue in her throat and looked down at Richard's body. The panic gave way to shock – a cold, white alarm that rang inside her brain. There were no tears – just this blank and broad disbelief. Her mind rejected what had happened; concocted an entirely different story. *I came in and found him like this.* Her denial was seductive in its simplicity. *I saw nothing, heard nothing, know nothing* – but she knew it wouldn't wash. She literally had his blood on her hands.

The doorbell rang and Lily pressed harder against the gash in his throat. She felt her bile rise and swallowed it down. Sweat coated her skin; the pall of held-back vomit. She flinched at the sound of splintering wood. Moments later, two uniformed police officers charged into the living room, tailed by paramedics.

'What's his name?' One of the paramedics knelt next to Lily.

'Richard.'

'You're Lily, right?'

'Yes.'

'Okay, Lily. We're going to need you to back away.' The paramedic placed her hands over Lily's and nodded as she eased them out. Lily moved back and stood, giddy on her feet. She felt a hand on her elbow. One of the officers, a broad-shouldered man with a kind face, escorted her out of the room. Lily twisted towards the paramedics, but the officer tugged her away, along the hall to the second reception room. He told her to breathe and Lily realised that she was trembling.

'I'm cold,' she said.

'It's okay, Lily. We're going to get you a change of clothes. I'm PC Danbury and my colleague here is PC Burke.' The other officer was a gangly woman, all hard edges and angles.

'Can you tell us what happened?'

'It was an accident.'

'What happened?'

'I didn't mean to do it. He came at me and I picked up the knife as a warning and I told him to stop but he didn't.'

The officer nodded calmly. 'Okay, Lily, here's what's going to happen. I'm going to have to arrest you on suspicion of grievous bodily harm, okay? You do not have to say anything. But, it may harm your defence if you do not mention when questioned something which you later rely on in court. Anything you do say may be given in evidence. Do you understand?'

Lily twisted towards the doorway. 'Is he alive?'

'Lily, face me please.' Danbury asked her more questions but she struggled to process them. Her neurons weren't quite firing, dampened by a need to know if Richard was alive or dead. She sensed movement behind her and turned in time to see the paramedic shake her head at Danbury. Horror bloomed in Lily's bones.

'There's no pulse,' confirmed the paramedic.

Lily stared at the woman blankly. On some base level, she knew she should signal grief, but her tears would not oblige. In their place was a scrabble for survival. She felt like a rat caught in a maze, wild in its search for escape.

'Face me please,' Danbury repeated. 'Lily, you are under arrest for murder. The same caution applies, do you understand?'

She nodded dumbly.

'We're going to ask you to change your clothes – PC Burke here will escort you – and then we'll take you to the station, okay? We need to ask you some questions about what happened here, okay?'

Lily was blank with shock. 'My son,' she managed. 'He's at his friend's house.'

'How old is he?'

'Thirteen.'

'That's okay. You can give us the address and we'll pick him up. Is there somewhere he can go?'

'Go?'

'Tonight?'

Lily felt her throat close. She would be in jail tonight. 'My sister. Natalie Baker,' she said with a choke.

Her mind detached from her body as the officers made her change her clothes. They wrapped plastic bags around her hands to preserve relevant evidence and then led her to their car. The journey to the station had a hollow, surreal quality as if viewed through a distorted lens. Lily had often heard that witnesses were unreliable and she finally understood. Richard had died mere moments ago but Lily couldn't say for certain the exact sequence of events. She remembered the ugly snarl on his face, his charge across the living room. It had all happened so quickly.

She jolted as Danbury parked outside Bethnal Green Police Station. She followed him inside, blinking rapidly in the harsh fluorescent cast. She was booked in and taken through an extensive process: fingerprints, hair samples, nail scrapings, photographs.

Through her narcosis, a warning sounded in her brain. 'I want my lawyer,' she said finally. 'His name is Jonathan Sinclair.' It registered only vaguely that he was the Astors' family lawyer. Would he represent her given that she'd admitted to killing their son? It was either that or take her chances with the duty solicitor.

She was led to a cell – a small grey room with a plastic mattress. She sat on it in a daze. Soon there would be paparazzi and journalists – vultures waiting for meat. The thought of them sobered her into logic.

Harry. Would they get to him before he was taken to Natalie? She drifted to the door and pressed her face to the window.

'Where's my son?' she shouted. When there was no response, she knocked against the reinforced glass to flag down an officer. 'Where's my son?'

'He's being picked up,' he told her.

'When?'

'I don't know.'

She rapped the window. 'When?'

'Can you calm down?' he said tersely.

Lily felt the pull of hysteria – a broad and deep abyss. She wanted to dive inside it and let off a banshee scream. If only she could cry, this awful, pent-up horror might ease. 'Please,' she begged.

'Miss, just wait for your brief.' He shut the window and left Lily with her panic.

*

Safa arrived at the scene just in time to see Lily go past in the back of a police car. It moved too fast for her to catch any details other than the fact that Lily looked calm. The house itself was abuzz with police but had the muted mood of a wake. Safa strained at the edge of the yellow police tape and tried to see inside. The hallway was blocked by officers and the living room curtains were drawn. Safa looked for gallows banter, but found an eerie quiet. She felt a deep sense of unease; knew on a gut level that something was seriously wrong. She looked up at the windows and their frames of creeping ivy. Just yesterday, she had stood in that very same spot. What terrible thing had happened since?

She skirted along the edge of the tape in search of a better vantage point. She peered into the side passage and saw the brass tap with the hosepipe and bikes in red and white. She squinted at the shapes in the dark.

'Excuse me, may I help you?' a voice cut into her thoughts.

Safa turned to find a uniformed policeman watching her from inside the tape. He had reddish hair and a nascent beer gut. Safa pulled on her reporter's voice like a protective cloak. 'My name is Safa Saleem. I'm a reporter from *The East London Echo*. Can you tell me what's happening?'

'I'm afraid not. Now please step back.'

'Has someone been hurt?'

He sighed. 'Look, you know this is going to take a long time. The SIO will give you an update when they're ready so can you just leave us to do what we need to do?'

Safa obediently took a step back. She knew that with these

low-level officers, goodwill was key. 'Who's the SIO?' she asked, pitching it in a gamely tone. There was a chance that Safa knew the senior investigating officer.

He glanced back over his shoulder and was on the cusp of speaking when he was summoned back inside.

Safa paced the length of the tape. She implored the officers for information but was duly ignored. Eventually, she heard movement in the hallway. The officers parted to reveal a large black body bag, motionless on a gurney. Safa felt a lurch of alarm. Her mind slowed as it tried to make sense of the details: the lamplight bouncing off the cheap black plastic, the clatter of metal wheels, the furrows left in the golden gravel. It hit her with chilling impact; an ice cube held to a nerve. Somebody had died inside that house.

It wasn't Lily and it couldn't be Harry, or Lily would have been hysterical. A sickening thought rose in her mind. *Do you really think I'd let myself become a battered woman?* Had Lily struck back? Was it *Richard* in that bag?

Just as she thought it, she overheard the answer from a nearby officer. Lily had been arrested on suspicion of murder.

Safa's shock felt chemical: a metal tang in her mouth, the acid wrench of her gut. Her fear for Lily was instant and immense. She pictured her friend in the police car, impossibly calm and composed. They were lucky there were no photographers here. Safa was astounded that she was the only reporter here. Her professional instinct told her to send a tweet, get the scoop, but she had to make sure that Harry was safe before she broke the story. She had been told at *The Clarion* that she lacked killer instinct, but she couldn't let the press descend on him. She wouldn't put it past some of them to reveal the news to Harry just to film his reaction. Safa may not have seen him in years, but he was the only child she had ever loved and that hadn't changed with time. She *had* to find out where he was before she broke the news.

She jogged to her car, a battered Clio, and headed to Bethnal Green Police Station. That was where Lily would be and that's where she might find some answers.

Fifteen minutes later, she hurried into the station and was relieved to find Billy at the desk. She could tell from his jittery energy that something big was happening.

'She's here, isn't she?'

Billy held up his hands. 'Safa, I can't tell you anything.'

'That means yes. Where is she?'

'I can't tell you anything.'

'Who's the SIO?'

Billy pointedly looked down at his paper, squinting at a crossword.

Safa tried to think of a strategy. These were the times that she wished she was better at flirting. Her persuasive powers came more from being scrappy, like a persistent puppy that yaps at your heels until you lean down to pet it. 'Please, Billy. I told my editor that Lily was a non-story. I'll get fired if I don't nail this.'

Billy stuck the tip of his pencil in his mouth. 'Hm, eight down. "Punishment beating on the soles of the feet",' he said, perusing the crossword clue.

She placed her hand over the crossword. 'Come on, Billy. I wouldn't ask if I didn't need this.'

'Oh, yes, you would.' He looked up at her puppy dog eyes, then shook his head with a huff. 'The SIO is Emmanuel Barent, but he's a stickler for protocol.'

Safa didn't recognise the name. 'Do you think you could get me in to see Lily?'

At this, Billy laughed – not a performative snicker but a genuine belly laugh.

'Fine,' she said, nodding gamely. She turned and headed down the corridor.

'You know I can't let you in there.'

'Bastinado!' she yelled over her shoulder.

'You what?' Billy was insulted.

'The crossword clue,' she called just as she slipped through the closing door. *So much for protocol.*

She took the lift upstairs and spotted Imran at his desk. The sight of him – so certain of his place in the world – made her pause for a moment. He looked up, sensing her gaze on him.

'Safa?' He shot to his feet. 'How the hell did you get up here?'

'Is Lily Astor here?' she asked, aiming for businesslike but sounding curt.

Imran ignored the question and ushered her out to the corridor. 'You're going to get me in trouble.'

'What can you tell me?'

'I can't tell you anything.'

'Can you get me in to see her?'

He scoffed. 'Who am I? Harry Houdini? Of course I can't do that.'

'Can you at least tell her I'm here?'

'No, Safa. You need to leave.'

'Can you please do me a favour?'

'Absolutely not.'

'It's not for me. Can you just make sure that her son is safe?' She dug her hands deep in her pockets and held Imran's gaze. 'You know he means a lot to me.' She hated to trade on their former intimacy, but knew that this would make him take her seriously. Imran was the only person who knew how much she had been hurt when Lily ended their friendship. Safa had opened up to him as they watched *Arise* one Bank Holiday morning, cocooned in their crumpled sheets. She told him about their childhood in Withy House and how Lily had left it behind. She spoke about Harry and how strange it was that someone you once loved fiercely could be removed from your life. Imran, who loved fiercely or not at all, had folded her into his arms, crushing the sadness out of her.

She looked up at him now, her eyes rounded in plea.

Imran sighed quietly. 'Harry Astor is with his aunt,' he said.

'Already?' Safa pictured Natalie Baker – a skinny, wiry girl who looked mean and bony next to Lily.

'Yes.'

'You know that for sure?'

'Yes.'

Safa slackened with relief. 'Thank you, Imran.' By instinct, she squeezed his hand, catching him off guard. He held on for a second too long before she pulled it back. His face flooded with sentiment, but his voice was brusque when he spoke.

'I've got to get back to work.'

'Okay.' She stepped back. 'Thank you.'

In the lift, she drafted a tweet: *Lily Astor has allegedly killed her husband, Richard Astor, following a domestic dispute.*

Then, she pressed 'Post'.

Chapter 6

Lily's nerves twanged every time she heard a footstep. She needed something to happen; couldn't bear another hour in this cell. Jonathan Sinclair, the Astors' family lawyer, had declined to represent her, so Lily had left a panicked message for a solicitor friend of hers. That had been two hours ago and Lily was losing hope. At this rate, she would rather face the police alone than fester in this cell. The walls themselves seem to bulge and tilt, deepening her anguish. Questions fired in her mind. Should she have denied it altogether? Or was she better off confessing?

An officer looked in through the window. 'Your brief's here,' he told her.

Lily stood in a rush, desperate for someone familiar. She followed the officer into a small interview room. She moved to hug Victoria but her friend held out a hand instead. Lily looked at it before she shook it. Victoria Hersham was an HCA, or Higher Court Advocate, a solicitor who could also defend her in court – if she agreed to do so. They had first met at a mutual friend's book launch and though they weren't the best of friends, Victoria was one of the very few people who Lily could be herself with.

'What happened, Lily?' Victoria set down her notebook.

'I need your help.'

'No shit, Sherlock. Why are you here?'

'Am I allowed to tell you the truth?'

Victoria folded her arms. 'Nothing you tell me will go beyond these four walls, but you should be aware that I can't say anything in court that I know to be untrue. Do you understand that?'

'Yes.'

'So,' Victoria spoke carefully, 'knowing that, do you want to tell me what happened?'

Lily shook her head. 'No comment.'

Victoria sighed. 'You don't *no comment* your own brief, Lily.'

'I don't want to say.'

Victoria arched her perfect brows. 'That's not going to wash in court. We have to put forward a defence.'

Lily had been in a hurry to see Victoria, but now realised that she needed more time. She had publicly stated that her bruise came from a tennis match. Could she backtrack now and say that Richard beat her? She realised with a sickening lurch that she didn't have a choice. She had admitted to killing him and faced a lifetime in prison. Those were her choices: say that Richard abused her or risk a life sentence. In the face of this simplicity, the choice was all but made.

'He hit me,' she said quietly.

Victoria studied her. 'Is that true?'

'Yes,' Lily said evenly. 'It's true.'

Victoria exhaled. 'I'm sorry. I had no idea.'

'It's okay.' Lily averted her gaze. 'Most people didn't.'

'Does Harry know?'

Lily's head snapped up in panic. 'I don't want him anywhere near court.'

Victoria held up a hand. 'Lily, please don't make any decisions now. Let me work out the best way to help you.'

Lily pictured her son in court, alone in the witness box, forced to recall the violence. She paled at the thought.

'Did Harry witness what took place tonight?'

'No. He was at a friend's house. Thank god I told him to go.'

Victoria's features tensed with regret. It was clear that she would rather Harry had been there. It made Lily uneasy, but she needed Victoria's killer instinct if she was going to get through this.

Victoria opened the notebook. 'Okay, talk me through the evening step by step.' She looked at Lily pointedly. 'But remember what I said.'

Lily braced herself and prepared to censor her story.

*

Lily sank into her shapeless grey hoodie. The material had a starchy texture that made her skin itch, but it helped stave off the bone-deep chill that permeated the interview room. Victoria sat next to her and two officers sat opposite: DS Emmanuel Barent, a sharp-angled man with a calculated manner, and DS Kate Walker, a mousy-haired woman with good skin but plain features.

'Take us through it again,' said DS Barent.

Lily closed her eyes and tried to muster patience. She had been through the evening twice already. It was shaming and exhausting to play up the role of battered wife, but this was no time for pride.

'As I said, we were celebrating the launch of Richard's book,' she started. She explained a third time that Richard had been in a bad mood. She told them how he had reacted when he saw her talking to her cameraman, Ben, and marched her to the kitchen, then snatched the glass from her hands. All of this was objective truth and could be verified by witnesses. Perhaps it was a good thing that Talia had been eavesdropping.

'You said that the last guests left at 8.55 p.m.,' said Barent, checking his notes. 'Take us through what happened next.'

'As I said, things came to a head when Harry, my son, said he wanted to go to a friend's house. I told him he could go and

Richard got angry with me. He thinks that Harry and I collude against him, but really we just close ranks because he gets the way he does.'

'Which is?'

'Violent,' she said quietly. She explained that the clashes had started during the pandemic, repeating what she had said in group therapy.

'Did Richard ever hit Harry?' asked Barent.

'No, but he got close to it. I felt like it was coming.' She knew that Richard's name would be savaged by the press, her long and happy marriage recast as bogus.

'Were you scared of him?'

'Yes.' Lily swallowed. 'I felt like I was living on tiptoes.'

Barent made a note. 'You told Harry to go. What happened next?'

'Harry left and Richard was furious. He thought I was weak for giving into him. I swore at him which I never do, and that was like a red flag. He charged at me. I panicked. I saw the knife and picked it up. I said that I would hurt him if he came for me. I was waving it in the air, just to warn him. I thought he would stop, but he didn't. It happened so fast. It was almost like he ran into it to prove I wouldn't do it.' Lily's skin prickled with heat, but still no tears would come.

'What happened next?'

Lily pictured the scene, mapping herself in the room, and the distance between her and Richard. 'He staggered backwards and I realised what had happened. I dropped the knife and went to him. I pressed my hands around his throat to stop the bleeding.'

Barent glanced at the file in his hands. 'Is that right?'

'Yes.'

'Did you do anything else first?'

She paused. 'No.'

'You went straight to him?'

'Yes.'

'Did you get anything else to stem the flow?'

Lily remembered now. 'Yes, I grabbed a tea towel.'

'From where?'

'From the ice bucket.'

'Before or after you pressed your hands around his throat?'

Lily considered this. 'After.'

'Okay, what happened next?'

'I pressed the towel to his throat. He was making these glugging sounds and there was all this blood. His eyes closed. I was screaming and I called the police.'

'How?'

Lily looked up. 'What do you mean "how"?'

'Well, you had your hands on his throat. So how did you call the police?'

She blinked. 'I told Siri to call the police. I told them that my husband was hurt.' Barent studied her, suspended in that space between doubt and belief. He made Lily feel guilty, even though she was admitting guilt.

'Was anyone else in the house with you?'

'No.'

'Harry?'

'No, I told you. He was at his friend's house.'

'What about Ben, the cameraman?'

Lily jolted. How quickly his mind had made that connection. 'No. It was just me and Richard.' She pictured those horrifying seconds. Richard's snarl as he charged forward, his face half in shadow. The knife catching the candlelight in the seconds before it landed in his throat. The vibrance of his blood. The dull glug of a fading life.

The memory made Lily retch and she jerked to one side just in time to miss her lap. Vomit splashed on the floor and splattered up the table leg. Her body broke into a shivery sweat. Then, the tears arrived. For the first time in three years, Lily was fully overwhelmed. All the pain and rage in her body burst out all at once. She bent at the waist and started to bellow. Richard was dead. Richard had bled out in her arms. Richard had left her alone. She cried into her hand, sobbing with fury and grief. As her body mourned in ways her mind didn't sanction, she was left with the feeling that everything was lost.

Chapter 7

Safa turned into Globe Road, driving just below the speed at which the rattle in the chassis set in. Despite its small size, her car was heavy to handle, like an unwieldy beast that would veer as soon as the reins were eased. She knew she needed to upgrade it, but her journalist's salary barely paid her bills. She pulled into a side street where the parking was ample on a Sunday morning. She walked to Withy House and was hit by the smell of stale oil; a smell she remembered from her childhood home up on the third floor. Sometimes, she used to wonder if the wet patches in the walls were oil rather than damp.

She walked past the square of concrete that claimed to be a courtyard. A soiled mattress was propped against a wall next to an upturned pram, a scrambled scene of domesticity. Safa walked straight into the building and headed up to the first floor. As she climbed, she felt a clench of unease, pitched straight back to childhood and the day she lost her mother. Everything about this place – the bubbles in the orange paint, the black strips on the concrete steps, the vacuous space – seemed utterly unchanged. It hurt her that a place so ugly reminded her most strongly of her mother. They hadn't had enough time together to recast each other in beauty. Safa pushed the thought away and headed to flat 55.

She pressed the buzzer and waited. She noted with relief that she was the only reporter there. Presumably, no one had guessed that the sister of beloved Lily Astor lived in such a dive. She heard movement inside and, a moment later, Natalie Baker opened the door. She was older than Lily, gaunt, with lank hair and thinning brows. The chasm between her and Lily had only grown with time. Her skin was pale and lined, and her thick transition lenses were at least a decade out of style.

'Hi, Nat. Do you remember me?'

Natalie squinted at her. 'Fuck me. Safa Saleem?'

Safa gave her a doleful smile. 'The one and only.'

'Jesus Christ.' Natalie scooted forward and gave Safa a bony hug. 'How the hell have you been?'

'Yeah, good.'

'How's your dad?' Natalie's face bloomed with warmth. 'I loved that man so much.'

Safa smiled. 'He's all right. He's got arthritis so struggles a bit, but generally he's well.'

'Man, I'd love to see him again.'

Safa nodded but didn't extend an invite. 'Can I come in?'

Natalie shifted nervously. 'Does Lily know you're here?'

Safa couldn't lie. 'No, but I really need to talk to you.' She hesitated. 'And check on Harry if I could?'

Natalie frowned. 'I can't do anything without talking to Lily.'

'I'm not here as a reporter, Natalie. Not right now.' She could see that Natalie was thinking. 'You're going to need help, Nat,' she added gently.

Natalie grimaced, then allowed Safa inside. Lino crackled beneath their feet and Safa saw that the plastic had turned brown from years of grime. Natalie made tea and they sat at the tiny table in one corner of the kitchen.

'How is he?' Safa asked.

'I can't really tell. He went straight to bed last night.'

Safa knew that Natalie and Lily weren't close. When Lily had left for university, she had left her family behind in more ways than one. Natalie, a hair stylist, was out of place in Lily's new world, which made her shy from contact. Something about posh people stripped her of her confidence, so even though Lily had tried for a while, the sisters drifted apart. Now, they only saw each other once or twice a year – on Christmases and birthdays.

In a way, Safa had taken on the mantle of an aunt. She remembered sitting with Harry on Lily's carpet, drawing clock faces onto sheets of paper and teaching him to read the minutes and hours. He had been five, or maybe six, and infectious with laughter. He had always brought out a lightness in Safa. *You're here now,* he'd told her once. *You can take off your brave.* The memory raised a bitter-sweetness – but now was not the time to reminisce.

'How much does he know?' asked Safa.

Natalie fiddled with her mug. 'He knows that Richard is dead and that Lily has been arrested. He's in shock I think. I've tried to talk to him, but . . .' She motioned helplessly. 'Maybe you can do a better job?'

'I could try, if you want,' Safa said carefully. She knew what her colleagues in the media would do: barrel over to him and get him on the record, but for Safa this was personal, and protecting Harry was key. 'Do you want to come with me?'

Natalie hesitated. 'It might be better if it's just the two of you.'

'Okay.' Safa preferred it that way, but had wanted to check first. She drained her tea and stood. 'Lily's room?'

'Yeah.'

Safa made her way along the dim corridor. It was enclosed on all sides by walls and had no natural light. She was surprised to see that it had the same carpet as when she and Lily were children: a brown and green blend of paisley, now worn to thread in patches. Safa wondered if Harry had even been to Withy House before. In her experience, people who came from poverty raised their children in one of two ways. Some were keen to expose them to the realities of their roots. Others, like Lily, did everything they could to shield them. Leaving Harry at Withy House was like dropping him into a foreign land.

Safa paused outside Lily's door and heard a tinny sound. She recognised it as the female text-to-speech voice on TikTok – mechanical and strangely modulated.

She knocked gently but Harry didn't answer. After a moment, she tried again.

'Harry? It's Aunt Saffie. Can I come in?'

The tinny voice fell quiet and the door flew open. 'Aunt Saffie!' Harry darted into her arms, nearly knocking her back. She felt a rush of love as she hugged him hard. He had grown so much since the last time she had seen him, years ago now. To her surprise, Harry immediately began to cry – loud, big-boned sobs as if he'd been holding them back for a very long time.

'Hey,' she soothed. 'It's okay, Harry. I'm here.' She pressed him into her shoulder. He was too tall now to tuck beneath her chin like she used to. Harry's chest trembled and Safa held him tight, trying to squeeze the grief from him. They stayed like that for a long time and slowly Harry calmed. When she released him, she had a chance to look at him for the first time in years. Sadly, puberty hadn't been kind to him. His wavy brown hair had tightened into unruly curls, his delicate nose had thickened at the bridge and his twinkling cuteness was gone. He must have read her thoughts because he turned inward, shoulders folding as if he were cold.

She wiped the look off her face. 'Harry, I've missed you.'

'I've missed you too.'

Safa glanced around Lily's childhood bedroom. It was sparsely decorated: a wood-framed bed in Ikea beech and a thin slab of mattress, worn carpet and a bedside table with a plastic lamp. The sight made Safa ache. The least he deserved was consistency. To be stripped of familiar comforts after such upheaval felt unduly cruel. Safa briefly considered offering him a place in her own flat, but it was hardly a match for Harry's own house. Instead, she ushered him to the bed and put her arm around his shoulders. He curved forward, his spine listing beneath the grief.

'It's okay, Harry.' She heard the sound of his throat as he swallowed.

'They think Mum did it.'

Safa pulled away to study him. 'You don't think she did?' She caught a flicker of doubt and watched him carefully. 'Harry, do you know something?' He didn't answer and she gently touched his knee. 'You won't get in trouble if you tell me.'

His features hardened. 'I'm glad she did it,' he said in a rush of spite.

Safa was quiet. She wouldn't tell him that he didn't mean it. She had seen too many people put through too many horrors by the people who were supposed to love them. She knew that emotions like this – anger, hate, spite – were real, at least in the moment that people felt them. She gave Harry a moment to cool, then asked, 'Was your dad hurting your mum?'

He fixed his gaze on the carpet, laced his hands and then nodded.

'Does anyone else know?'

'No. Just us.'

Safa considered her next question. Gently, she asked, 'Has he ever hit you?'

Fresh tears glazed his eyes. 'Wanted to, but never actually did it.'

'I'm sorry, Harry.'

His features creased. 'I never stood up for her. I told myself to. Every time. *Just go and stand in front of her*, but I never did.'

'Harry, you couldn't have possibly done anything. You're a child.'

'I'm just as big as her.' His voice shook with indignation. 'I should've stood up for her.'

'That wasn't your responsibility.'

'I should've told someone about it.'

Safa gently touched his arm. 'Do you want to talk about it now?'

His lips twisted in a grimace. 'Are you going to write about this?'

'No, I'm not,' Safa said firmly. 'For now, I'm trying to get to the truth so we can help your mum.'

Harry thought this over. He nodded, but it took him a minute to start. 'Mostly, they hid it from me. Mum had read this thing that said the most important thing for a kid to see is their parents in love, so she hid their problems from me. I never saw them argue, but after Dad lost his job, he got angry at the smallest things.' Harry gripped the threadbare duvet. 'It started over dinner one day. Mum asked him to put away his phone and he just threw it at her head.' Harry's face was pale. 'Mum and I were stunned, but Dad carried on eating like nothing had happened. We didn't know what to do so we just carried on too.' Harry shook his head. 'I don't know why we did that. If we'd said or done something, maybe he would've stopped.'

'Did she talk to you about what happened?'

Harry let out a shaky breath. 'No. Mum's always been good at pretending.'

Safa knew that was true. 'She never mentioned it to you at all?'

'Only to tell me not to tell anyone.' Harry wiped the sweat off his upper lip. 'When my grades got bad, she came and saw my teacher. She said it was because my granddad had died. I never even knew him. She just kept saying that we couldn't tell anyone.'

Safa was chilled by this. Harry was the most important thing to Lily. How desperate she must have been to deny him help he needed.

Harry tugged at his neckline, stretching the cotton fabric. 'Dad got more controlling. If Mum looked too nice, he would make her go upstairs and take off her makeup. She said no the first time and learnt that it was easier to do what he said.' Harry clenched his fist, the veins in his hand a livid purple. 'He used to *pinch* her when we were out. He thought that no one would see, but I did. I asked her about it, but she said I was imagining it.'

Safa listened with a racing heart.

'It was always in places that people wouldn't see. Her earlobe, the back of her neck, her stomach.' Harry's voice was thick with emotion.

'She didn't tell anyone at all?'

'No. She just wore longer, baggier stuff.'

Safa closed her eyes. It wasn't lost on her that both Lily – rich, white, famous – and Rukshana – poor, brown and disadvantaged – were too ashamed to reveal their secret. Silence, it seemed, was their common language.

Harry wiped his palms on his jeans. 'Mum was nervous before the party yesterday. She was hoping that Dad would be in a good mood. When that happens, both of us sort of tag-team to keep it up. Mum's all giggly and happy like she is on TV and I stay quiet and out of the way. But Dad was already in a mood before it started. I knew he'd be fake and happy in front of his guests but he'd make us pay as soon as they left. When I heard the last of them go, I went downstairs and asked if I could go to Stephen's house. I left Mum there even though I knew that Dad would be angry.' Harry hung his head. 'It was my fault.'

'It was *not* your fault, Harry.' Safa's tone was clipped and final, leaving no room for argument.

Harry didn't respond.

Gently, Safa asked, 'Do you know what time you left your house?'

'It was nine o'clock. I know because Dad said it was too late to go to someone's house.'

'What time did you get to Stephen's house?'

'It takes twenty minutes to walk there so about nine twenty. Maybe a bit later because I stopped on the way to call him.'

Safa made a mental note of the timings. 'Harry, would you mind if I talked to Stephen?' She saw a shadow cross his face. 'You can absolutely say no if you want to.' She wasn't being entirely fair to him, but she also knew that she was well placed to help Lily.

'The police have already talked to him.'

'Could I talk to him as well?' Safa pressed. 'I think I can help your mum.'

He agreed hesitantly and gave Safa the address.

She squeezed his hand. 'I'm going to be here, Harry. I can't promise that everything is going to be okay, but whatever happens I'm going to be here.'

He squeezed hers back. 'Thank you, Aunt Saffie.'

She stayed with him awhile, wanting to make sure that he was all right – at least for today. When his attention wandered back to his phone, Safa kissed his hair and headed back to the kitchen where Natalie was nervously waiting.

'Did you know that Richard was hitting her?' asked Safa.

Natalie was forlorn. 'No, I didn't.'

'I can't believe it. Lily of all people.'

'What do you mean?'

'She's Lily Astor, the nation's sweetheart. I would have thought that someone would have noticed.'

Natalie scoffed. 'Yeah, right.'

'What?' Safa was confused.

'Do you really believe that Lily sat back and took his abuse for years?'

'You don't?' Safa knew from her work that abuse didn't just happen to subdued women in drunken homes. It happened to strong, capable ones as well.

Natalie raised her palms, denying responsibility. 'You know

what Lily is like,' she said. Before Safa could digest this, Natalie picked up her cigarettes and headed out the door.

*

Safa walked along Harford Street, past Shandy Park. The dreary patch of grass had an outdoor gym and basketball court, and was generally frequented by teenage boys. Safa was surprised that Lily had let Harry come by here at night. A posh white boy after dark might as well have a target on his back. In fact, she was surprised that Lily let him have a friend who lived here, so keen was she to escape her roots.

Natalie's words came to mind. *You know what Lily is like.* Safa hadn't pressed her, but the implication made her uneasy. Safa was sure that Lily was telling the truth but she also knew that her former best friend couldn't stand to be wronged.

Safa thought back to the year that they had turned fourteen and a particular day in school. They were in their Religious Studies class and their teacher, a thin-lipped woman named Ms Burton, was describing the crossing of the Red Sea.

'Moses held out his staff and parted the sea, creating a gap wide enough for passage.'

Patrick, the class clown, turned in his seat. 'Hey Lily-Ann, did Moses also part your teeth?'

It took a moment for the joke to hit and, then, the class erupted. Lily turned beetroot-red as hoots of laughter rose around her. 'Very clever,' she said, lifting her chin a few degrees to signal nonchalance. Safa, however, noticed the way her lips clamped hard over her noticeably bad teeth. She tried to catch Lily's eye, but she just stared ahead as Ms Burton tried to quieten the class. Safa didn't mention it on their walk home. Instead, she waited until they were safely in her room at Withy House.

'Hey Lily,' she started tentatively. 'What Patrick said today. He was being a real dick.'

Lily's eyes were cool and hard. 'I don't care about him.'

Safa studied her. Lily lied all the time about what she really felt – to her sister, to her teachers, to her classmates – but Safa usually got the truth from her if she dug hard enough. 'I know but it wasn't very nice.' Lily didn't say anything. 'If he'd said it about me, I would've been upset.'

Lily's cheeks flushed pink. 'It's not like I don't *know* that my teeth are bad. I see people looking every time I smile. Why say that in front of everyone? I can't change how they look. Mum doesn't take us to the dentist, so what am I meant to do?'

Safa grimaced with sympathy. Her father took her to the dentist like clockwork, marking each appointment on his calendar with a big red cross. 'Your teeth aren't bad,' she lied, but Lily wasn't listening. Instead, she was pacing the room.

'That prick thinks he's so funny.'

'He's an idiot, Lily. Forget about him.'

Lily continued to pace. 'And everyone just goes along with it, laughing like fucking monkeys.' She clenched and flexed her fingers.

'They'll have forgotten it tomorrow,' Safa said soothingly.

Lily paused by the window, a faraway look in her eyes.

'Come on, Lily.' Safa tapped her maths textbook. 'Let's get on with this.'

Lily's jaw was hard and stubborn as she looked out at Globe Road.

'Lily,' Safa urged gently. She managed to coax her to the textbook, but she remained cold and sullen for the rest of the evening. Her mind was clearly somewhere else, working on some other problem. When Lily left, Safa wanted to say something else; to make sure she was all right, but she decided to let it be. It was clear that Lily needed time.

Two months later, Lily was walking to school one day when she saw Patrick in a car with a man. The man had his hand in Patrick's trousers. Lily rushed to school in a panic and told a teacher who reported it to the police. Patrick vehemently denied it but the news spread. Soon, everyone knew that Patrick Meaden in year 10 had been felt up by a paedo.

Lily seemed aghast that the news had got out, but Safa saw her expression one day as she stood in the classroom doorway, looking across at all the pupils gossiping about Patrick. It was a look of satisfaction; a quiet, secret pride. It raised a sick feeling in Safa's stomach. It couldn't be – could it? Later, in the school bathroom, Safa brought it up.

'Lily, you remember a couple of months ago when Patrick made that joke?'

'What joke?' Lily asked lightly as she studied herself in the mirror.

Safa frowned. 'About your teeth.'

'Oh right. That.' She shrugged one shoulder. 'That was just Patrick being Patrick.'

'You were pretty upset about it.'

She puckered her lips. 'Was I?'

Safa glanced at the stalls to make sure they were empty. 'Hey, can I ask you something?' She lowered her voice. 'You didn't make up that stuff about Patrick, did you?'

Lily met her gaze in the mirror. 'Why would I do that?'

'I don't know.' Safa paused. 'For revenge?'

'Revenge?' Lily seemed amused. 'Are you mad? Of course I didn't make it up.'

'So it's all true?'

Lily turned towards her. 'Of course it's true.'

Safa hesitated. 'Because there are less messed up ways to get revenge. You could've have just said he was gay.'

There was something cold and adult in Lily's smile. 'Don't be silly. Being gay is cool now.' With that, she turned and walked out.

Safa was chilled. Had Lily calculated how to cause maximum damage? Outing Patrick as gay would furnish him with a certain cachet. Branding him as abused, however, was a stroke of cruel genius. There was nothing cool to be gained from that. Patrick's denial would be taken as that of an anxious victim and Lily would look like a saviour.

Patrick continued to deny it for a year and eventually he and his family moved away. Lily, meanwhile, got braces.

As adults, Safa had never asked Lily about it, but it had always gnawed at her. So, yes, Safa *did* know what Lily was like – or at least suspected what she was capable of – but there was simply no way that she had killed Richard for a reason other than self-defence.

Safa set the thought aside when she arrived at Stephen's house. This conversation would need her focus. She pushed open the gate, which announced her with a high whine. A curtain twitched on the upper floor and Safa pretended not to see. The house was one of the modern builds that lined Harford Road. It had a neat row of plants outside and a trellis with creeping ivy, like a miniature version of Lily's. Safa rang the bell and waited. A woman opened the door – white, in her late thirties, pretty in a wholesome way, but clearly tense with worry. Behind her was a busy hallway: a tall rack of shoes and an overflow row beside it, a sideboard with browning flowers, a noticeboard studded with keepsakes and reminders.

'Hi, I'm Safa Saleem. I'm a family friend of Lily Astor's.'

The woman's face grew pinched. 'How can I help you?'

'I spoke to Harry earlier and he told me that he was here last night?'

The woman shifted uneasily. 'Yes.'

'Could I come in for a moment?'

'The police have already come round to question Stephen.'

Safa grimaced with sympathy. 'I'm so sorry to hear that. It's just that Harry is alone at his aunt's house and I'm trying to help him and Lily.'

The woman checked over her shoulder, then asked, 'Is it true that she killed Richard?'

Safa knew that she had to give a little in order to get something back. 'That's what it looks like. I'm trying to fit the pieces together.'

'Why don't you let the police do that?'

'Because they want to put her in prison and, if what I believe is true, that's the last place she belongs.' Safa saw the 'Time's Up' pin on the noticeboard. Heartened, she added, 'Abused women shouldn't be put in prison for defending themselves against their abuser.'

The woman thawed a little. 'Look, you can come in for a moment, but I'm afraid you can't talk to Stephen.'

'That's okay. I just want to check a few things with you.'

The woman introduced herself as Hannah and led Safa to the living room. She offered to make tea, but Safa declined politely, recognising the clipped tone that implied she'd rather not.

'Do you remember what time Harry came round yesterday?'

'Yes. It was about quarter past nine.'

'Is it normal for Harry to come by at that time in the evening?'

'Not really, no.'

Safa didn't take out her notebook, wary of spooking Hannah. 'You said it was "about quarter past nine". Can you be more specific?'

'You're like the police. That's exactly what they asked.' Hannah tapped her watch. 'It was 9.20 p.m. I checked the time when the doorbell rang as it was a bit late for visitors. I didn't mind of course, but we're normally winding down at that time.'

would never fill in someone's sentence but, as a friend, she needed the postscript.

Lily was quiet.

'Right?'

Lily nodded.

'Harry said that Richard was hitting you.'

'You had no right to talk to him.'

Natalie had given her permission, but Safa knew that this was a feeble excuse. 'I'm not sorry,' she said, surprising Lily. 'I'm sorry that you feel betrayed but I can't say I'm sorry that I did it because I would do it again. We lost touch, but that doesn't mean I stopped caring. About you *or* Harry.'

'I never said you did.'

'What happened that night, Lily?'

Lily's jaw hardened. 'I can't talk to the press.'

'I'm not here as "press".'

'Aren't you?'

Safa flushed. 'Okay, look.' She placed her hands on the table in a show of candour. 'I *am* working on a story, but it's not—'

'Of course you are. Gossip and clickbait. How incredibly gratifying.'

Safa ignored the sting. 'It's not like that. It's going to be a long-form feature. Lily, I have *eight thousand* words to play with.' She spoke quickly to convince her of what the piece would be: a deep dive into the psychology of abuse and how it drives women to the brink. 'I promise you it's going to nuanced and intricate and comprehensive. It's going to break down the justice system and how it fails women that—'

'Well, good luck with it,' Lily cut in.

Safa stopped, frustrated. She knew she was being unfair, but she expected more from Lily. There were women out there who literally couldn't communicate the horrors they had faced. The Glassman handpicked his victims for this exact reason. Lily, meanwhile, had

'How did Harry seem to you?'

'A little preoccupied, but his mood lifted as soon as they raided the snack drawer.' She smiled warmly. 'He's a sweet kid.'

Safa felt a well of affection for him. 'Did Harry seem agitated in any way?'

'No. He was normal.'

'So he arrived and they raided the snack drawer. What did they do after?'

'They went upstairs to Stephen's room. I always get them to leave the door open. You don't know what they're looking at on the internet these days, but they're usually just on TikTok.'

'What happened next?'

Hannah angled her head. 'Nothing. I left them to it until the police knocked on our door at around ten o'clock.'

'How was Harry when the police collected him?'

'Scared. Shaking. I think he thought that something had happened to Lily.'

Safa spent the next half hour charting out the details of the police visit. She briefly considered asking to speak to Stephen, but Hannah had already said no and Safa wanted to respect that. She stood and thanked her for her time.

'If you speak to Lily, please tell her that we're thinking of her and we're glad that she's okay.'

'I will.' Safa pictured Lily in a jail cell. She was physically unharmed but far from 'okay'. Safa felt guilty for letting Natalie get in her head. *You know what Lily is like.* Yes, she *did* know. Lily was tough and brave and resilient. Ruthless, yes, but she had *had* to be to lift herself out of poverty; to escape her mother's addiction; to make something of herself. She wasn't perfect, but neither was Safa – *that* was for damned sure.

Chapter 8

Safa filled her flask to the brim, needing the extra caffeine to get through Monday morning. The weekend had been frenetic. *The Echo* had got the credit for breaking the Lily Astor story thanks to her tweet and a follow-up piece on the website. Lily had been officially charged with Richard's murder, inciting a media frenzy. Even now, the TV in the newsroom kitchen was tuned to Lily's story. There was a panel debate show on screen, hosted by former tabloid editor Max Lockwood, known for his forthright presenting style. Against her better judgement, Safa paused to listen.

'I'm afraid I just don't buy it,' Max was saying. 'I don't believe that Lily Astor – who by the way I think is a brilliant presenter – was getting abused by her husband behind closed doors.' Max spoke into the camera, directly to the viewer. 'Here's something that the good folks at home should know: when stories like this break, people in the industry usually go *Finally! Someone told the truth!* Because, often, we know when someone is misbehaving. Sometimes, it's an open secret in the industry, whether it's a Hollywood producer in the US or a popular presenter in the UK. And as much as we want to tell you – as much as you *deserve* to know – we can't because of libel laws. With Lily Astor, there was nothing. No rumours, no hints, no stories. In fact, I've met Lily and her husband several times and they seemed blissfully happy.'

'Max, hold on a minute,' Naomi, his long-suffering co-presenter, cut in. 'You're not seriously saying that because they *looked* happy, there can't possibly have been something darker happening.'

Max gave her a withering look. 'That's not what I'm saying at all. What I'm saying is that people in the industry have a good sense of things and *my* sense is that Lily Astor is a strong, intelligent, capable woman. Why on earth wouldn't she report it if something was wrong?'

Safa grit her teeth. Men like Max weaponised a woman's own competence against her. By his definition, Lily was too strong to be a victim. And Safa was willing to bet that Rukshana was too *weak*.

As Max wittered on, a seed of an idea came to Safa. She stared at the screen, lost in thought for a minute. Then, she spun and marched to Kevin's office.

'Good work this weekend,' he said, waving her in. 'What's the latest?'

Safa took a seat. 'The Mags can't grant Lily bail so, for now, she's in custody.' The Mags – or Magistrates' Courts – was the first port of call for all crimes, the more serious of which were passed on to the Crown Courts. 'If she's denied bail, she'll probably be transferred to Bronzefield.'

'Is that likely?'

'I'm hoping she'll get bail. She's not a flight risk, it was an act of self-defence, and she has a child. I don't think it benefits anyone to put her away.'

'Did the kid see anything?'

'No. I've spoken to a source at the Met and Harry's whereabouts checks out. Two witnesses – Talia Wilde and Edward Harrison – were guests at the party and saw Harry leave the house at 9 p.m. just as they drove away. His phone records show that he called his friend, Stephen, at 9.10 p.m., halfway between their homes, and both Stephen and his mother have verified that Harry arrived at 9.20 p.m. I've done the walk between their houses myself and it takes twenty minutes at a decent pace.'

'So you think Lily is telling the truth?'

'I believe her, yes.'

'Okay.' Kevin waited for more, recognising the look on her face. 'What?' he asked carefully.

'Kevin, do you remember Snow Fall from 2012?'

He nodded. 'Of course.' Snow Fall was a ground-breaking feature about a lethal avalanche published online by *The New York Times*. It seamlessly wove interactive graphics, animated simulations and aerial video into the written narrative to create an immersive experience. It won a Pulitzer Prize, a Peabody Award and a Whitney, and changed the way in-depth features were reported across the globe.

Safa wheeled her chair closer to the desk. 'I'm being courted by a startup which specialises in interactive features. They emailed me in January offering our first story for free to test out the platform. I've been brushing them off because we haven't had anything meaty enough. I was going to suggest it to you for the Robert Knox feature, but there have been several deep dives on that guy already. Could Lily's story work instead?'

Kevin pursed his lips in thought. 'It could do.'

Safa sat up straighter. This feature would allow her to examine the epidemic of violence against women through the lens of Lily's case. Even Francesca at *The Clarion* would surely deem it as *news*. Safa grabbed a pen off the desk and flipped open her notebook. 'There's so much we can explore through Lily's case: the broken veneer of a charmed life, miscarriages of justice against victims of abuse, the media's fascination with female killers, the albatross that is the "perfect victim"—'

'Hold up,' Kevin cut in. 'I said it *could* work. That doesn't mean it *will* work. Snow Fall took six months and eleven people. There's only one of you.'

'I can do a scaled-down version.'

'Scaled down to an eleventh? That's not going to work, Safa.'

'Then give me another person.'

He clucked with impatience. 'You know I can't do that. I can't even spare you. It's a good idea but we just don't have the resources.'

'What if I did it in my spare time?'

Kevin gestured dismissively. 'You're already here all hours of the day. Where exactly will you get this spare time?'

'I'll work on it in the evenings. On the days I need to be in court, I'll catch up on my normal work afterwards.'

'I don't think this can be done by halves, Safa, and I can't commit any budget. Our IT guy is already invoicing overtime which I can't afford.'

'Then I won't use him at all. The startup can help with the tech instead.' Safa gripped the edge of the desk. 'Look, what if I did it as a freelance project, outside of my remit at *The Echo*? As long as I can use the paper's name to pull strings, you can pay me a nominal fee at the end to "buy it" so to speak. All I want is a bit of flexibility in my schedule.'

Kevin sighed, clearly unconvinced.

'Look, can I tell you a story?' asked Safa, knowing that Kevin could not resist. 'Last year, I was in Vienna with my ex, Imran. We had a delicious dinner at a charming local restaurant and were walking back to our hotel when we came upon a group of men. There was hardly space on the pavement, so Imran and I had to walk in single file. Immediately, I tensed because a woman walking by herself is perceived differently. It can be as subtle as that: a man leaves your side and immediately you go from protected to prey.

'But here's the kicker. When I actually looked at the men, I realised that they were wearing Pride flags. They were gay men on some sort of demonstration – and the way my body just relaxed . . .' Safa exhaled, her shoulders no longer hunched. 'It was the first time I properly realised what it's like to be a woman in a public space and I just don't think men understand that. The closest parallel I can think of is the way you might act in front of the police. Your body becomes aware; you subconsciously adjust your behaviour; you're mindful of where they are until you're safely away. It's a poor comparison, but that's why I need time and space to work on this feature, Kevin. The complexity of it can't be summed up in a neat metaphor.'

Kevin leaned back in his chair and laced his fingers behind his head. For a moment, he was lost in thought, then his gaze came back to her. 'If you do this, you have to do it properly. No half-assed local-paper garbage. It has to compete.'

'It will.' Safa nodded vigorously. 'Kevin, this feature could convince hundreds of women to speak out.' Just as important to Safa, it would explain why so many women *don't*.

Safa understood that all the features in the world would not convince Rukshana to talk. The Glassman's victims had things in common with Lily – suffering at the hands of men, silence that protected those men, a deep and ossified shame – but Safa would need different tools if she were to help them. She couldn't shine a torch on them; she needed to let them grieve in long, desperate hours at home. It hurt her to picture Rukshana moving alone through her evening routine. Undoing her hair from its neat grey bun, so thin now that it showed her scalp. Rubbing lotion into her hands, unable to meet her own eyes in the mirror. The drumbeat of dread that comes with nightfall. The fear. And the exhaustion of holding that fear all by herself. All these women. All this hurt. If they all screamed at once, they might deafen the earth.

'Please,' Safa said softly. There was something in the texture of her voice that changed Kevin's expression: fatherly now, and strangely sentimental.

'Okay,' he said with a gentle nod.

'Okay?'

He cleared his throat. 'Okay, but if it affects your usual duties, all bets are off.'

Safa clasped her hands together. 'Kevin, thank you.'

'You think you can do it? Then go and fucking do it,' he said gruffly.

Safa laughed with nervous relief. 'You, sir, are a gentleman and a scholar.'

'Get out. And take that fucking cliché with you.'

She stood quickly. Kevin rarely showed softness and was embarrassed when he did. She thanked him again and hurried back to her desk. Her workload would be crushing but, for now, she felt a great weight lift.

*

Lily was aware of how eerie she must look, accepting her prison tracksuit with a full-watt smile on her lips. By now, it was an instinct, a socially-acceptable nervous tic, but she knew it must looked unhinged. It remained fixed as she followed the guard around the wing of HMP Bronzefield, the largest women's prison in Europe. She was led to an empty cell that smelled of disinfectant and faint vape fumes – fruity and artificial. When the cell door locked behind her, there was no momentous reckoning or swift undoing. Instead, she sat on the hard-boned bed in a quiet state of narcosis. Her mind reached for shards of memory and tried to glue them into a single piece. Through this gentle ordering, perhaps she could make sense of the violence.

Visions of Richard whirled through her mind, each too gory to dwell on. The gaping wound, the whites of his eyes, the life draining out of him. It had been an accident. She had to convince others of that fact, not least of all Harry. She pictured the police collecting him. How had they broken the news that his mother had killed his father? There was no chance he would get over this, no chance they could be normal – but Lily had to try. All of this she had done for Harry.

She balked at the thought of him in her cramped childhood bedroom, living alongside Natalie. Her sister was a severe woman with little affection to offer. She had no children of her own and was prone to depressive episodes. She had dealt with their mother's alcoholism for many more years than Lily and it had drained all the patience out of her. Lily had kept her at arm's length from Harry, an error she now regretted. She prayed that they would find some common ground, a way to co-exist.

The sound of high-pitched laughter cut into her thoughts. It was brief and mean and filled her with anxiety. She took long, slow breaths to calm herself. Whatever nightmare followed, it had to better than the daily stress and fear of home. She pictured Richard's face as he charged across the living room. She thought of the different ways that she could have defused the argument. Instead, fuelled by anger and alcohol, and a brazen self-destructiveness, she had let it get out of hand. In that moment, she hadn't cared what would happen to her. After years of pretending, it was almost euphoric to experience a moment of pure uncaring. But that brief lapse in vigilance had led to disaster: a murder charge and now six long months at Bronzefield until her trial date in October.

Lily Astor, national treasure, on trial for murder.

There was a bitter irony in all of this. She had spent so many years resenting this creation of hers, but it may be the thing that saved her. The *Arise* audience – the 'Tower Block Traceys' as her team had cynically dubbed their viewers – adored Lily. It was a trick that even *she* didn't know how she'd pulled. After all, she never traded on her council flat roots, preferring the image of an English rose. She had stores of goodwill and knew that the public would be outraged that Lily was on trial for murder for defending herself against her abuser.

They would believe it too. Lily was certain that none of them would fathom any other reason why she would kill her husband.

*

Safa checked her phone and swore. No emails or messages. She had put in a request to visit Lily at Bronzefield, but hadn't received confirmation. She felt restless and impatient, unable to focus. The thought of Lily in prison filled her with a crackling dread. In any other arena – a shark-tank workplace, an infamous council estate – Lily could handle herself, but the daily reality of prison was surely too much for even her.

Safa refreshed her email one more time and then headed to the meeting room that flanked the main newsroom. The heating was broken and the air inside snapped with cold. Safa huddled into her scarf and rolled her chair next to Tim, the intern. He had asked Safa for help on his article about Robert Knox, the controversial influencer. Tim slid a DPS – a double page spread – across the table to Safa. She took a few minutes to read it, then rolled back her chair a few inches.

'So this is a feature, right?'

'Yes,' said Tim.

'Okay, so news is very different to features. You're giving us the facts about this guy – his follower count, his biography, his bank balance – but there needs to be *emotion*. Why are young men drawn to his toxic masculinity? What is wrong in their lives that they have to resort to a TikTok influencer for their moral compass? And how do *you*, a working-class white male, relate to this? Are you swayed by any of it? If not, why not? If so, be honest. Don't be scared to expose yourself a little bit. Tell us how you really feel. Show us compelling reasons why young men are being seduced by him.'

Tim noted down her questions, nodding rapidly as he wrote.

He had a nervy energy and Safa wanted to take his hand and say, *it's okay, you've got this.*

'Send me the second draft once you're done and we'll look at it again,' she told him.

'Thank you – and sorry.' He frowned at the DPS, clearly disappointed.

'Hey.' Safa waited for him to look up at her. 'This is an excellent start. Switching from news to features isn't easy. It takes practice and finesse. I'll be here until you get it right, okay?'

He gave her a shy smile. 'Thanks, Safa. You honestly don't know how much you've helped.'

She grinned at him. 'You've got this. Now go and fucking do it,' she said, echoing Kevin's words. She watched him leave and then turned to her phone, the smile still on her lips. A new email appeared in her inbox.

Your request to visit HMP Prisoner # 25619 has been approved.

Safa leapt to her feet. Lily had agreed to see her. She grabbed her coat and bag from the newsroom and hurried out the door. The journey to Bronzefield was an hour and a half, but in her car it was closer to two. When she finally got there, she was welcomed by a blue-and-silver sign into what looked like an industrial business park. She parked her Clio furthest from the building, needing to stretch her legs. The air smelled of industrial cooking: boiled carrots and tinned green beans, which reminded her of school lunches. She walked across the car park and headed inside to clear security. It wasn't her first time here. She had interviewed other inmates for features but never someone that she actually knew.

Safa scanned the visitors' room. The space was large and rectangular and looked like a community centre: epoxy flooring in speckled blue, frayed chairs with plastic tables and a chaotic playpen for visiting toddlers. Safa spotted Lily in one corner. She wore a grey tracksuit and her hair was no longer in its trademark curl. Instead, it fell lank and straight. Safa hugged her but Lily was limp like a mannequin. Safa tamped down her dread. She had to take this step by step; to ask small, answerable questions. But Lily spoke first.

'How could you, Safa?' Her tone was flat, but her eyes were bright with anger.

'How could I what?'

'You spoke to Harry without my permission. I expected it from all the other hacks sniffing at my door, but not you.'

Safa coloured, because she knew that Lily had a right to be angry. 'I went to see if he was okay.'

'You crossed a line.'

'I wanted to check he was safe. That's the only reason I went.'

'Not to collect exclusive content for the *East London Echo*?'

Safa was hurt. 'That's not fair, Lily. You know I wouldn't use anything he said. I went to help.'

'I don't need help.'

Safa looked pointedly around at the room. At the table closest to them, a woman was coughing phlegm into a tissue. At another, an inmate was shouting at her visitor, a gaunt male with knotty features. 'I think you do,' she said gently.

'Why are you here, Safa?'

'To ask you that very same question.' They stared each other down and a lifetime fell away, revealing the girls that they once were. Lily kneaded the cuff of her sleeve, a childhood tic that surfaced whenever she was distressed. In Safa, it prompted an old and fierce protectiveness. She leaned towards Lily, her shoulders hunched in a try for privacy. 'Tell me why you're here.'

Lily cleared the glue-like sound in her throat. Her breath was audible – shallow and uneven. 'I killed him,' she said softly.

Safa waited. 'In self-defence,' she added. As a reporter, she all the tools, but declined to use them. Safa *had* to try to convince her. Gently, she asked, 'Would you talk to me for the piece?'

'I told you: I can't talk to the press.'

'Nothing would be published until after the trial.'

'No,' Lily said plainly.

'Lily, your story needs to be told.'

'Oh, you're doing this for *me*?'

'I'm doing it for the women who feel they can't speak out about their abuse. Lily, there is an *epidemic* of violence against women in this country, but when one of them gets hurt or killed, it isn't deemed *news*. Through your story, we have a real opportunity to expose the true horror of it.'

Lily was cynical. 'So this isn't your ticket to the big-time?'

A familiar anger rose in Safa. 'Yes, Lily, it might be. Not everyone was given one by their university.' Safa knew that this was petty, but she still felt the sting of that old teenage betrayal.

Lily exhaled harshly. 'God, you've always had a chip on your shoulder about that.'

'You don't know what it was like. You went off to Oxford and got on the fast track. And the *one* time I asked you for help, you dropped me.'

Lily looked at her curiously. In the next instant, her hostility fell away. 'You think I dropped you because you asked about a job?'

Safa stalled. 'Wasn't it?'

'Oh, Safa. So clear-eyed and yet so terrifically wrong. Of *course* it wasn't.'

'Then why?'

Lily gripped her cuff in her fist. 'That's when he started to hit me.'

Safa lurched with surprise. 'He's been hitting you for *three* years?'

'Yes.'

'Oh, Lily.' Safa felt a clasp of emotion close over her heart. A dozen questions rose in her mind – *Why didn't you tell me? Or tell anyone?*

Why didn't you leave? – but she knew that these questions put to a victim shifted the blame to them. Instead, she said, 'I wish I'd been able to help you. I'm meant to rescue you, remember?'

Lily tried to smile, but it collapsed into a sob. 'I couldn't face the shame of you knowing.'

Safa winced at her own self-righteousness. Lily had suffered in silence for three long years. That's what shame did to a victim; it took all their power and strength and cut it down to nothing. What use were the tools given to Lily if her hands were tied at the wrists?

'I didn't help you,' Safa said gently, 'but together we can help others like you.'

Lily shook her head. 'Safa, I can't even think straight right now.'

'Okay.' Safa wouldn't push. 'Take some time to think about it. If you decide against it, I'll still be here. There's a lot we can do to get the public to support you; to define the narrative; and to pressure the CPS for treating a DV victim like this.'

There was movement in the room, signalling the end of visiting hours.

'In the meantime, please be careful. This isn't a place for that famous Baker bravado.'

Lily balked at the mention of her maiden name and Safa instantly regretted using it. Lily hated everything about her old life and even the most innocent reference to it felt loaded with judgement.

'I mean it, Lily. I know you're tough but please keep your head down. This isn't Withy House. You can't survive on posture and smarts.'

'I know.'

Safa reached forward, halfway across the table. When Lily reached out too, they gripped each other's hands – hard like an arm wrestle. 'I'm in this fight with you.'

Lily nodded, her eyes glassy with tears.

The buzzer sounded and Safa withdrew. 'I should go.' She rose quickly to her feet. 'I'll see you soon, Lily.' She didn't pause for a longer goodbye. Lily had never seen her cry and she wasn't about to let her now.

*

Lily watched Safa leave and felt a sense of displacement. They had been friends for over twenty years and Lily was one of the few people that had seen beneath the veneer. Sure, Safa never cried but softness didn't always show in tears. It was in the faraway look that shadowed her face in unguarded moments – something like nostalgia, but a darker, sadder flavour. Or the way Safa pulled away from physical touch, as if she didn't deserve it. Or how her lips twitched just a little at the faintest hint of emotion – her own personal reminder to buck up, bear down, be strong. Lily remembered Safa's reaction to her news about Oxford. That eerie Arctic smile. *Okay, wow. Well, I'm happy for you.* False cheer papered over the betrayal – and it *had* been betrayal. Lily had known that if she told Safa about Oxford, then she would apply too and likely get accepted. Safa had always been the smart one, the ambitious one, the one who pushed Lily to try. If it hadn't been for her, she would still be on the estate, scraping together a living.

So, yes, Lily had kept quiet about the application. She'd assumed that she would be rejected – that part wasn't a lie – but she *hadn't*, and she remembered the look on Safa's face when she heard the news, delivered so breezily to downplay the crime. Lily had always felt guilty that Safa – the better writer by far – had lagged so far behind.

Now, their lives had collided again, and Lily knew that she had to be careful. There was a deep-rooted comfort in having Safa near, but the cool, clear voice in Lily's head warned her that it was risky. Safa had a hawk's eye for detail and could sense unspoken truths like vibrations in the air. Lily couldn't allow her to get too close again.

Instead, she would use her as insurance. Safa could sell the narrative that Richard had been abusive; that Lily was a survivor who had hit back at a violent partner. This was the narrative that would redeem her in the eyes of the public and she needed Safa to seed it.

Lily was sure that she had got the balancing act right. If she had agreed to the feature too easily, Safa might suspect an ulterior motive. Instead, she had been reluctant, so that Safa would keep on pushing.

She would wait a few days before telling her what she wanted to hear. She would let her write her mammoth feature. She would cook up emotions for Safa to capture in her spare but beautiful prose. She imagined her friend dwelling on just the right metaphor and the thought almost made her smile with warmth.

Yes, she would use Safa just as Safa was using her. Winning public sympathy could be her saving grace in the future. Lily could bear this cell for a summer until her trial in October, but she wouldn't survive a lifetime of this – and not just metaphorically. She knew with a cold and lucid certainty that she couldn't, *wouldn't*, spend her life in prison.

But they were a long way away from that. Lily had six months to prepare. Six months to fine-tune her story; to storyboard it scene by scene until it was crystal clear. She would mine past bruises and injuries in lieu of better evidence, and repeat and recite the details until they were seared in her brain. She couldn't stumble or hesitate if she were to convince a jury that she was telling the truth. Richard abused her and she had killed him in self-defence. That was the story that would save her and that was the story she would sell.

PART II

Chapter 9

The air was crisp with the first hint of autumn. It had been a brutally hot summer and London felt like a held breath: hot and stale, in desperate need of exhalation. Safa threw a ball for Mint, her father's latest foster dog, and listened to the crunch of leaves underfoot. Harry dawdled next to her, awkward with his newly long limbs. He had grown taller in the last six months, taller than Lily too, already on the cusp of manhood.

Mint retrieved the ball and Safa let Harry throw it. He loved dogs but couldn't have one of his own. There was no room at Natalie's. Safa was secretly grateful. These Friday evening walks gave her a low-pressure way to spend time with Harry. Somehow, talking side by side in Victoria Park made room for intimacy in a way that sofas and tables did not.

'How are you getting on at school?' she asked.

'Okay.'

'No more trouble?'

Harry shrugged.

Earlier in the summer, he had got into a physical fight with a fellow student. The school had made an exception given what had happened with Lily. A few weeks after that, however, he got into a second fight, this time giving a boy a black eye. The school had warned that, next time, he would be expelled. The alternative was Stepney Green School, and Safa was well aware that a boy like

Harry would be eaten alive there. Natalie wasn't a disciplinarian, so Safa had taken a more active role in making sure he behaved.

'Have you had any more trouble at the gates?' Safa had been angered to hear that reporters and photographers had approached Harry after school.

'No, it was just those times I told you about.'

Safa nodded, satisfied. 'And how's Ella?' she asked, hoping to lighten the mood. Harry blushed and the sight made Safa smile.

When he spoke, however, it wasn't with shyness but anger. 'Ella's a bitch. I asked her to the end of year prom and she laughed at me. She asked in front of everybody if I was going to *murder* her.'

Safa balked. 'Oh, Harry, I'm so sorry.'

'It's fine,' he said, though it clearly wasn't.

'That was really unkind of her.' They walked in silence for a while as Mint whizzed back and forth across the path. After a minute, Safa said, 'But, hey, maybe don't call her a bitch.'

Harry looked at her quizzically.

'It was nasty of Ella to say that, but it's not very gentlemanly to call her a bitch.'

'Gentlemanly?' Harry was amused. 'What? Like in Dickens?'

'You know what I mean.'

He shrugged. 'Bobby says that girls don't like gentlemen.'

'Well, you shouldn't always listen to your friends.'

Harry made a wry face. 'Okay, what should I call her instead?'

'I dunno. Something not gendered, like "jerk" maybe.' Safa realised that she wasn't very good at this.

'"Jerk"?' Harry laughed. 'Maybe I should try "scamp" or "rapscallion" instead.'

Safa nudged his shoulder with hers. 'All right. I get the point.' She enjoyed this lightness between them; the easy camaraderie that had been missing from so much of her life. Safa didn't have siblings, didn't even have many friends. The romcom ideal of a young quartet of friends brunching or lunching was alien to her. This easy push-and-pull with Harry gave her a sense of what she had missed.

They arrived at the lake and stood at its edge in companionable silence.

'How are you feeling about next week?' asked Safa. Lily's trial was due to start but, as a witness, Harry wasn't allowed to attend until after his evidence.

'I'm okay. I'm worried about Mum.'

'If you have any questions – about her or the court process – you can ask me, okay?'

'Okay.'

'And how's Natalie?'

Harry toed a stone out of the soil. 'She's okay. I don't think she likes me.'

'Why do you say that?'

Harry's lips parted but he didn't speak.

'Harry?'

'She told me that Mum was too young when she had me.'

Safa winced. She had to tread carefully because, in truth, she agreed with Natalie. Lily had fallen pregnant in her final year at university – her bright trajectory disturbed by unplanned motherhood.

'I don't know if you know, but they tried to get rid of me,' Harry said quietly. 'Mum tried to abort me.'

Safa caught her breath. 'Who told you that?'

He looked out at the shore. 'I heard them talking about it a couple of years ago.'

Safa considered denying it, but honesty between them was important. 'Did you talk to your mum about what you heard?'

'No. She would have just lied. Pretended that everything was fine.'

'Did you talk to anyone else?'

'No. I kept it to myself.'

Safa felt a weight settle on her. Harry was right. When Lily and Richard found out she was pregnant, they had immediately booked an abortion. '*We have years to start a family,*' Lily had told Safa, matter of fact. '*It's simply illogical to start now.*'

But the pill failed and the very fact of Harry's survival switched something in Lily. To Safa's surprise, she decided to keep the baby. Richard had reacted with a cold and stoic fury, unable to believe that this had happened to a man like him. *You can take a girl out of a council estate,* he had told Lily in a particularly cruel mood.

Safa wondered now if the violence in Richard could be traced back to that one decision; to the realisation that mistakes could not always be erased by a clean sweep of privilege.

She touched Harry's arm. 'Your mother has always loved you, Harry.'

His gaze remained fixed on the shore, but when he blinked, tears rolled down his cheeks. 'Then how come she tried to get rid of me?' His shoulders curled inward, embarrassed by his own need.

Safa felt a loping sorrow. 'That was before she knew who you were, Harry. And who you would be. As soon as she had you – before that, in fact – she fell in love with you.' Harry wiped his eyes and Safa looked away, giving him space to grieve. He slid down to the grass and hugged his knees to his chest. Safa sat too and put an arm around him. He leaned into her, his weight unsteadying her. She could feel the sadness rolling off him and wished that she knew how to ease it. 'Your mum would do anything for you. You know that, right?'

Harry wasn't yet able to speak; only nodded instead.

'I know things feel hopeless right now, but they will get better. I promise.'

'You don't know that,' he said, shrugging out of her grip.

'No, but I know your mum and one thing she knows is how to survive.'

'What if they don't let her out?'

Safa spoke carefully, wary of making false promises. 'We'll deal with that if it happens. For now, let's take each day as it comes, okay?' He didn't respond and Safa lightly touched his hair. 'Okay?'

He wiped his tears on his sleeve. 'Okay.' For the next few minutes, he watched the surface of the lake, pleated by the breeze. 'How come you never had kids?' he asked unexpectedly.

Safa tensed. She had fielded this question so many times but it caught her off guard now. 'I never wanted them.'

'How come?'

She reached for her roster of excuses. *I like my life as it is. I'm far too busy. I'm far too broke.* Then, for a reason she couldn't pinpoint, she told him the truth. 'I don't think I'd be a very good mother.'

Harry was surprised. 'You'd be a great one.'

'Oh, I don't know,' she said, studiedly casual.

'Why?'

Safa felt old emotions stir. 'I think I'd be too worried about messing up,' she said vaguely.

'Yeah, but you wouldn't.'

She scoffed and Harry looked at her curiously, hearing the bitter note in it. She focused on the lake, but felt his laser gaze on her. She laughed a little then. Talking to a child forced one to be frank. You couldn't dodge hard questions through euphemism and humour. She took a bracing breath. 'When I was a kid – younger than you – I messed up badly and that made me afraid in ways that I don't really like to talk about.'

'What did you do?'

Safa's ears hummed with blood. Her memories of that time had taken on a sort of malevolence; warned her that if she unearthed them, the balance in her life would cave. The depth of Harry's pain, however, forced her to be honest. If he could bear his, then maybe she could bear hers.

'It happened when I was eight years old,' she said, lacing her fingers tight. 'My dad didn't speak English back then. He came over from Bangladesh in the seventies and worked long hours in a garage; never had time to learn. I had to translate for my parents: calling the council for repairs, paying their gas bill at the post office – things like that.'

The thought of her dad asking her for help made her feel uneasy. 'A lot of the time, it confused me but I sort of muddled through.' Safa could still feel the churning anxiety of being out of her depth; of knowing that she had to advocate hard for her parents but lacking both the courage and vocabulary.

'For a long time, we managed okay, then Mum got pregnant and I was dealing with her medical appointments.' Safa spoke with weighted precision, knowing that these words could crush her. 'The doctors were always nice to me, but the tone that they'd put on – this childish way of speaking – made me feel worse. It made me feel my age more keenly if that makes sense. Like, here I am – a child – and I'm trying my best to act like a grown-up but the way they spoke to me only made it clearer that I was a kid; that I didn't know what I was doing.'

The humming in her ears grew louder. 'We were coping, but then Mum went into labour early. We went with her to the hospital and Dad couldn't answer any of the questions. They didn't have a Sylheti interpreter so I had to do it.' Safa touched her cheek to try to cool the burning. Her throat felt thick, swollen with the words she was trying to say. She pictured herself at eight, in her Princess Jasmine nightie, tasked with a duty that none of the adults were able to do. Part of Safa ached for that child. And part of her hated her.

'I didn't understand some of what they asked but I did my best.' Safa paused to steady her voice. 'They asked if Mum was allergic to antibiotics. I knew what allergies were because a friend at school couldn't eat peanuts and I thought that's what they meant. I remember thinking *Mum loves peanuts*. She would shell them for us and the peel would get everywhere, so I told them no.' Safa dug a nail into the ridge of her knee. 'Mum went into shock. She stopped breathing. They tried to save her but we lost her. And the baby.' Shame washed through her, closing her throat.

Harry reached out and touched her hand, but she pulled hers back, knowing that the slightest softness would wholly undo her.

Her pain was corrosive, spitting heat and acid. *I told you so,* it said. *I told you to leave it alone.* She swallowed hard and forced herself on. 'At first, I didn't realise it was my fault, but they eventually found an interpreter to talk to my dad. I was across the hall but I heard them talk.'

Safa remembered the dull shine of her patent leather shoes, the pretty little bow that was slightly askew. Her bare legs were cold but her palms were clammy as she listened to the muted voices. *Your daughter gave us the wrong information.*

Safa remembered hearing those words: the flash of neon panic, the room starting to spin. Her child's mind was just old enough to comprehend the horror of what she had done. 'Mum died because I was too scared to tell the doctors that I didn't understand the question.' Her lips drew a hard, thin line. 'Dad never blamed me but it *was* my fault,' she finished.

'No, it wasn't.' Harry was fierce, almost angry.

Safa tried to smile but it came out a grimace. 'That's sweet of you, Harry, but it *was*.'

'Your dad shouldn't have expected you to do that.'

'It wasn't his fault. He tried. He learnt English after that; did everything he could to give me a good life.'

'But the hospital should have had someone to help!'

'I know, but there weren't always provisions for my community.'

'That's why you don't want kids? Because you think you'll mess up?'

Safa cleared her throat – a harsh, abrasive sound. 'Maybe I feel like I don't deserve them.' The thought, finally articulated, made her blanch with grief. She pressed her palms in the grass to hold herself upright.

'It wasn't your fault, Saffie.'

When she didn't respond, he placed a clumsy arm around her. At first, she was stiff and unyielding, her tears too close to the surface. Then, she leaned her head on his. He gripped her hand and, together, they watched the autumn evening fold in on the sun.

*

Safa walked down the long corridor, her boots squeaking on the plastic flooring. She pushed into the visitors' room. It was Sunday afternoon, a day before Lily's trial, and the space was surprisingly empty. Families, she supposed, reserved their prison visits for earlier in the day. Lily was sitting in a corner and stood up to greet her. When they hugged, Safa could feel her ribs through her thick grey fleece. Her cheeks were gaunt and bony, and her wrists looked like they might snap if she picked up something heavy.

'Are you eating?'

'Jesus, Safa, not this again.'

Safa studied her. 'Lily, what's going on? Is someone taking your food?'

Lily tutted. 'This isn't *Bad Girls*, Safa. The food's awful – that's all it is. Besides,' she flicked her wrist in the air, 'if there's one thing I know, it's how to starve.'

Safa flinched, unable to maintain the usual glibness of their monthly meetings. 'Lily,' she said softly, remembering the bare cupboards of Lily's childhood, the bread-and-butter sandwiches, the lankness of her hair in the six-week summer break when nutrients were scarce.

'Do you want to get started?' Lily asked brusquely. She motioned at Safa's notepad and pen.

Safa regarded them for a moment, then set them on the table. 'I was thinking we could just hang out today.'

Lily arched a brow. 'Okay,' she said cautiously.

'Seriously. We're off the record today.'

Lily rolled her shoulders in an effort to relax.

'How was your visit with Harry?'

Lily's features darkened. 'The same.' He'd visited over the course of the summer, but always under the watchful eye of a court-appointed supervisor. 'There's so much to say, but we sit here like we're at a fucking tea party.' Lily couldn't discuss the trial with Harry given that he was a witness. 'Do you know that we haven't talked about Richard? Not even once?'

Safa listened to Lily vent. Then, tentatively, she asked a question that she hadn't yet dared. 'Do you ever miss Richard?'

Lily averted her gaze and was quiet for a moment. 'Every day,' she said. 'And do you know what? It kills me not to be able to talk about that.'

Safa shifted uneasily. She knew that Lily would be pilloried if she expressed in public the slightest affection for Richard. In the age of social media, things were black and white with no room for nuance.

Lily continued: 'Even now, even after months in this fucking place, I wake up and for a second – one split second – I think I'm in bed at home and that I'll turn around and fling an arm over him and he'll crack his grin and look at me with his big brown eyes. And then reality hits and I feel like I'm falling into this *void*.' Lily swallowed. 'Sometimes, I get so angry, I want to hurt myself.'

Safa was startled. 'Are you serious?'

Lily shrugged.

'And *have* you?'

'No.' She balled a fist in her lap. 'But I get furious with myself. Why didn't I tell someone? Why didn't I ask for help? Why did I hide it like some fucking Victorian mouse?'

Safa grimaced. She had wanted to ask these very same questions when Lily had first been charged. She knew from her work as a crime reporter that contemporaneous evidence was important in cases like Lily's. Any messages, conversations or notes from the actual period of abuse were more convincing to a jury than a claim made in retrospect. If Lily had told someone about the abuse three years ago, that would matter more than telling the jury now.

Safa thought of the Glassman's victims, all of whom held their silence. She was willing to bet that there wasn't a shred of contemporaneous evidence among them. Safa had sent Rukshana a pleading letter after that first meeting, but she never replied. Safa hadn't called again, wary of harassing her, but knew that if she *did*, Rukshana would just pretend that they had never met. It was why the Glassman targeted these women in the first place. They wouldn't dare commit his atrocities into notes or diaries, let alone tell their families. Their pain would go unacknowledged and poison these women's final years. Safa wondered if Rukshana had laughed with joy even once since the Glassman's attack. Would she ever feel true peace with so much darkness weighing her down?

Safa felt her anger simmer. She felt impotent with it – swollen and ungainly. She reached out and gripped Lily's hand.

'Don't you *dare* blame yourself,' she said, low and ferocious.

Lily withdrew it gently. 'Some days, I think it was ego,' she said. 'In my most honest moments, that's what I think it was.

I didn't want people to pity me. I didn't want them to peel back everything from my life until there was only abuse. I didn't want to be a victim.'

'That's not ego, Lily. That's shame – and that *is* some Victorian bullshit.'

Lily dug her fingers between her knees. 'Safa.' Her voice trembled. 'What if they find me guilty?'

Safa recognised the Lily of her childhood: tough but achingly vulnerable. She wanted to reassure her, but Safa was a pragmatist and couldn't deny that this was possible. 'Let's take each day as it comes, Lily. That's the best that we can do.'

A lull opened up between them, but Safa wasn't ready to go. 'You'll never guess what,' she said, switching to a lighter tone. 'Dad asked me about Bumble this week.'

Lily's surprise cut right through her mood. 'No!'

'Yes. He said that one of his friends from the foster centre was on there and told him he should get on it.'

Lily was open mouthed. 'And *is* he?'

'I took him to the park with his dog to take some pictures for his profile picture.'

'Oh my god!' Lily threw her head back and laughed.

'He asked me if I could Photoshop the grey out of his beard.'

Lily laughed harder and Safa watched with warmth. On the eve of the trial, when heaviness pressed so close, she would give Lily the gift of distraction. She carried on talking, and as the world moved on around them, she folded Lily into the comfort of her oldest friendship. Tomorrow, her life would be put up for public viewing, but for now, at least for a while, she was safe with Safa.

Chapter 10

Safa sat on the press bench of courtroom eight at the Old Bailey. In the centre of the room, four rows of wooden desks were reserved for barristers and solicitors. These desks faced the judge's bench which was directly opposite the dock. To the judge's right was the jury box and press bench and, to the left, the witness box and public gallery. From Safa's vantage point, she had a clear view of the dock and Lily inside it. She sat with her knees primly together and wore a black Chanel suit, a sleek bun and minimal makeup. From a distance, she looked every inch the TV star but Safa knew from her visits that Lily was struggling.

The press bench and public gallery were packed – a full house for a celebrity circus. As Judge Edmund Turner took the jury through court formalities, Safa spotted Natalie in the public gallery. She wore a white shirt with a wide collar, a weathered green cardigan and a tartan skirt. She seemed flighty and nervous – far less composed than her sister in the dock. Safa tried to catch her eye but Natalie's dark transition lenses prevented any contact.

Lily's advocate, Victoria Hersham, sat closest to the jury. She was in her forties, slim and white, with long black hair tucked beneath a horsehair wig. Safa knew her a little and whenever they crossed paths outside court, found her to be funny and charming. In court, however, she was distinctly icy.

The prosecutor was Lucien Garrett KC, a craggy white man in his mid-fifties. He had spent thirty years at the Crown Prosecution Service and had the jaded air of someone who had seen things – like a slightly less rakish Oliver Reed. He smoothed his black silk gown and stood to give his opening speech.

'Members of the jury, there is no doubt that Lily Astor killed her husband. She has admitted that she slashed his throat and you will hear evidence that he died as a direct result of his injuries. But is Lily guilty of murder? That is what we're here to find out – today and over the course of the coming weeks.

'A person is guilty of murder if they unlawfully kill another person and, at the time of doing so, they intend to kill that other or to cause them really serious injury. Lily Astor denies murder and her defence rests on two claims. First: a lack of intent to kill. Second: the loss of control. So let's examine each in turn.

'The first is easy to dispense with. Lily says that she did not intend to kill or cause serious injury to her husband when she slashed his throat – but, ladies and gentlemen, you might well ask yourself this question: if you cut a person's throat with a knife, what can you intend to do but at the very least cause really serious injury? Quite what she intended at that moment we may learn as the evidence unfolds.

'The second claim is more complicated. Loss of control, if it applies, would not excuse her completely but would reduce murder to manslaughter. So what *is* loss of control? It is not the same as acting out of revenge. It's not the same as doing it because you were drunk or wound up or goaded, or you were just angry. For loss of control to apply, there must be a qualifying trigger – in this case the fear of serious violence. We must also be convinced that a person of Lily's sex and age, with a normal degree of tolerance and self-restraint, might have reacted in a similar way to Lily in the same circumstances.

'So, the pertinent question is not "did Lily kill her husband?" but "*why* did Lily kill her husband?" In her statement to the police, she claims that Richard Astor mounted a campaign of violence and control that lasted years, that he attacked her on the evening in question and that she acted to save herself. You will not hear me or any of the prosecution team seek to defend domestic violence. Any right-thinking person would consider that to be abhorrent. But we must be frank in presenting the evidence and there is none to suggest that Lily suffered any form of violence or mistreatment in her fourteen-year marriage to Richard. There is no medical history of broken bones and injuries, no calls to the police, no confessions to best friends or therapists. We submit that this story about violence and control is merely that: a *story* made up after the fact to hide the ugly reality of what happened that night.

'It is our case that Lily Astor was of sound mind and knew exactly what she was doing when she slashed Richard's throat with a knife. We submit that she had other reasons to be angry with him – not least the fact that Richard was planning to leave her.'

A murmur rose in the courtroom and Garrett paused to let it air. There was movement around Safa as her fellow reporters hurried to share the news. Safa studied Lily, but she showed no signs of emotion.

Garrett continued. 'From where you sit, it may look like Lily and Richard had a strong marriage, but you will hear from witnesses that they argued frequently. You will hear from neighbours that had seen them fighting. You will hear that Richard was gentle in conflict; that he tried to calm Lily when she had her rages – and she *did* have rages, despite the bright and bubbly persona that you see on TV.

'Lily is a smart, Oxford-educated, strong, determined woman. What she is *not* is a victim of abuse or coercive control. Now, we, the prosecution, bring the case, which means that we must prove every element of it. If Lily relies on the defence of loss of control, we must disprove it. We will do this by presenting the facts in a clear and logical order. If you are convinced of those facts, then we ask, members of the jury, that you find the defendant, Lily Astor, guilty of murder.'

Garrett turned to the judge. 'My Lord, we call our first witness, Ms Audrey Astor.'

*

Audrey Astor was an elegant woman with snow-white hair in a high, tight bun, a softly lined face and a healthy tan. She exuded class and – worse for Lily – a warmth that was rare among Old Money. Safa had only met her once, years ago at Lily's wedding. She remembered how the woman had taken her by the elbow and brought her into the fold. The memory filled her with goodwill. What a talent it was to disarm everyone you meet.

'Mrs Astor, can you explain your relationship to Lily Astor?' asked Lucien Garrett, the prosecutor.

'She is – *was* – my daughter in law.' Audrey cleared her throat. 'She was married to my son, Richard.'

Garrett offered his condolences. 'And what was your relationship with Lily like?'

Audrey's bright eyes dimmed. 'Up and down, I would say.'

'In what way?'

'Well, we didn't meet under the best circumstances. Lily fell pregnant very young and when Richard told us that they were to be married, we were taken aback.' Audrey gestured philosophically. 'But I told Harry – Harry Senior that is, my late husband – that we had to embrace it or we risked losing our son. We welcomed Lily into the family with open arms, threw them a beautiful wedding.'

Garrett nodded. 'And then what happened?'

'After they got married, I came to see that there were two sides to Lily: a warm, bubbly side that she showed in public and a different version that she hid.'

'What do you mean "different"?'

Audrey hesitated. 'I saw flashes of nastiness in her.'

'In what way?'

'She would say certain things when she thought no one was listening. For example, we went riding once and when we stopped for lunch, she received a phone call and took it outside. She thought she was out of earshot when she said, "Do you think posh old women love riding horses so much because they're no longer getting 'effed' by their husbands?"'

Safa saw the jurors wince. Here, in the harsh acoustics of the courtroom, the words sounded callous, but *this* was the Lily she knew: sharp, irreverent, acerbic – and, mostly, harmless.

'Did you ever confront her about this "different version" as you call it?'

'Yes, I did. It was early on in their marriage. Richard was out in the garden and I was with Lily in the conservatory. I told her that she could be herself around me. She gave me a quizzical look and said, "Whatever do you mean?" I told her that I could see she was uncomfortable being herself around us.' Audrey grimaced and the lines around her eyes crinkled. 'Maybe I put it less charitably. I think I said that I felt like she was putting on an act around us.'

'And how did she react?'

'She dropped one my antique china cups. They were a family heirloom and she knew how much I cherished them. She said it was an accident but . . .' Audrey shook her head, 'there was something in the way she did it. She moved the cup to one side and dropped it while making eye contact. I was shocked by it – shaken even. Richard came in and Lily sort of sprang into action, cleaning up the china and fussing over it, making a big show of how devastated she was. Things like this continued to happen, but there was always deniability.'

'Did you talk to Richard about it?'

'No. They were all small things, like opening the oven door when I was baking a soufflé or leaving a red sock in the white wash. I would sound petty if I brought them up, so I never did.'

Safa thought back to their school days. Once when Lily was angry, she loosened the screws in a teacher's chair so that it collapsed when he sat down. Another time, she poured glue in his classroom keyhole. Her pettiness created a real nuisance, but surely she had outgrown it.

Garrett continued: 'Mrs Astor, in the many years that Lily and Richard were married, did you ever see them argue?'

'Oh, yes.'

'Did you ever witness violence between them?'

'No. It was always verbal.'

'What's the worst argument you saw between them?'

Audrey considered this. 'A few years ago, my husband and I came to London to stay with Richard. At some point in the evening, Lily had texted Richard to ask him to pick her up from the station at a specific time. He was busy getting us settled and didn't see her message. When she came home that night, she was fuming.'

'How do you know?'

'She began shouting at him as soon as she came in the house. We were in the dining room, a little way down the hall. When he told her we were home, she lowered her voice but we heard the awful things she said.'

'Such as?'

'I remember this clearly. She told him, "If I'd got raped on the way home, it would've been *your* fault."'

Heads snapped towards Lily in the dock. The jurors, who only knew her from TV, were shocked by the nastiness of this, but Safa could *hear* Lily saying it.

'How did Richard react?' asked Garrett.

'He pleaded with her to calm down. He begged her not to say things like that. They argued for a while and then Lily stormed upstairs without saying hello to us.'

'Mrs Astor, how long have Richard and Lily been married?'

'About fourteen years.'

'In all that time, how many times have you witnessed disagreements between them?'

'Oh, dozens. Maybe twice a year.'

'In all those years and all those disagreements, did you ever witness Richard acting violently?'

'No. Never.'

'Did you ever see Richard hit Lily?'

'No.'

'Did you ever see Richard threaten to hit Lily?'

'No.'

Lily's lawyer hissed something at Garrett – no doubt a demand to stop labouring the point – but he smoothly ignored her.

'Mrs Astor, in all those years and all those disagreements, did you ever witness *Lily* acting violently?'

'Yes.'

'What did you see?'

Audrey shifted uneasily. 'I saw her slap Harry, her son, once.'

Safa jolted, certain she hadn't heard correctly.

'I'm sorry, can you repeat that?' asked Garrett, playing to the gallery.

'She slapped Harry,' said Audrey. 'It was a couple of years ago now. We were having a picnic in Hyde Park. Richard and I went for a walk and on our way back, we saw Lily slap Harry.'

'You're sure that this is what you saw?'

'I'm certain.'

'How did Harry react?'

'He sort of shrivelled up on himself.'

'Did you confront Lily about this?'

'Yes, absolutely. She said he was misbehaving and she lost her temper but that she hadn't hit him hard. Richard told me to let it go; that Lily was going through a hard time.'

'"A hard time." What did he mean by that?'

'I'm not sure. I think she was under pressure at work and had a lot of pent-up stress.'

'Did he mention any mental health issues? Depression? Anxiety?'

'No, nothing like that. She just lost her temper.'

'"She just lost her temper."' Garrett nodded gravely. 'Mrs Astor, did you see any signs that Lily was afraid of Richard or that he was exerting control over her?'

'No. Never.' She made a wry face. 'And I appreciate that I'm his mother so of course I would say that, but I've campaigned against domestic violence for years. I donate to Women's Aid and Refuge and have hosted a fundraiser for Southall Black Sisters. If I ever saw the slightest hint of violence in my son, I wouldn't stand for it, but Richard never, ever raised a hand to a woman or sought to control her. I promise you I raised him better than that.'

'Thank you, Mrs Astor.' Garrett turned to the judge. 'I have no more questions, My Lord.'

Judge Turner nodded. 'I think this is a convenient moment to break for lunch. Members of the jury, thank you very much. Let's take a break now until 2.15 shall we?'

Safa left the press bench with the other reporters. She tried to catch Lily's eye to no avail. There *had* to be missing context to what Audrey had just shared. Lily had many faults – cynicism, spite, perhaps a certain callousness – but she was cool-tempered and rarely ruffled. Safa couldn't believe that she would ever hurt Harry.

As she mulled this over, she heard her name behind her. She turned to find Imran in the foyer. His hair was freshly cut and he wore a suit and tie. Safa arched her brows.

'Well, don't you scrub up well?'

'I was giving evidence in a trial,' he said by way of explanation.

Neither made a move to touch the other. 'Is there any news?' asked Safa.

Imran shook his head. 'Nothing yet.' At this stage, their discussions about the Glassman were hewn down to shorthand.

'What can I do, Imran? *The Clarion* have blackballed me, the Met won't believe me and Rukshana won't talk to me.'

'We wait.'

'For him to attack someone else?'

Imran gestured helplessly. 'Until one of them is willing to speak.'

Safa covered her eyes with a palm and made a long, bone-weary sound.

Imran let her wallow for a second. When she dropped her hand, he asked, 'Are you going in or out?'

She gestured towards the door. 'Out.'

He fiddled with a cufflink. 'Do you want to grab lunch before I head back?'

Safa was surprised. They had seen each other only twice over the course of the summer and both times he'd been keen to leave. She hesitated, then checked her watch to buy her time. 'Um, sure,' she said, carefully casual. 'If we're quick.' They walked to a local café and settled in with coffee and soggy paninis.

'How's your dad?' asked Imran.

'He's okay. He had a diabetes scare so is eating better now.'

'That's good. Is he still fostering dogs?'

'Yeah.'

'That's nice. I guess it keeps him healthy.'

'Yeah.' They looped into an awkward silence. 'How's Amina?' Safa asked out of politeness.

'She's okay.' Imran twisted his coffee cup. 'Actually, we broke up a while ago.'

Safa was taken aback. 'What? When?' The last she had heard from Billy at the station, Imran was going to Scotland to meet Amina's parents.

'Three months ago.'

'How come?' Quickly, she added, 'We don't have to talk about it if you don't want to.'

He shrugged lightly. 'It's okay. I just didn't see it going the distance.'

'Oh, right.' Safa hesitated. 'How come you didn't say anything?'

Imran fixed his gaze on her. 'Would it have made a difference?'

Safa's heart did a little turn. She didn't know how to answer that. *No? Maybe? Almost certainly?*

In the face of her silence, Imran changed the subject, back to Jahangir. 'I miss your dad's cooking.' A pause. 'And I miss seeing him.'

'He misses you too.'

Imran was on the cusp of saying more, and though Safa had told him in the past not to, she wanted to hear him say it: *I miss you.* Instead, he clenched his jaw, biting back whatever it was that he was about to say.

Their waitress, a cheerful young woman with a swinging ponytail, appeared at their table.

'Can I get you guys more coffee? Maybe some cake?'

Safa checked the time. 'No, thank you,' she answered for them both. She wanted to be back in court in time for Audrey Astor's cross exam.

The waitress smiled a little sheepishly. 'Sorry, I overheard you guys talking about food.' She slid her phone onto the tabletop, opened to an Instagram post. 'My sister, Sabina Begum, is doing a supper club in Bethnal Green this Thursday. She makes proper home-cooked Bangladeshi food. Would you guys like to come?'

Imran and Safa looked at each other, suddenly exposed.

The waitress saw their hesitance. 'Sabina's an amazing chef. She's had recipes in Waitrose magazine and is trying to get enough support to open her own place. It would be so great if you guys could come.'

Imran shifted uncomfortably under her hopeful gaze. 'I suppose we could?' he said unsurely. He glanced at Safa. 'Unless you're busy?'

She couldn't gauge if this was a genuine question or merely an SOS to help him escape the commitment. 'We could I guess. If *you're* free that is.' She was wary of her workload but could catch up on the weekend, so put the ball back in his court.

He surprised her by saying, 'I'm free.' His expression gave nothing away. Was this a date, or simply a bid for friendship? Or, worse, an Englishman ceding to pressure in an awkward situation?

'That's amazing! Sabina will be thrilled!' The waitress beamed. 'What name shall I put on the booking?'

Imran surrendered his details, then waited until she was out of earshot. He laughed self-consciously. 'I think we just met the best saleswoman this side of Whitechapel Market.'

Safa frowned. 'We could always cancel the booking if you'd rather not go?'

'No,' he said quickly. 'I want to go. Unless you don't?'

'I do.'

'Okay, then it's settled,' he said firmly. 'I'll see you on Thursday.'

'Okay.' There was another lull and Safa made a show of checking her watch. 'I better get back.'

Outside, they hunched against the rain. Imran leaned in, protecting her from the worst of it. She tilted her face up to him, hoping and not hoping. He touched the small of her back and Safa held her breath. But then he broke the spell; kissed her brusquely on the cheek and headed to the tube. Safa watched him for a moment before she too turned to go.

*

Victoria Hersham took off her glasses and fixed her ice-grey eyes on Audrey.

'Mrs Astor, do you tend to hold grudges?'

'No, I do not,' said Audrey, her tone now clipped and formal.

'In your evidence-in-chief, you referred to an incident that happened in your conservatory "early on" in Richard and Lily's marriage. What year was this?'

Audrey thought this over. 'I can't be sure but my best guess would be 2011.'

'So – thirteen years ago?'

'Yes.'

'Thirteen years and you still remember that Lily broke a cup. Wouldn't you call that a grudge?'

'As I said, it was an heirloom and meant a lot to me. And the way in which she did it stuck with me.'

Victoria glanced at her blue notebook. 'You said, "she moved the cup to one side and dropped it while making eye contact". Isn't it true that you can't be certain whether or not the act was intentional?'

It took Audrey a moment to decode the question. 'Yes, but I'm fairly certain.'

'Mrs Astor, "fairly certain" means that you're not 100 per cent sure. So you're not certain, are you?'

Audrey's tone grew sharp. 'Why are we talking about a cup when that woman killed my son?'

Victoria raised a brow. '"That woman",' she repeated with a quick glance at the jury. 'Mrs Astor, you said that your relationship with Lily was "up and down". You listed a litany of petty infractions. In addition to the cup, you accused Lily of opening the oven door when you were baking a soufflé and leaving a red sock in with your white wash. Isn't that correct?'

'Yes.'

'May I ask: do you have any other daughters-in-law?'

'Yes. My living son, Charles, is married to Becca.'

'And what's your relationship like with Becca?'

'We get on.'

'Is your relationship with Becca better or worse than your relationship with Lily used to be?'

Audrey cleared her throat. 'Maybe a little bit worse.'

'Why is that?'

'I felt that she was controlling.'

'Has she ever done petty things to mess with you?'

Audrey flushed. 'I believe so, yes.'

'What things?' Victoria waited, but Audrey didn't answer. Tartly, she added, 'Okay, let me jog your memory. Did you tell your son, Charles, that Becca trampled your daffodils on purpose?'

'Yes, but—'

'Did you tell him that Becca spilled red wine on your white shirt on purpose?'

'I didn't "tell" him. I asked him if he thought it was possible.'

'Did you tell him that Becca tracked mud onto your antique carpet on purpose?'

'Yes, but I'm certain she *did* do that.'

'And, finally, did you tell him that Becca smashed one of your heirloom china cups on purpose?'

Audrey was stone-faced. 'Yes. I did.'

'So Lily wasn't the problem at all, was she?' Victoria didn't wait for an answer. 'Mrs Astor, you referred to a picnic in Hyde Park where you say Lily slapped Harry. How did she slap him?'

Audrey frowned. 'Well, she reached out her hand and hit him.'

'On which cheek?'

Audrey blinked. 'It wasn't on his cheek. It was on his shoulder.'

'On his shoulder?' Victoria feigned surprise. 'That's a very different proposition to slapping someone's face, isn't it?'

'Well, yes, but a slap is a slap.'

'Not if it's a tap on the shoulder.'

'It wasn't a tap.'

'It sounds like it wasn't a slap either.'

Audrey sighed, losing patience. 'Look, I know what I saw.'

Victoria picked up her blue notebook and appeared to examine something carefully. Safa was familiar with this tactic. It made the witness believe that there was some evidence to which they weren't privy.

'Mrs Astor, I have a simple question for you. Have you ever seen your son, Richard Astor, hit your grandson, Harry Astor?'

Audrey stiffened, hit with a realisation. 'Yes,' she answered quietly.

'How many times?'

She grimaced. 'Three, maybe four times – but only to discipline him.'

'How did he strike him?'

'He didn't "strike" him. It was just light discipline to show Harry that he wasn't behaving. He didn't actually hurt him.'

'Light discipline? Like what exactly?'

'Like a pat on the bum,' said Audrey.

'Or a tap on the shoulder?'

'Yes,' said Audrey instinctively. And, then, she realised her mistake. She tried to backtrack, but Victoria was too quick for her.

'You don't like Lily very much, do you?'

Audrey's lips were a tight, thin line. 'No, I don't,' she admitted.

Victoria nodded, satisfied. 'I have no further questions. I know this has been difficult for you, Mrs Astor.' And, then, she added, 'I hope you won't hold a grudge.'

*

Safa was relieved when the judge adjourned for the day. The courtroom had grown stifling, pulsing with the heat of a hundred bodies. Outside, the air was cool and she let the breeze move over her. She headed to the tube station and heard a voice behind her.

'Need a ride?'

She turned and saw Oliver Witherow leaning on his silver Jaguar. He wore a white linen shirt with salmon-pink trousers and navy blue boat shoes. Safa rolled her eyes and carried on walking.

'I have a proposition for you,' he called after her. Met with silence, he added, 'It's about the Glassman.'

Safa stopped in her tracks. 'What about him?' she asked, turning back towards Oliver.

'I'll give you all the Glassman materials.'

She narrowed her eyes, but took a few steps towards him. 'Why would you do that after all this time?'

He crossed his arms. 'Because there's something you can do for me.'

Safa waited.

'I'll give you all the Glassman materials if you set up an interview with Harry Astor.'

Safa tensed with frustration. 'Oliver, have you even looked at the materials? Don't you understand the horror of what this man does?'

Oliver gave a casual wave. 'I want to speak to Harry.'

Safa was disgusted. 'You are a ghoul, you know that?'

'See, this is why you'll never get far as a journo. You're tough, sure, but you lack killer instinct. You don't have what it takes.'

'And *you* do?'

He shrugged.

Safa took another few steps closer to him. 'Oliver, you are a walking example of the adage "if I've heard of your father, I don't need to hear from you".' She scoffed. 'It's ironic because nearly every one of you ends up with a national column.' She angled her head in confusion. 'Except *you* it seems. I guess daddy doesn't have time to mark your homework.' She saw the colour rise in his face and smiled wickedly. 'Have a nice day, Oliver.' She spun and marched away, leaving him open-mouthed on his silver Jaguar.

She headed to St Paul's tube station and made her way to Stepney Green. It was four thirty and Harry would be back from school. She was keen to talk to him about Audrey's evidence. She couldn't share specifics because he was a witness, but she could skirt around it.

At Withy House, the entrance lock was broken as usual, so she headed straight up to Natalie's flat. She rang the bell and strained to hear it ring. She had texted Harry to say she was coming. A curtain twitched and he looked out, before promptly opening the door.

'Hey, Harry.' She gave him a hug. 'Is Natalie back? I lost her on my way out of the courtroom.'

'No. She texted to say that she's popping to Tesco.'

'Okay. Can I come in?'

'Sure.' He opened the door wider.

Safa followed him to the kitchen and wrinkled her nose at the smell of stale oil.

'Um, Aunt Nat isn't much of a cook.' He gestured at the recycling bin which was overflowing with boxes of ready meals.

'Oh, Harry. I'm sorry.'

'It's okay.' He smiled and a dimple appeared in his cheek. 'It makes a nice change actually. Mum always made sure that I ate *all five food groups*,' he said primly.

Safa laughed but saw a shadow cross his face. 'Are you okay?'

He nodded. 'How is she?' he asked quietly.

'She's okay. She bore up well today.' Safa beckoned him to the table and they spoke for a while about idle things: school, work, weather. Then, Safa broached the tricky subject.

'Harry, I know you and your mum always had a good relationship, but can I ask: did she ever discipline you physically?'

Harry frowned. 'What do you mean? Like hit me?' He didn't have to think about his answer. 'No. Never.'

Safa mulled this over. If what Audrey had said was true, then Harry would surely remember it. 'She never gave you a tap on the wrist or slap on the bottom or anything like that?'

His frown deepened. 'Why? Is that what they're saying?'

Safa knew she shouldn't say any more. 'No,' she lied. 'I'm just trying to get a picture of Lily as a mother.'

'Mum never hit me.' Harry picked at a flake in the table top. 'But sometimes I wished she would.'

The words jarred, but Safa didn't react; let him fill the silence.

'Whenever she was mad, she tried not to show it. She just acted normal but I could see the difference. It's like when you're forced to be nice to someone you don't like. The niceness isn't real and that's how it felt with Mum. If she would have got angry at me, shouted at me, hit me or whatever, then at least it would have been real.'

'She was under a lot of pressure,' said Safa. 'She was trying to give you the calmest childhood she could.'

'But if she'd asked for help instead of pretending that everything was okay, none of this would have happened. It wouldn't have got this far.' Harry broke off another small flake. 'Sometimes, I feel like it's her fault.'

Safa grimaced. 'Harry, in my years as a crime reporter, I've spoken to maybe a hundred victims of abuse, and every single one has blamed themselves at some point. Whatever you think of your mother, I can guarantee you she's thought it herself. What she needs now is kindness. There's so little of it in her day to day.'

Harry's shoulders curled inwards, bearing fresh guilt. 'I'm sorry.'

'Don't apologise. Just be there for her, okay?'

Wordlessly, he nodded.

Safa motioned at the bin. 'Do you want me to order you some takeout?'

'No, it's okay. Aunt Nat is making roasted lamb tonight.' He made a doleful face. 'I'll text you if I need a Deliveroo rescue.'

Safa laughed and stood. 'Okay, kid. I'll see you soon.' She kissed his hair and left him alone in the flat.

*

Safa pulled off her long down coat and then her knitted jumper. Her dad's house was far too hot after their bracing walk. He took off his gloves and held his hands over the radiator. When Safa was younger, he would force her to join him on rambling walks, but as he grew older, he began to feel the cold. Now, even short outings to the local park would turn his fingers white.

Safa caught them in her hands and rubbed until the colour came back. Mint fussed around them, keen for some affection too. Safa laughed and scratched her between the ears.

'You two play,' said her dad, unzipping his coat. 'I'll heat up the curries.'

'I'll help.' Safa followed him to the kitchen. She carried three pots to the stove. Her mother had always cooked three varieties of dishes when Safa was a child: a meat, a fish and a vegetarian option, and often additional sides. As an adult, Safa had tried to talk her father out of this tradition. *Look at white people*, she told him. *They have either meat or fish or veggie as a main – not all three.* But he wouldn't listen. It was yet another way that he tried to give her a sense of normality.

She helped herself to a large plate of rice and *alu bhazi*, and realised that she was ravenous. That soggy panini at lunch hadn't done the job.

'How's the case going?' he asked.

Safa nodded through a mouthful of rice. 'The prosecution had their first witness today. Richard Astor's mother, Audrey. She said something weird; that she saw Lily hit Harry once.'

Her dad frowned. 'Is it true?'

'Harry doesn't remember it. It was only three years ago, so he should do. Audrey doesn't like Lily, but would she just make it up?'

'Her son died. People will do all sorts for justice. Or maybe Lily just lost her temper. Parental rage is a real thing.'

Safa chewed her food. 'How come you never lost your temper with me?' After her mum died, Safa would fall into deep sulks whenever things went wrong. It took her years to grow out of them.

'You needed love,' he said.

Safa grew sombre. 'I wasn't angry with you. You know that, right?'

'I know,' he said with a tenderness that made Safa want to hold him.

'I was angry at myself,' she said.

'And you never stopped.'

Safa stiffened. 'That's not true.'

'Anger can be cool,' said her dad. 'It's not always the red-hot rage of youth. It can be icy and hard and turn your heart to stone.'

'All right, Dr Phil,' Safa reached for humour.

'I mean it, Safa. I see you closing yourself off from everything good in the world. Love, joy, family.'

'Dad, I come and see you every week.'

'Not me. A proper family.'

Safa looked at him sideways. 'So this is about you wanting grandkids?'

'Can you be serious for one moment?'

Safa rolled her eyes, but set down her fork.

'I worry about you. You work too hard. You barely eat. You barely have friends.'

'Says the man who mostly talks to dogs.'

'Safa,' he chided. 'You think that if you can control everything, the world will work as it should – but you can't control it. I'm going to die one day and you're going to be alone.'

'Well, that's a cheery thought.'

He shook his head, disappointed. 'You never forgave yourself.'

His grief, and the way it changed the texture of his voice, cut right through her glibness. 'Dad, can we not do this?' she said quietly.

'What happened to your mother wasn't your fault.'

Safa pushed away from the table. 'Dad, you don't need to coddle me. It was objectively and categorically my fault. They asked me a question and I got it wrong and then Mum died. Cause and effect. Just because you say otherwise, it doesn't make it true.' She spoke in short, sharp bursts, asserting her own guilt. If she could own it, if she could hold it in her palm like onyx and tell the world *here it is*, then others couldn't use it.

Her dad gestured helplessly. 'Safa, you shouldn't have been the one talking to the doctors.'

'Well, I *was* – and I failed.'

His face flushed with sorrow. 'My darling daughter, don't you have the slightest sympathy for an eight-year-old child?'

Safa pulled back in surprise. The question in its simplicity lifted her briefly from guilt; showed her an aerial view of it. 'Dad,' she said softly, colour lacing her neck.

'You see now? You were just a child, Safa.'

She felt choked with anguish over what she had put her eight-year-old self through.

'It's time to set it down, Safa. All that anger inside you.'

She didn't speak as she didn't trust her voice. She felt fat with emotion, clumsy from the weight of it all.

'Safa, my *jaan*, you have to let it go.'

She hung her head. 'I don't know how to do that, Dad.'

'It's actually really simple,' he said tenderly. 'You start by choosing the fun thing. Whenever you're faced with a choice, you choose the fun thing. Should you go home early or stay at work until 10 p.m.? Go home. Should you eat ice cream or go for a run? Eat ice cream.' The slightest pause. 'Should you watch your dad die alone or go on a date with Imran?'

Safa didn't laugh. 'It's not that easy,' she said.

'Actually, it is. You just have to try.'

She made a cynical sound.

'Please, Safa, just try.'

She didn't speak and he reached out and touched her hand. Gently, he asked, 'Don't you think you owe it to that eight-year-old child?'

Safa looked at the ceiling, a blink away from tears. After a long silence, she nodded once.

'Promise me you'll try.'

'I'll try.'

'Promise?'

It took her a moment to speak again. 'Yes, I promise,' she said.

Chapter 11

Safa hurried into the Old Bailey to escape the October chill. Her cheeks stung with colour and her flyaway hair was full of static. She had stayed up late last night following an intense second day in court. The prosecution had called a pathologist to speak to the cause of death, followed by the senior investigating officer. The two witnesses had covered a lot of ground, filled with technical detail, all of which Safa had to distil for readers. She was tired and restive, and desperately needed a coffee, but couldn't take it inside. At courtroom eight, she spotted a familiar figure waiting by the door.

'I was hoping to catch you,' said Erin Quinto. She held out a folder, creating space between them. Erin had never been one for hugs.

'Did you find something?' Safa took the folder and flicked through the pages inside. Her head snapped up. 'How did you get a hold of this?'

Erin smiled sardonically. 'Do you really want to know?'

'Not if I'm gonna get court-martialled over it.'

Erin's laugh was deep and throaty, catching the attention of passers-by. Safa saw the way men looked at her, clearly intrigued. Erin was striking in an anime-goth sort of way: lily-white skin, cropped black hair and big dark eyes. She wore a leather jacket and buckled cuffs around her wrists. She worked as a private investigator and Safa had asked her to look into the witnesses in Lily's trial. *Nothing illegal*, she had stressed, knowing that Erin had a knack for uncovering classified information.

'Thank you, Erin.' Safa indicated the folder. 'This is big.'

'Enjoy.' Erin zipped up her jacket, readying to leave.

'Hey, can I ask for another favour? Do you think you can find Juliet Culpen's contact details for me? I want to talk to her for a feature, but my emails have bounced back.'

Erin angled her head. 'You know she's notoriously wary of the press, right?'

Juliet Culpen, now fifty-six, had received a life sentence in 2011 for the murder of her abusive husband. After ten years in prison, Juliet was released when her sentence was reduced to manslaughter. It was a landmark case that brought coercive control into the public consciousness, but the press had not been kind to her. Juliet had a timid, nervy manner – all bones and wrists and jaundiced skin. She spoke too softly, which frustrated those around her. She was 'the sort of woman you wanted to shake' one columnist had stated in a national paper. The comments beneath the piece were worse: 'it's hard to *not* want to hit her', 'why does she act like a fucking mute? Use your voice, you bint', 'I can't stand this wallflower bullshit. You're a woman, not a dormouse.' It went on and on, driving Juliet inwards until her home became a prison of a different sort.

'I can get you her details, but I doubt she'll want to talk,' said Erin.

'I'd like to try. I feel like she might talk to me.'

'Why do you think that?'

Safa hesitated. Haltingly, she asked, 'Have you ever heard anyone mention the Glassman?'

Erin looked blank. 'What is that? A Marvel movie?'

Safa grimaced. 'No. He's a serial rapist who targets elderly Asian widows in Tower Hamlets.'

If Erin was shocked, she didn't show it. 'Is he in custody?'

'No. The police don't think he's real, but I know he is.' Safa briefly told her what she knew of the Glassman.

'Okay. I've got a million questions, but what does this have to do with Juliet?'

Safa checked her watch, mindful that court would begin in ten minutes. 'Juliet was pilloried for being weak, for not speaking out or seeking help proactively. The Glassman's victims are the same – worse, even. Can you imagine the comments when this gets out? *"Maybe if they'd learnt English, they would've been able to report it." "How can these women expect justice when they literally can't speak to the police?" "They're the ones who let this happen."* We blame women for "allowing" themselves to become victims rather than asking why men have victimised them. Juliet understands this more than most and I think she would have interesting things to say, even if she says them softly.'

Erin nodded once. 'Okay. Give me 'til the end of the day.'

'Thanks, Erin. I owe you one.' Safa wasn't ready to break the story of the Glassman, but she hoped to lay some groundwork with her feature on Lily; to prime the public to be sympathetic towards imperfect victims. She indicated the folder. 'I better get this to Victoria.' She thanked Erin again and headed to the courtroom.

'Hey, Safa,' Erin called her back. 'Would you choose the bear?'

Safa let out a small laugh. 'Choose the bear' was a debate that had exploded on the internet over the summer. It posed the question: if you were alone and unarmed in the woods, would you rather encounter a bear or a man? Swathes of women chose the bear, deeming it a lesser threat, which in turn had enraged swathes of men.

'I don't know,' said Safa. 'The only good constant in my life has been a man. My father.'

Erin gave her a doleful smile. 'And is he typical of a man?'

'No,' Safa said sadly. 'He's not.'

'And so your answer is?'

'I honestly don't know.' Safa nodded at Erin. 'What about you?'

Erin traced the buckles on her wrist. 'I have a friend, Portia, who won't leave her daughter, Jessie, alone with a man apart from Jessie's father. Not Portia's own brothers, not even Portia's father. She says that she *knows* they wouldn't hurt her, but why take that risk?'

'Wow. That's . . .' Safa trailed off.

'Crazy? Extreme? I used to think so too.'

'And then?'

'And then Portia got distracted one day when staying at her family's holiday home. She walked in on the male housekeeper kissing Jessie on the lips. It wasn't in an obviously sleazy way, and he'd known Jessie all her life so there's an argument to be made that it was purely affectionate, but he'd never done it in front of Portia before, so why do it the first time he has Jessie alone?'

Safa grimaced. 'You really think it's as grim as that?'

Erin gestured to the air. 'A woman somewhere probably thinks it's okay to leave her daughter with her brother, but what if her brother is the Glassman?'

Safa shuddered. The thought was utterly chilling.

'Not to put too fine a point on it, but if my choice is death, or rape and *then* death, I'm choosing the bear for me, Portia *and* Jessie.'

Safa's dismay settled like mist on her skin: cold and oppressive. Erin inclined her head as if to say *exactly* and then turned and walked away.

*

The judge was yet to enter so Safa slid discreetly to Victoria. She crouched next to the defence barrister and spoke rapidly. Victoria listened and jotted down some notes.

'Very nice,' she said.

Safa nodded and scurried back to the press bench. She spotted Natalie opposite, in the public gallery. Today, she wore a fraying yellow shift dress, a cheap and chunky silver necklace and her thick transition lenses. Safa felt ashamed for thinking that she looked like a dime-store Jackie Kennedy – or, as was the case, a dime-store Lily Astor. Natalie was surrounded by other spectators, mainly tourists and rubberneckers. Some of Safa's colleagues mocked these 'gawkers', but Safa never blamed them for coming. Curiosity was a human trait. In fact, it fuelled her livelihood. Yes, people read the news to be informed but, at the root of it all, was curiosity and she would never criticise a person for indulging it.

A knock on the door announced the judge's entrance and the clerk declared that court was in session. Lucien Garrett stood to question his first witness of the day – an elegant white woman who wore a cream silk shirt with a designer suit. She was aged forty-seven, Safa knew from the research, and had clear skin and curly blonde hair.

'Dr Miller, can you explain for the jury what it is that you do?' asked Garrett.

'I am a consultant forensic psychiatrist at Synergy Health, an independent provider of mental health services across the UK.'

'Do you have a specific area of expertise?'

'Yes, I work with victims of domestic violence and abuse. I have nearly twenty years' experience and have worked with hundreds of victims. I have written two books and co-authored over a hundred academic papers.'

'What specifically do you do for these victims?'

'It varies. Mostly, I work in a therapeutic capacity, helping them recover from trauma. Sometimes, I help them regain custody of their children, or make a judgement call on why they shouldn't. Other times, with NHS referrals for example, it might be picking up slack from other systems, like helping victims secure housing or benefits.'

'Have you worked with the defendant, Lily Astor?'

'Yes. I was asked to assess her following the alleged murder of her husband. I spent several hours talking to Ms Astor on topics ranging from her childhood, career, motherhood – and, of course, the night that her husband died.'

'What was she like during this time?'

'Calm, intelligent, eloquent.'

'Dr Miller, what are the long-term effects of domestic violence or abuse?'

'There are myriad effects, ranging from emotional to psychological and physical. Mental health problems include depression, anxiety, panic attacks and post-traumatic stress disorder. There might also be misuse of drugs and alcohol as a coping mechanism and a whole host of physical ailments.'

'Did Lily Astor exhibit any of these?'

'No.'

'Did she seem clinically disturbed in any way?'

'No.'

Garrett led the doctor through a maze of questions, designed to show the jury that Lily showed no signs of abuse. 'Dr Miller, in your professional opinion, what was Lily's state of mind on the night she attacked her husband?'

'Lily Astor was clear-eyed. She knew right from wrong. She understood the consequences of her decision.'

'Did she understand that slashing her husband's throat with a knife might cause his death or, at the very least, cause him really serious injury?'

'Yes, she did.'

'And she did it anyway?'

'Yes, she did.'

'Thank you, Dr Miller.' Garrett nodded, satisfied. 'Please remain there for a moment. My learned friend will have some questions for you.'

Victoria stood and opened her notebook. 'Dr Miller, you say you have worked with hundreds of women over the course of your career.'

'Not always women,' said the doctor. 'Men can be victims of domestic violence too.'

Victoria's face grew pinched. She clearly didn't like being corrected. 'How many of them were you right about?'

'Excuse me?'

'Let me be more specific. You said that sometimes you make a "judgement call" on whether victims should regain custody of their children. How many of these "judgement calls" were, in fact, the right call?'

'That's a very difficult question to answer. It's hard to quantify mental health and my organisation isn't directly involved in aftercare so—'

'Let me rephrase then,' Victoria cut in. 'How many of them were you *wrong* about?'

The doctor tensed. Now she understood where this was going. 'In this profession, you get false positives and false negatives so, sadly, it's an inherent part of the job.'

'No, I understand that. But my question is very specific: how many have *you* got wrong?'

Garrett stood. 'My Lord, I'm not sure that these questions are going to assist the jury.'

Victoria scowled at him. 'My Lord, Dr Miller is the prosecution's expert witness. I am merely examining her expertise.'

'Ms Hersham's right, Mr Garrett,' said the judge.

Victoria nodded obsequiously and turned back to the witness. 'Dr Miller, how many have you got wrong?'

'Again, that is difficult to say.'

Victoria sighed in a stagey manner. 'Is it one? Two? In the tens? Dozens?'

'I can't say for sure but I would guess in the tens.'

Victoria glanced at her notebook. 'Was Paris Bell one of them?'

The doctor looked to Garrett for help but he had his head down. 'Yes, she was.'

'You assessed her as a patient, didn't you?'

'Yes.'

'And you gave her a clean bill of mental health, didn't you?'

'I did, but these things are nuanced.'

'And the day after, what did Paris Bell, *your* patient, do?'

'She had an episode, which led to a fatal traffic incident.'

Victoria eyed her coolly. 'What happened, Dr Miller, is that Paris Bell drove her tiny Peugeot 206 into oncoming traffic, killing herself, her two children and two other adults, isn't that true?'

The doctor coloured. 'That's true.'

'What did the pathologist rule?'

'Murder by suicide.'

'Murder by suicide,' repeated Victoria. She let this steep for a second. 'Dr Miller, didn't you say that Paris Bell showed no signs of depression, anxiety, panic attacks or post-traumatic stress disorder?'

'Yes.'

'Didn't you say that she showed no signs of being clinically disturbed?'

'Yes.'

'Didn't you say that she was "clear-eyed, calm and intelligent"?'

The doctor hunched defensively. 'Yes.'

'Do you still believe that Paris Bell was in perfect mental health?'

'With the benefit of hindsight, no.'

'Hindsight is not available to us, Dr Miller, which is why we have experts like you. We rely on you to be clear and accurate.'

'Every expert has false negatives.'

'How do you know that Lily Astor isn't one of them?'

'They are different pathologies. Paris Bell was—'

'Dr Miller,' Victoria cut in again. 'You were wrong about Paris Bell, weren't you?'

The doctor grimaced. 'Yes.'

'So you can't say for sure that you're right about Lily?'

'Well, no one can say for sure but—'

'No one can say for sure,' Victoria repeated. 'That's exactly right, isn't it, Dr Miller? No one can say for sure what Lily's frame of mind was on the evening her husband died.'

'I can give my professional opinion.'

'Ah, yes, and we know how much *that* is worth.' Victoria turned to the judge. 'I am finished with this witness, My Lord.' As Victoria took a seat, she caught Safa's eye and winked.

Safa didn't enjoy seeing a woman torn down in public, but her friendship with Lily was stronger than her duty to the sisterhood. When it was Lily's turn to give evidence, the prosecution would pull no punches, and the defence had to act the same.

She watched Dr Miller leave the witness box, red-faced and shiny, and made a mental note to buy Erin Quinto a drink.

*

After lunch, the prosecution called their next witness: a forty-eight-year-old man with a dramatically receding hairline. He had a beaky nose that would have looked harsh were it not for his kind blue eyes. He wore a white shirt beneath a knitted blue jumper with neatly-pressed khaki trousers. He took the oath and stated his name and relationship to the defendant: Matthew Weaver, Lily's neighbour. Safa knew from her research that he was an unmarried teacher who had inherited the house from his grandmother. He was softly spoken and Lucien Garrett had to ask him to speak up.

'Mr Weaver, how long have you lived next door to the Astors?'

'About six years. I've lived there for fifteen years and they moved in about six years ago.'

'Did you have a good relationship with them?'

'Oh, yes. I always said hello when I saw them.'

'Have you spent any time with them aside from saying hello in passing?'

'Yes. I've attended barbecues and parties at their house and they have come round to mine for dinner and drinks.'

'Were you at their house on the night of Saturday 6th April?'

'Yes, I went to a party there.'

'What was the mood like at the party?'

Matthew considered this. 'At first, it was fun and relaxed. Richard had just published a book and was in high spirits. He had lost his job during the pandemic, but his career seemed to be back on track.'

'Did he look happy?'

'Yes.'

'Did Lily look happy?'

'Yes, she was on sparkling form. Laughing and flirting.'

'Flirting? With whom?'

Matthew's gaze flicked guiltily to the dock. 'Um, well, there was this one specific gentleman. She was sort of nudging him with her body when he made a joke, touching his arm. I think she lay her head on his shoulder at one point.'

'Did Lily seem at ease flirting with another man in front of her husband?'

'She seemed to be.'

'How did Richard react?'

'He was sort of sheepish. He led her away to the kitchen.'

'Sheepish?' checked Garrett. 'Did he look angry?'

'Oh no, nothing like that. It was very light and casual, more like he didn't want her to feel embarrassed in the morning.'

'I see. Did you stay until the end of the party?'

'No. I left at about 8 p.m. Lily and Richard seemed fine at that point. Lily was a bit unsteady on her feet but nothing to worry about.'

'In your six years of living next door to the Astors, have you ever seen Richard get angry at Lily?'

He thought about this. 'No.'

'Have you overheard any arguments?'

'Only once,' he said with another glance at the dock.

'What happened?'

'It happened a few months ago, on Christmas Eve. I think it started off in the kitchen. I heard shouting so I looked out. Lily stormed into the garden. She was angry at Richard, shouting at him. Saying things like "leave me alone", "what's wrong with you?"'

'Was he shouting back?'

'No, he just stood meekly by the door. I'd never seen Lily behave like that. I thought she was having some sort of breakdown. It went on for a couple of minutes.'

'Then what happened?'

'Lily did something that made my blood run cold.'

'What did she do?'

'She looked at Richard with this coldness in her eyes and said, "Don't you understand? I'm scared I'll kill you one day."'

Safa heard the shock spread through the courtroom: the low murmurs in the public gallery, the rustle of clothing as people leaned in to whisper. Safa studied Matthew closely, seeking clues to the truth. She couldn't picture Lily saying this. A cruel barb delivered precisely? Yes. But this small and strange bid for help amid her naked rage? It wasn't Lily's style.

Garrett let the shock settle. 'Mr Weaver, just to confirm, you heard the defendant, Lily Astor, say to her husband, "Don't you understand? I'm scared I'll kill you one day"?'

'Yes.'

'What happened next?'

'Richard tried to comfort her. He sort of corralled her to one corner of the garden and spoke to her in a soothing tone. She pulled away from him at first. I could tell she was still angry. Every time he reached out to comfort her, she sort of batted him away, but eventually he talked her down and she let him hug her and she sort of broke down and cried. They stayed like that for about five minutes and then Richard brought her inside.'

'Did Richard show any signs of anger throughout the exchange?'

'No.'

'Did Lily seem scared?'

'Not scared. Furious.'

'"Not scared. Furious",' repeated Garrett. 'Thank you, Mr Weaver. I have no further questions, My Lord.' Garrett sat down and aimed a sporting smile at the defence table. Safa caught the subtext. *Game on.*

*

Lily watched Matthew Weaver slink out of the witness box. She had never liked him. He was ostensibly a liberal – "a failed socialist", he would say with a faux guilty laugh – but Lily could tell that he had a chip on his shoulder. Everyone else in their enclave had earned their place there while Matthew had simply inherited it. Lily had tried to make him feel comfortable but there had always been distance there. Still, to have him stand up in court and expose a private moment like this felt like a betrayal.

Usually, Lily would never argue in public, but she had reached breaking point that day. The world had stopped for Christmas, which meant that she couldn't escape to the studio, or even to social gatherings. She was stuck at home, under that dreadful atmosphere. She couldn't even remember how the argument started. No doubt it was something trivial: she hadn't checked his jeans before a wash and left tissue in his pocket, or forgot to order peppercorns so that his favourite dish didn't taste the same.

She did remember leaning over the sink with a bloody nose. Richard had fretted around her, vowing it would never happen again. She had pushed him away; told him not to make impossible promises. She had been furious, mostly at herself for letting it happen again. She feared that one day she would hit back and that it wouldn't feel like an act of violence but reclamation – of her pride, her self-worth, her very identity.

It was in that state of disarray that she had fled to the garden. The fact that her neighbour had seen her and cast her as the aggressor made her clench with resentment. She tried to catch Matthew's eye as he left the courtroom but he scurried out without looking upwards.

The judge adjourned for the day and Lily was led out of the dock. She spotted Natalie in the public gallery and lifted a hand to wave, but Natalie didn't see her. She wanted news of Harry; of how he was *really* doing. The court-appointed supervisor at their meetings prevented any real intimacy. On several occasions, Lily had wanted to tell the stuffy old bitch to back off, but she had to be on her best behaviour. Lily's celebrity was a double-edged sword. On one hand, it made her stand out – not a good thing in prison – but on the other, it protected her from physical violence. Her fellow inmates knew that insults would be overlooked, but none of them wanted the wrath of the guards for physically harming *that famous bitch*. Her profile had earned her a level of solicitude rarely given to others. She remembered how, in her first week at Bronzefield, an inmate had to flood her own cell to get attention.

Lily had spent many long evenings in her cell, thinking about the ways her life had gone wrong. It had started with her mother's alcoholism. Lily could still feel the excruciating embarrassment of being dropped off by her mother in her fluffy bathrobe. She had seen the judgement in other parents' eyes and the way they averted their gaze when they saw her looking. She had been thankful when she was finally old enough to go to school with her sister. When Natalie moved to the big school, Lily had to do the walk alone but she preferred that to being dropped off by her mother's boyfriends, who always seemed amused by a joke that Lily wasn't in on.

When Lily was fourteen, her mother got serious about one boyfriend. He was an addict and Lily had had to hide everything: her clothes, her books, even her pound-store jewellery. One time, she bought some new underwear and found it missing the next day. She was horrified to realise that Dave had sifted through her drawer and picked out whatever looked fit to sell. The breaking point came when Lily found a stash of handbags hidden in the cupboards under the stairs. At first, she had thought that they were off the back of a truck and that he would flog them at cut-price, but then she noticed the wear and tear: the splitting of leather, a frayed clasp, the chewed ends. It hit her that these belonged to people; Dave had taken them from actual women. She pictured the violence: Dave smacking a woman in the face, snatching her bag away – or had he used a weapon? Lily was disgusted.

In the end, getting rid of him had been easy. When he was doped out of his mind one day, Lily got into his camera phone – stolen no doubt. She thumbed through his MMS messages and, sure enough, there were several lewd photos sent to other women. Lily forwarded one to herself along with a suggestive message. The next time he was sober, Lily got him alone in the living room. She stood over him as he lay on the sofa.

'Listen to me, Dave,' she said, slowly so her voice wouldn't shake. 'You need to get up. You need to pack everything you have in this flat. You need to leave. And you need to never come back.'

He gave her a lazy, sleazy grin. 'If I don't, will you make me?'

Lily felt wrongfooted. She had expected anger, or maybe confusion, not this dozy amusement. 'Yes, I will,' she said.

He arched his back so that this belly protruded towards her. 'How?'

Lily was damp with sweat. 'I'll tell my teacher that you've been grooming me.'

The smile left his face, replaced with a sneer. 'Who's going to believe you?'

'Why wouldn't they believe me?'

'Because it's not true.'

Lily had the upper hand now. 'But it *is* true.'

The look on his face changed. 'This isn't funny.'

'Do I look like I'm trying to be funny, Dave?' She gestured towards the door. 'I told you. Leave and never come back and I won't cause any trouble for you.'

'Your mum's gonna hear about this.'

'Good, I think she *should* know that her boyfriend's been coming on to me.'

'I haven't,' he said, worried now because so much of what he'd said to her *could* be read that way.

'But you *have*.'

'You're a liar,' he said, groping for his cigarettes.

'You can't smoke in here,' she told him despite that fact that he always *had*.

His hand froze mid-air. 'You don't get to tell me what to do,' he said but there was no backbone in his words.

Lily's face crumpled and she feigned distraught emotion. '"Ms Allen, I didn't know who else to tell."' She wiped imaginary tears. '"It started months ago and I was too scared to tell my mum."'

Dave shot up, rigid with worry. 'They won't believe you.'

Lily was impassive again. 'Even when I show them the photos?'

Dave paled. 'What photos?'

She gestured casually. 'Check your sent messages.'

He grappled for his phone, thumbed the buttons for a few seconds, and then his face fell. 'You little slut,' he snarled.

Lily clung to her bravado. 'I have a copy and so do three of my friends,' she lied.

'You wouldn't,' he said breathlessly.

Lily let out a sob. '"He said my mum would blame *me* if she knew. He told me not to tell anyone."'

Dave's face was ghostly white.

'You don't even *like* my mother,' she said. 'You're using her, so go and find someone else.'

Dave's right hand formed a fist and there was spittle on his lips. For a moment, it seemed that he would charge at her, but Lily held her ground. Then, his shoulders slumped. In the end, he left without uttering another word. Lily learnt that day how easy it was to manipulate if you were willing to play the game. She learnt how to plan, evade, hustle and charm to get what she wanted. It was why, when she met Richard, she was so taken by him. He had wealth, status and pedigree – far easier routes to stability.

Getting pregnant had been a stupid move, but the two of them had survived. They had married and set up a life. So many times, Lily had thought *this is it, my dreams have come true*. The sentiment was pure, unmarred by guile or cynicism. Lily had genuinely loved Richard. In fact, there were days when she missed him so much, her heart seemed to constrict with it. She wished desperately that she had been able to set a different course for them; to tap into the precise moment when sadness turned to violence, and reroute their lives elsewhere.

*

Safa turned south towards Narrow Street instead of heading home. Natalie had asked her to pick up some of Harry's belongings as neither could face it themselves. Safa didn't tell them this, but she wanted a chance to look around so readily agreed. She slipped through the open gate, her boots crunching on the California gravel. The house looked neat from the outside despite lying empty for a full six months. The service charge was clearly designed to keep up appearances. Only the side passage showed signs of vacancy. The hosepipe had come loose and lay like a snake in the drain and a spider had spun a web across the bikes, the red and white now speckled with rust.

Safa let herself into the house. It smelled musty but faintly fragranced with something warm and expensive. It was still and quiet, and Safa felt a trill of unease, as if she were trespassing. She thought of the day that Richard had turned her away at the door. *Has it ever occurred to you that you're just a cheap hack, Safa?* He had always been somewhat cool towards her. Perhaps he thought she was a hanger-on, working Lily for her contacts or, worse, financial help. She *had* wondered early on if Richard had a problem with people of colour, but he was a card-carrying *Clarion* reader and she came to understand that it was *disinterest* more than dislike. Clearly, he did not think that someone who worked at *Asian Bride* was worth engaging with.

She walked along the hall, past a shaft of light that exposed motes of dust. She looked into the living room. This is where the killing had happened. Her reporter's brain pictured the scene: Richard in a rage, Lily picking up the knife by instinct. Safa had seen hints of Richard's controlling behaviour: monitoring how much Lily drank, getting tetchy if she became too loud. As Safa had learnt from her beat, the pandemic could easily have tipped this to violence.

She scanned the room from the threshold, wary of stepping inside. It was large and airy and had two sash windows with tasteful white blinds. The sofas looked old and sunken – heirloom pieces from Audrey no doubt – and were arranged around a vintage rug. A custom-made oak sideboard held an array of trinkets: brass candlesticks, a model of a clipper ship, an empty vase and tasteful lantern. It was a world away from Withy House.

She continued to the kitchen where she rifled through a cupboard for Harry's Spiderman mug. She set it on the counter, which was custom-made with the same oak as the sideboard. Next, she went to the utility cupboard and rooted around for Harry's duffel bag. She ducked as a cascade of things came crashing down: three bicycle helmets landing on her like in a cartoon. She negotiated around a shoe rack and found a set of duffel bags, recognising the red one that Harry needed for a school trip. She dragged it out and placed it next to the mug in the kitchen. Then, she ventured upstairs to the top floor. Harry had given her a list of things he needed from his room: a sleeping bag, a head torch, his hiking boots and a waterproof watch. It was the first time she had ever been in a teenage boy's bedroom and it was every bit as chaotic as she expected. There was a touch of innocence in it too. Spiderman curtains, action figures on the windowsill, posters of footballers and a boxer in red shorts posing inside a ring. She collected the items diligently, then headed back downstairs. She paused on the landing on the middle floor and peeked in the master bedroom. Instinctively, she went to the window and its sweeping view of the Thames. Today, the river was rough and murky, but nonetheless romantic. Safa watched the roiling water and wondered what it was like to wake up to this every day. She sighed wistfully and turned to go, but something snagged in her mind and she turned back to the view. She looked into the neighbour's garden and frowned in confusion.

She double-checked the view from Harry's room and an idea came to her. Downstairs, she grabbed Harry's blue bicycle helmet. She left Lily's front door open and rang the neighbour's doorbell. A man answered and Safa did a subconscious safety check: it was indeed Matthew Weaver, the teacher who had spoken in court that day.

'Hello. I'm a friend of the Astors.' Safa motioned at Lily's open front door. 'I popped round to collect some of Harry's stuff.'

Matthew peeked out. 'Oh, I see. How may I help you?'

Safa held up the helmet. 'Harry asked me to collect his bike. I can't find it in the house, but don't have a key to the garden. Do you mind if I take a look from your window to see if it's there? It'll save me coming back for it if it's not.'

Matthew looked at the helmet, then back at Lily's open door. 'Um, of course.'

Safa asked for a minute to lock Lily's house and then followed him into his. It was identical to Lily's but a mirror image, and in dire need of redecorating.

'What a lovely home,' she said as she followed him upstairs. 'I'm sorry about what happened next door.'

'It was certainly a shock,' said Matthew. 'The media have been relentless. They want to know everything: did I hear Richard beating her? Did I ever think about calling the police? Did I ever intervene?'

Safa paused on the landing. 'Did you?'

'Heavens no. I barely heard a peep. They seemed very happy, but I suppose he *did* change somewhat after losing his job in the pandemic.'

'Oh?'

'Yes. Before that, he always had this . . . arrogance.'

'Oh, yes.' Safa gave him a knowing look and that seemed to disarm him.

'He was always a bit of a know-it-all, you know?' said Matthew. 'Always wanting to make a show of how clever he was. But after he lost his job, he became a different person. Moody, downbeat. I thought he'd snap out of it once the pandemic ended but he didn't.' Matthew paused by a door and gestured into the room. 'Be my guest.'

'Thank you.' Safa walked to the window and strained towards Lily's garden. She tutted. 'It doesn't seem to be there.' She glanced back at Matthew. 'Do you mind if I take a picture, just to show Harry that I checked?'

'Of course not. Do you want to look upstairs as well? You might have a better vantage.'

Safa was careful not to smirk. There were benefits to being a small brown woman – people assumed you were harmless. 'That would be great,' she said and followed him upstairs. He hovered at the threshold as she scanned the view. 'It looks like it's not there.' Safa snapped another picture, then turned ruefully. 'Thank you so much for your help,' she said. 'I should let you enjoy your evening.'

'I'm glad to have helped. I'll show you out.'

He turned his back and Safa followed with a secret smile.

Chapter 12

Victoria Hersham studied the two pictures, then looked up at Safa.

'Safa Saleem, you fucking genius.' She slid the photos into a folder. 'I could kiss you, but I won't because frankly these lips are professional-grade perfect.'

Safa laughed. Victoria's red lipstick was indeed immaculate, a nice contrast to her black robe and horsehair wig. 'I'll see you in there,' she said and headed to the courtroom.

Today, Lily wore a pale blue suit and a cream coloured shirt with a lace Peter Pan collar. She clearly knew how to dress the part, thought Safa.

Matthew Weaver, Lily's neighbour, was back in the witness box. Safa had deliberately sat in the back row where her short height meant that she was all but hidden from view. She hadn't broken any laws but was skating on thin ice ethically.

Victoria began with some basic questions to put Matthew at ease.

Then, she asked casually, 'Mr Weaver, in the evidence you gave yesterday, you said that you witnessed an argument between Lily and Richard on Christmas Eve, is that correct?'

'Yes.'

'For accuracy, I'll read a few extracts from your evidence: "Lily stormed into the garden. She was angry at Richard, shouting at him . . . He just stood meekly by the door . . . She looked at Richard with this coldness in her eyes and said, 'Don't you understand? I'm scared I'll kill you one day.'"' Victoria read it in a monotone, stripping it of impact. 'Mr Weaver, were you telling the truth when you gave this evidence?'

Matthew was confused. 'Yes, of course I was.' He gestured towards the usher. 'I take the oath very seriously.'

Safa suppressed a smile. He sounded like a jobsworth, and if there was one thing the British public disliked, it was that.

Victoria traced a line of text in her notebook. 'Okay, let's focus on this: "he just stood meekly by the door." Which door did you mean?'

'The kitchen door that leads into the garden.'

'How do you know he was standing meekly by that door?'

'Because I saw him.'

'Did you hear him or did you see him?'

Matthew frowned. 'Both.'

'Are you sure?'

'One hundred per cent.'

'Can you give us any details about Richard? What was he wearing that day? What was his facial expression?'

'Well, yes. He was wearing an orange jumper. I remember because it was the same colour as my curtains. He seemed really worried about Lily.'

'While he was standing meekly by the kitchen door?'

'Yes.'

'And you're sure?'

Matthew grew impatient. 'Yes, I'm positive. I don't know how else to say it.'

Victoria inclined her head as if to say *very well*. 'Mr Weaver, do you recognise this?' A photograph was shown on screen.

He squinted at it. 'Yes. That's my garden.'

'It was taken from Lily Astor's house. And do you recognise this?' A second picture was shown.

Matthew frowned. 'That's . . . Lily's garden.' He jolted a little and scanned the courtroom.

'That's right,' said Victoria. 'And this is also of Lily's garden.' A third picture came up on screen. 'Do you recognise where pictures two and three were taken?'

'Yes, they were taken from my house. A woman knocked on my door and—'

Victoria cut him short. 'What do you notice about these pictures, Mr Weaver?'

He searched them blindly for nearly a minute. Safa saw the moment that realisation hit. 'But . . .' He trailed off, clearly at a loss.

'What do you notice?' Victoria waited. Finally, she answered for him. 'You can't see the kitchen door, can you, Mr Weaver? In fact, you can't see that half of the Astors' garden at all. So how do you know that Lily was talking to her husband?'

'Because I saw him.'

'Standing meekly by the kitchen door?'

Matthew searched his memory. 'Maybe not exactly, but he did follow her to the part of the garden that *was* in view. I remember that very distinctly because of the orange. And I definitely saw his face. He looked worried and I heard him trying to calm her.'

'But you also remember him standing by the kitchen door. Did you not say you were one hundred per cent certain of that?'

'Well, it was a logical conclusion based on what I saw next.'

'How do you know she wasn't talking to her son or her gardener or her babysitter, or any number of other people with whom she might have been angry?'

'Because she wasn't.'

'The truth is that you did *not* witness Lily saying those words – "I'm scared I'll kill you one day" – to Richard, did you?'

'I made a logical conclusion. You're making a mountain out of a molehill.'

'No, Mr Weaver. I am trying – very carefully and precisely as the law requires – to understand the truth. And the truth is that you did *not* witness Lily saying those words to Richard, did you?'

Matthew looked to the jury, as if they might intervene.

'Did you?' pressed Victoria.

Matthew's shoulders sagged. 'No, I didn't, but I know he was there.'

Victoria angled her head. 'And let me guess. You're one hundred per cent sure.' She turned to the judge before Matthew could respond. 'My Lord. I have no more questions for this witness.'

*

Safa checked her reflection in the mirror and winced at the lighting in the courthouse bathroom. She looked and felt exhausted, but did her best to rescue to her face.

The door swung open behind her and Victoria walked in. Their eyes met in the mirror and Victoria winked wickedly.

'Good work today, Safa.'

She nodded and turned to face the lawyer. 'How do you think it's going?'

'It's hard to say. You know better than most that juries do whatever the fuck they want.' Victoria paused and narrowed her eyes. 'You look nice. Is it an occasion?'

Safa blushed and immediately felt foolish. She was in black jeans and a T-shirt, but had put on some lipstick and eyeliner. 'Maybe.'

'Do tell.'

'It's a date I guess. Or maybe not. I don't even know. We were on-again-off-again for ages and now I'm not sure.'

'Are you talking about Imran Anwar?'

'Yeah,' said Safa sheepishly.

'Oh, he's hot.'

Safa agreed dolefully. 'Any tips?' she asked, only half-joking.

Victoria rolled her eyes. 'Like you need tips.'

'If only that were true.'

'Come on. You've got the whole "tough chick" thing going on. Men love that.'

Safa scoffed. 'Trust me, they do not.'

'Seriously?'

'Seriously.' Safa wasn't just being self-deprecating. She *did* get asked out, that was true, but apart from Imran, she couldn't remember the last time she got a second date.

Victoria frowned. 'Well, it's not your looks so it's clearly the chemistry.'

'You mean my personality,' Safa said wryly.

'You *do* come across a bit . . . serious.' Victoria waved delicately. 'Look, I would never tell you to change to please a man, but there *is* one thing you need to know. It's not what you do for a man; it's how you make him *feel*. You need to have *fun* on the date. You can't be uptight, wary, cynical. You can't have your journalist hat on. You can't be asking *does this have a future?* You have one job: have as much as fun as possible. Try not to think any further than that. If you have fun together, he'll want more time with you and then *you* get to decide if you want to give him that.'

'"Have fun"?' said Safa. It wasn't lost on her that it was the same advice she'd got from her dad.

'Yes! For starters . . .' Victoria reached out and took the clip out of Safa's bun, letting her hair fall to her chest. 'And would it kill you to wear a dress once in a while?'

'Thanks for the advice, Mrs Tradwife.'

'Oh, go fuck yourself.' Victoria arched her brows sportingly. 'Clearly no one else is.'

Safa let out an ugly hoot of a laugh. She always enjoyed seeing Victoria outside the courtroom. Other than Lily, Safa had never had close female friends and this barest glimpse reminded her how good it could feel. She almost asked if Victoria wanted a coffee sometime, but suspected she would be too busy.

'Seriously, Safa. Just have fun.'

'Okay.' She plumped out her hair in the mirror. 'I have one job and that is to have fun.' She thanked Victoria, pulled on her coat and headed into the autumn evening.

*

Safa parked her Clio on a side street in Bethnal Green and took a moment to collect herself. She felt the waltz of nerves, like she had on their very first date. Back then, she had relied on her usual tools – sarcasm and detachedness – but today she would strive for fun. Today, she would let her guard down. She locked her car and headed to Root19 for Sabina Begum's supper club.

She paused outside the venue and stripped off her long down coat, shivering in the wind. Inside, she found an intimate venue with soft cushions and low lighting. She was five minutes early and Imran hadn't yet arrived. Unlike her, he wasn't a stickler for time. She was shown to their table and saw that the place settings had their names written out in English and Bengali.

The waitress placed a jug of water on the table. She was dressed in a canary-yellow sari and Safa felt a sudden yearning for femininity. She had spent so much of her youth hiding the softest parts of herself, so that her dad would never worry about raising a daughter alone. In doing that, the colour and fun of girlhood had entirely passed her by. At Asian weddings, she would stand around awkwardly in a shalwar kameez that she had bought online, the creases still faintly visible from her hasty ironing. Her jewellery collection comprised a cheap neckpiece from an Ancient Egypt-themed party that she had attended years ago and an ill-advised gift of a necklace from her colleagues at *Asian Bride*. She rarely wore anything dressier than the jeans and T-shirt that she was in now. She glanced around the room and wished that she had chosen something prettier.

She heard the door swing open and Imran walked in. He wore black slacks and a pale blue shirt, and smelled like something delicious. When he kissed her cheek, she felt a pang of pride that *she* was the one he was here with.

'Shall we start with a cocktail?' he asked.

'Oh, I'm driving so . . .' She caught herself. 'Actually, yes. Let's do it. I can always get an Uber.' She ordered a mojito while Imran asked for an old fashioned. She gulped hers down, knowing that she'd need the help if she was going to be 'fun'.

Imran tilted his head. 'Are you okay?' he asked.

'I'm really happy to see you,' she said, allowing herself to be honest.

His smile was slow and warm. 'I'm happy to see you too.'

The smile became a grin and Safa was jealous at how easy it was to be him. He had a job he loved; he was fit, happy and healthy; he had a great family; and even had hobbies, for god's sake. Twice a week, he went boxing and on free weekends, he went camping with his brother.

'What are you thinking?' he asked.

'Whoever heard of a Bengali boy going camping in Britain?'

Imran laughed. 'You should come. It's peaceful.'

'I'd rather come boxing.'

He perked up. 'Would you really?'

'Maybe.'

'You would love it. It's great for anger.'

She arched a brow. 'Am I angry?'

Imran considered this. 'I feel like you are, yes.'

Safa frowned. This wasn't going the way she had planned. 'No matter where I go, there I am,' she said with resignation.

He looked at her quizzically. 'I think we need more alcohol.'

They ordered a second round and Safa let herself be lulled by it. Soon, she was in fits of laughter at his stories of hapless criminals.

She liked listening to him: the resonance of his voice, the quickness of his wit, his easy way of teasing. Together, they enjoyed five courses of the best Bangladeshi food that either had ever tasted.

Emboldened by the alcohol, she looked at him with her best guess at seductive. 'Do you know, I fancied you the very first time I saw you?'

He grinned. 'Of course I knew.'

'You did not!'

'Do you think I would have pulled that move in the canteen if I hadn't clocked your raging lust?'

'Fuck off,' she said, laughing.

'I'm one hundred per cent serious.'

She recalled the very first time she saw him in court, wearing that stab-proof vest. 'Fuck,' she said in a nostalgic tone.

Imran threw back his head and laughed. 'I told you!'

'Yeah, you did tell me.' She reached out and lightly touched his fingertips. The muscles in his forearm tensed and she thought he would pull away, but then he closed his hand around hers. A shadow moved across his face, in conflict with itself.

'Safa.' He laced her fingers with his. 'Why don't we give it a try? A proper one?'

For a moment, Safa allowed herself to imagine a life with Imran. Waking up with him on a lazy Sunday morning, the patter of feet, and then tiny laughing bodies leaping on them in bed. The thought took her breath away and she had to push it back, bury it deep beneath the realm of possibility.

'I want to, Imran, but things haven't changed for me.'

'I know that, Safa. I know you're not going to wake up one day and decide that you want kids with me after all. But you know what *I* can't do? I can't wake up and not think of you.' He squeezed her hand to the point of pain. 'I tried with Amina. And if that life was so important to me, I would have stayed with her because,

Jesus, she was perfect in so many ways. But that life doesn't matter to me.' He half-shrugged as if this were the simplest thing in the world. 'Not if it means not being with you.'

Safa unlaced her hand from his. 'Do you know, there's this bit in *When Harry Met Sally* that got to me when I watched it. In it, Sally is explaining how she'd always felt lucky not to have kids, but then one day she's in a car playing I Spy with her friend's daughter who's saying *I spy a tree, I spy a dog* or whatever. As they're driving, they see a man and a woman, and the man is carrying their child on his shoulders. The girl says *I spy a family* – and Sally just starts crying.'

Safa felt the press of sorrow. 'If you never have kids, Imran, that sense of loss will define who you are. I can't be responsible for that.'

Imran made a cynical sound. 'That's bullshit, Safa. You're assuming to know how I'll feel and you're martyring yourself because of it. I'm an adult. I can take responsibility for my own choices.'

Safa wished she could believe him; that she could shrug off her part in this. 'Imran, please be honest. Do you really think you can be happy without ever becoming a father?'

It took him a moment to answer. 'I really do think I can, Safa.' His tone was firm but his voice was thick with emotion.

'And what happens when you realise you can't?'

Imran's face flushed with sentiment. 'Is that what you're scared of, Safa? That I'll decide otherwise and leave you behind?'

'I don't know.' A pause. 'Maybe,' she admitted.

'If we *don't* do this, if we say *enough is enough* right now and we go our separate ways and you never see me again, would you not miss me? Would you not regret it?'

The thought made her recoil. 'Yes,' she managed to say.

'Then, Safa. Why don't we try?'

She couldn't answer the question. She couldn't tell him that opening herself up to him when everything – friends, films, culture – said they would never be happy without a family *terrified* her. 'I need time,' she told him.

'Then I'll give you time,' he said without missing a beat.

Safa smarted with guilt. She had taken so much of it from him already. 'Just a couple of weeks,' she said, 'so I can think after the trial.'

'Okay,' he said, carefully patient.

Safa grew morose. This was supposed to have been a fun evening. She fiddled with her empty glass, not skilled enough to shepherd them onto safer territory.

'I'll get the bill,' said Imran, sensing her discomfort.

Outside, they hovered on the pavement.

'I better call my Uber,' she said, far too tipsy to drive.

'I could walk you?' he suggested. It would take half an hour, mostly along Regent's Canal from this end of Victoria Park. He added, 'I don't want to end the evening like this.'

Safa felt the same and though usually she was desperate to be alone after conflict, she needed to be near him. They walked along the water, moonlight glossing its surface. It made her sentimental and she found herself back in that hospital corridor, learning what had happened to her mother. Had Safa decided in that instant that she didn't deserve the softness of motherhood? Or was she trying to retrofit a reason why society thought her abnormal? She dared not share this with Imran, for it would only give him hope. Of healing, softening, a cracking open of herself.

'What are you thinking?' he asked, glancing at her sideways. Their fingertips were a paper's width from touching, but never quite did.

She smiled mildly. 'Seriously though. Are you guys the only brown boys that camp in Britain?'

Imran smiled too and led her towards home.

*

Safa let herself into her flat and leaned against the door. She felt drunk and somewhat breathless. Imran had left her at the entrance to her building and though he hadn't kissed her, the way he had leaned over her, his stare laying claim to her, had left her a little stunned. She let herself bask in the feeling. Still smiling, she kicked off her shoes and tossed her keys on the Ikea bookshelf that took up her tiny hallway.

Then, she froze, sobering in an instant. Something in her flat wasn't right. She didn't understand why but there was a slow and dreadful sense that someone had been inside. She stood there, not moving, and listened. There was no sound other than the thump of her heart. She took a damp breath and crept down the hall to her living room. Every dark shape inside leapt up towards her. She clenched her fist to stop the panic. She pressed the light switch, certain it would reveal an intruder standing in the middle of the room. She yelped with fright even though the room was empty. Everything was where it should be: the cushions in a heap on the sofa, the flimsy table with its gifted succulents, the large leafy plants with a film of dust – but she couldn't shake the feeling.

She turned towards her bedroom and a bud of dread opened in her gut. Safa always left her door ajar – but today it was shut. She watched it for a second, expecting it to fly open. She moved towards it even as her instincts reared. Soundlessly, she reached for the handle and gave the door a push. A shape flew towards her and a scream rose in her throat. She reeled backwards and hit the wall. Panic flared before she managed to register that it was just the flitting shadow of the door. She slackened against the wall, slick with sweat. The room was empty. *Of course it was.*

'Come on, Safa.' She spoke out loud to muster her courage, but her dread remained. She couldn't understand it, but she *knew* that something was wrong. Her pulse raced as she unlocked her phone to call Imran. He picked up after one ring.

'Imran, have you gone far?' she asked, her voice shaking.

'No. What's wrong?'

'I think someone's been in my flat.'

'I'm on my way,' he said, already running. 'Safa, I need you to get out and go to a neighbour's flat. Stay there until I get there. Don't move, don't answer the door, don't do anything. I'll be there in literally a minute.'

'There's no one in here now.'

'Just do it, Safa. And stay on the phone.'

Safa was at the far end of her flat, furthest from the front door. That's when she felt it: a presence in the room, the heat of an extra body. She realised that she hadn't checked the wardrobe. She turned towards it, barely daring to look. Her gaze fixed on the crack in the doors – and that's when she saw him move.

She shrieked and careened out of the room. She ran towards the front door and blanched when a figure appeared in the hall, her mind taking too long to recognise Imran. She spilled into his arms and he rocked back to slow her momentum.

'Safa. What's wrong?'

'The wardrobe. In the bedroom.'

He understood and pointed her towards the exit. Silently, he advanced along the hall. Safa stood at the threshold and watched him disappear around the corner. She waited, her whole body rigid. He was gone for far too long. Her flat was *tiny*. What could be taking so long?

'Imran?' She took a tentative step inside. 'Imran?' She heard the creak of a floorboard, but Imran didn't answer. She pressed a fist to her mouth to suppress her panic. And, then, he rounded the corner.

'There's no one here.'

Safa bent forward, slack with relief.

Imran came to her. 'Hey. What happened?'

She took a moment to calm herself. 'As soon as I came in,

something felt wrong. It's like . . .' She shook her head, knowing it sounded illogical. 'The grain of the carpet is wrong. You know how when you vacuum it? I always go this way.' She mimed running a vacuum forward and backward. 'But today it's this way.' She pointed side to side. 'Or here.' She pulled him into the living room and showed him the adhesive pads beneath the legs of her desk, designed to protect the flooring. 'These are always lined up but you see how it's tipping over here?'

Imran frowned. 'What else?'

'I always leave my bedroom door open but today it was closed.'

'Do you have any valuables?'

'No. Just my passport, a little bit of cash and a couple of nice pens.'

'Have they been taken?'

Safa checked her desk drawer. 'They're still here.'

'How sure are you that someone's been in here?'

She scanned the room again. There was nothing concrete but it was all a little off, like someone had moved everything a centimetre, just to mess with her.

'Maybe eighty per cent,' she said.

Imran's expression was unreadable. 'All the windows are locked. They could have come in through your front door but they'd have to have the key. Who else has one?'

'Just my dad.'

'Not a neighbour? An old colleague?'

She grimaced. 'I think there was a copy in my desk when I left *The Clarion*. I remember asking if I could come back to check and they didn't let me. They said nothing had been handed into lost property.'

'Is there anyone at *The Clarion* that has a grudge against you?'

Safa thought of Oliver Witherow. 'There *is* one guy, but I'm positive he wouldn't do this.'

'Give me his name.'

Safa typed Oliver's name into Imran's phone. Together, they did a circuit of her flat. They were all subtle things: the angle of her table lamp, the placement of her dishrag. Would someone break in just to mess with her mind?

She rubbed her temple. 'God, maybe I just had too many mojitos.'

Imran watched her with concern. 'Would you feel more comfortable elsewhere? I can drop you at your dad's or you can come and stay at mine?'

'No, I don't want to worry him. Thank you, Imran, but I think it's okay.'

He hesitated. 'Or I could stay here?'

'Would you mind?' Safa knew she wouldn't sleep all night if she was alone.

'Of course. I can take the sofa.' He regarded the tiny two-seater that he had helped assemble.

'No, that's silly,' she said, knowing he wouldn't fit on it. 'You've seen the size of my bed.' The super-king, a gift from her dad when she bought her flat, nearly touched both walls of her bedroom.

Imran agreed hesitantly. It was late, but Safa needed to calm her nerves so made them both a drink. By the time they went to bed, they were pleasantly drunk again. They lay there in the dark, clear distance between them. Imran cleared his throat.

'You know, there were easier ways of getting me to stay.'

'Very funny,' she said.

They lay for a little while longer, Safa hyper aware of his body next to her. She could feel the warmth and heft of him, within touching distance. They lay like that for a long while, sleep nowhere near. When she turned towards him, he was already waiting.

Chapter 13

Safa could tell by looking at the jurors which of them would dominate the verdict. There was a man in his late forties who wore a thin tie and a short-sleeved shirt. His hair was thinning on top and he had the look of a smarmy middle manager. Another was an older woman, in her early sixties, with tightly coiffed hair and a prim pinch about her mouth. One strong personality could sway an entire jury and these two could prove pivotal.

Lucien Garrett stood. 'My Lord, the prosecution calls its final witness, Ms Talia Wilde.'

A slim, elegant brunette walked to the witness box. She had long hair and a soft fringe, and warm blue eyes that seemed to twinkle. She wore a dark suit with white trim and large Navy-style buttons. She looked calm and comfortable as she took the oath and confirmed her occupation: the founder of a high-end fashion reseller website.

'Ms Wilde, how do you know the defendant, Lily Astor?'

'I'm an old friend of Richard Astor's. He and I were in the same year at Oxford. I met Lily through him.'

'When was the last time you saw Lily?'

'On the night of 6th April this year. I was at their party.'

'What time did you leave the party?'

'At 9 p.m.'

'That's very exact.'

'Well, we were the last to leave – me and Edward, a fellow guest. As we were pulling away in the car, we noticed Harry, Lily's son, leave the house and storm off down the street. I remember looking at the time on the dashboard and remarking that it was a bit late for him to be going out.'

Garrett nodded meditatively. 'You said you were the last guests at the party. What was the mood like in the house when you left?'

'It started off like any good party – fun, lively, with a good mix of people – but by the time we left, it was tense.'

'Why?'

'Well, Lily had spent the evening flirting with a colleague – Ben if I remember correctly – and she was being obvious and showy about it, almost as if she wanted to goad Richard, which I suppose makes sense.'

'Why is that?'

'Well, a few months before, Richard told Lily that he wanted a divorce and she lost it. She guilt tripped him, grew hysterical.'

Victoria stood. 'My Lord, this is hearsay evidence.'

The judge nodded. 'Ms Wilde, can you stick to what you saw and heard yourself, not what someone told you?'

'Yes, sorry,' said Talia smoothly. She was far too polished to be ruffled.

'Did Richard tell you he wanted a divorce?' Garrett asked.

'Yes.'

'Do you know why he wanted a divorce?'

'Yes.' Talia's voice was clear and firm. 'Because Richard was in love with me.'

Safa startled in surprise. From her position, she could see Lily in the dock clearly. Her features were a picture of pain but, unlike the jurors, Safa had caught the look before it: glazed and impassive; the look of a woman who'd just been told something she already knew.

'There had always been a spark between us,' Talia continued.

'Ever since we met at university and even after Lily appeared on the scene. But then she fell pregnant and our potential future together was abruptly wiped clean. Ever since then, we both felt that there was something . . . incomplete.'

'Did anything romantic happen between you and Richard?'

Talia hunched guiltily. 'I'm not proud of it, but, yes. It happened a few years ago – in 2021. Richard had lost his job in the pandemic and I took him out to cheer him up. It was summer and we were at this rooftop bar with a beautiful view and both had a bit too much to drink. Richard kissed me. It was a spur-of-the-moment thing but all my emotions came spilling out. I told him that I loved him; that I had loved him since I was eighteen.' A softness came to her eyes. 'He told me that he had felt the same way at uni, but once Lily gave birth to Harry, he was committed to her. He said that he wouldn't walk out on his family.' She exhaled slowly. 'Nothing happened for a long while after that, but in 2023, we began a physical relationship.'

Safa felt her blood heat. Richard had lost his job, likely felt emasculated by Lily's success, and turned to another woman. How fucking predictable.

'I never expected him to leave,' said Talia. 'I knew he had a family and I would never ask that of him and for a while it was fine, but then he said he wanted to leave her. That things at home had got too much. I told him no, I wasn't a home-wrecker.' Talia cringed. 'I know that sounds like a contradiction. I was in love with him and he was in love with me but I didn't want to hurt his wife or family. Tragic as it sounds, I was satisfied being on the sidelines.'

'Did Lily know that you were the reason Richard wanted a divorce?'

'No.' Talia spoke with conviction. 'I told him that if he wanted a divorce, that was up to him, but to take me out of the equation. I didn't want a bearing on it.'

'So Lily was unaware of your affair with Richard?'

'Yes, but . . .' Talia hesitated. 'She found out on the night she killed him.'

Safa looked to Lily. She had said nothing about an affair.

'How did Lily find out?' asked Garrett.

'Richard was upset on the night of the party. He felt that Lily was parading her attraction to Ben in front of him. At one point in the evening, I went to the bathroom upstairs and when I came out, Richard was on the landing. He had this look in his eye – this careless, almost self-destructive look. He kissed me brazenly. I pushed him off. I didn't want to do anything in his family home. For me, it was never about the excitement or the thrill like it may be with some other women. Being discreet was important to me.

'I pulled him into the bedroom and told him to stop behaving irrationally. He said he was stressed and needed a moment away from everyone else. He kissed me and I kissed him back.' Talia took a breath, jerky and full of regret. 'That's when we heard a noise out on the landing. We sprang apart and when I looked out, I saw Lily rushing down the stairs.'

'Did she see the two of you kiss?'

'Yes, I'm certain she did. She was rushing, tripping over the hem of her dress, and it was clear that she was panicked.'

'What did you do?'

'I wanted to follow her, but Richard stopped me. I was mortified and wanted to leave immediately but I had promised to drive Edward home and knew it would be odd if I left early. I stayed on the periphery of the party and Lily avoided me all evening; wouldn't even catch my eye. I wanted to apologise, but Richard told me to act like nothing had happened.'

'And when you left, what was the mood like?'

'Tense. Strained. Like something was about to erupt.'

'Did Richard seem angry?'

'No. He seemed worried.'

'What about Lily? Was she angry?'

'Lily was livid.'

Garrett steepled his fingers. 'Thank you, Ms Wilde.' He turned to the judge. 'I have no more questions, My Lord.'

*

Safa picked at her panini, too preoccupied to eat. She thought over Talia's evidence. Had Lily seen the kiss? Had she known that Richard was cheating? And would it be enough to drive her to violence? Safa couldn't picture it. Lily could be prideful, and she certainly knew how to hold a grudge, but she was rarely reckless. Calculated, yes, but not reckless. Although, if you had asked Safa in childhood which was more likely, that Lily would grow up to be a *perpetrator* or a *victim* of violence, she would not have chosen victim.

As she ate, Safa studied Lily's Instagram and noted how the picture-perfect reel revealed little of her actual life. Next, she went to Facebook where Lily would occasionally share biting insights into the London media scene. She hadn't posted anything since 2022 and even the months before it had been scrubbed of anything remotely snarky. Safa clicked Lily's friends list and searched for Talia's name but found no results. After a moment of hesitation, she clicked onto Richard's profile. It had been memorialised and was filled with condolences. This time, Talia did appear in the list of friends. Before Safa could probe, however, her phone began to ring. She saw that it was Imran and took the call outside.

'Hi, Safa,' he said with a hum of noise around him. 'I checked out Oliver Witherow and he's clean. Old Harrovian. His dad got him a job at *The Clarion* and he's been failing upwards ever since. Last night, he happened to be on stage at the Cheltenham Literature Festival.'

'That sounds about right,' said Safa sardonically. 'So it couldn't have been him in my flat.' She turned her back to the traffic to shield her phone from the noise. 'Listen, maybe I wasted your time. I was tired and drunk and might've imagined the whole bloody thing.' She waited for reassurance, but Imran didn't disagree. 'What do you think?' she prompted.

'I can't say either way, Safa. You've always been able to pick up details, but if nothing was missing and nothing tangible was moved, then it seems too weird to be true.' He paused. 'If you're worried, I could come and stay again?'

She heard the hope in his voice. 'I've got to work tonight,' she said. She needed time to think before she pulled him close.

'Okay, I'll see you soon,' he said. Another pause. 'Let me know if you change your mind. I'll be home tonight anyway.'

She said goodbye and hung up. When she looked up, she noticed a figure across the street staring at her intently. He wore dark clothes and glasses and a cap pulled low. She studied him and when it became clear that he was indeed looking at her, she moved to cross the road.

A double decker bus made her pull back and by the time it passed, the man was gone. Safa scanned the street but couldn't see any sign of him. Her instincts bristled and she sensed that something was wrong. Like thousands of women did every day, she mapped herself to safety. *Five seconds to get back in the café; one scream away from the aid of strangers; witnesses in passing cars; maybe CCTV.* Reassured by this whip-quick inventory, she remained there on the street, scanning and scanning. She exhaled hard to release the tension. Was it just paranoia fuelled by last night's supposed break-in? She told herself as much, but a sickly anxiety settled in her gut. She searched the street one last time, then headed back to court. She didn't let herself look over her shoulder once. She was determined not to show fear, but her hair stood on end all the way back.

*

The jurors filed back to the courtroom, freshly fed and watered. The man with the short sleeves sat in the front row, straining his neck like a meerkat scanning the room for threat. Two seats along, the woman with the pinched mouth sat with a straight back, like a favourite student awaiting instruction. Safa felt uneasy about them. She knew that they were here to serve their civic duty but it was always clear which jurors enjoyed it unduly. There was something about passing judgement on others that appealed to certain people.

It occurred to her that this was a good idea for a feature and reached for her phone to make a note. The screen unlocked onto Talia's Facebook profile and Safa flicked through it furtively. Talia's recent photos included a dozen from Lily's party. Safa had seen them before thanks to Erin Quinto, but she looked at them with fresh eyes, now aware of Richard's affair. She studied Talia and Richard, but saw nothing untoward. The other photos showed a mix of well-to-do people, high on life and money.

'Court rise,' the clerk instructed.

Safa stood and just as she was about to lock her phone, a picture snagged her attention. She zoomed in and out, then startled. Clumsily, she thumbed the screen.

A moment later, Victoria's phone buzzed with a message. Safa watched her snatch it up and set it quickly back down. It wasn't clear if she had read the message or simply silenced her phone. Safa thought about trying to catch her attention, but the judge would surely notice.

Victoria stood in one fluid move and began her cross-exam. 'Ms Wilde, if being discreet was important to you, why did you go to a party that Richard co-hosted with his wife?'

'It would have been odd not to.' Talia was unperturbed. 'We have always been good friends.'

Victoria smirked. 'This morning, you told my learned friend that Lily was being "obvious and showy" when she was flirting with Ben. You said that she was trying to "goad Richard". What did you mean by that?'

'She was touching Ben's arm, making prolonged eye contact, laughing in an exaggerated manner.'

'So in other words, being a good hostess?'

'Well, she wasn't acting that way with anyone else.'

'She didn't touch anyone else's arm?'

'Well, she may have, but not in a pointed way.'

'And what is a "pointed way" to touch someone's arm?'

Talia measured her words. 'Repeatedly touching their arm.'

'Were you counting?'

'No, but—'

'So how do you know how many times she touched his arm?'

Talia scowled. 'I don't know.'

'No. You don't know,' Victoria said tartly. 'You told the jury that Richard was upset because he thought that Lily was flirting with Ben. That he, in fact, was *so* upset that he was acting "careless, almost self-destructive". But if he was in love with you, why would he have got so upset?'

'I guess it was a point of pride. Lily was disrespecting him.'

'"Lily was disrespecting him".' Victoria arched a brow. Talia clearly didn't see the hypocrisy. 'So Richard didn't like feeling disrespected?'

'No, but who does?'

'And this made him angry?'

'Not angry. Upset.'

'To the point of being self-destructive?'

Talia gestured irritably. 'I guess so.'

Victoria gave her an icy smile. 'Ms Wilde, you said that you're not a home-wrecker. You said, "I know that sounds like a contradiction, but . . . I didn't want to hurt his wife or family. Tragic as it sounds, I was satisfied being on the sidelines." So you didn't pester him to divorce his wife?'

'No, never.'

'Are you certain?'

Talia sensed a trap. 'Maybe in a moment of pique but never seriously.'

'What counts as a moment of pique?'

'Maybe when he had to leave early one night, I might have said something about wishing we could be together.'

'And that's all?'

'I would say so, yes.'

Victoria nodded at the clerk. 'During the investigation, the Met were given access to Richard Astor's phone records.' She indicated the screen. 'Ms Wilde, do you recognise these texts?'

Why haven't you told her yet?

- Talia, I can't. Things are fraught right now. I need to keep an eye on Lily.

You promised me you would. I'm not a cheap whore that you can fuck and leave whenever you like. Make your fucking decision.

- Talia, come on. Please.

Talia's cheeks filled with colour. 'They were in the early days of our relationship when I was idealistic.'

'Okay, well, how about these from January of this year?'

If you don't tell her, Richard, then I'm walking away. It's been A YEAR.

- Talia, you don't understand. I can't just walk away from her. There's too much history.

Tell her this week or we're done.

Richard, did you tell her?

Hello???

WTF, Richard? I've just had a save the date from Lily about your book launch. You are such a fucking coward.

Victoria angled her head. 'It doesn't sound like you were happy on the sidelines, does it?'

Talia grew tetchy. 'If you follow that conversation, you'll see that I apologised for acting like that. I was drunk that night and lonely.'

'What is it they say: *in vino veritas*?' asked Victoria.

'That's not fair. I wasn't being logical. I apologised. You're selecting certain messages to make me seem unhinged. There are plenty of calm, rational, loving messages between us.'

'Do you know what there wasn't, Ms Wilde? There wasn't the faintest sign that Richard had asked Lily for a divorce.'

Talia was visibly tense. 'He told me over dinner that he'd asked her.'

'And you never referred to it via text? You never discussed logistics, timeframe, the future, your plans? Not even once?'

Talia raised her chin, her neck long and rigid. 'I was happy to be patient.' Her voice snapped on the t. 'Divorces take time and I was willing to wait for him.'

'Here's what I think happened, Ms Wilde. You were desperate to be with Richard and you resented Lily. You resented her because he chose her over you every time. You were angry at her, so you made up this divorce to make her look vengeful.'

'That's not true.' Talia's tone was brittle.

'Then why isn't there proof? Richard says in those texts "I can't just walk away from Lily." "I need to keep an eye on Lily." You yourself said that he was driven to *self-destruction* because Lily merely touched another man's arm. This doesn't indicate a man who was in love with you, does it? This indicates a man who was fixated on his wife.' Victoria narrowed her gaze. 'There was no divorce, was there?'

Talia's mouth tightened. 'There was.'

'Ms Wilde, you rather liked the idea of Lily finding out, didn't you? You liked the idea of her seeing you and Richard in a hot embrace under her own roof?'

'That's not true.'

'When you saw Lily rushing down the stairs, you felt a pang of satisfaction, didn't you?'

'No. I did not.'

'When you looked into her eyes and knew that she knew, you felt like you had won, didn't you?'

'No, I didn't.' Talia's patience was slipping.

'Didn't what? Look her in the eye or feel like you had won?'

Talia waved a jerky hand in the air. 'Either. Both. She was running down the stairs. I didn't even see her face.'

Victoria stopped short. 'You didn't even see her face.' She stared at Talia with wide-eyed gravity. 'Ms Wilde, you said you were certain that Lily saw you.'

'I was. I am.'

'But if you didn't see her face, how do you know it was her?'

'Because she had the same blonde ponytail, the same blue dress.'

'Ah, that's right. You said this morning that she was tripping over the hem?'

'Yes.'

'This dress?' asked Victoria.

A picture of Lily at the party appeared on screen. Her blonde hair was indeed in a ponytail and she wore a dress in shimmery midnight blue.

'She was tripping over the hem of *this* dress?'

Talia's face grew mottled and pink. In the picture, the hem of Lily's dress stopped just below the knee.

'Or is it *this* dress you saw?'

A second picture came up on screen. This one also showed a woman with a long blonde ponytail. Her blue dress, however, was in a lighter shade and the hem skimmed the floor.

'Is it *this* woman you saw?'

Talia's mouth parted in dismay. She hadn't lied but she *had* made it up. The woman she saw on the stairs hadn't been Lily at all.

'The truth, Ms Wilde, is that Lily Astor knew nothing about a divorce or an affair. She wasn't flirting with guests. She wasn't goading Richard. She was being a normal hostess. Richard wasn't going to leave his wife for you. He was fixated on her to the point where he became self-destructive because she was speaking to Ben. It wasn't Lily at all who was angry and bitter. It was Richard – and it was you.'

Talia didn't answer and Victoria let the silence talk. She took her time to square the edges of her notes, then looked up at the judge. 'I have no further questions, My Lord.'

Safa let her breath out and the courtroom seemed to exhale as well. Victoria caught her eye and gave her the slightest nod. Safa nodded back and deleted the pictures of the dress from her phone. Victoria took a seat, her expression entirely neutral for someone who had just destroyed the prosecution's final witness.

*

Safa dumped her laptop on her tatty sofa and collapsed beside it. It had been a long week in court and she was exhausted. She wanted to talk to Lily about Richard's affair but her visitation request was unlikely to be granted over the weekend. Something about the case still needled at Safa. It was too neat – or not neat enough – and she couldn't get a handle on it. She wished she had been at the party that night to observe the events first hand. As a proxy, she cycled through the same pictures on Facebook but spotted nothing new. She sighed and closed the tab, then winced at the number of emails in her inbox. She opened one from Kevin.

Where's the Deliveroo story?

Safa cursed and checked her watch. She had promised to write a story this week about a spate of muggings targeting delivery workers. She had exactly twenty-four minutes before the week officially ended. She collated the facts at lightning speed and wrote directly into WordPress. She hurriedly found a picture of a Deliveroo worker and added it to the piece.

'Thank you, shopblocks,' she said to the photographer who had uploaded the rights-free image to Flickr. She checked her watch, pressed publish and sent the link to Kevin with two minutes to spare. She couldn't afford to drop the ball. Kevin had given her permission to work on her feature as long as she kept up her normal duties. She wished that she could work on the feature full time, but didn't have that luxury. She felt a pang of nostalgia for her job on Special Projects. It had been a dream and she still felt an intense resentment every time she thought of how she lost it.

A new email from Kevin landed in her inbox.

Touché. Now get some rest.

She closed her laptop and placed it on her desk-cum-dining table. She poured herself a large glass of Malbec and took it back to the sofa. It made her think back to her first date with Imran. They had met in a buzzy Italian place and dithered over the drinks menu for an awkward minute.

Eventually, Imran asked the question: 'Shall we get some wine?'

'Oh, thank god,' said Safa. 'I thought that maybe you didn't drink.' They fell into an easy camaraderie and the shorthand shared by second-gen Muslims. Many didn't drink alcohol but others, like Safa, did. So much of Imran made sense to her. So much of their lives would be easy.

Yesterday, he had told her that she was martyring herself to protect him from future regret, but it was also cowardice. She wanted to protect *herself* from that moment when he finally realised that she alone wasn't enough. Could she be brave enough to take the risk? Could she handle getting five or ten years down the line and having Imran say to her, *you were right after all. I spied a family and it made me cry*?

The thought made her heart contract. But what was the alternative? Spend the next five or ten years alone? Try to find someone who wasn't Imran? She couldn't imagine meeting anyone who lifted her so cleanly out of a bad day, who made her laugh through stress, who was kind and strong and fearless. She wanted that. She wanted *him*. She just had to be brave and make the decision.

She reached for her glass of wine with a low, frustrated sound. She needed her brain to stop whirring for just one night. She drank the wine quickly, letting it warm her blood. Another glass later, she headed to the shower.

The hot rush of water washed the day off her. She rolled her shoulders to ease the ache in her blades. The steam filled the cubicle so that she couldn't see outside it. She lingered there in her own tiny cocoon. When her fingers began to prune, she turned off the water and gently wrung her hair.

That's when she heard the rustling sound right outside the

cubicle. She whirled towards it, her heart thumping as she searched through the fog. Nothing. No one.

But then she heard it again, seemingly closer this time. A drumbeat of panic started off low. With a damp breath, she slowly opened the shower door. The water had cooled on her skin and she began to shiver. She took a careful step outside and slid into her robe with her gaze fixed on the bathroom door. Had she left it unlocked? She reached for the handle, but then heard the sound behind her – with her in the bathroom. She spun. Nothing. No one. With a jolt, she realised that the sound was in the walls. God, did she have *rats*? These flats were built cheek by jowl and rats in one meant rats in all. It would take an age to get rid of them.

She pressed an ear against the wall and strained to hear the sound. That's when she felt the draught. Was there a hole somewhere? She knelt and studied the skirting. She heard the sound again, higher up this time. Was there something in her fern? It was a spindly thing on her windowsill and often collected bugs. She straightened and poked at it, expecting something to wriggle out. Nothing.

Carefully, she dragged it to one side. It took a moment to register what she was seeing. And, then, she was shrieking. She careened backwards, her body reacting before her mind caught up. She crashed into the bathroom door, seized by fear and shock. Because there, behind the plant, in the window, was a small but perfect square cut into the glass.

Chapter 14

Imran put an arm around Safa as the locksmith finished up. Her flat was on the twelfth floor and the bathroom window looked onto a side of the building that was practically sheer. There were no stairs, balconies or fire exits, which meant that the glass had been cut from *inside* Safa's flat. Somewhere beneath her panic, she had understood that the cut wasn't fresh; it had happened on the night of the break-in and, somehow, both she and Imran had missed it.

'He was here,' said Safa. 'The Glassman was in my flat – and he wanted me to know.' Her mind was numb – blanked by shock. What she felt was physical: the bristle of hair on her arms, clamminess in her palms, thinness in her breath. She felt acutely exposed: on a high precipice with only a slippery foothold. The room seesawed around her and she touched a wall to steady herself.

'Safa, I'm so sorry.' Imran flushed with guilt. He had checked her flat himself and locked every point of entry, but hadn't looked behind the plant pot.

Safa was too shaken to respond. The Glassman had been inside her flat. He knew that she was after him. The Bengali community was small and Safa poking around must have caught his attention. That's what she chose to believe. The alternative – a villain who was somehow omniscient – was too chilling to entertain. Safa swallowed and her throat felt dry and painful. *Hold on, girl,* she told herself. She was on the verge of losing her composure – from fear but also frustration that she had been made to feel this way. Safa had always thought of herself as strong, calm and resilient, but today she was thoroughly shaken. Today, she understood how *embarrassing* it was to be made a victim. You try and try to be strong, but this person made you meek.

The locksmith snapped his toolbox shut, making Safa startle. He stood and held out three sets of keys.

'Take care of these.' He motioned at Imran. 'And make sure your boyfriend keeps a spare. The Ultion locks are near impossible to break into. Trust me, if a burglar sees this symbol, he's doing a runner.' He gave her a crooked smile, which briefly smoothed his jowls. 'And if you lock yourself out, don't call me 'cause even *I* can't get in.'

Safa took the keys and gripped them in her palm. They felt heavy and reassuring. 'Was the old lock easy to get into?'

'Oh yeah. Some of these new builds are basically cardboard. Developers use the cheapest stuff possible.' He held up her old lock, a cheap golden thing. 'This you could pick with a butter knife.'

She grimaced. 'Thank you for fixing it.'

'I'll send you an invoice,' he said with a nod. 'You take care now.'

Safa let him out of the flat and leaned against the door. She felt drained, and strangely disconnected. Her mind was wired but her body was exhausted.

'Imran. Thank you,' she said in a voice that sounded young to her. He had shot over after her panicked call and arranged a visit from his colleagues in the force.

He smiled, but couldn't hide the haunted look in his eye. 'Come on.' He gestured at her duffel bag. 'I'll drop you off.'

Safa gingerly pulled on her coat and followed him outside, making sure to triple-lock the door. Imran had urged her to stay with him, but tonight she needed her dad. She had told him that her boiler had broken down, not wanting him to worry. His response was to immediately start cooking.

It was a short walk to her dad's, but she was grateful to have Imran with her. As they passed beneath the streetlamps, she couldn't shake the feeling of being watched. She scanned the street around them, ready to find a pair of eyes gleaming in the darkness. She leaned closer to Imran and walked a little quicker.

They arrived minutes later to a house filled with the scent of frying onions. Safa almost started crying at how comforting it felt. She took a moment in the hall to compose herself: to wipe the sweat from her upper lip, smooth her hair and tamp down her nerviness, then followed Imran into the kitchen. Her dad hugged them both and ushered them to the table.

'The food's pretty much ready,' he said. He busied himself with plates and glasses. 'Do you know what's wrong with the boiler?' he asked.

'Someone will look at it tomorrow,' she lied.

'Well, you can stay here as long as you like.'

'Thank you, Dad.'

He filled her plate with rice and curry and Safa felt the tension ease. Here, with her father, she finally felt secure. Safa was grateful that Imran had stayed. He was able to bring an ease and cheer that her churning mind could not.

After dinner, Imran joined them on their walk with Kipling, her dad's new foster dog. Safa listened as her dad gently fussed over the dog. She noticed that he spoke only English with his dogs as if they were monolingual. Hearing him speak brought back memories of him learning the language. She would overhear him sometimes, running through his exercises, so often getting things wrong. He would pronounce a long 'e' at the end of words so that *done* became *don-ee* and *gone* became *gon-ee*. It had always hurt her when native speakers sniggered at his efforts.

Kipling bounded to her with a twig and she knelt down to retrieve it. She stayed there for a moment, stroking Kipling's ears, while Imran fell in step with her dad. She watched them, shoulder to shoulder as they cut through the darkness.

I spy a family.

She crouched there on the path, struck with a breathless sense of clarity. This – Safa, Imran, her dad, a dog – was, in fact, a family; one she wanted to keep. In the purity of that thought, her decision was finally easy. She wanted to be with Imran. She wanted to give herself – and, by proxy, her dad – a proper shot at happiness. After years in the shadow of grief, it was the least they all deserved.

She pressed her cheek to Kipling's fur. 'Let's give it a go, eh, girl?' she said softly. 'Let's be brave.' Kipling barked and the two men looked back. 'Come on, girl. They're waiting for us.' Safa straightened and walked up the path, closing the distance between them all.

Then, as if it was the most natural thing in the world, she took Imran's hand. He looked at her, a question on his brows. When she nodded, he didn't show surprise. Instead, there was a sense of acceptance, as if things that were inevitable were finally starting to happen.

*

Lily compulsively smoothed her skirt. She didn't know who would do better in court today: Lily-Ann Baker or Lily Astor. Would the working-class version curry more sympathy or the cut-glass presenter fare better? More importantly, what emotions did she have to show? Remorse? Certainly. Vulnerability? Yes, but that's the one she had most trouble with. Neither of her guises knew how to do it. Lily-Ann was too tough and Lily was too cheerful, albeit now officially sullied. Lily's recasting as victim-slash-killer had inspired endless coverage. Even her colleagues on *Arise* were running segments on the trial, a thought that made her certain she would never return to public life. She saw one of them now, slinking onto the press bench, which was filled to the brim as usual.

At the centre of the courtroom, Victoria Hersham stood. Lily felt a stab of anxiety. She wasn't ready for this, was scared that she'd get her story twisted.

'My Lord, the defence calls its first witness, Ms Lily Astor.'

For an awful moment, Lily thought her knees would buckle, but she managed to walk to the witness box. She was aware that her favourite suit now hung off her frame. Six months at Bronzefield had worn her down in ways she hadn't imagined. There were obvious things – her hair now like straw, her skin sallow, her nails ragged – but there were other, more profound, effects. Like how she now grew anxious in silence, so accustomed was she to sound and fury. Or how her senses were always hyper-aware so that reds and yellows in the outside world hurt in their brightness. She couldn't imagine finding her way back to normality. Even if the jury believed her, even if she was freed, she would never be the same person: Harry's mother, Richard's wife, award-winning presenter. Despite everything that had happened, those were things that she had been proud of.

Inside the witness box, she raised her hand and took the oath, swearing to tell the truth, the whole truth and nothing but the truth.

Victoria began with a picture of Lily's life: how she and Richard had met, when they got married, when they had Harry, where they lived, their jobs and their lifestyle. She then charted a timeline of the abuse: from Richard's mood swings in January 2021 to his first act of violence in April that year. The back-and-forth of factual information steadied Lily's nerves, but then Victoria began to dig deeper, asking more from her.

'Lily, if Richard's friends were to describe him, what would they say? Give us five words they would use.'

Lily considered this. 'They would say he was intelligent, confident, charming, ambitious and successful.'

'And if Richard's *enemies* were to describe him, what would *they* say?'

Lily thought about this for a little longer. 'They might say he was impatient, arrogant, self-involved, a little ingratiating and sometimes insecure.'

'Would any of them be wrong?'

'No. Richard could be all of that.'

'Is it fair to say that he had a relatively good image in his social circle? After all, those negative traits aren't particularly offensive.'

'Yes, that's fair.'

'Was there a side of him that friends and indeed enemies did not see?'

Lily shifted uneasily. 'Yes.'

'And how would you describe that side of him?'

She picked at a cuticle on her ring finger. 'He could be petty, volatile, selfish and vicious.'

'Did others ever see that side of him?'

'Sometimes, yes, but they never saw the full picture.'

'Can you give us an example?'

Lily had a story ready. 'A couple of years ago, we were on a trip to Boston. Some of Richard's family live there and we all went to a lobster restaurant. There were maybe nine of us. It was a potluck place where you put your plate up and the chef gives you a lobster. Richard was convinced that he was given a small one. When we got back to the table, he began to hiss and complain about it. That's what he did a lot of the time; hiss at me, expecting me to put it right.'

'What did you do?'

'I offered to swap my lobster for his and he said no, but he kept complaining. The others noticed and they offered to swap as well, but he just fell into a sulk. Usually, he would expect me to sort it out or we'd leave, but we couldn't just leave. I couldn't make everyone give back their lobster, so I tried to ignore him. He got angrier and angrier, and just spoilt the evening for everyone. They saw a hint of who he could be, but they didn't see the full picture.'

'And what was the full picture?'

Lily took a shaky breath. She needed the jury to believe that she had spent so long hiding her plight, it felt obscene to reveal it now. 'Underneath the table, he was pinching my thigh.' Lily cleared the gummy sound in her throat. 'At one point, he managed to catch my arm. He pinched it so hard, it brought tears to my eyes, but he kept it there, hurting me for as long as he could. The memory of me just sitting there, in front of our family, with this creepy smile on my face, still makes me so ashamed.' Lily blinked back tears.

'Was this a one off?' asked Victoria. 'Was he having a bad day?'

Lily swallowed her anguish. 'No. It happened all the time. One time, it was because I didn't order coffee at the same time as dessert. Another time, because there was no cheeseboard on the menu and I didn't ask them to make us a custom one. I had to be alert as to what might trigger a mood and try to stave it off.'

'How did that make you feel?'

'It gave me anxiety. I was jumpy and unsettled. I did things big and small to placate him. I changed the sheets twice a week because he complained that they were dirty, I cooked his favourite meals, I kept a calm and quiet environment at home, I never questioned where he was going or with whom. We used to talk all the time and I would think of a hundred things to tell him each day and I just kept them to myself because I didn't know what would trigger him.'

Victoria was sympathetic. 'Did these triggers ever result in worse violence than pinching?'

Lily's palms were damp. 'Yes.'

'Can you give us an example?'

Lily searched her vast stock of stories, built with Technicolour detail over her six months at Bronzefield. 'At the start of the year, we visited Richard's mother, Audrey, in her home in Buckinghamshire. She had sent us a hamper for New Year's and I thanked her for the gesture. She asked what the wagyu steaks were like and I said that they were delicious. I mentioned that we had them with a lovely Cabernet and she seemed pleased, but later, when I went to the bathroom, I came out to find Richard waiting for me.

'He asked why I had made a point about the Cabernet. He said that it looked like I was criticising Audrey for not sending us wine with the hamper. I told him not to be ridiculous.' Lily took an audible breath, holding back emotion.

'He punched me in the stomach.' Lily's shoulders hunched, still feeling the impact. 'It winded me and he could see that I was struggling, but he just walked back downstairs as if nothing had happened.' She clenched a fist on the rail. 'It's not the physical pain that broke me. That only lasts a few seconds and adrenaline masks the worst of it. It was having to go back down and try to sit upright and act normal, pretending that nothing had happened. The shame of doing that, repeatedly, for years, is what did it.'

Victoria lingered on the pause. 'Lily, how frequently did violence like this – a punch, a slap, a kick – happen to you?'

Lily had already calculated this. 'I would say once a week.'

'For three years?'

Her gaze dropped. 'Yes.'

'So over one hundred and fifty times?'

Her voice was small. 'Yes.'

'How did that make you feel?'

Lily felt a lump in her throat. 'I was anxious. I was stressed all the time. I couldn't sleep. I was late to set, which had never happened before.'

'Did anyone witness the abuse?'

'Harry, my son, but I tried to shield him as much as possible.'

'Did you tell any friends or family?'

'No.'

'Why not?'

'I was ashamed. I had spent so long building this perfect life, I was too ashamed to admit I was being abused.'

Victoria spoke gently. 'Lily, some would say "you're a rich and famous woman with a sizeable platform. If you can't speak out, then who can?" What would you say to them?'

Lily squared her shoulders. 'I would say that I loved him. Money or fame doesn't immunise you from that. I'm a woman, and the person I loved more than anything else in the world hurt me not *despite* the fact that I loved him but *because* of it. Because he knew I would protect him. I would let him punch and kick and pinch my flesh for *years* before I considered exposing him. Fame in the face of love is nothing.' Lily squeezed a tissue in her fist.

Victoria gave her a moment. 'Lily, we've spoken about your life with Richard. Now I would like to concentrate on the night of his death.' She paused to instruct the jury to turn to Lily's police interview in the jury bundle. 'In your account to the police, you said that you and Richard were hosting a party that day. What was his mood like?'

Lily kneaded the tissue, sending a shred to the floor. 'He was tetchy before it even started. I think he blamed me for encouraging him to have a launch. He had worked hard on his book and I thought we should celebrate, but it didn't look likely to hit the bestseller list and Richard was upset. As the party wore on, he became increasingly tense.'

'Did it affect your own mood?'

'Yes. I grew more tense myself. I tried to give him space, but that only made him madder. It was like I was supposed to stay by his side; to absorb his complaints and leave him unburdened. By the end, he was like a spark about to flare.'

'Is this after the last guest left?'

'Yes. I could tell that he was wound up and tried to work out the best thing to do: placate him or ignore him and carry on.' Lily took the jury through the next few moments: Harry storming out of the house, Richard blaming her.

'What happened next?'

'He threw a glass at me and it exploded over the wall.'

Victoria motioned at the screen, which showed shards of glass scattered across Lily's living room floor.

'I knew he would come for me so I instinctively picked up the cake knife. I said, "Don't you dare. Not tonight," and he gave me this look.' Lily's voice turned bitter. 'A pitying look as if he knew I wouldn't use it. And then he charged at me. It happened so fast. He was coming at me and my head was blaring with panic. I waved the knife in front of me to warn him to stop. But he didn't.' Lily's hands began to shake and she gripped the rail to still them. 'When I realised what had happened, I just started to scream. I saw the blood and the best way I can describe it is that my mind split in half. One half was just standing there screaming in horror and the other understood that I needed to act. That's the half that took over. I knelt by him and stemmed the blood.'

'How?'

'There was a tea towel around the ice bucket. That's what I grabbed.'

Victoria pointed at the screen. 'Members of the jury, you will find these pictures on page 114 of your bundles. The first was taken from previous witness Talia Wilde's Facebook page. It shows the tea towel wrapped around the ice bucket on the sideboard. The second picture was taken by the crime scene photographer and shows the bloodied tea towel that Lily held to her husband's throat.' Victoria turned back to Lily. 'Why did you reach for that towel?'

'I wanted to save him.'

'Why?'

'I didn't want to hurt him. I just wanted him to stop.'

Victoria nodded gravely. 'In your police interview, you said that you immediately dialled 999. Is that correct?'

'Yes. I had both hands on the tea towel so I told Siri to make the call.'

Victoria took this opportunity to play Lily's call to the emergency services.

My husband. He's hurt. He's bleeding. Oh god, please help.
'You sound distressed,' said Victoria.

'I was devastated.'

'Lily, did Richard ever ask you for a divorce?'

'No. Never.'

'If he *had* asked, would you have given it to him?'

'I don't know,' said Lily honestly. 'I would have asked him to go to therapy, to try to keep our family together. I genuinely believed that he could get better.'

Victoria's tone grew gentle. 'Did you know if Richard was having an affair?'

Lily swallowed. 'No, I did not.'

'Did you suspect that he was having an affair?'

'No. I knew there were things wrong with our marriage, but I never thought there was someone else.'

'Did you see Richard with Talia Wilde in your bedroom on the evening of the party?'

'No.'

'Did you see anything to indicate that they were having an affair?'

'No.'

'Was there any part of you that wanted to wreak revenge on Richard?'

'No.'

'Why did you pick up that cake knife?'

'I did it to defend myself. I couldn't handle another attack. I needed it to stop.'

'In that moment, when he charged at you, were you genuinely scared for your safety?'

'I was terrified.'

'Did you mean to kill him?'

'No.'

'Did you mean to seriously injure him?'

'No, I was just trying to protect myself.'

'If you could do that night again, would you do anything differently?'

Lily's voice trembled. 'I wouldn't have picked up that knife. I would have let him punch me, slap me, take his anger out on me.'

'Would you have sought help?'

Lily blinked and tears rolled down her cheeks. 'No,' she said, her voice low and pitiful. 'I would have carried on until *he* killed *me*.'

'Thank you,' said Victoria. She turned to the judge. 'I have no more questions, My Lord.'

*

Safa read over her article about Lily's evidence in chief. It was factual and succinct – as news is meant to be – and betrayed none of the turmoil that Safa had felt in court that morning. She pictured Lily in that restaurant in Boston, smiling even as Richard pinched her skin. The thought of him striking Lily over a hundred and fifty times filled Safa with not rage but something darker, something quiet and venomous: a slithery cobra of a feeling. If Richard weren't already dead, Safa would have found a way to hurt him, maybe not physically but in some other, irreversible way.

Safa's hand tensed on her mouse. Had Lily thought this very same thing? *He hurt me, so I'll hurt him.* And would Safa blame her if she *had*? This was the essential question that Safa would ask in her feature. She had a title and an angle now. *A Killing on Narrow Street* would ask the central question, 'Do women who kill their abusers really belong in prison?'

For the longest time, men who killed a cheating lover could claim loss of control, but women subjected to years of abuse had no such recourse. Mercifully, the law had changed, but victims who hit back still faced life in prison.

Safa imagined the stress of living with constant threat. The Glassman had pierced her own sense of safety: a tiny pinprick that leaked all day. For women like Lily, that pinprick was an open wound that seeped with constant dread. It was this vulnerability that Safa sought to capture in her feature. She wanted to reveal the Lily behind her public persona and explore the tragic legacy of abuse. Safa had to tread carefully, for she knew that the feature could end their friendship for good. She wasn't betraying Lily per se, but she *had* pulled out old photos and repurposed personal anecdotes to deepen the reader's sense of Lily. There were details in the piece – like the bare cupboards of her childhood – that she knew Lily would not want exposed. Safa was also keen to explore the idea of the perfect victim: resilient but never bold, fragile but not weak, upset but not irate. Conversely, she would look at the flawed victim, but this would be hard to do without looking at Lily's flaws. And if she did *that*, she would have to be honest.

She sighed, pushed back from her desk and headed to the newsroom kitchen. She would need coffee for this.

Kevin passed by and spotted her. 'Shouldn't you be in court?' he asked, sticking his head in.

'A juror had a commitment so we finished early.'

'How's the feature going?'

'Good. I've got lots of material.' She paused. 'I do have a dilemma though.'

Kevin motioned at the rickety table and they both took a seat.

'One thing I want to explore is how flawed victims are treated by the courts. We all know that women can be passively flawed – women like Juliet Culpen who didn't speak out or seek help – but what about those who are *actively* flawed? I also want to speak to women like Penelope Jackson, who stabbed her husband and refused to help when the paramedics on the phone begged her to.'

'Go on.'

'Okay, so we all know that Lily is passively flawed – she didn't speak out or seek help – but she's also actively flawed and I don't want to gloss over that.'

Kevin frowned. 'Why do you believe that?'

'Well, she has an edge that she hides from the public. I think she's done things that would turn people against her and I don't know if I should leave it alone for the sake of a clean narrative.'

Kevin mulled this over. 'What things?'

Safa shifted uneasily. 'Something happened when we were fourteen. There was a boy in our class – a loud, jokey kid. You know the type, needs attention, thrives on laughs. One day, he managed to insult Lily quite badly.' Safa recounted the story of Patrick Meaden and how Lily claimed to have seen him being abused. When she finished, Kevin leaned back in his chair, fingers laced behind his head.

'Well, you know what you have to do,' he said.

Safa grimaced. 'I need to talk to Patrick Meaden.'

'You need to talk to Patrick Meaden.'

'Dammit.'

Kevin shrugged as if to say *them's the breaks*.

'You're right,' Safa said wearily. 'Thank you.' She grabbed her flask and stood.

'You're doing good work, kid.'

Safa was startled by the praise. 'Thanks, *bawss*,' she said in a terrible New York accent. She headed back to her desk with colour in her cheeks and Kevin's laughter trailing her.

She set down her flask and pulled up the logical first port of call: Facebook. There were several Patrick Meadens but she dismissed each in turn for being too short, too dark, too pale, too ginger. None of them were the Patrick she was after. She cycled through all the obvious channels – social media, the electoral register, records from Companies House – but found nothing. She wracked her memory for details of him and jotted down a list:

    was funny

    was good at maths

    wore glasses

    moved away to south London – Plumstead?

It wasn't very much to go on, but it was a start. She began with a search for 'opticians in Plumstead' and found that there were seven. If Patrick had worn glasses as a child, there was a good chance he would still need them now. She scanned the list, knowing what Oliver Witherow would do: call each one and pretend to be Patrick Meaden hoping to change his address: '*SE18 7EA. No? Oh, there must be a typo. What do you have instead?*'

Safa, however, was bound by firmer ethics. She set aside the list and tried various other searches – 'maths tutors in Plumstead', 'maths clubs in Plumstead', 'amateur comedy Plumstead' – but came up empty. She scoured old reports about the alleged abuse and found an old picture of Patrick, his fine-boned face swamped by glasses. As she studied it, she remembered that he used to like cricket. He had tried out for a local team but had been rejected on account of his glasses.

He'd see two balls instead of one! one of their classmates had teased. *Oi, Patrick, ain't that right? You often play with two balls?*

Safa searched for cricket clubs in Plumstead. Nothing. She widened her search to Woolwich and scoured names and faces. Three rows down, she saw him: still slim, and taller, with sandy brown hair that was just a touch too long. When she read the caption, however, it said that his name was Patrick Fuller. Safa zoomed into his face, certain that it was him. He had a scar above his right eye, in the same place as Patrick Meaden.

Safa found the club's email address and drafted a short note asking to be put in touch with Mr Fuller as shown in the attached picture. 'I went to school with him,' she wrote, 'and have something important to discuss with him – if he would be willing.' As far as she could remember, the two of them had been on friendly terms. Patrick was funny and bolshie but also clever, which is something Safa could appreciate. She had always been nice to him, but hoped that her friendship with Lily wouldn't put him off.

Safa regarded the email with hesitation. It could open a can of worms and she had to be sure it was the right thing to do – not just for Lily but Patrick. As she hovered over the 'Send' button, she heard hurried footsteps behind her. She turned to find Tim, the intern, pink-faced with exertion.

'Safa!' He skidded to a stop by her desk. 'Safa, you won't believe this!' He shoved his phone at her.

She took it and frowned at the greasy film of fingerprints. Before she could read the email on screen, Tim blurted out his news.

'The BBC want me to do a documentary! A producer got in touch this morning! They said they loved my feature about Robert Knox.' Tim grabbed his phone back and scrolled. 'Here! They said they thought it was "extraordinarily sensitive and offered a rare and illuminating portrait of the working-class male experience."' He beamed. 'Safa! My own BBC documentary!'

Safa leapt up and hugged him. 'Tim, that's huge! Congratulations!'

'Safa, I couldn't have done it without you. Thank you so, so much.' He stammered a little when he added, 'You're the first person who's ever helped me like this.'

Safa felt a rush of affection. 'I'm proud of you.'

Tim seemed taken aback and Safa saw tears in his eyes. He coughed, embarrassed. 'Thank you,' he said again.

Safa checked her watch. 'Listen, come back in an hour and we'll go for a drink to celebrate.'

He lit up. 'Great. Thank you, Safa!' He scooted off, practically humming with energy.

Safa watched him go and felt a bittersweet pride. She was happy that Tim had got a foothold, but it also reminded her of what she so desperately wanted. Not a documentary per se, but recognition from the mainstream. *A Killing on Narrow Street* was her best shot and she had to go all in. She returned to her email for Patrick, took a deep breath and pressed 'Send'.

Chapter 15

Safa sat on the press bench and compulsively scanned the courtroom. Her gaze snagged on a figure in the public gallery, but he was too old to be the Glassman. She had spent four restless nights at her dad's house and was due to return to her flat this evening – a thought that filled her with dread. She kept picturing the Glassman, a stealthy, darting figure, moving through her flat, thumbing through her things, shifting everything just an inch. She imagined him in her bathroom, setting down his tools, calmly cutting the glass. The thought was so disturbing, it raised a sense of panic.

Safa pushed her nails into her thigh to bring herself back to the courtroom. The Glassman wasn't here. She wasn't being watched. The air in the room didn't help. There was a vulture-like hunger in it; the promise of something bloody. Today, Lily would face the prosecution and people were ready for a show.

Safa watched her in the witness box. She wore a dark suit with a rose-gold shirt and a pair of modest pearl earrings. Her blonde hair was loose, and Safa knew that this was no accident. It made her seem soft and approachable, more like the Lily from morning TV. This Lily, though, was nervous. She smoothed the lapel of her blazer, tucked a strand of hair behind her ear, laced her fingers together.

Lucien Garrett assessed her coolly. 'Ms Astor, you met Richard when you were eighteen years old, is that correct?'

'Yes, that's correct.'

'How old were you when you married him?'

'Twenty-one.'

'And how old are you now?'

'Thirty-five.'

'So that means you were married for . . . fourteen years, correct?'

'Yes.'

Garrett made a sound to show he was impressed. 'That's a mighty long time. You were in love, yes?'

'Yes.'

'You said in your evidence yesterday that people would describe Richard as intelligent, confident, charming, ambitious and successful. Did you think he was all those things?'

Lily shifted uneasily. 'Yes, I did.'

'According to you, Richard was violent towards you in the last three years of your marriage. Had he showed any signs of violence in the eleven years before that?'

'No. It was like he was triggered during the lockdowns.'

'Before that, did he ever pinch you under the table while dining with friends and family?'

'No.'

'Not once in *eleven* years?'

Lily exhaled slowly. 'No.'

'Did he ever punch you? Slap you? Kick you?'

'No.'

'Not once in eleven years?'

Lily's voice took on the slightest tension. 'No.'

'So let me see if I understand this correctly. You and Richard were happily married for eleven years during which he showed no evidence of violence whatsoever. Then, because of lockdown – something we *all* went through – he suddenly turns into a serial abuser who punches, kicks, slaps and pinches his wife and continues to do so with impunity for the next three years. Is that correct?'

'It wasn't as simple or as sudden as that,' said Lily, the tension in her voice rising. 'There were lots of things happening in his life. He had lost his job. His freelance work had dried up. He was feeling insecure.'

Garrett angled his head. 'Are you saying that your confident and charming husband – who himself had a media profile – decided to become a serial abuser *eleven years* into a loving marriage because he was feeling "insecure"?' Garrett rubbed his temple as if the mere *idea* of this pained him. He didn't wait for Lily to answer the question. 'You mentioned an incident at a lobster restaurant in Boston. Do you remember what restaurant this was?'

'No,' she said tersely.

Safa willed her to be calm. *Upset but not irate.*

'You said there were about nine people there. Who were they?'

Lily held back a sigh. 'There was me, Richard and Harry, my son. Then there was Richard's aunt and her husband, their two children and I can't remember who else.'

'You said that Richard spoilt the evening for everyone. How so?'

'As I said, he was griping about the lobster. Everyone offered to swap with him, even one of the kids, but he was determined to be mad.'

'"He was determined to be mad",' Garrett repeated. 'Ms Astor, if Richard was indeed pinching you beneath the table, how difficult would it have been to say, "Oh, Richard, you're hurting me" in a light tone as if it might have been by accident? Just as a gentle nudge to him to stop what he was doing?'

Lily grit her teeth. 'If I had done that, I would have paid for it threefold later. When he got like that, I had to appease him at all costs.'

'When he got like what?'

'Sullen, moody, angry.'

'And he had already spoilt everyone's evening?'

'Yes.'

'What if I told you that Richard's mother, Audrey Astor, knew exactly where and with whom you had dinner that night because she helped you coordinate with her side of the family?'

'I would have no reason to doubt you,' she said icily.

'What if Audrey Astor was able to provide us photographs of that evening? Would you want to reconsider your story?'

Safa saw the subtle change in Lily's face: from confusion to concern.

Garrett pointed at the screen. 'Your booking was for 7 p.m. These photos were taken at the harbour at 9.40 p.m., presumably after you had finished dinner.'

On screen was a collection of seven photographs. In each, Richard was shown with members of his family, all of whom were laughing or smiling. In one, Richard carried his young cousin on his shoulders. The cousin had covered Richard's eyes but his grin was clear: bright, warm and happy. In another, Richard leaned lovingly against his aunt. Her face was caught mid-laughter, blurry in her joy.

'Ms Astor, does this look like a family whose evening has been spoilt?' He paused. 'In fact, does this look like a man "determined to be mad"?'

Lily's gaze darted from picture to picture, as if they might offer up an answer. 'Pictures don't always tell the truth,' she said. 'Anyone can smile for a second.'

'Pictures don't always tell the truth, but neither do people. Isn't that true?'

Lily spoke carefully. 'Sometimes, yes.'

'Ms Astor, while you were at the lobster restaurant, who were you sitting next to?'

There was an eerie look in Lily's eyes that Safa couldn't place: anger, contempt or unease?

'I was between Richard and Harry,' she said.

Garrett motioned at the screen again. 'This photo was taken at 8 p.m. and it looks like you're about halfway through dinner.'

Safa examined the picture. It showed their party of nine around a circular table filled with plates of lobster in varying degrees of mess.

'What do you notice?' asked Garrett.

Lily's face was ashen.

'What you notice, Ms Astor?' When she didn't answer, Garrett did it for her. 'You are sitting between your son and Richard's aunt, *not* Richard.'

Safa looked at the jury; saw their surprise and confusion. It was clear that they had believed Lily's story.

'Tell me, Ms Astor, how exactly did Richard reach across his aunt and repeatedly pinch your thigh and arm?'

Lily weaved a little and Safa worried that she might faint. She steadied herself on the rail, her fingers gripping hard.

'He must have moved at some point,' said Lily, her voice brisk and edged with panic. 'Audrey didn't give you all the pictures.'

Safa winced. The dinner plates were filled with bits of shell and meat – not the sort of meal during which you can easily shift.

'I don't think he did move, Ms Astor,' said Garrett. 'I think you fabricated a story about Richard hurting you.'

'I didn't.'

'You said that Richard could be "volatile" and "vicious", and you used this dinner as an example of when others witnessed this, but the photos speak for themselves, don't they?' The first set of pictures was back on the screen. 'Does this look like a family who's had a terrible time? Does that look like a man who's "determined to be mad"?'

Lily seemed small and defeated, lost in Garrett's rhetoric. Safa willed her to bear up, but could see why she was wrong-footed. It *was* possible that Richard had moved during dinner, but it was patently untrue that he had spoiled everyone's evening. Richard's smile beneath his nephew's palms was clearly warm and genuine, and the pictures showed a family in the midst of a lovely evening.

Garrett fixed his steely gaze on Lily. 'I'll give you another opportunity to answer the question put to you by my learned friend: did others ever witness the so-called "volatile" and "vicious" side of Richard?'

Lily faltered. Garrett had debunked her last example and she was clearly wary of giving him more. 'I'm not sure.'

'Yesterday, you claimed that your husband had been violent towards you over one hundred and fifty times. Did this ever result in injuries?'

'Yes. Bruises, sometimes a bloody nose.'

Garrett made a note. 'Did you ever go to the doctor about these injuries?'

'No.'

'The hospital?'

'No.'

'Did you see any medical professional?'

Lily flexed her fingers. 'No.'

'Is there *any* medical evidence to prove these one hundred and fifty injuries?'

'No.'

Garrett sighed as if losing patience. 'Ms Astor, what exactly did you do about these injuries?'

'I tended to them myself.'

He tutted as if this somehow inconvenienced *him*. 'Did you tell any friends or family about the abuse?'

'No.'

'Why not?' His voice was hard with accusation.

'I was ashamed about it.'

'If *you* were the victim, why were *you* ashamed?'

Lily clenched her fist, then hid it behind her back. 'That's what victims do. You're made to feel ashamed, like it's your fault.'

'But in three whole years, you didn't tell any friends or family?'

'No,' Lily repeated.

Safa's chest was tight with anger. She felt powerless as she watched Garrett browbeat Lily. Justice had to be rigorous, Safa knew, but seeing a victim prodded and doubted always made her bristle. Safa imagined these same questions being put to Rukshana and the Glassman's other victims. The idea that those women could make it all the way to the witness box and be able to give answers that would satisfy a man like Lucien Garrett seemed like utter fantasy. Safa felt a sense of hopelessness, but pushed hard against it. Her job, her work, her *purpose*, would be empty if she didn't believe it was possible to arm the weak against the strong.

Garrett continued: 'Ms Astor, isn't it true that you have spoken on social media about your "difficult relationship with food"; that you advocate "openness, facing problems and talking it out"? That is a direct quote from your Instagram account, is it not?'

Lily was visibly uncomfortable. 'Yes.'

'So why *didn't* you? Why didn't you face your problems and talk it out?'

'I . . .' Lily faltered. 'I didn't want the attention. I didn't want people to rip apart my private life. I didn't want paparazzi following me around or entire podcasts dedicated to whether or not I was lying.'

Garrett looked at her slyly. 'You were worried that your story wasn't credible?'

'It's a vicious cycle. Women don't speak because they won't be believed. And then they're not believed because for so long they didn't speak.'

'And yet you still didn't speak?'

Lily was at a loss, still caught in the cycle.

He barrelled on: 'Ms Astor, we have established that you didn't seek medical help nor did you confide in family or friends. Tell me: did anyone see these one hundred and fifty bruises?'

Contempt showed on Lily's face. 'My bruises weren't always visible. Mostly, they were on my body, sometimes I would cover them with makeup, other times it was a light slap or something that didn't cause a bruise.'

'Did *anyone* see them?'

'My makeup artist on *Arise* saw a couple. One of the bruises was picked up by the news.'

'Just one? Out of a hundred and fifty?'

'Yes. As I said, the injuries were usually on my body.'

Safa grimaced. Lily's tone was tart and combative – not what juries wanted from a victim. She wished she could catch her eye, muster their old telepathy and tell her friend to be calm.

'This bruise that was picked up by the news. What caused it?' asked Garrett.

'Richard. He hit me because I had made dinner before he had had a chance to shower when he came home.'

Garrett nodded at the usher who handed Lily a clipping. 'Please read out the highlighted lines,' he instructed.

Lily's features grew pinched as she read. 'I'm very heartened by the nation's concern over my bruise. I was playing a rather overzealous game of tennis with my husband, Richard, on Saturday and a stray ball caught my temple. It's a good lesson to take to the future: we are not, and neither should we pretend to be, one of the Williams sisters.'

Safa recognised the quote from her own article. At the time, she had wondered about including the joke. Reporters owed a duty of care to their sources when they said something problematic, but this hadn't quite crossed the line and so Safa had left it in. Now, read out in court, it took on far more weight.

'Isn't it true that you got the bruise while playing a game of tennis?' asked Garrett.

'No. That's just what I told people.'

'Isn't it true that there is no proof of violence because there was no violence?'

'No.' Lily was tense, coiled tight like a spring. 'I'm not lying.'

'Then or now?'

Lily's voice was strained. 'Women lie all the time to hide their abuse. I was lying then, but I'm not lying now.'

'I see,' said Garrett archly. 'Ms Astor, in your interview with the police, you said that you attended a support group for victims.' He flicked a page in his notebook. 'Specifically, the "Violence Against Women and Girls" group that meets at the Poplar Community Centre. Is that correct?'

'Yes.'

'If that's true, why can't a single woman from that group remember you?'

Lily paled. 'I disguised my identity,' she said. 'I was wary of my story being sold to the papers and so I guarded my privacy.'

'Ah, yes. You described this "disguise" to the police: brunette wig, bottle-top glasses, ripped jeans and a baggy hoodie. Ms Astor, the facilitator has run the group *every* Thursday since 2018 and is certain she hasn't met you, or any other woman fitting that description. You can't explain that, can you?'

'She must be mistaken.'

'The truth is that you didn't really go to these sessions, did you? There's no proof at all that Richard was abusing you, so you concocted your attendance at this violence group.'

'That's not true.'

'If you needed therapy so desperately that you would wear a *disguise* to the support group, why not just pay for a personal therapist? I assume that you can afford to do so?'

'I told you. I didn't want anyone to know about the abuse. Group therapy meant less scrutiny.'

'I submit that Richard Astor never laid a finger on you. Men don't decide after eleven years of marriage to start beating their wives. What they *might* do is decide to have an affair, just as Richard did with Talia Wilde. I submit that you found out and decided to confront him. You picked up that knife, knowing full well that it could cause serious injury and are now using one bruise – *one* bruise after so-called *years* of abuse – to fashion a story of domestic violence. Isn't this right?'

All colour was gone from Lily's face. 'That's not true.'

'Answer this, Ms Astor: were you scared of your husband?'

'Yes, I was.'

'But we have heard evidence that you were flirting with your cameraman at the party. That's very odd behaviour for someone who fears her husband, wouldn't you say?'

Lily squared her jaw. 'I wasn't flirting with him.'

'We have heard that you touched him repeatedly, were laughing with him and seemed very much at ease. Isn't that the case?'

'I was being a good hostess,' Lily said helplessly.

'But to only one guest?'

'To all my guests.'

'You were getting your own back, weren't you?'

'No.'

'You knew that Richard was having an affair with Talia Wilde, didn't you?'

'No.'

'You picked up that knife with intention of using it.'

'No. I never meant to hurt him.'

'But you *had* threatened to, hadn't you? A few months earlier, on Christmas Eve?'

'No.'

'Your neighbour *heard* you. Why did you threaten Richard?'

'I didn't threaten him.'

'Your neighbour says you did.'

'He's mistaken.'

'Tell the truth, Ms Astor. You knew about the affair, didn't you?'

'I didn't.'

Garrett pulled a bundle of paper out of his notebook. 'Ms Astor, we came across a curiosity when we looked at Richard's search history.'

Lily tensed, sensing danger.

'We noticed that Richard used "Find My Device" frequently. Initially, we assumed that he was forgetful, but it happened too often – two to three times a week – to be natural.'

Safa bristled. Lily's defence team would have had access to the same data but this sometimes ran into thousands of pages and a 'curiosity' could be easily missed.

'Were you keeping tabs on Richard's whereabouts?' asked Garrett.

Lily's face was drawn. 'Yes, but only so I would know when I could and couldn't relax.'

'There were two search results that placed him at 125 Cedar Drive in Bow, East London. Do you know who lives at that address?'

Lily measured her words. 'It's familiar, but I couldn't say without looking it up.'

Garrett assessed her coolly. 'That is the address of Richard's mistress, Talia Wilde, but you already knew that, didn't you? You knew that Richard was with her on these two occasions.'

Lily didn't answer.

'You confronted him about it, didn't you?'

Again, she didn't answer.

'Here's what's curious,' said Garrett. 'The two dates that place Richard at Talia's house match exactly with two events we've already heard about in this trial.' Garrett paused, making the jurors crane forward. 'The first date was Christmas Eve last year; the same day your neighbour heard you say *I'm scared I'll kill you one day.*

Garrett let that sink in. 'The second was the morning of Saturday 6th April.' Another pause. 'The day you killed your husband.'

There was motion in the courtroom: a scuttling haste on the press bench as journalists vied to break the news. Safa felt the swing of dread. Lily's evidence had been called into question. There was simply too much coincidence to account for the discrepancies, which left one explanation: Lily was lying to the jury.

*

Safa was jostled out of the courtroom in a thicket of people. She dodged a horde of photographers as they converged on Lily's departing van. They held their cameras up to the blacked-out windows, hoping to get a picture of the fallen national treasure. Safa looked on with disdain, but knew she was complicit. This was, after all, why she had got into journalism: the addictive thrill of a landmark story.

The van joined traffic, losing the crowd around it. Safa spotted Natalie on the opposite side of the road, huddled in an alcove. Her cheeks were gaunt as she sucked on a cigarette. Safa nipped across between two passing buses.

'Natalie, hi. I haven't seen you in a while.'

Natalie lowered her cigarette. 'Yeah, sorry.' She gestured towards the photographers. 'I try to sneak out before court gives out, so I can avoid the circus.' She adjusted her glasses and tousled her hair, but it remained lank on her scalp. The ends had become frayed and desperately needed a cut. 'Safa, can I ask you a question?' She took a nervous drag of her cigarette. 'Do you think Lily will be put away?'

Safa feared that this was a real possibility. 'Don't lose hope, Natalie. Harry's evidence could turn it all around. He can prove that she's telling the truth.'

Natalie watched Lily's van until it was out of sight. 'What happens to Harry if she does? Do I have to keep him forever?' She shook her head. 'I never even wanted kids. Not after Mum.'

Safa felt a rush of solidarity. She knew what it was to forgo motherhood. As the older sibling, Natalie had borne the brunt of her mother's alcoholism. She had had to look after a child with neither the tools nor funds. Now, history was repeating itself with Harry.

For a brief moment, Safa wondered if he could live with her, but dismissed it out of hand. Harry had a deep-seated sense of rejection. He knew that his mother had tried to abort him. Learning that his aunt didn't want him could be devastating. Natalie had to step up and be there for him.

'Natalie, just hang on,' she told her. 'It won't be long before we know either way and then we can look at your options.' She paused. 'Is money a problem?'

Natalie flushed. 'No. Lily is sending me something every month. It's not that, Safa. I've barely got a GCSE to my name. I don't know how to raise a child like him.'

Safa recalled her father's words. 'I think what he needs is lots of love. He's lost his father and essentially his mother, and he just needs love, Nat.'

Natalie looked away. 'I never had that. I don't know how to give that.'

'We'll figure it out together.' Safa touched her arm. It was thin and birdlike under her palm. 'What if I came by later? I've got a meeting now, but we could talk about it then?'

Natalie waved, leaving a trail of smoke. 'No, that's okay. We can talk another day.'

'Are you sure? I could bring takeout.'

'No, no, that's okay. I've got stuff in the freezer.'

Safa thought of the pile of ready meal boxes stuffed into her bin. 'Okay,' she said, not wanting to push. 'You'll call me if you need me?'

'Yeah, course.'

'Okay.' Safa checked her watch. 'I should go.' She gave her a quick hug, then turned and headed to the tube en route to Plumstead.

*

Safa stepped off the bus and glanced around quickly to get her bearings. She rarely ventured to southeast London, but Patrick Meaden worked from home and had agreed to let her visit. She made her way to a housing development where the houses looked so similar, she hadn't been able to tell one side of the street from the other when she'd looked it up on Google Street View. The development was neat and expansive, but at least two decades old and showing signs of wear: discoloured bricks where pipes had leaked, guttering that hung askew, potholes that hadn't been filled.

She located house number seven and rang the doorbell. Her throat felt dry and she swallowed hard to work up her nerve. She heard footsteps approach and, a moment later, Patrick opened the door. He was slim with thinning hair and wore rimless glasses.

'Hi, Safa. Long time no see.' He rolled his eyes. 'God, how banal. Come in, come in.'

Safa was transported back to childhood where Patrick's droll humour was a familiar feature in the classroom. 'I'm sorry to have got in touch out of the blue like this,' she said.

He gave her a strange, wistful look. 'You know, I always expected *someone* to, but I thought it would be Lily.' There was an awkward pause. 'Anyway, come in.'

The living room was large but cosy, and clearly home to someone unbothered by guests seeing mess. There were piles of books everywhere, blankets strewn across the sofa and plants invading living space. Patrick cleared a place on the sofa for her.

'I'll be back with tea,' he said, not asking how she liked it. He returned moments later with two individual teapots, a jug of milk and a bowl of sugar balanced on a tray. He slid it onto the table, making two books spill over, and sat opposite Safa.

They skirted around the subject at first, opting to reminisce over simpler memories: the intense sugar hit of the school's sticky toffee pudding, the dinner lady who gave extra helpings to skinny kids.

'So I guess you know why I'm here,' she said eventually.

'Yeah.' He dug his hands beneath his thighs.

'You must have seen the news about Lily?'

'Yeah, she's been pretty hard to avoid,' he said with a sardonic nod.

'I'm doing a story and I wanted to see if you'd be willing to talk to me. It's a long read about women who kill their abusers.' Safa explained her vision for the feature.

Patrick grew tense as he listened. 'It sounds like a crusade to free Lily.'

Safa couldn't deny that this was partly her goal. 'Patrick, I want to explore the idea of the flawed victim. We both know that Lily isn't perfect and I don't want to skirt over that.'

'I don't know, Safa. I don't want to resurrect those demons.'

She held his gaze. 'Maybe it's time to exorcise them.'

Patrick bristled, but when he spoke, his tone was gentle. 'Maybe. I think that's why I agreed to see you.' He bobbed his head wryly. 'Therapy hasn't bloody managed it.'

Safa set down her phone. 'How about we talk for a while and if you don't feel comfortable, we press pause?'

'Okay,' he agreed quietly. He gripped his empty cup and sat up a little straighter. 'It was like a freight train,' he began. 'One day I was a normal kid. And the next I was . . . I didn't even know what.' He made a bitter sound. 'I had the whole range, you know? From kids calling me gay to adults saying I had Stockholm Syndrome to my parents treating me like a delicate flower. Throughout it all, no one would believe me. Things got so bad, we had to move.'

'Is that why you changed your name?' Safa nodded at the pile of mail. 'Your picture in the paper said Patrick Fuller.'

'No. That's because I took my husband's name.'

'Oh, I see.' At school, Patrick hadn't spoken about his sexuality.

'Yeah, I'm gay,' he said with a shrug. 'Here's the thing, Safa. I never had a problem with being gay. Fine, I wasn't "out" but it's not like I tried to hide it. I was just who I was. Lily must have seen me with a boy and instead of just outing me like a garden-variety arsehole, she made up this fucking monstrous lie about me being abused.'

Safa digested this. 'Might Lily have misunderstood what was happening? Maybe she thought you were being forced?'

'There was never any car, Safa. Don't you think I'd remember? It's not like I had so many sexual experiences that I forgot a bunch of them. Tower Hamlets was hardly awash with gay kids. There was never any car. There was never an adult. I was never abused.'

Safa simply couldn't believe that Lily had fabricated the entire thing. 'Was there a time you were in a car with someone else? An uncle? A family friend?' she pressed.

'No, Safa. Do you think we could afford a car? My mum had to take the 309 bus to Lidl and would come back with marks in her hands from the weight of the bags. If there was ever a car I'd know.'

'Patrick, are you sure?'

'I'm one hundred per cent certain.'

Safa felt a darkness settle over her. 'You really think she made it all up?'

'I know she did.'

Safa was chilled. She remembered the detail in Lily's report: the way the man's hair curled into his ear, the green cast in his stubble, the crescent of dirt in his thumbnail; detail that a fourteen-year-old would struggle to concoct. On top of that, there was the *consistency*. When Lily's mother, her teachers, the police asked her about it, she never once wavered.

'Could she have seen another boy and mistaken him for you?' said Safa in a final plea.

'You already know the answer to that.'

Safa did know. Lily had specifically described Patrick's scar: a two-centimetre slash above his right eye. Safa had been convinced that Patrick had been abused. The possibility that Lily had made it up was too appalling to consider. 'Did you ever talk to her about it?'

'Yes. I saw her in Stratford one day. I remember approaching her with my hands up because I didn't want to scare her off.' His lips twisted bitterly. 'But she was completely unruffled. She told me that I should stop pretending and tell the truth. It was eerie, like she'd convinced herself of the lie. Then, before she left, she gave me this little smile. She *knew*, Safa. And she wanted me to know that she knew.'

Safa was disoriented. The foundations of what she believed about Lily shifted, leaving her unsteady. Could it be that the things Safa admired about Lily – her spine, her drive, her mettle – calcified into something harder underneath the surface? Safa knew that Lily could be ruthless, and occasionally vindictive, but if what Patrick had said was true, then she took real pleasure in malice. Safa pictured that look on her face when she stood at the edge of the classroom watching the gossip spread. And, later, her glib dismissal: *Don't be silly. Being gay is cool now.* Hadn't that always gnawed at her?

A line from court came to her: *there is no proof of violence because there was no violence.*

Patrick watched her grapple with it. Softly and without accusation, he said, 'I never understood why you were friends with her.'

Safa was quiet for a moment. 'Did you know that, sometimes, she didn't have enough to eat?'

Patrick frowned. 'What do you mean?'

'I mean literally. There was nothing in the cupboards at home.

Sometimes, she and her sister, Natalie, would eat rice and salt – just plain rice and salt. And although I tried to help, and share my food with her, we never talked about it, you know? I never sat her down and said, "Hey, I know you don't want to get your mum in trouble but you don't have enough to eat and maybe we need to tell someone." She just learned how to survive.

'I was her friend because she was tough and resilient and resourceful and brave.' Safa swallowed. 'But maybe all that survival turned something mean inside her.'

'Does that excuse what she did?'

'No.' Safa was wistful. 'It doesn't.'

A silence opened up between them and Patrick set down his cup. 'Are you likely to see her?'

'Yes.'

'Can you tell her that I'd like to talk to her sometime? Tell her I'm not angry. I just . . . I want her to say sorry.'

Safa saw his throat contract, his pain right near the surface. 'I will, Patrick. I promise.'

He talked for a while longer: the whiplash of moving to southeast London, coming out to his parents, falling in love and starting a career as a graphic designer. Eventually, when they ran out of things to say, Safa moved to leave. She didn't know if or how to touch him, so just shifted on her feet awkwardly. 'Thank you for meeting me.'

'I'll see you out.' In the hallway, they shared a quick hug.

Safa stepped into the October night and felt a sense of vertigo. Patrick's certainty had put her world on a tilt. Her mind spun with a question: had she been wrong to trust Lily?

Chapter 16

Safa awoke with a jolt. Her heart raced as she sifted through the sounds: the hum of the fridge in the kitchen, the flush of a toilet in the flat above, the rumble of a plane in the sky. There was no errant footstep, no foreign clink of glass. She was in her bedroom, safe. The sheets were damp with sweat despite it being October. Safa threw them off and sat up, her heart still beating fast.

Imran had offered to stay with her, but she had insisted on spending the night alone. It was her way of reclaiming her space; of convincing herself that she wasn't afraid. Imran had spent the last few days poring over CCTV of the surrounding streets, but had found no trace of the Glassman. Safa shivered and grabbed her robe. In the bathroom, she showered with the door wide open; her small act of defiance. *Come and get me*, she thought with bravado she knew was false. She dressed quickly and left for court. On the train, she found herself scanning the carriage at every stop. She flinched when she saw a figure in black step on, but it turned out to be a woman. Safa was angered by her own skittishness and took slow, deliberate breaths to try to calm herself.

At the Old Bailey, she passed through security and took her place in courtroom eight. She pushed the Glassman out of her mind. They had reached an important stage of the trial and she couldn't lose focus now. She assessed the witness, an older gentleman taking the oath. He had thick white hair, clear skin and good teeth, and wore a well-cut suit. He introduced himself as Dr Julian Evans, a consultant forensic psychologist with over three decades of experience. He spoke with authority and had the polished manner of someone comfortable in a public forum. Victoria Hersham stood to examine her second witness.

'Dr Evans, you mentioned that you have three decades of experience. Now, "forensic psychology" is a bit abstract. Can you explain in layman's terms what you do?'

A flash of white teeth. 'Yes, of course.' He spoke to the jury instead of Victoria as any experienced expert witness would. 'In a nutshell, I assess people and situations. That can be anything from risk of violence or risk of recidivism to suggestibility in people with learning disability. Now, I know that's a mouthful so, in essence, I try to answer questions like "is this person likely to harm their spouse?" or "is this person likely to re-offend?" or "has this person been coerced into giving a confession?"'

'Thank you, doctor. And did you assess Lily Astor?'

'Yes, I did.'

'What question were you trying to answer?'

'"Did Lily Astor act in self-defence on the night she killed her husband?"'

'How did you go about answering that?'

'I spent several hours with Lily talking to her about her relationship with her husband and the events of 6th April. In doing so, I was trying to identify whether her response was proportionate and reasonable.'

'Regarding the night in question, Lily said that she picked up the knife and told Richard to stop moving towards her, but he carried on regardless. Given that he didn't strike her, can her actions still be classed as self-defence?'

Dr Evans nodded sagely. 'Yes. There is no rule in law to say that a person must wait to be struck first before they may defend themselves. Nor is there a rule to say she should retreat. Lily was under extreme stress and picked up the knife as a result.'

'Was she was panicked in the moment?'

'Yes, but it's important to note that victims of domestic violence react not just because they're panicked in a single, isolated moment. Their response doesn't have to be sudden and temporary; it can be a buildup over time because of abuse. In fact, the law changed in 2010 because victims of domestic abuse were being short-changed. Men who killed their partners as a result of, say, sexual infidelity were said to have enacted a crime of passion and that gave us the language to acquit them. Victims of domestic violence, on the other hand, don't tend to act in a single crime of passion. The breakdown happens over time and that often culminates in a single incident, so we must judge them as part of a timeline.'

'And what did Lily's timeline tell you?'

'Lily's behaviour was consistent with other victims of domestic violence. She was suffering insomnia, she showed signs of disordered eating, she was withdrawing from her social circle and experiencing anxiety. When her husband charged at her that night, it triggered a stress response. In that moment, Lily feared serious violence. Picking up that knife was indeed an act of self-defence.'

'But he hadn't yet hit her.' Victoria pre-empted the prosecutor's questions to take the wind out of his argument.

'In cases of self-defence, a *fear* of serious violence is enough. In Lily's case, her history with her husband would have certainly made her fearful enough.'

Victoria nodded meditatively. Over the next hour, she led the doctor and the jury through the psychology of abuse, mapping symptoms to Lily at every opportunity. 'In summary, Dr Evans, did Lily act in a manner which could be expected of a reasonable person in her situation?'

'Yes, she did. Everything about her behaviour is consistent with someone who has experienced domestic violence over a prolonged period of time.'

'Could one of us have done what she did had we experienced the same abuse?'

'Yes, any one of us.'

Victoria nodded solemnly. 'Thank you.' She turned to the judge. 'I have no further questions, My Lord.'

Safa leaned back in her seat, the air in her coat deflating. She studied Lily in the dock. Her face was like marble: smooth and expressionless. Before Safa had met with Patrick Meaden, her support for Lily had been simple. *Believe the woman* was not just a rallying cry, but a moral compass that marked a clear path. Now, that path was muddy, marred by half-truths and outward lies. There was one thing that Safa knew for certain: Lily was cleverer than most people thought. Both Lily-Ann Baker, the skinny kid from a council estate, and Lily Astor, the bubbly presenter on morning TV, had more cunning than others suspected. The more Safa thought about it, the harder she found it to believe that Lily hadn't known that Richard was cheating – but would she have physically attacked him for it? Would she then have been so cavalier to claim abuse without any proof?

With a cold jolt, Safa realised that it wouldn't be the first time Lily had concocted a story of abuse in an outsize act of revenge. Isn't that what she had done to Patrick for a far lesser offence? Safa couldn't make sense of the case. It was like picking for the lip of tape, going round and round in circles. When she finally found it, things would begin to unravel.

*

Lucien Garrett fixed his wizened gaze on the witness. Dr Evans was calm and authoritative and Safa hoped that he would hold up under the prosecutor's scrutiny.

'Dr Evans, I would like to check a few things about the evidence you gave this morning.' Garrett paused as if he had just thought of something. 'I'm sorry, are you a *medical* doctor? You weren't very clear this morning.'

'No. I have a PhD in forensic psychology.'

'From where?'

'From the University of Newcastle Upon Tyne,' said the doctor.

'Oh? I haven't heard of that.'

'It's more commonly known as Newcastle University.'

'I see.' Garrett arched his brows. 'Dr Evans,' he said with the slightest inflection on *doctor*. 'You said that the defendant Lily Astor feared serious violence. How would you describe serious violence?'

'Violence that results in physical harm: wounding where the skin is broken either internally or externally, bleeding, bruising or a broken bone would all be examples.'

'In your assessment of Lily Astor, were you able to look at her medical history?'

'Yes, it's in my report.'

'Did you find history of wounding?'

'No, but it's very normal for victims to not seek treatment for their injuries.'

'Was there history of bleeding?'

'No, but—'

'A simple yes or no will do. Was there a history of bruising?'

The doctor sighed. 'I see where you're going with this but as I said, it's very normal for victims to not report their injuries.'

'Okay, let's be very clear here. Have you seen any *physical* medical evidence to support the narrative of abuse? Yes or no?'

'No, but—'

'Okay, so there is no medical evidence of serious violence. Dr Evans, do you *know* that Richard was going to physically hurt Lily that evening?'

'No, but even if he were not, if Lily feared and believed that he would – even incorrectly – she would still be acting in self-defence.'

'How do you know that she feared it?'

'Because I assessed her.'

'But there is no evidence to show that he was violent towards her.'

The doctor sighed. 'My assessment *is* evidence.'

'Ah,' Garrett said in a mocking tone. 'She *told* you she was scared and therefore she was scared, is that how it works?'

'No. I may not be a medical doctor, sir, but there *is* a science to what I do.'

Safa winced. His retort came off petty and defensive.

Garrett continued. 'Lily Astor picked up a knife and slashed her husband's throat with it. Would you say that this was reasonable force?'

'Based on my assessment, yes.'

'Would a reasonable person – a member of this jury, say – use the same level of force as Lily did?'

'Yes. That's precisely what reasonable force *means*,' said the doctor. As the hour wore on, he grew increasingly tetchy. Safa feared that, in the eyes of the jury, it would dignify Garrett's earlier jibe. If the doctor was truly secure in his expertise, he wouldn't be so defensive. It was these subtleties that could turn a jury against an expert witness.

Garrett closed his notebook but he wasn't finished. 'Dr Evans, you have given evidence in a number of cases. Tell me: does self-defence still stand if a defendant acts out of revenge?'

'No, it does not.'

'So, if someone kills their spouse because they're having an affair, that would not be an act of self-defence?'

'No, but—'

'Thank you.' Garrett turned to the judge. 'I have no further questions, My Lord.'

*

Safa checked her watch. She had only an hour before visiting hours were over at HMP Bronzefield and security was taking an age. When she finally got into the visitors' room, she spotted Lily in the furthest chair, her knees primly together. Her hair and her makeup – still neat from court that day – were at odds with her grey sweater and joggers. It occurred to Safa that Lily was truly a chimera. In her experience, social climbers were never truly convincing. There was something innate about a good pedigree that was hard to fake. Most people lacked the polish – the good skin, the quiet luxury – to do it successfully. Lily, however, had mastered the poise and accent, and seemed entirely out of place in Bronzefield.

Safa sat down opposite her. 'How are you feeling?'

'I'm okay.' Lily angled her head, sensing Safa's mood. 'What's going on?'

Safa set down her pen and notebook. 'I'm going to ask you something, Lily, and I want you to tell me the truth.' She watched Lily closely. 'I saw Patrick Meaden yesterday.'

'Patrick Meaden?' Lily frowned as if she were searching her memory. 'That loudmouth kid from school?'

'Yes,' Safa said stiffly. 'That kid from school.'

'Okay. And?'

'And he told me what happened back then.'

For a moment, Lily was neutral but then her features darkened. 'You're seriously going to do this now?'

'Patrick said that you lied about what happened back then.'

Lily grew rigid with hostility. 'Where did you even find him? Why are you digging into this?'

'Is he right?' Safa kept the edge from her tone. 'Patrick said there was never a car. What did you really see?'

'Why are you bringing this up now?' Lily's voice was acid. 'Are you trying to spice up your story? "The two faces of Lily Astor" – is that it?'

'I'm trying to get to the truth.'

'And a Whitney wouldn't hurt, right?'

Safa's cheeks coloured. 'That's not what this is about.'

'Don't lie, Safa. It doesn't suit you.' Lily leaned forward. 'You sold this to me as a crusade to help victims but it's really about making your name. Who the fuck wants to read eight thousand words on domestic violence? No one gives a shit about violence against women – it's the oldest story in the world – and no one will give a shit about your moralising. But a hit piece on Lily Astor and her long history of lies? Now *that's* going to get attention, isn't it? That's going to get the clicks.'

Safa was intent on staying calm. 'That's not what I'm doing. You know that.'

'Then why are you tracking down Patrick Meaden? What does he have to do with any of this?'

'I'm trying to work out who you are.'

Lily stalled. 'What's that supposed to mean?' Her hostility faded, giving way to something else: surprise, or maybe even sorrow. 'Why would you say that?'

'Because sometimes I wonder.' Safa could see that this hurt Lily, but had said it because it was true. All her life, Safa had believed that Lily was strong and smart and fearless and therefore *good*, but there were things she had overlooked. Lily with that adult smile: *'Don't be silly. Being gay is cool now.'* Lily applying to Oxford in thief-like secret. Lily bragging about how she had got rid of her mother's boyfriend. All her snark and wit hidden from the public. Safa shivered as goose bumps rose on her skin.

Lily shook her head. 'You *know* me, Safa. You said it yourself: some days, it feels like you're the only one who does.'

'Then tell me,' Safa said quietly. 'What really happened with Patrick?'

'Safa, I was in court yesterday being ripped to pieces. Today, I had to hear how I *must* be lying because I didn't tell anyone that my husband was beating the shit out of me. I don't have the headspace to deal with something that happened when we were kids.'

'He said he would like to see you.'

'That's not going to happen.' Lily knotted her hands in her lap and Safa saw that they were shaking.

'Not now, but maybe after the trial?'

'So he can get his piece of Lily Astor? I don't think so.' She tried to push her chair back but it was bolted to the floor.

'Lily, don't you think you owe him a conversation?'

'Safa, what you don't understand is that everyone from my past thinks I owe them something. Why has Patrick reared his head now? Because he believes he can get something out of this.'

'It's not like that. *I* approached him.'

'Then maybe you should ask why *you* believe that I owe you something.'

The question silenced Safa because of course she believed that very thing.

'You know what? I'm done,' said Lily. 'I am done with the headlines and the speculation and the *glee* of all these fucking journalists who were meant to be my colleagues.' Lily shoved Safa's notebook. 'I'm done with this.' She stood and turned to go.

Safa caught her sleeve. 'Can you just answer me this?' She stood so that she was level with Lily. 'Did you know that Richard was having an affair?'

Lily exhaled slowly, gathering her patience. 'No, I didn't know, Safa. I was too busy surviving.'

Safa let her hand drop. 'I'm sorry to ask you that.'

Lily scoffed. 'It's okay. Everybody believes women until what they say is unbelievable.' She stepped back and signalled to the guard that she was ready to go.

Safa slackened. How could it be that after all these years, Lily was still an enigma? And how could Safa preach about believing women and somehow still not trust her?

Chapter 17

Jenna McAlister was dressed like a schoolgirl: white shirt, grey skirt with knee-high socks and court shoes. Her hair had a streak of purple and jewellery tinkled everywhere: her ears, her neck, her wrists. She was what Safa would describe in print as 'alternative'. The girl took the oath and glanced at Lily repeatedly. She was clearly nervous as she explained who she was: a makeup artist who worked with Lily at *Arise*.

Victoria Hersham began with some basic questions. Jenna was a witness for the defence and it was important to put her at ease before moving to trickier territory.

'Jenna, did you do Lily's makeup on the morning of 25th March?'

Her eyes flicked to the dock as if seeking confirmation. 'Yes.'

'Did you notice anything unusual while you were doing her makeup?'

'Yes. Lily was wearing large shades, which in itself isn't unusual, but when she took them off, she had a big bruise around her left eye.'

'Did you ask how she got the bruise?'

'No. Before I could ask, Lily told me that it was an accident; that it happened during a game of tennis.'

'Did you believe her?'

Jenna considered this. 'Ultimately, yes, but I did notice that she seemed nervous, like she was keen to jump in with a reason. I felt that if it was truly innocent, she would have been a bit more relaxed about it.'

'Did you press her on this?'

'I told her she should get it checked out but she insisted it was fine. What worried me is when she asked me not to tell anyone. It was a real concern for her.'

'Was that the only time Lily came to work with bruises?'

'No. The next week, she was on air and she accidentally spilled coffee when her co-presenter nudged her. She didn't want to take off her cardigan. She got into a real tizzy about it, saying that she was cold and all sorts. I started to take it off her and that's when I saw that her shoulder had a massive bruise.'

Safa remembered that a crewmember had tipped off the press. This was the bruise that had sent her to Narrow Street and that strained conversation with Richard. She wished now that she had forced her way inside.

Victoria motioned at one of the screens in the courtroom. 'You can in fact see it here, can't you?' A clip showed Lily on the set of *Arise*. She was stiff and awkward, unlike her normal self. Her long blonde hair was tossed over one shoulder and, if you looked closely, you could see that it was masking a bruise. A zoomed-in screenshot showed the bruise more clearly. Seeing the purple-green of it made Safa ashamed of her clash with Lily. How alone she must have felt concealing this from everyone. Safa remembered the lightness in her tone when they spoke in March. *We are not, and neither should we pretend to be, one of the Williams sisters.* How skilled she was at hiding the truth.

'Did you talk to Lily about this new injury?' asked Victoria.

'Yes. I went to her dressing room, but she said it was a riding accident.' Jenna made a face. 'This time, I didn't believe her and I told her so. She denied that anything was wrong, tried to make light of it, but I could see she was on the verge of tears. That's when I knew she was being abused.'

*

Before he spoke, Lucien Garrett took a moment to assess Jenna McAlister. It was clear what he thought of her outfit and excessive jewellery: frivolous, puerile, not to be taken seriously. Jenna neatened the purple swatch in her hair, then closed her fingers over her bangles to stop their cheap rattle. Safa knew what it was like to be held in disdain by an older white man. For all her grit and brass, she too had been made to feel small by men like Lucien Garrett.

'Ms McAlister, how long have you been Lily's makeup artist?'

'Five years,' said Jenna.

'How many times a week do you do her makeup?'

'Five days a week.'

'Once a day?'

'Once in the morning and then small touch-ups throughout the morning.'

'I'd like to do a rough calculation if that's okay. Lily takes eight weeks of holiday per year, which means she works forty-four weeks of the year. Five years multiplied by forty-four weeks multiplied by five days equals 1,100. So you have done Lily's makeup at least 1,100 times, is that correct?'

'If the maths are right, then, yes.'

'In the 1,100 times that you have done Lily's makeup, how many times have you seen bruising on her?'

Jenna's gaze flicked to the dock. 'Two,' she said with hesitation.

'In addition to the two you talked about this morning?'

'No. Just two.'

'Just two,' Garrett repeated theatrically. He spent some minutes on Lily's first bruise, mainly to remind the jury of Lily's quip at the time: *we are not, and neither should we pretend to be, one of the Williams sisters*. 'Ms McAlister, can you remind us how Lily explained the second bruise?'

'She said it was a horse riding accident.'

'As far as you know, does Lily ride?'

'Yes.'

'Do you know how often?'

'I believe she rides weekly.'

'So it was a perfectly valid explanation?'

'Yes, but—'

Garrett didn't let her finish. 'You said that Lily denied that anything was wrong. Do you recall what she said exactly?'

'She sort of laughed it off and said, "Come on, Jenna. You know me. Do you really think I'd let myself become a *battered woman*?"'

Safa winced. Lily had said those exact words to her in that exact tone: careless, breezy, more than a little judgemental. This was contemporaneous evidence, but not in Lily's favour. In fact, it was evidence of the worst sort. It showed Lily directly contradicting herself, but almost worse was the *tone*. Juries and indeed the public liked victims who were sedate, modest, earnest. Any hint of bite or verve could turn a jury off.

'"Do you think I'd let myself become a battered woman?"' Garrett repeated. 'How did you respond to this?'

Jenna's hand went to her hair, then came back down again. 'I tried to get Lily to open up, but she brushed it off. We sort of joked about it and then I left it.'

'You *joked* about it?'

Jenna grimaced. 'Not like making light of it, more just . . .' She didn't know how to finish the sentence.

'What was the joke?'

Jenna coloured. 'I said I was going to be watching her body like an incel.'

Garrett stared at her. 'Are you saying that you *genuinely* believed that Lily was being abused and yet you joked that you would be watching her body like an incel?'

'Yes, but it was just gallows humour.'

'Forgive me, Ms McAlister, but I don't understand the joke.' Garrett tapped his notebook imperiously. 'In your earlier evidence, you said, "That's when I knew she was being abused." You *knew*, you said. But instead of encouraging her to speak out, or reporting it to an authority, or trying to get her help, or doing any of the dozen things a responsible adult would do for a victim of abuse, you "joked about it" and then "left it". Is that what you're saying?'

Jenna twisted one of her bangles. 'It wasn't like that. I was respecting her privacy.'

'But you said you *knew* she was being abused. If *I* knew that my very good colleague was being abused, I wouldn't "leave it" just because she wanted me to. Why did *you*?'

Jenna was at a loss. 'I don't know. I should have said something.'

'I put it to you, Ms McAlister, that the reason you didn't say something is because you *knew* the bruises were innocent. It's only in retrospect that you have been convinced otherwise.'

'That's not true.'

'Then why didn't you say something at the time?'

Safa noted that this was the very same question put to thousands of victims. *Why didn't you say something at the time?* It was a grim truth that taking time to gather your courage made you more likely to be doubted. *Speak at your weakest or hold your tongue* was the prevailing message.

'I didn't know how to help,' said Jenna.

'I have one more question, then. When you joked about watching Lily's body "like an incel", how did she react?'

Jenna's face darkened. 'She laughed.'

Garrett's eyes were pantomime wide. 'She laughed?'

'Yes.' Jenna was defeated.

Garrett turned to the judge. 'I have no more questions, My Lord.'

Victoria Hersham stood to re-examine the witness.

'Jenna, in the 1,100 days you worked with Lily, how many times did you apply makeup on her abdomen?'

Jenna was confused. 'Never.'

'How many times did you apply makeup to her buttocks or her breasts?'

'Never.'

'What about her arms and her legs?'

'Never,' repeated Jenna.

'Is it true, then, that Lily could have had 1,100 bruises on her stomach, chest, back, buttocks, arms and legs and you would never have seen them?'

Jenna brightened a little. 'That's true.'

'Is it true that the only reason you saw the bruise on Lily's shoulder is because her co-presenter happened to spill coffee on her?'

'Yes, that's true.' Jenna nodded vigorously.

'So, all those other times that he *didn't* spill coffee, could Lily have been hiding bruises?'

'Yes.'

'In that case, is the 1,100 number essentially meaningless?'

'Yes.' Jenna grabbed the lifeline. 'It's completely meaningless.'

'Thank you. I have no more questions, My Lord.'

Safa left the Old Bailey feeling deflated. Jenna was one of few witnesses appearing in Lily's defence and Garrett had done a good job in discrediting her. Victoria had repaired some of the damage, but that eternal question remained. If Jenna really thought that Lily was in danger, *why didn't she say something?* In reality, it would have made little difference – the police had scant resource to deal with suspicion – but Jenna's silence undermined her.

As Safa mulled this over, she spotted Natalie ahead of her. She jogged after her, making her startle when she called her name. Today, she wore a grey pin-striped trouser suit that sagged at the knees and elbows – a sign that it had been worn too long – with a shiny paisley scarf. Her hair had a deep parting and was clipped to one side like a child's.

'You look well,' Safa lied.

Natalie scoffed, too astute to be fooled.

'Do you have time for a coffee?'

Natalie didn't check her watch. 'No. I've got to get back before Harry.'

'How is he?'

'He's okay. He's nervous about tomorrow.'

Safa pictured Harry in the witness box, facing up to Lucien Garrett. His evidence would be key in convincing the jury that Lily was a victim. 'Do you want me to come back with you? I could talk to him?'

Natalie waved away the offer. 'No, that's okay. He'll be okay.'

'I'll be driving tomorrow. Do you want me to give you both a lift?'

Natalie considered this. 'Will it be quicker than taking the tube?'

'It depends on traffic, but probably, yes.'

She grimaced. 'Maybe we'll take the tube just to be on the safe side.'

'Well, what if we leave half an hour early? That way we'll have plenty of time.' Safa wanted to be there to smooth any last-minute nerves.

Natalie fiddled with the clip in her hair. 'Okay, maybe. If you're sure.'

'Of course.' Safa smiled reassuringly. 'While I have you, Natalie, I want to talk to you about something.' She moved to one side of the pavement in a bid for privacy. 'I saw Patrick Meaden yesterday. You remember him, right? That kid from school who was abused.'

Natalie adjusted her glasses in what seemed like a stalling gesture.

'Patrick told me something. He said that Lily made the whole thing up back then. Do you think that's possible?'

Natalie stepped back. 'I don't know, Safa. I'm sorry, I don't really want to talk about that.'

'Why?'

'I just don't.'

Safa saw the tension in her shoulders, the nervous twitch of her hands. 'You know something.'

'Look, I can't talk. I've got to get back for Harry.'

'Natalie, just wait a minute.' She reached for her but Natalie pulled away. Safa stepped sideways to block her route to the station. 'When I came to your house a while back, you said to me "you know what Lily is like". What did you mean by that?'

Natalie grew frustrated. 'That was just sibling talk. Lily can be a pain. You know that.'

'But you were talking specifically about Richard abusing her. Did you not believe her?'

'Look, I've really got to go.'

'Did she lie about Patrick?'

Natalie was pale. 'I can't talk about this, Safa.'

'Is she lying now?'

Natalie's voice climbed a register. 'You know her just as well as I do.'

Safa bristled. 'What does that mean?'

'I'm sorry. I have to go.' This time when Safa tried to stop her, Natalie barged past, walking so fast, it seemed like she might start to run.

Safa watched her go and a sickly feeling turned in her gut. Natalie knew something; something that frightened her. And though Safa didn't yet know what it was, somehow it frightened her too.

*

The DLR rocked gently as it wound its way into East London. The light outside had faded and Safa felt exhausted. She leaned her head on the window, comforted by the train's low rumble. She might have closed her eyes but that pinprick of fear kept her on alert. There were three other people in the carriage: an elderly man and a young couple opposite Safa.

'Hey, look at this,' said the girl, hunching over her screen. She was dressed in a pink bomber jacket with cargo pants and boots. The boy was all ears and elbows – lanky and awkward. On reflection, Safa decided that they weren't a couple after all. More likely, they were students on the same university course or maybe colleagues in a retail store.

The boy raised a brow. 'Bloody hell, what a creep.' As they watched, Safa gleaned that it was a video of a female tourist being followed in Rome. Safa listened as the woman flagged down a passing cyclist and asked him for help. The cyclist was clearly nervous as he confronted the woman's stalker. His initial warnings didn't work, but his final gambit – *look, she's my girlfriend, okay?* – did the job of warding him off. The video played on and the girl in pink shook her head.

'Thank god that guy was there. Can you imagine what could have happened?'

'Yeah, she was lucky,' said the boy. Then, he sniggered. 'Although I didn't see her running to a *bear*.'

The girl laughed. 'You have a point.'

The boy flushed with pleasure. Emboldened, he continued. 'Seriously though, all that *choose the bear* stuff is just bullshit, right? Like, no woman would seriously choose the bear. Not in real life.'

The girl shrugged.

'It's a bandwagon. Women are literally like *me too!* so that they feel included. It feels like a competition. Who's had the worse experience? Who's got the worst story? It's almost like if you *haven't* been assaulted, then you're not part of the gang.'

The girl grimaced. 'That's a shit thing to say.'

'Why? It's *true*.'

'Because they're not saying it to be part of the *gang*. These women have actually been assaulted.'

He scoffed, but then saw the look on her face. His own expression changed – from light into dark. 'Wait. Have *you*?'

The girl fiddled with her zip, eyes downcast.

'For real?'

She lifted a shoulder.

'Fuck.' He ran a hand through his greasy blond hair. 'I'm sorry, Izzy. I didn't know.'

'It's not a big deal,' she said.

There was a moment's pause, then Izzy scrolled to the next video, this one of a clumsy panda. She laughed and scrolled on. The boy watched her for a moment. Then, he turned to the screen and his frown dissolved. Safa watched the exchange with bone weary sorrow. The girl was so young, with so much life in front of her. How many more times would she shrug off something unspoken?

Her own phone pinged with a message and Safa checked her screen. It was an email from Juliet Culpen, the woman whose case had brought coercive control into the public conciousness. The email was short and to the point.

Dear Ms Saleem,

Thank you, but I don't want to take part in your feature. I know you were hoping for a different answer, but please take this as my firm and final one and do not contact me again.

I rarely reply to journalists but felt compelled to when you shared the dreadful story of the Glassman. The only thing I would like to say to his victims is this: *Tell one person. The purpose of shame is to isolate you and when you are isolated, you are vulnerable. So tell one person. Just start there.*

Thank you,
Juliet Culpen

Safa exhaled. The message was simple but affecting. She had hoped for an in-depth interview and envisioned pages of Juliet's insights but this message in its purity was unexpectedly powerful. *Tell one person.* This one act could have changed Lily's life. If she had told Safa about Richard's abuse, then things would have been different. Safa would have whisked Lily and Harry out of there and kept them away from Richard. She would have installed them in her flat and built entire barricades.

Tell one person. Safa understood that she was that person for the Glassman's victims. They wouldn't tell their relatives or neighbours, but Safa was ready to listen. She thought back to Rukshana's instruction: *Don't come here ever again.*

Could you force a victim to talk? Should you even try? Would you retraumatise them by insisting they face their pain? That it shouldn't be ignored, minimised, trivialised? That it *was* a fucking big deal? Safa put her head in her hands, weary and dejected. She stayed like that all the way home while Izzy and her friend carried on scrolling through videos.

*

Safa pulled aside the fern and checked the window again. Since the break-in, it had become a compulsion: looking behind the plant to ensure that the glass was still intact. She exhaled, frustrated with herself, then snatched up the plant and moved it to the coffee table in the living room. She prowled the length of her flat, feeling stressed and restless. Her mind felt jumbled, and pulled in different directions: Lily, Patrick, Harry, Imran, her dad – and the Glassman. Being stuck here, in this tiny box in the sky, made her yet more anxious. She threw open the doors to the Juliet balcony. She hadn't put up net curtains yet, but needed to let in some air. She leaned on the railing and watched the sky. As it lost its light, she felt a strange sensation – the hair-on-end feeling of being watched. She scanned the view. Her flat was boxed in on three sides by other flats. A central courtyard served as a store for communal bins, along with dumped fridges and mattresses.

Safa scanned the dizzying array of windows. If someone was indeed watching her, they could do it safely from behind all that dark glass. She moved to close the doors and that's when she saw it: the figure on the pavement. He was dressed all in black and was staring in her direction. Was she imagining that he was looking at her? A trick of perspective? She leaned over the railing to get a closer look. His features were a blur but he definitely seemed to be looking at her.

A marble of fear rolled in her gut. *Could it be?* The figure raised a hand and waved at her.

Safa lurched in fright. As she jerked backwards, her calves hit the coffee table. The plant wobbled and her hand shot out to steady it. When she looked back, the figure was gone. Wildly, she scanned the courtyard: the space between the bins and the ground floor flats in case he had found an open window. There was no movement at all. He had to be in the courtyard. He couldn't have escaped so quickly. Her instincts told her to retreat, to lock the doors and call the police, but she stayed on the balcony, convinced he would flee any minute. She spent a full twenty minutes waiting, but the only things that stirred were the whirlpools of rubbish. Finally, her heart rate calmed and she shivered from the cold. Gingerly, she closed the doors, still alert for movement.

She felt exposed by all that glass in her window. She marched to her utility cupboard and pulled out her yellow toolbox. She rifled through the drawers and found two golden hooks, which she drilled into the wall. One thing her mechanic dad had taught her was how to fix her car and home.

She didn't have any curtain wire, so connected three of her belts and looped them into the hooks. She pulled out some bed sheets from her cupboard and folded them over the belts, blocking out the view.

That's when she heard the knock on the door – a slow, calm sound. Safa's heart thumped in time. The locksmith had said that no one could get in the Ultion lock, but that did little to reassure her. Another knock. The same measured calm. Safa crept towards the door, wincing at a creak beneath her feet. He knew that she was home.

'Safa?' called a voice.

Safa folded in relief. *Imran*. She checked the spyhole and opened the door.

He frowned. 'You're not ready.'

She scooted into his arms.

'Hey.' He kissed her hair. 'What's wrong?'

'I think he was here.' Her voice sounded small and foreign to her. 'The Glassman.'

His body tensed in high alert. 'Where?' Carefully, he detached himself.

'Not in here.' She pointed towards the living room. 'Out there in the courtyard about half an hour ago.'

He went to the window. 'You saw him?'

'I think so.'

'What did he look like?'

'About six foot. Average build. He was wearing black canvas trousers and a black jacket with a cap. No logo. Beyond that, I don't know.'

'His race?'

'I couldn't say.'

'Asian?'

'I don't know.'

'Are you sure it was him?'

'No. It could have been anyone, but he was looking directly at me.'

Imran looked at the makeshift sheets. 'Safa, you should come and stay with me for a while.'

She lifted her chin. 'He's not going to drive me out of my home.'

'Then I could come and stay here.'

Safa was unsure. That would be too much, too soon. The offer hung in the air until Imran spoke again.

'Would you prefer to stay in tonight?'

Safa remembered that she had promised to go boxing with him. 'No, let's go.' She needed to slow the whir of her mind. 'Give me five minutes.' She changed into a running top and an old pair of leggings, and triple-locked the door behind them.

Fifteen minutes later, they were at Limehouse Boxing Club. It was a large rectangular space with high ceilings and a boxing ring at one end. The walls were adorned with posters and flags, and the space was filled with men.

'Is this pointless?' asked Safa, charting the difference in size between her and them. 'Am I really going to be able to hurt anyone?'

Imran shook his head at her defeatist attitude. 'Listen to me. Make a fist,' he told her. Safa curled her hand into a tight fist. Imran closed his own over it and shook it a little. 'That is a really fucking horrible thing to be hit by.'

She looked at her hand as if seeing it for the first time and realised that he was right. She may not be able to overpower a man, but she could give herself a fighting chance.

'Let's get to it. First things first, we need to protect your knuckles.' Imran brandished two hand wraps – long ribbons of elasticated fabric – and wrapped them around her wrists and knuckles.

Safa examined her hands. 'This doesn't seem like enough padding,' she said.

'They're not there for padding as such,' he explained. 'Rather, they keep your joints and bones in place so they don't misalign when you punch.'

Imran led her to the ring and held up the rope so that she could step inside. He took her through the basic boxing stance: feet apart, hands up, chin down, eyes on her opponent's chest. He taught her basic defences and how to put more power in her punches. Once she was familiar with the jab and the cross, he made her punch different combinations into the pads, occasionally adding a blow of his own. She punched with all her might and, over the next hour, felt the tension leave her. Her confusion, paranoia and anger fell away completely. By the end of the hour, she was dripping in sweat. Her hair was plastered across her scalp and her breath came thin and fast.

'Fuck, that's hard work,' she gasped.

Imran smiled, clearly pleased to have inducted her into his hobby. A cheeky gleam came to his eye. 'You look so sexy right now.'

'Fuck off,' she said but her gaze darted to the mirror behind him to check. He caught her looking and laughed. He did a silly dance and started singing *'Sexy and I Know It'* by LMFAO. Safa tried to cuff his shoulder but he slipped it easily. He ducked and weaved around her, then pulled her into a sweaty hug. She squealed in objection – a high and girlish sound that was foreign to her ears. She felt the strength in his arms as he locked her in place against his chest.

'Hey,' she said softly.

He looked down at her, his smile fading a little. 'What?'

'I'm sorry it took me so long to figure things out.'

He gave her a lopsided smile. 'Safa by name. *Suffer* by nature.' He brushed back a strand of her hair. 'Come on. Let's go home.'

'Okay. Let's.' She felt light and happy as she slipped her hand in his. 'Thank you for bringing me boxing. I feel good.'

'I told you it was good for anger.'

She puckered her lips. 'I guess you were right.'

They walked in silence for a while before he asked, 'Have you ever thought about seeing someone about that?'

Safa slowed. 'What? Like a therapist?'

'Yeah.'

'Brown people don't do therapy,' she said glibly.

He arched his brows. 'Yeah, but every single last one of us needs it.'

'Fair point,' she conceded.

'But, seriously, have you ever thought about it?'

'I don't know,' she said mildly. It had been a long time since they had spoken with this sort of intimacy. 'Firstly, I couldn't afford therapy even if I wanted it. Secondly, I think I'm more or less okay, you know? I go to work and I do a good job and I pay my mortgage and my crippling fucking service charge, and I take care of my dad.' She gestured vaguely. 'It's not like I was in a war, or got attacked, or any of the stuff you really need therapy for. I lost my mum. Everyone does – and *that's* if they're lucky.'

Imran stopped. The light from a nearby lamp turned his lashes an orange-yellow. 'But it wasn't that straightforward.'

'I know and some days that's harder to deal with than others, but I'm okay.' She exhaled sharply. 'Mum's gone and that's okay.' She saw the pain in Imran's face and felt hers ease a little. For the first time in her life, she trusted someone else to carry it awhile. She beckoned with her head. 'Let's go.' She tugged him gently and they both moved forward, beyond the pool of light.

Chapter 18

Safa sounded the horn, but her battered Clio only managed a feeble toot. She tried calling Harry and Natalie again, but neither answered the phone. She sighed and turned off the engine, then got out and locked the door. Inside Withy House, the lift was out of order, so she started the climb to the fifth floor. She rang the bell and checked the time.

Harry threw open the door, clearly in a panic. His hair was ruffled, his tie was askew and his socks were a mismatched black and green.

'Harry, what's going on? We need to leave soon.'

'I know!' he cried.

'Hey, it's okay.' Safa ushered him inside. 'One thing at a time. First, your tie.' She helped him fix it – an expert after years of helping her dad. 'Next: the hair.' She went to the bathroom to look for hairspray. 'Where's Natalie?' she called over her shoulder.

'She has a migraine.'

'What? She's not coming?' She rummaged through the cupboard but couldn't find anything. She wet her hands and hurriedly neatened the unruly strands of his hair. He was wild eyed with worry and Safa clamped her hands on his shoulders. 'Harry, it's okay. Let's take a breath.'

'But we'll be late!'

She gave his shoulders a shake. 'Come on, let's breathe.' It took him a moment to focus but he did as she instructed. Together, they took a few deep breaths until she felt the nervy energy ease. She plucked his black blazer from the chair. 'Did Natalie not wake you in time?'

'No. She sleeps in when she has a migraine.' He pushed his feet into his shoes, bending them out of shape in his rush.

'Do you have your house keys?'

'Yes.'

'Should we check on Natalie?'

'No. She'll be annoyed if we wake her.'

Safa hesitated. 'Okay, let's go.'

Outside, she spotted a traffic warden further up the road. She checked her windshield – mercifully clear – and ushered Harry inside. She zoomed off towards the city, thankful for the extra half hour she had planned. 'It's okay. We have plenty of time,' she told Harry.

He neatened his hair and smoothed his tie, bouncing his knee compulsively. Safa reached out and stilled it gently.

'What shall I tell them?' he asked.

Safa glanced at him. 'What do you mean?'

'The court. What shall I tell them today?'

'You should tell them the truth.'

His knee started bouncing again. 'What if it's bad?'

Safa deftly manoeuvred around a bus. 'The truth can be hard to hear, Harry. In fact, it usually is, but after love, it's the most important thing.'

He fell quiet and they drove in silence for a mile. He gathered his hands in his lap and asked, 'Do you always tell the truth?'

'In my work, yes. It's a little cheesy but I think of it as my north star; the thing I always follow. When I'm lost, I ask myself what the truth is. If I know, I tell it. If I don't, I try to find it.'

'So telling the truth is always right?'

'In court, yes. If you feel lost, ask yourself what the truth is. If you know, tell it. If you don't, then just say that, okay?'

'Okay.'

Safa wanted to say more; to tell him how sorry she was that his life had gone awry, but she didn't want to stir him up before his appearance in court. 'I'll be on the press bench, okay?' She plucked her navy-coloured jumper. 'If you can't find me, look for this blue.'

'Thank you, Aunt Saffie.' Harry cleared the choke in his throat.

Safa kept her eyes on the road, and coughed to clear her own.

*

Safa left Harry with a witness liaison officer and hurried into the courtroom. The press bench was full, bar a single seat. She squeezed her way to it and sighed when she saw who was next to it. Oliver Witherow raised his brows. Safa responded with a look of contempt. She slid in next to him and he leaned in towards her.

'Saved you a seat.'

'Wiped it down with ricin, did you?'

'Careful now. A woman of your "disposition" shouldn't say words like that in public.'

'Did you get your wit from your dad, Oliver? Like everything else in your life?'

'All rise,' called the usher.

Judge Turner took his seat and Victoria Hersham stood to call her final witness.

Safa glanced at Oliver's notebook. It gave her a petty satisfaction to see that he didn't know shorthand. It was an outdated technique, but the stalwarts of reporting still expected it and otherwise didn't take you seriously. Oliver was distracting and Safa angled her body away from him so she could focus on Harry.

He stood in the witness box and smoothed a wayward lock

of hair before he took the oath. When his voice broke to reveal a pubescent squawk, his shoulders curled inwards. He looked small and exposed, and it hurt Safa to watch him. Lily in the dock was watching him too. Her face was a mask but Safa could see her distress: her fingers gripping her sleeve, the tightness in her jaw as she tried not to cry.

Victoria started with some simple questions to put Harry at ease: his age, where he lived, his school. She waited for the tremble in his voice to steady before she moved on.

'Harry, I know this is difficult, but I'd like to talk about the night of your father's book launch. If at any point you would like to take a break, please just tell me. Does that sound okay?'

Harry wiped his hands on his tie and even from where she sat, Safa could see the faint print of his sweaty palm. 'Yes,' he answered quietly.

'On the day of the party, did you notice any tension between your parents?'

Harry's gaze flicked to the jury. 'Yes. Mum and Dad were arguing before it even started. The weather looked bad, like it was gonna rain, and Dad was saying that he knew a garden party was a bad idea. Mum said it was good because it meant that most people would be gone by eight or nine. Dad told her, "Unlike you, I actually *like* spending time with my friends," and that made things worse. They only stopped arguing when people began to arrive.'

'Did you talk to any guests?'

'No. Dad told me to stay out of the way. I didn't mind. I knew it'd be boring so I stayed in my room, just playing games and stuff on my phone. Stephen, my friend, texted later to say he'd got the new *Grand Theft Auto* and did I wanna go and play. Obviously, I said yeah. I went down to ask Mum if I could go. The party had finished and Mum and Dad were arguing about the cleaning up.

I said I was going to Stephen's and Dad lost it. He said I wasn't going anywhere at that time. I was sick of hearing them argue, so I left.'

'You walked out of the house?'

'Mum said I could go.'

'What time was this?'

'Nine o'clock.'

'Do you usually go out at this time?'

'No but if I go out at, say, six, they let me come home at ten or even later sometimes, so I didn't get what the big deal was. It was a Saturday and I'd been stuck in my room all day, so they owed me.'

'What was your father's mood when you left?'

'He was mad. I didn't want to deal with it so I left. I went to Stephen's house and we played GTA for a while.' Harry flushed with colour. 'Then, the police came.'

'I know this is difficult, Harry, but I need to ask a little more about your mum and dad. Did they argue a lot?'

'Yeah. It started in the lockdowns.'

'Did your dad ever shout at you or your mum?'

'Yes. Both of us.'

'Did you ever see him throw things?'

Harry chewed his bottom lip. 'Yes.'

'Did you see him hit things?'

'Yes, he hit the cushions.'

Victoria spoke softly. 'Did he ever hit you?'

'No.'

'Did you ever see him hit your mum?'

Harry's jaw worked with stress. He searched the press bench until he found the dark blue of Safa's jumper. They locked eyes and Safa nodded gently. *Tell the truth, Harry.*

'Harry, did you ever see your dad hit your mum?' Victoria repeated.

He smoothed his tie again, exhaled, and then he said, 'No.'

Safa jolted. Harry had told her himself that Richard was hurting Lily. Why had he changed his story? A sick feeling turned in her gut. After all this time, was *this* the actual truth?

Victoria stared at Harry, clearly wrong-footed. 'Harry, in your statement to the police, you said that you had seen your father strike your mother on several occasions.'

The colour in his cheeks deepened. 'I was trying to protect her, but I never saw that.'

'Harry.' Victoria paused to even her tone. 'You were very specific in your interview. You said your mum had cooked slow roasted lamb for dinner and when she asked your father to put his phone away, he threw it at her head. Do you remember saying that?'

'I remember saying it but I didn't see that.'

Safa struggled to understand. Harry had been *so* angry with himself for not protecting Lily. *I never stood up for her. I told myself to. Every time. Just go and stand in front of her.* Was that all a lie?

'Harry, it is very important that you tell the truth.' Victoria was ruffled for the first time in the trial.

Garrett was on his feet. 'My Lord, the witness has answered the question.'

'He's right, Ms Hersham. Please move on.'

Victoria groped to collect her thoughts. Clearly, this had destroyed her strategy.

Safa looked from Harry to Lily. It felt like a second conversation was happening underneath.

'Harry, were you scared of your dad?' asked Victoria.

He considered this for a moment. 'Sometimes.'

'Why?'

'He had a temper.'

'Have you ever been scared of your mother?'

Harry looked immensely sad. 'No. Never.'
'Does she have a temper?'
'No.'
'Have you ever seen her hurt your dad?'
'No.'
'Have you ever heard her threaten to hurt your dad?'
'No.'
'Okay.' Victoria tried to hide her frustration.

There were other things she could ask at this juncture – *can you think of any reason why your mother would want to hurt your father?* – but after Harry's curveball, every further question was a risk. What if he answered *yes*?

'I have no more questions, My Lord,' Victoria conceded.

Safa watched with despair. Harry was meant to be the linchpin in Lily's defence; the witness who would finally corroborate her claims of abuse. Instead, he had sent her into free fall, careening towards a verdict that carried a life sentence. *Guilty of murder.*

*

Lucien Garrett smiled warmly. He had been handed a rare gift this morning and was sure to treat it carefully. Harry had placed Lily in a treacherous position and Garrett's job was to slowly, tenderly, push her over the edge.

'Harry, I understand that you got into a fight at school in May of this year. Is that correct?'

Harry looked at Safa on the press bench. She didn't understand Garrett's strategy, but nodded at Harry to answer.

'Yes.'

'How did it start?'

'A boy in my class, Darren, was bullying my friend, Rashid. I told him to stop, but he wouldn't listen. He started saying horrible things to Rashid like "*Oh, look, is your boyfriend backing you up?*" I got between them. Darren pushed me and I pushed him back and we got into a fight.'

'So you were standing up for your friend?'

'Yes.'

'That was a brave thing to do.'

Harry didn't respond.

Garrett smiled kindly. 'Would you say that you tend to get involved when you see someone in danger?'

Safa felt her blood heat. It was too adult a question for a thirteen-year-old child.

'Yes,' Harry said hesitantly.

'Harry, do you love your mother?'

Safa clenched her fists to stop herself from springing to her feet. *What the* fuck *sort of question is this?*

'Yes,' said Harry with the slightest crack in his voice.

'So you would want to protect her if you sensed she was in danger?'

'Yes.'

'When you left your house on the evening of the party, did you fear for your mother's safety?'

Harry swallowed, then shook his head. 'No.'

'You said your dad was angry. Were you scared, even a little bit, that he would hit her because of it?'

His eyes grew shiny with tears. 'No.'

'Because you had never seen anything to suggest that he would hit her? Isn't that correct?'

'Yes.'

'If you thought he would hurt her, what would you have done?'

His chest quivered with the effort to keep composure. 'I would have stayed.'

'You would have stayed,' Garrett repeated. 'Harry, in the weeks before your father's passing, did you notice your parents arguing more than usual?'

'Yes.'

'Do you know what they were arguing about?'

'No.' Garrett started to speak but Harry added, 'but . . . '

'But?'

'But I think it was to do with the divorce.'

Quiet settled on the room.

'Divorce?' Garrett's voice was almost a whisper, wary of spooking him.

Harry shifted. 'A couple of weeks before the party, Dad asked me who I'd wanna live with: him or Mum. I asked if they were getting a divorce and he said maybe.'

Garrett controlled his voice. 'Did your dad talk to your mum about divorce?'

'I don't know.'

A pause. 'Did you?'

Harry hesitated but only for a beat. 'Yes.'

Tension boiled over into noise. The reporters surrounding Safa jostled to report this while those in the public gallery buzzed with audible shock.

'Was your mother surprised by this?'

'No,' said Harry.

'So it seemed like she already knew about it?'

'Yes.'

'What did she say in response?'

'She said that Dad was confused right now.'

Garrett sensed that there was more. 'And?'

Harry's voice trembled ever so slightly. 'And he'd die before he left us.'

Chapter 19

'Members of the jury, there is a difference between self-defence and revenge,' said Lucien Garrett as he began his closing speech on dreary Monday morning. 'There is a difference between self-defence and overreaction. And there is a difference between self-defence and a retro fitted excuse. Here is one thing that we know for certain: Lily Astor killed her husband. She is responsible for his death. The defence have tried to put the deceased on trial instead.

'They claim that Richard Astor was abusive and that Lily feared serious violence to such an extent that she took a *knife* to his throat and killed him. I would like to submit four points to help you come to a verdict.

'Number one: Richard Astor did not hit or abuse or control Lily. We have not seen an iota of evidence to support this. There is no medical evidence. No witnesses to the abuse. No confessions to a therapist or a friend or family member. Much has been made of the two bruises she was seen with in the lead-up to the killing. By her own admission, these were completely innocent. The first was from a tennis match and the second from a riding incident, but they were refashioned as sinister once it suited her. Don't forget that she joked about it with her makeup artist, saying that she wouldn't let herself become a *"battered woman"*. If her husband really were abusive, wouldn't there be some evidence? Even her own son denies this.

'Number two: Lily Astor did not fear serious violence. Consider her behaviour on the evening of the party. Witnesses have said that she was openly flirting with her cameraman. If she were morbidly scared of her husband, would she have done this? If she genuinely feared serious violence, would she have done this? It simply isn't logical.

'Number three: Lily Astor did not use reasonable force. She picked up a knife and she slashed his throat. This isn't an act of self-defence. It is an act of violence. We have heard evidence that Lily slapped her own son when she lost her temper at a family picnic. We have heard that she threatened a person – most likely her husband – with the words "Don't you understand? I'm scared I'll kill you one day." This speaks to a streak of violence that the public doesn't see.

'Number four: The real reason Lily Astor killed her husband is revenge. Revenge for having an affair and revenge for daring to leave her. She told us that she knew nothing about a divorce, but her own son told us that she *did* know. Lily told him that Richard "would die before he left us". Well, he did, members of the jury. He died at the hands of Lily Astor who then retrofit innocent bruises into a false narrative of abuse.

'Based on the evidence, we submit that Lily Astor attacked her husband while she was sound of mind, knowing that her actions could and very likely *would* lead to his death. She then co-opted the domestic violence movement, knowing it would invoke public sympathy.

'Now, this is very important: self-defence does not apply when the motive is revenge. Lily picked up that knife because she was angry, because she wanted to wreak revenge on Richard, because she wanted to make him pay for even thinking about leaving her.

She didn't pick up a knife because she was scared for her life. She didn't wave it around and happen to catch his throat. She was angry. She was out for revenge. For that reason, we put it to you that the only just and correct verdict in this case is *guilty*. If you are convinced of these facts, then we ask that you find the defendant, Lily Astor, guilty as charged.'

*

Victoria Hersham took her time. She lay out her notebook, scanned the open page, uncapped her pen and made a small amendment. The message was subtle but effective: this task and, with it, the jury's decision, deserved time and care. She set down the pen, took off her glasses and met the jury's waiting gaze.

'Members of the jury, men tend to kill for a multitude of reasons. Power, jealousy, greed, pride, revenge. Women, on the other hand, tend to kill in self-defence: when they or someone they love is threatened. What women *don't* kill for is when their husband asks for a divorce.

'Throughout this trial, the prosecution have tried to portray Lily as a liar, a fraud, a histrionic woman hell-bent on revenge. They have tried to persuade you that Lily saw her husband in a passionate embrace with his mistress. They used this to fashion a motive of rage and revenge – but it simply isn't true. Lily never saw them. It was someone else that ran down the stairs that day. The prosecution have tried to gloss over this. They want you to forget that they tried to persuade you of this. What their case boils down to then is that Lily Astor – a successful and beloved broadcaster with a glittering career, beautiful home and loving son – killed her husband simply because he asked for a divorce. Just think about that for a moment. Is that really likely, or is there something else going on here?

'Let's examine the prosecution's four points in turn. Number one: they deny that Lily was abused simply because she did not report it, but abuse happens behind closed doors. It is taboo. We do not advertise it. We hide it from even our closest friends and family. We reach for gallows humour to cover up our pain, like Lily did with her makeup artist friend. A forensic psychologist with three decades of experience confirmed that Lily's behaviour is consistent with other victims of domestic violence. She was suffering insomnia. She shows signs of disordered eating. She was withdrawing from her social circle and experiencing anxiety. All of those things are true. Lily is indeed a successful and beloved broadcaster, but that doesn't make her immune to the dark impulses of men.

'Number two: they deny that Lily feared serious violence – and their reason? Because she was nice to a guest. They are asking you to convict Lily because she *smiled* at a guest. Because she touched his *arm*! It is ludicrous to suggest that she cannot be a victim because she was being a good hostess.

'Number three: they deny that Lily used reasonable force. Members of the jury, have you ever faced the threat of violence? If so, you will know that self-defence is not a process of calm detachment. Self-defence is not the preserve of law books. Self-defence is an instinct that nature herself recognises – a recognition that any living creature is going to act, or react, a certain way when faced with threat. It often happens in a split second, but not in isolation. We heard from an expert that the fear of threat can build up over years and culminate in a single incident. In hindsight, a defendant may themselves say that they should have acted differently, but we are not dealing in hindsight here. Rather, we are putting ourselves in Lily's position on the night that her husband charged at her. We are trying to feel the danger she felt, to understand her desperation, and asking ourselves: might we have picked up a knife to defend ourselves? If your answer is maybe, then *that*, members of the jury, is reasonable force.

'Finally, number four: they claim that the motive was revenge – but for what? Divorce? That is not a motive. It is a gross exaggeration based on a late-night heart-to-heart with her son. In an attempt to assure her son that his father would not leave them, Lily used wording that could be – and *has* been – misconstrued. Lily never saw Richard with a mistress. There is no evidence that she was even aware of a mistress. This was not a crime of rage or revenge. Lily has unfailingly shown remorse for what happened. She immediately stemmed his wound, she immediately called for help, she stayed with him and tended to him until the paramedics arrived. These are not the actions of a vengeful criminal bent on revenge. These are the actions of a victim who acted out of desperation and who has been seeking redemption ever since.'

Victoria's tone was grave. 'Members of the jury, Lily Astor faces a serious offence. She is charged with murder. Her life as she knows it is on the line. Are we to put her in prison for life because we don't believe that a man might hurt his wife in secret? Doesn't Lily Astor deserve better? Don't all women?'

Victoria's voice was clear and firm and carried across the court as she finished. 'The prosecution has not proven that this was an intentional act. Hold them to their burden. A conviction in this case would be a travesty, so I ask you, members of the jury, to do the just thing and find Lily Astor not guilty.'

Chapter 20

Imran held up the pads and Safa landed a jab. The pad barely moved and she tried again harder. Still, no progress.

'You need to step with the punch,' said Imran. 'Transfer your weight into it. At the moment, you're punching with your arm rather than your body.'

Safa screwed up her face. 'Okay, *sensei*,' she said tartly.

'You're mixing up your sports, Safa-*san*.'

'Just show me what to do,' she said with a hint of impatience. She had felt antsy and restless since leaving court yesterday. She wanted to speak to Lily about Harry's evidence, but she had refused to see her following their run-in over Patrick Meaden. All Safa could do was wait for the verdict and it might be days before that was in. She needed some way to work out her anxiety, so had agreed to an early-morning boxing lesson.

She punched the pads in a one-two pattern.

'Harder,' said Imran.

She punched again.

'Harder.'

She punched them once, then twice, then thrice. Then, with a cry, she tried again. This time, Imran was forced to step back. Safa yelped with delight, pleased for even this small bit of progress.

'Again,' said Imran. This time, he counter-punched with a light tap against Safa's head. 'Keep your guard up,' he said, pulling up her gloves to protect her face. 'Chin down,' he lightly glanced her jawbone, 'or you'll catch an uppercut.'

She amended her stance.

'Better,' he told her. He worked her on the pads until she was red in the face. 'Do you want a couple of rounds on the heavy bag?' He led her to a large bag suspended from the ceiling. He called out combinations and she pummelled the bag in the accordant pattern – jab, jab, cross; jab, cross, hook; jab, slip, hook. She punched until she was drenched in sweat. Imran pushed her on and it was only when she was gasping for air that he let her stop. She slumped against the bag, exhausted but weirdly elated. All the worry of the past few weeks seemed to lift right off her. She sat on the edge of the ring and took long, slow breaths to calm herself. Imran sat down next to her and helped her out of her gloves.

'How are you feeling?' he asked.

'Honestly? I feel a little high. I think I could get into this.'

He smiled, but there was no light behind it.

Safa studied him. 'You okay?'

He opened and closed the Velcro strap of her boxing glove. 'Safa, I need to tell you something.'

She angled her body towards him, sensing that it was serious. 'What?'

'There's been another case.'

A band of pressure squeezed her chest. 'The Glassman?' she asked in a whisper.

'Yes.'

Safa put her face in her hands, still encased in their wraps. 'When?'

'The night before last.'

'A widow?'

'Yeah.'

'How old?'

'Seventy-four.'

Safa let out a frustrated growl. 'What are the police *doing*, Imran? Why can't you find this monster?'

'You *know* why, Safa. The women won't talk.'

'Tell me what you know about the new victim.' He protested but Safa cut him short. 'Come *on*, Imran. This is more important than protocol. You know I won't print anything.'

He rubbed the furrow between his brows. 'A woman came to see us yesterday. She's thirty-four and lives with her in-laws in Bethnal Green. Her own mother lives alone on Ben Johnson Road after being widowed last year. The daughter woke up this morning to three missed calls from her mother. She called back and her mother said that someone broke into her house in the early hours. She rushed to her mum's house and found the back window with a square pane of glass cut out – big enough for a person to fit through – but there was nothing missing. Her mother said it was probably because she owned nothing of value. The daughter noticed the ligature marks on her mother's wrists. She asked about them, but she made up some bullshit excuse about her bangles getting stuck. The daughter was worried. She tried to take her mother to the doctor, but she flat out refused. She didn't know what to do, so she came to report it to us.'

Safa felt a shoot of hope. 'Has anyone talked to the mother?'

'Yes, but she insisted that nothing else happened. Nothing was missing so it's been recorded as a case of criminal damage.'

'Criminal damage? For fuck's sake, Imran. They need to put a dedicated team on this.'

'We're so short staffed, Safa. We can't chase imaginary crimes.'

'It's not an imaginary crime!'

'*We* know that but if the victims say nothing, then what can we do?'

Safa squared her jaw. 'Give me her details.'

'You can't get involved, Safa. Forget protocol for a moment, you're already on the Glassman's radar. What if he's watching for you?'

'Then you come and watch for him.'

'I can't put you at risk like that.'

'But you'll put these other women at risk?'

His eyes flashed with hurt. 'Safa, that's not fair.'

She gripped his sleeve. 'He'll keep going, Imran. And no one is going to stop him.' She gave it a little shake. 'Witnesses are *so* scarce in this case. I need to talk to her.'

Imran was weary. 'Okay,' he said finally. 'But I'm coming with you.'

She jumped to her feet. 'Okay, give me five minutes to shower.'

'You want to go *now*?'

She checked her watch. 'You still have time before your shift, right?'

'Not really.' He saw her face. 'But I'll figure it out.'

'Thank you.' She squeezed his arm and headed to the shower.

Twenty minutes later, they parked by Dalbury House on Ben Johnson Road. Safa told Imran to stay in the car and watch. She walked up the road to the squat block of council flats and located number seven. She rang the bell but no one answered. She waited, then tried again. Still, no answer. She hesitated, then bent and peeked through the letterbox.

'*Sasi, afna dorza kulbayni?*' she called, swapping to Sylheti to ask the woman to open the door. '*Afnar furi amdar logeh zugazug korsila. Zikayson amda afnar logeh matam.*' She explained that the woman's daughter had asked them to talk to her. She waited a few minutes, then tried again, but there was no answer. She skirted around to the side of the building to see if the broken window had been fixed. She counted down the flats and saw that the square had been boarded up. If the woman was lucky, it would be weeks rather than months before the council replaced the glass.

Safa watched for signs of movement inside. Nothing. She turned just as the front door opened to Haughton House opposite, drawing her gaze to it. Instinctually, she made eye contact with the man in the doorway. He was six foot tall, dressed in black canvas trousers and a black jacket and cap. Safa jolted with recognition. This was the man who had waved at her from her building's courtyard. He recognised her too and, for a split second, froze with indecision. Then, he spun and bolted into the building. By instinct, Safa tore across the road after him. She caught the door just in time before it closed and locked.

'Safa!' She heard Imran's voice behind her but didn't have time to wait for him. She charged inside after the man. Footsteps echoed in the stairwell and she looked up to see the man racing up.

'Stop!' She sprinted after him. He ran up in a methodical pattern, taking the stairs by three. Safa's lungs burned as she strove to keep up with him. 'Stop!' she cried again.

That's when he made a mistake. He glanced over the banister to see where she was, giving Safa her first clear view of his face. She drew momentarily closer but he was faster than her. She chased him to the quieter upper levels and felt her first stab of fear. Logic told her to retreat; to slow down and wait for Imran. She did not want to be on a high roof alone with this man. But it was too late. He was already out and she couldn't let him escape. She spilled onto the roof, a hair width away from panic. Her senses pulled at the detail in the landscape: the soft putter of bird wings, the cold blade of wind, the taste of rain in the air.

'Oi!' she cried out, putting a lid on her fear. 'Show your fucking face!' Emboldened by adrenaline, she ventured onto the tarmac. 'I saw you, you fucking coward. I know exactly what you look like. I saw your pretty little beauty spot above your lip like Cindy

Crawford's. I've got your ticket, you fucking bastard.' She scanned the perimeter.

Metal whined behind her and she spun to find Imran on the roof.

'Safa! What the fuck is going on?'

'He's here. The Glassman is here.'

Imran's body went rigid with the threat of danger. He held a finger to his lips and guided her behind him. In a slow circle, he canvassed the roof. The only place they couldn't see was the half-metre of space behind the door's concrete housing. Imran kept Safa close behind him and crept towards it silently. They rounded the corner but the space was empty. Safa cast about frantically.

'It was him, Imran. I know it was.' He tried to calm her but she darted to a corner of the roof and scanned the surrounding rooftops. It was too wide to jump. 'Where did he go?' She headed back towards the door.

'I wasn't far behind you, Safa. He didn't go back inside.'

'Then where is he? Where did he go?' She whirled in a circle.

'How did you realise he was watching you?'

'He wasn't watching me,' said Safa. 'He was shocked to see me. He wasn't expecting it. Imran, I think he might live here in Haughton House.' She groped for her phone and spoke into it, recording everything she had seen. 'Tall, six foot I would say, strong, muscular arms, brown eyes, black hair, Asian, early forties. Thinning hair at the temples, kind eyes slightly downturned, a mole or beauty spot above his top lip on the left when facing him.' She closed her eyes and scanned her brain for detail. 'Wore black hiking shoes with a shiny base, grooves on the bottom. Fast, athletic. His jacket had a logo: a cross between a bird, a plane and an arrow.' She rummaged for a pen and drew it on her hand.

'Diadora,' said Imran. 'Keep going.'

She tried to snatch more detail from the ether of her memory. 'His boots had a label. Yellow writing on black.'

'Timberland?'

She held up a hand to quieten him. 'No. Not black on yellow; yellow on black. It was a single word, maybe six or seven letters long, printed on the side of the sole.'

'What else?'

'Wispy hair. Dark circles beneath his eyes – puffy, like he hadn't slept. A slight cleft in the middle of his nose. Ears a little too long for his face, fleshy at the lobes.' Safa searched for more, but all other detail was lost to her. 'Where did he go, Imran? He can't have made this jump.' She mapped the distance between them and the nearest rooftop.

'It's about four metres,' said Imran. 'It's not impossible but you'd have to be mad to try it.'

The thought of it made Safa queasy. 'You're sure he didn't go down the stairs?'

'He couldn't have without passing me. There's only one way down.'

Safa frowned. 'How far behind me were you?'

'One floor.'

Safa went back inside the building and down one flight of stairs. She looked upwards and her throat closed. Between them and the rooftop was a single door. It was made of sheet metal and had a broken lock. Imran ushered Safa to one side and gently pushed the door. It swung open with a screech. The room inside was filled with an industrial hum: the clang of rusted pipework, the whir of a fan. The air held the damp smell of a laundrette and felt furry with dust. Imran took a step inside, ducking between the pipes, scanning left and right. Safa followed him in but saw that the room was empty.

'Imran.' She pointed at the far wall. Another door, made of the same sheet metal, this time with no lock. Imran opened it and Safa heard him swear. She joined him and saw that the door led to an exterior fire escape that criss-crossed the building all the way to the ground. Safa started down it and Imran followed, though they surely both knew that the man was gone.

Safa took the steps two by two. 'He must have ducked back inside just as I got to the rooftop. His timing was fucking immaculate to have avoided you too.'

Imran kept pace. 'Safa, he could have escaped to any one of these floors.'

'I don't think he'd take the risk. I think he would have fled.'

Back on the ground, they cased the surrounding streets, but the man had disappeared. Doggedly, Safa reeled off a list. 'Imran, we need to canvass every flat in this building. We need to give every resident a description of the man I saw. We'll make a note of anyone who doesn't answer the door and keep coming back till they do.'

Her phone cut in before she could finish. It was Natalie.

Lily's verdict was in.

*

Safa hurried into courtroom eight and took her place on the press bench. Her nerves jangled as she watched Lily stand up, her gaze impassively fixed ahead. There were no outward signs of distress. Was she hopeful or had she accepted her fate? Safa wished that she could speak to her, squeeze her hand like she used to in their youth, tell her *it's okay, it's me, you can stop pretending.*

'Mr Foreman, have the jury reached a verdict upon which you are all agreed?' asked the clerk.

The juror who looked like a middle manager got to his feet. 'Yes,' he answered firmly.

'On count one, do you find the defendant guilty or not guilty of murder?'

The silence in the room was absolute. And even outside, the wind and rain seemed to stop their onslaught. Lily closed her eyes and in that tiny concession, Safa saw her unbearable strain. Even Lily, it seemed, couldn't stare a life sentence in the face and refuse to look away.

The foreman took a wet-sounding breath. Then, he said a single word. 'Guilty.'

There was a rupture in the air, not yet audible – like the charge before a sonic boom. And, then, it hit. Noise exploded in the public gallery while reporters scrambled to break the news. Even two of the jurors were talking. And, in the midst of it all, Lily blank-faced with shock.

'Ms Astor, you have been found guilty of murder,' said Judge Turner. 'You will remain in custody until sentencing.'

Lily covered her face and folded into her chair. Safa looked on with dismay. On seeing her in that state, her faith in Lily snapped back into place. She realised with jarring clarity that she hadn't ever believed that Lily would be found guilty – or that she deserved to. Safa could see there were holes in Lily's defence, but on hearing the world 'guilty', she *knew* in her gut that the verdict was wrong. Safa had fallen into the same old trap of doubting a victim because she was flawed.

Lily's shoulders shook and Safa realised that this was the first time she had cried all trial. If she had shown more vulnerability, would there be a different verdict? Now, finally, her pain was on display.

When she dropped her hands, however, and looked up at the ceiling, there was a different emotion on her face entirely. Relief. Garish, bare-toothed relief that morphed into high laughter. Safa watched her, unnerved. Instinctively, she went to the dock and shielded Lily from view.

Lily was crying but also laughing. 'It's okay,' she said as she was led out by the dock officer. 'It's okay, Safa. It was always going to end this way.' Tears streamed down her face. 'Please take care of Harry. Tell him I love him. Tell him to remember me. To forgive me. Tell him,' she swallowed a sob, 'tell him I want to be his mother. Tell him to please let me.'

'I will,' promised Safa. 'It's not the end, Lily. I'm going to raise hell for the DPP. We're going to appeal. You're not going to prison for life over this.'

'No, Safa. It's okay.' Lily walked up the narrow aisle and looked over her shoulder at Safa. 'One of us was going to get killed. And it wasn't me.' Her laughter edged into hysteria as she turned and followed the dock officer. Safa felt a cold bud of dread open in her chest. She had never seen Lily like this before: her shrill hyena laugh, the wildness in her eyes, the jerky arc of her shoulders. Lily had endured years of trauma, only to be convicted of murder. The injustice of it, the sheer and brutal cruelty, was enough to drive her mad. Would Lily endure this, or had Safa just witnessed a mind already sliding apart?

Chapter 21

Safa watched the exit carefully. One benefit of being a small woman was that you could loiter with impunity. Few would consider you a threat or report you as suspicious. She checked her watch – 7.42 a.m., exactly three minutes before Thomas Cox, the Director of Public Prosecutions, or the DPP as he was known colloquially, would exit St James's Park tube station. She waited patiently until she saw him emerge. He was huddled into an overcoat and wore a black Fedora above his shock of white hair. Safa crossed the road, dodging a passing bicycle.

'Thomas,' she called out.

He spotted Safa and the lines on his face grew deep. He shook his head and picked up his pace, down Petty France towards the looming Brutalist building that housed the Ministry of Justice.

Safa kept pace with him easily. 'Thomas, I need to speak to you about Lily Astor.'

'You may contact the press office, Ms Saleem.'

'They blackball me every time and you know it.' Safa had had plenty of unfriendly dealings with his office.

A hint of a smile crossed his lips. 'I see they're doing their job then.'

Safa scowled. 'Thomas, come on. Do you really believe that Lily Astor deserves a life sentence?'

'We have a justice system, Ms Saleem, and this is how it works.'

'So she didn't get harsher treatment because she happens to be a celebrity?' Last year, the Crown Prosecution Service had come under fire for being soft on celebrities: a footballer accused of rape, a politician who broke his wife's nose, an actor who threw a phone at his crew. None of them had been charged let alone prosecuted so the CPS was now out for blood. 'She's not a danger to the public, she's not a flight risk, and she has a young son. Why wasn't she given bail?' asked Safa.

He picked up his pace. 'As I said, we have a justice system and this is how it works.'

'Thomas, if you think you got bad press last year, wait till you see what's coming. Lily has 8.5 million followers on Instagram – a veritable *army* of women. An army of feminists, in fact. The Centre for Women's Justice have been in touch and will use all their channels too.'

There was amusement in his features. 'You know, you would have made a great lawyer.'

'And what? Drop a level in the circles of hell?'

He raised a brow. 'I'm fairly sure that journalists rank lower than lawyers.'

'Can I quote you on that?'

He laughed but didn't break stride. 'Please contact my office, Ms Saleem. I can't comment on individual cases.'

'Thomas, just tell me this. Do you think Lily deserves life in prison?' He paused at a junction and Safa stepped into his eye line. 'Thomas, she's not a glossy celebrity. She's from the estate – like me.' She paused. 'And you.' Conflict crossed his features and Safa knew she had him.

'The prosecution did not oppose bail, Ms Saleem. If she had applied, they would have agreed conditions.'

Safa scowled. 'Lily was at Bronzefield for *six months* awaiting trial.'

'As I said, they would have been neutral on bail, but they never got to consider it.'

Safa stalled. 'Are you saying that Lily's team didn't *apply* for bail?' A pause. 'But they *always* apply for bail.'

'Take it up with them,' said Thomas. The pedestrian light turned green and he marched away, leaving Safa alone on the pavement. She was baffled. Why hadn't the defence applied for bail? It was standard practice.

'Well, look who it is,' said a voice behind her.

Safa recognised it immediately and turned to find Oliver Witherow in a ridiculous three piece suit. He looked her up and down with disdain. Safa remembered how, in her first week at *The Clarion*, he had told her to 'dress for the job you want, not the one you have'. Back then, she had to pretend that he was there on merit.

'Whose door are you darkening today?' he asked, looking over her shoulder.

'Get your own stories, Oliver.'

'Touchy touchy,' he said with a smarmy smile. 'I'll have you know that I have a very spicy story on the boil right now. They call him the Glassman,' he mocked.

Safa clenched her fists. She briefly considered telling him that she had been personally targeted, but she wasn't sure he would care. She opted for a different tack.

'Oliver, do you know there's been another victim?' She caught the look on his face. Interest – but also a hint of guilt? Did he have a conscience after all? 'She's seventy-four. She lives alone. She had ligature marks on her wrists but told her daughter she got them from her bangles.' Safa waited, watching for the slightest give. 'Please, Oliver. Give me the materials. You know I'm the best person to do this story.'

His face hardened. 'Then you shouldn't have screwed up, Safa.'

'Is that what you really believe, or are you just toeing the party line? Because you must know it wasn't *me* who messed up.'

'I can't help you.'

'Oliver, please. The police aren't going to commit resources to this until a victim speaks up. The one I had was almost ready.'

'I can't help you,' he repeated. He half-shrugged, then turned and walked off with nonchalance.

'Oliver!' she called with frustration. She hated to beg him, but this was more important than her pride. She scrabbled for something to offer him, but a man like Oliver was born with everything and Safa had nothing to trade him.

*

Safa's car was draughty and she blew on her hands to warm them. The heater whirred with labour but to little effect. She turned onto Mile End Road, nearly back at work, when her phone began to ring. She groped for it, but missed the call from Natalie. She slid to a stop at a traffic light and tried to call her back. A car horn sounded behind her and she realised that the light was now green. She raised a hand in apology and swiftly moved on.

'Hey Siri, call Natalie,' she instructed her phone. Natalie's voice was on the end of the line. 'Natalie, hang on, one second. I'm driving.' Safa struggled to hear her response. 'Hey Siri, put the phone on speaker,' she said. It didn't heed her and she tried again. She sighed and manually switched to speaker. As she looked up, a car cut into her lane and she slammed on the brakes, narrowly avoiding the back of it. The driver wore a black cap and jacket and she stared at him for a beat. She had started to map the Glassman everywhere: on dark street corners, next to her in a deserted lift, behind her at the cash machine. Imran had enlisted a colleague to help him canvass Haughton House, but the Glassman had almost certainly fled.

The driver in front turned in profile and she saw that he was Black. She exhaled and told herself to get it together. She apologised to Natalie and kept a closer eye on the road.

'Sorry I missed your call. Is everything okay?' she asked.

'Safa, I need to speak to you. Lily's told me to move into her house with Harry.'

'Okay.'

'I can't do that.'

Safa grimaced. 'I know it's not ideal asking him to live in the house where his dad was killed, but I think you'd be more comfortable there, Natalie. Surely, it's better than Withy House?'

'No, you don't understand, Safa. I mean I can't do it. I can't take on a thirteen-year-old kid. I have my own place. My own life.'

'Natalie, he doesn't have anyone else.'

'What about his grandmother? Audrey?'

'She might be an option, but Lily wants him to live with you.'

'I don't know how to look after a kid. We're barely coping as it is.'

Safa remembered the heap of ready meals spilling out of Natalie's bin. 'Listen, what if I came round today after work? We can have a chat about it. Maybe talk to Harry? See how he feels?'

'He won't want to talk. He had a temper tantrum today about his cricket whites.'

Safa felt a ping of worry. She knew that this was the age at which children began to lose their way. 'Listen, why don't I swing by his house and collect his kit for him?'

Natalie was quiet.

'Is there anything else he needs?'

'This is too much, Safa.'

'I know. It must be overwhelming but I'm here, okay? In fact,

I'll drop by now and get it. I still have my key.' Natalie protested but Safa insisted it was no trouble. She hung up and did a U-turn, back towards Narrow Street.

Weeds sprouted in the seams of the concrete that lined Lily's doorstep while flyers plugged the letterbox. What was the etiquette for this? Does one ask a neighbour to perform death duty? Safa suspected that, after Matthew Weaver's appearance in court, neighbourly goodwill was at a low.

She unlocked the door and pushed against the heap of unopened mail. Natalie didn't have a car, so would find it hard to keep up the maintenance. The most obvious solution was for her and Harry to move here.

Safa stepped inside and dust hit the back of her throat, making her release a guttural cough. She felt like an intruder as she moved upstairs to Harry's room. Everything was as she last left it: posters of footballers and a boxer posing inside a ring. She recognised him from the walls of Limehouse Boxing Club. She opened Harry's closet and rooted around for his cricket whites. She was relieved to find them in a bag along with his bat and pads. She heaved it up and then, with a smile, picked up the stuffed toy behind it. It was a plush red rhinoceros that Safa had given him as a present. She had christened him Gosling as in *Rhino Gosling*, and was touched that Harry had kept him all these years.

She was struck with sadness as she thought of the ways his life had changed. Bereaved of his father, deprived of his mother, stuck with an aunt who didn't want him. He deserved more than that and Safa vowed to help him. Her threat to Thomas Cox wouldn't prove empty. She would rally Lily's fans and enlist support from justice groups and, together, they would fight. Together, they would free Lily and bring her back to her son.

Chapter 22

Safa sat opposite Lily in the visitors' room. Today, it smelled of lemon disinfectant but with undertones of vomit – its acid tang still sharp in the air. Lily looked gaunt and her blonde hair looked brassy. There were dark circles beneath her eyes and her nails were short and jagged.

'Lily, while we wait for your appeal, there are things you and I can be doing. I've been in touch with a PR firm that does pro bono work for victims of abuse. They can enlist public support, turn this into a cause célèbre of sorts.'

'Safa—'

'Also, the Centre for Women's Justice have been in touch. They helped Juliet Culpen. They understand cases like yours.'

'Listen—'

'Trust me. We haven't even begun to exhaust everything we can do.'

'Safa, stop.' Lily's voice was hard. 'I don't want your help.'

'Lily, this isn't the time for your *me-against-the-world* bullshit, okay? Harry needs you and if you won't help yourself, then I'm going to do it for you.'

'I don't need your help. I have Victoria.'

'Victoria didn't even try for bail!'

'I asked her not to.'

Safa blinked. 'Why would you do that?'

'I didn't deserve bail. I didn't want it.'

'That's crazy. Victoria should never have agreed to it.'

'Just finish your feature and leave me alone.'

'I'm not going to do that. Harry needs you. Natalie needs you. We need to figure this out.' Safa pulled out her notebook and read from a list. 'Look, these are all the people and organisations who are willing to lend support. Women's Aid, Refuge, Solace, Mind, IDAS, Aanchal.'

'Safa—'

'The Fawcett Society, The Women's Institute.'

'Safa!' Lily barked. Several other prisoners turned to look their way. Lily didn't move for a moment, like a model holding a pose. 'I'm going to tell you something now.'

Safa quietened.

'You were right. About Patrick.' She gathered her cuff in her fist. 'I never saw him in a car with anybody. I just said that I did.'

Safa felt an immense weariness close over her. 'Why?' she asked, knowing that nothing Lily could say would answer that adequately.

'It was a lie that got out of hand.'

'It—' Safa had to stop to calm herself. 'It didn't "get out of hand", Lily. It destroyed Patrick's life.'

'Don't get so indignant, Safa. Deep down, you knew what I did.'

'That's not true.'

'Isn't it?'

Safa remembered Lily's breeziness – *Don't be silly. Being gay is cool now* – and that look on her face as she stood at the edge of class and watched the rumour spread. Safa had told no one else about her suspicions. 'Why did you do it?'

'To get him back for making fun of me.'

'It was just a childish insult. You *saw* what it did to him.'

'I didn't mean for it to become such a big deal.'

'Then why not take it back?' snapped Safa. 'Why not say you were mistaken?'

'I didn't want to get in trouble,' Lily said evenly.

'Lily, how the fuck have you lived with yourself knowing what you did?'

Lily's expression was coldly stoic. 'That's what I'm trying to tell you, Safa. I can live with things that ordinary people can't.'

Safa stared into her flat grey eyes. 'What's that meant to mean?'

Lily licked her cracked lips. The silence between them began to hum. 'What I'm trying to tell you, Safa, is that I killed Richard.'

'I know that.'

'No. You don't understand. I *wanted* him to die.'

'Maybe in the moment it felt true, but you tried to save him.'

'No, Safa. Listen to me carefully.' Lily's voice was low and urgent. 'There's a reason I need you to leave this alone. Right now, everyone thinks I was helpless, but if you keep gnawing at this like a dog with a bone, they will begin to see the discrepancies.' Lily glared at her, the air charged with meaning. 'And they will know that I waited.'

'Waited?'

'I waited until I was sure he would die before I called the police.'

'You're not serious,' Safa said in a whisper.

'I watched the life drain out of him. I wanted to look him in the eye when he knew that the end was coming.'

Safa's hand went to her neck, her shock like a noose. 'Lily, tell me that isn't true.'

'It is true. He deserved to die, Safa. He was a selfish bastard who didn't give a shit about me.'

Safa blinked to clear her vision. 'How long did you wait?' she asked, groping for a way to rationalise this.

'Minutes – but it was long enough.'

Safa pitched forward, elbows on knees, bowed by the weight of what she was learning. 'No, Lily.'

'Yes.'

Safa covered her eyes for a brief, awful moment. The reality was too large, expanded too quickly, filling her with a beating panic. 'Oh god, Lily, what were you *thinking*?'

Lily's voice was calm. 'I was thinking about freedom, about getting up in the morning and not worrying if he would be in a good mood today. I was thinking about sunlight streaming into the kitchen at breakfast and feeling it on my face. I thought about what it would feel like to be myself again.' Her face took on a sunken look. 'Then, I thought about going to prison for attempted murder without having finished him – a lose-lose result. I thought about whether or not I could do it and I decided that, yes, I could. I could let him die.'

Safa rejected this. 'How could you do it? How can you live with a secret like this?'

'I'm paying the price. I've been found guilty of murder, Safa. What value is there in telling the truth now?'

Safa shook her head vigorously. 'Lily, we need to get you help. Someone to talk to. A therapist. A professional.'

'No, Safa. Just leave it alone.'

'But you've lost everything. You need a way to process this.'

Lily's gaze was distant. 'I haven't lost everything. I have my reputation. I have the goodwill of my audience and, most of all, I have Harry who won't forgive me if he ever learns the truth.' Her focus shifted back. 'So you understand why, Safa, I need you to finish your feature and then leave this whole thing alone.'

Safa struggled to order her thoughts. Knowing that Lily had waited – that she had *calculated* minutes and watched while Richard was bleeding – was utterly chilling. Safa couldn't accept that *this* had made more sense to Lily than walking out of her marriage. There was *support* for abused women. Had Lily really felt that Richard had to *die* in order to be free of him?

Her thoughts shifted like sand, blown this way and that. Then, a dark shard of knowledge revealed itself to her. 'The affair,' she said, eyes wide with horror. 'You knew about the affair.'

Lily's lips twisted in a sardonic moue. 'Don't be stupid, Safa. Of *course* I knew.'

Safa paled. 'You lied in court.'

Lily nodded.

Safa felt the cold seep of dread. 'That's why you waited.'

Lily gave her an eerie look of sympathy – a villain to a hero thwarted. 'Maybe.'

Safa pressed a fist to her mouth. 'Lily, what the *fuck* did you do?'

Lily crossed her legs, as sleek as a shark in water. 'You know the truth now, Safa, and you know why you need to leave it alone.' She stood. 'Please tell Women's Aid and Refuge and whoever else is interested that I don't want their help. I just want to be left alone.'

'Lily, we're not finished.'

'Yes, we are,' she said gently. 'We're finished now.' Halfway to the door, she paused. 'Good luck with the Whitneys, Safa.' Her smile was not Astor bright; instead, it was soft and warm. 'I'll be rooting for you.'

PART III

Chapter 23

Safa stared at her screen and scrolled up and down compulsively. The startup had done a brilliant job with *A Killing on Narrow Street*. The feature began with a childhood picture of Lily, smiling into the sun, her blonde hair wild in the wind. It then followed the trajectory of Lily's career, her marriage to Richard, the speeches at their wedding set next to pictures of the couple staring at each other adoringly.

As she scrolled, the colour turned darker, charting Richard's job loss and testimonials from his friends about his changing mood. And then the night of the murder, Lily's interview with the police and her evidence in court.

The feature hadn't yet been published, but a film agent had already been in touch to ask about the rights. It looked and read exactly as she had envisioned, but there was one sticking point; it didn't tell the truth – and to Safa, that's what mattered most.

Without it, the past seven months of work amounted to little. Technically, she hadn't agreed to Lily's request that they speak off the record so Safa could, from a professional standpoint, print what she had been told. She knew what Oliver Witherow would do. Her editor, Kevin, would do the same. Any killer reporter would put the truth out there. The truth was neither good nor bad. It just *was*, but it could be wielded to be cruel.

The media was a game of reputation and Lily could cling on to hers. Before long, she'd likely be writing a column for a progressive women's magazine about her experiences of prison. *The Bronzefield Bulletin* or something along those lines. More importantly, Lily could still be a mother to Harry. If Safa revealed the truth, then all of that would be gone and for what? A prize?

'Ready to go?' She heard Kevin's voice behind her. It had been two weeks since the verdict and he had been pestering her to finish the feature.

'I need another day,' she told him.

'For what? Safa, Lily is already old news. We need to publish.'

'I know, Kevin. I just . . . There's something I'm still trying to decide.'

Kevin pulled up a chair and sat down. 'Can you say what it is?'

She puckered her lips. 'I don't think so, no.'

'You know what I always say.'

'Tell the truth.'

'That's it, Safa. That is our most important job.'

She swallowed. If she told the truth, her relationship with Lily – and most likely Harry – would be over forever. Was she willing to sacrifice that? 'One more day,' she told him.

'Okay, but we press publish at 8 a.m. tomorrow.'

'Agreed.' She turned back to her screen. She had already drafted the alternative version and pulled up the document now. The lead image showed a close-up of Lily's face, smiling but in shadow. This ending – the truthful one – elevated the piece from good to great. *This* was a prize-winning feature. As she skimmed the final paragraph, she heard an excited commotion at the other end of the newsroom. She glanced up and saw that Tim, the intern, had brought in a box of cupcakes.

'The trailer for my documentary is out,' he explained to Safa when she joined the group. Safa had seen an early cut and turned to the newsroom TV to watch the final edit.

'Multi-millionaire entrepreneur. Influential speaker. Kickboxing champion. Ultra alpha male,' a narrator spoke over a montage of images: Robert Knox in a sharp suit, Knox on stage, Knox in a boxing ring wearing red shorts, Knox with a bevy of women. A close-up of his face as the narrator spoke again: 'Or a pimp, rapist, trafficker, and purveyor of toxic masculinity. We go deep into the world of Robert Knox.'

The camera cut to Tim and a cheer went up in the newsroom.

'I'm journalist Tim O'Leary and I'm here to investigate: what is the pull of Robert Knox? Why does he appeal to men as old as eighty and boys as young as eight?'

Safa watched with bittersweet pride. There was no reason to believe that Tim – with his borrowed suit, fresh haircut and only a hint of his local accent – wasn't an anointed journalist. She grabbed a cupcake and took a big bite, swallowing it without really tasting it. Tim caught her eye and made his way to her.

'Safa, can you come to the screening? I'd love for you to be there.'

'Of course I will.'

'I was thinking you could share the stage with me.'

Safa was touched. It was true that she had helped him shape the original feature, but she hadn't expected any credit.

Tim continued: 'They want someone to interview me and I thought you would be great.'

Safa stalled. Tim was her mentee and now *she* would be interviewing *him*?

'What do you say?' he asked.

Safa swallowed her pride. 'Yes, of course I will.'

'Amazing! I'll email you the details now.' He bounded over to his desk and Safa returned to her own.

There, she stared at her alternative ending. She copied it from the document and pasted it to the bottom of *A Killing on Narrow Street*. She didn't press save, so that only she could see it. Her stomach knotted at the thought of pressing publish – but this was about the truth. It wasn't about a prize, or the fact that Tim had outstripped her. This was the truth, pure and simple, and surely that was enough.

*

Safa scanned the street before she unlocked her car and slid inside. She had planned to leave the office before it got so late, but she had worked and reworked the ending of her piece until her vision had blurred. Now, it was nearing nine and she realised she was famished. She decided to swing by Imli Kitchen for a cheeky takeaway. It was a little out of her way but worth the extra distance. She crossed the A13 and turned into Narrow Street. As she drove, her gaze naturally went to Lily's home.

She frowned when she saw that the hall light was on. Only Safa, Natalie and Harry had keys. Had they changed their minds about moving in? Safa saw a flicker of movement and wondered if she should look in. She made her decision at the very last minute, nipping through the black gates onto the gravel courtyard. Her Clio looked out of place next to the array of expensive cars and she felt sheepish as she locked it. She rang the doorbell and waited, but there was no answer. She couldn't hear it ring and wondered if it had been disconnected. She grabbed her phone from her bag and rang Natalie, but it went to voicemail. She rang the bell again, then idly tried the handle. To her surprise, it twisted open. She hovered at the threshold, unsure of what to do.

'Natalie?' she called. Tentatively, she stepped inside. 'Harry?' She closed the door behind her. 'Guys?' There was no movement or sound. It occurred to her that she could be interrupting a burglary. It was public knowledge that Lily was in prison and her address would be easy to find.

Safa grew hot and her throat, dry and scratchy. She should leave and call the police. And tell them what? *I saw a light on.* It was almost certainly Harry and Natalie. She advanced along the hallway, making noise to alert anyone inside to her presence.

'Natalie?' she called again. Something toppled over and she tried to locate the source. It had come from somewhere in the bowels of the house and she followed its rough direction, past the living room and into the large kitchen. She caught movement in the garden. A fleeing intruder. She darted to the window and scanned the lawn. Then, she slumped with relief. It was only Natalie, stood by the open shed. Safa knocked on the window – gently so not to startle her – and went out to join her.

Natalie turned and, when she spotted Safa, leapt to her feet like a scalded cat.

Safa flinched at the sight of her. A deep bruise, livid and purple, bloomed across her eyes. The right socket seemed filled with liquid and was almost swollen shut. Safa's breath was like sand in her lungs. She took a step forwards but Natalie held up her palms.

'No, don't.' She grappled for something in her pocket and quickly slipped on some shades.

Safa's stomach lurched. Because that's when she realised that she hadn't seen Natalie without dark glasses since the start of the trial. And every time she'd been to Withy House, Natalie hadn't been around.

She's popping into Tesco.
She sleeps in when she has a migraine.
She'll be annoyed if we wake her.

Safa remembered Natalie's nervy energy, bordering on the manic: *I've got to get back before Harry.* Natalie fretting: *Maybe we'll take the tube to be on the safe side.* The dread with which she asked, *Do I have to keep him forever?*

Safa was aghast. She fixated on the bruise. A whispered name on her lips: 'Harry?'

Natalie looked at her with infinite sadness. 'Harry.'

Chapter 24

Safa's blood drummed in her ears as she approached Natalie – slowly so not to spook her. She couldn't see her eyes now, but her distress was clear.

'Harry did this to you?'

Natalie twisted her birdlike hands. 'Yes.' A pause. 'He did it all.'

Safa watched her carefully. 'What do you mean *all*?'

'All everything. Lily is many things – you and I both know that – but she's not a killer.'

Safa felt the ground sway beneath her. 'You're saying it was Harry?' She glanced around the garden for other signs of madness. 'But it *couldn't* have been him. He was at Stephen's house. The police confirmed this.'

'I don't know how he did it, but I know he did.'

Safa's thoughts swung like a pendulum, from one extreme to the other – offence, defence, offence, defence. 'You're saying *Harry* killed Richard to protect Lily?'

Natalie's gaze was hard and pleading. 'No, Safa. I'm saying Harry killed Richard because *Richard* was protecting Lily.'

Safa's mind whirred to catch up. Then, the heft of realisation hit her like a fist. 'But that's impossible.'

Natalie's jaw worked in silence. She was still for a moment, then she pushed up a sleeve. Safa gasped, for Natalie's arm was mottled with bruises. She pointed to one that sat on her wrist like a bracelet.

'This was because I asked him to turn down the sound on TikTok.' She pointed at another. 'This one was because I answered a quiz show question before him. This one was because I hadn't washed his trainers.' There was a choke in her throat as she pushed up the other sleeve. 'Lily begged me not to tell. She said he'd be put in an institution. She tried to get him private help, but he flat-out refused. How could we force him without the world finding out?'

Safa floundered for meaning. '*Harry* was the one hurting Lily?'

Natalie nodded. 'Richard never touched her. It was Harry all along.'

Safa stepped back unsteadily, the grass reaching up to grab her. Her mind careened with disbelief. 'But . . . he's thirteen.'

'Old enough to do this.' She indicated her body. 'Safa, I know that he killed Richard. He hints at it. Says things like, "I don't want to do something *else* I'll regret."'

Safa struggled to believe it. Her mind wheeled through her time with Harry and snagged on certain incidents: his fight with a fellow student, his anger towards a female classmate: *Ella's a bitch. Bobby says that girls don't like gentlemen.*

'I don't know what to do,' said Natalie.

Safa looked at the delta of bruises on Natalie's pale arm. 'You need to tell the police,' she said with more conviction than she felt.

'I can't.'

'You have to, Natalie. We can't let Lily rot for this.'

'She'll kill herself before she lets that happen.'

'You don't know that.'

'She said so, Safa. She told me that if I tell anyone, she will kill herself.'

'She wouldn't do that.'

'She'll do anything for him.'

'But he *hit* her.'

'Yes, but he's her son,' said Natalie plainly.

326

Safa was appalled that maternal love could extend this far – so strong and elastic that it could wrap itself into a noose. She shook her head, then spun and headed towards the house.

'Where are you going?' called Natalie.

'To Bronzefield,' said Safa without breaking stride. 'To find the truth once and for all.'

Chapter 25

The air at Bronzefield was stale and held the chemical smell of antiquated heating. Safa stripped off her down coat and sat opposite Lily. She had engineered this meeting under the guise of a final fact check and spent the first ten minutes going over minor details: Lily's college at Oxford, Harry's date of birth, the location of her wedding to Richard. Then, once Lily was at ease, she switched to the night of the killing.

'I want to check something, Lily. In the police interview, you said that you used your hands to stop the bleeding and then grabbed a tea towel to help you. If it's true that you waited for him to die, why did the towel have blood on it?'

Lily considered this. 'I did use it on his wound. I did that by instinct. It's only later that I eased the pressure.'

'So it's true that you initially stemmed the wound, first with your hands and then the towel?'

'Yes.'

'Where did you get the towel from?'

'The ice bucket on the sideboard.'

'You also said that you called the emergency services and asked for an ambulance. How did you call them?'

Lily was confused. 'I've been through this.'

'Humour me. Please.'

'I asked Siri to.'

'How?'

'I said, "Hey Siri, call the police."'

'At this point, both of your hands were on Richard's wound?'

'Yes.'

'How did you put the call on speaker?'

Lily sighed. 'I said, "Hey Siri, put the phone on speaker."'

Safa folded her arms. 'Here's the thing, Lily. Siri can't put a call on speakerphone once you're already on the call.' She studied Lily closely; watched the pallor spread. 'And there's something else.' She pulled out her notebook. 'None of the photos from the party show the ice bucket on the sideboard.'

'You're wrong,' said Lily. 'They showed one in court.'

Safa opened the notebook to a single photograph. 'This is the picture they showed. It was taken from Talia's Facebook page and shows the ice bucket with the tea towel.' She pushed it towards Lily. 'What do you notice about the bottle?'

Lily didn't look. 'What are you doing, Safa?'

Safa tapped the photo. 'There are spotlights reflected in the bottle – but you don't *have* spotlights in the living room. This picture was taken in the kitchen, on a countertop made of the same oak as the sideboard.'

'What's your point?'

'My point is that the tea towel wasn't within reaching distance, so either you went and got it yourself from the kitchen, in which case you would have just said that – or someone got it for you.'

Lily shrugged jerkily. 'So I got confused. I was stressed, Safa.'

'I don't think so, Lily. You have been very precise about everything. I know that someone else was there. I know that someone fetched you that towel. I know that they moved the bucket to make it look like you could reach it. And I know that someone else called 999.'

'That's ridiculous.'

'I know, Lily. I know that it was Harry.'

Lily scoffed but there was a falseness in it; the fatigue of upholding an intricate lie. Safa remained silent. She knew from her years of interviewing when to talk and when to wait; when to let the secret expand until it spilled out. She could hear Lily's breathing – soft and fractured. First, a gentle surrender and, then, breakdown. Lily leaned forward and covered her eyes, but there was no other movement or sound. When, a minute later, she looked at Safa, her eyes were red and raw as if she had wept for hours. There were no tears, however. Just a strange and lucid calm.

'I heard this thing once that there's a difference between trolls and goblins.' There was a faraway look in her eye. 'If trauma happens to you when you're older, then it's a troll. You can fight it and kill it or banish it. If, however, it happens in a formative year, then it's a goblin and you won't ever get rid of it. It will always be there. I think that it – whatever *it* is – got into Harry too early.'

Safa felt a jittery hum in her arms – finally, the truth.

'I blame myself.' Lily smoothed an invisible crease in her sleeve. 'Sometimes, I think that his anger is primal. Maybe he knew on some level that I tried to kill him in the womb. It's like his body absorbed the knowledge. I did everything to make up for it. I was the best mother I could be, I gave him everything, vowed that nothing would hurt him, but I fear that he somehow knew.'

Safa recalled her heart-to-heart with Harry. *Then how come she tried to get rid of me?*

'He was only eleven when it started.' Lily sat up straight, neatened her hair and laced her hands in her lap – a rosary of small acts designed to show composure. 'I'd cooked Harry's favourite meal: slow roasted lamb. It had taken me hours but he just sat there on his phone. I told him to put it away and with no warning, lightning quick, he threw it at my head. It hit the wall behind me. Richard and I just sat there, stunned. I remember that Harry was just as stunned as us. He sat there, waiting to see what I would do. I tried to be calm. I told him to go upstairs, but he didn't listen. There was this tension in the air, like something might rip through the walls and fold the room in two. Richard was practically humming with fury. He had never hit Harry, but men's instincts are frightening, so I shouted at Harry to leave.'

There was a tremor in Lily's hands and she squeezed them tight to snuff it out. 'I told myself not to overreact. We had just been through the lockdowns and hadn't we *all* gone a little bit crazy? But it got worse. He became obsessed with this vile misogynist on TikTok. Robert Knox. Or *Bobby* as Harry liked to call him.'

Safa jolted in surprise. *Bobby says that girls don't like gentlemen.* She and Harry had been walking in the park and she had responded glibly. *Well, you shouldn't always listen to your friends.*

A snatch of an image came to her. The poster on Harry's wall of the boxer in the ring. She had recognised the image not from her gym but the trailer for Tim's documentary. *Why does he appeal to men as old as eighty and boys as young as eight?* The boxer was Robert Knox.

Lily continued: 'Harry watched a video of Knox beating up this poor girl who then claimed it was consensual. How are we meant to combat that? I turned on all the parental controls, but they find ways to access things. His friends would save videos off TikTok and send them to him manually. And I don't know if all those videos warped him, or if that warp was always there and Knox just twisted it further – but that's how it started.'

Lily's skin was glossed with sweat. 'It was always me,' she said. 'He never hit Richard. It was like he was *furious* with me. I never thought I'd be the sort of woman that tolerates abuse but, Safa, no one expects it from their child.'

Safa felt a well of emotion. 'Lily,' she said gently. 'He told me that Richard used to pinch you when you were out. That wasn't true?'

Lily squeezed her hands harder, her knuckles now shiny and white. 'It was Harry who did that. The story about the lobster was true, but it was Harry who did it.'

Safa felt a wringing in her chest. Knowing that Lily would be out with Harry, and that he would hurt her like that, in secret, in unseen parts of her flesh, made Safa quail with horror.

'I felt completely alone, like I was the only one going through this, but then I found out about CPA – child to parent abuse – and that there were other parents going through the same thing. I found a group that met every Wednesday in Poplar and that gave me some relief.'

Safa recalled how Lucien Garrett had badgered Lily about this in court. 'So you *did* go to a support group?'

'Yes, but I went to the Wednesday night CPA group, not the Thursday night VAWG group. I couldn't tell the truth without exposing Harry, but neither did I want them to say that I hadn't sought help at all. In the end, it worked against me because of course no one at the VAWG group remembered me.' Lily swiped the moisture off her upper lip.

'Things got bad. Richard didn't know how to handle it. It got to the point where I wouldn't even tell *him* what happened each day, or I'd hide my bruises from him.'

Safa thought of the Glassman's victim who insisted that her ligature marks had been caused by bangles. Like Lily, she had hidden a literal body of evidence.

Lily continued: 'I was ashamed, and scared that something would ignite between them and so I played it down. But things got bad. I said things to Harry that no mother should say to her son.'

'*I'm scared I'll kill you one day,*' said Safa.

Lily nodded. 'I was screaming at Harry that day. Not Richard.'

Safa felt a cawing sympathy. 'Oh, Lily. I'm so sorry.'

'Richard felt lost. He didn't know how to help me. He kept

pushing for boarding school, but I was terrified of what would happen if Harry was violent there. It caused a rift between us and Richard turned elsewhere.'

'Talia?'

Lily nodded. 'He confessed the affair to me but, Safa, I didn't have the mental space to deal with it. I barely even registered it. He got so desperate, he said he'd file for divorce if we didn't seek help – but I knew he wouldn't leave me. Despite the firestorm we were in, we never stopped loving each other. He was the only man I've ever let into my heart. And if I could do that night again, I would give my life for his.' Lily balled her fist on the table, intent on finishing this.

'What you said about waiting for him to die. You made that up?'

'I had to get you to stop looking, Safa, in case you found the truth. I thought that if I lost your sympathy, you would stop trying to free me.'

Safa exhaled. 'What really happened on the night Richard died?'

The tension eased in Lily's shoulders – the relief of confession. 'The day before the party, Harry told us to call it off. He said that we shouldn't have organised it without consulting him. When I told him it was too late, he smacked me across the face. He may be a child but he hits hard enough to make me bleed.'

Safa recalled Imran's words. *Make a fist. That is a really fucking horrible thing to be hit by.*

'I ran to the bathroom. I was always so fucking ashamed. I tried to hide it from Richard, but he knew that something had happened. That's why he was so stressed when you turned up at our door that day.'

Safa remembered her run-in with Richard and now understood that his aggression was misplaced. *Has it ever occurred to you that you're just a cheap hack?*

'I watched you leave, Safa, and a part of me wanted to throw open that window and scream, *Safa, help me!* because I knew you would. You would crash through the walls to rescue me, but I had to protect Harry. Richard and I clashed about that constantly. He couldn't understand why *that* instinct came above everything else, even self-preservation.

'Richard tried to protect me the best way men know how: aggression. He went upstairs and began to bang on Harry's door, shouting at him to turn the music off. I knew it would escalate so I begged Richard to leave him alone.

'On the day of the party, I was on tenterhooks – maybe even a little bit manic in making sure things went smoothly. Richard checked in with me regularly, made sure I was okay, that I wasn't drinking too much. We managed to pull it off but after the last guests left, Harry came downstairs and said he was going out. It was late and Richard told him no, but Harry stormed out.' Lily smiled dolefully. 'In the end, the timing worked perfectly because it meant that Talia and Edward saw him leave.

'Richard came and held me and we stood there in this god-awful soup of helplessness.' Lily gestured delicately. 'And then I heard the front door open. In his rage, Harry had left his phone behind. When he came back to get it, Richard grabbed him by the collar. It was the first time that they'd ever got physical. Harry shoved him off and things happened so quickly. Harry picked up the knife and threatened him. Richard, of course, thought he was bluffing. He squared up to him and tried to grab the knife, but Harry swung it and the next thing I know, Richard is bleeding on the living room floor.' Lily's eyes took on a vacant glaze. 'I began to shriek, but even in the depths of my panic, there was another, sterner part of me that knew I had to act. I stemmed the bleeding with my bare hands. You worked it out already; Harry got the ice bucket. He was white like a sheet, shivering, on the verge of hysterical. He was never evil, Safa. He was angry and lost and misguided, but never evil. The world would never understand that, so I knew somewhere deep and primal that I had to take the blame.

'I had minutes to save Richard and it's like some higher consciousness inside me came alive. I knew that Talia and Edward would have seen Harry leave so I told him to put on a jumper and leave immediately. I told him to take his bike and ride to Stephen's house, but to call him when he was nearly there so that his phone data would place him elsewhere. When he got close to Stephen's house, he dumped his bike so he could later claim that he had walked. This gave him twenty minutes of alibi – the twenty-minute walk to Stephen's house – when really it took him five on the bike. I knew that if I confessed, the police wouldn't look at Harry too closely, so I just needed to put him elsewhere.'

Safa recalled how the red, white and blue bikes became just red and white. Harry had dumped the blue one. 'But didn't Harry have blood on him?'

'Yes. Underneath his jumper.'

Safa blinked. 'He went to Stephen's house with blood on him?'

'Yes. And spoke to the police. The safest place to dispose it was *on him*. I knew they weren't going to search him.'

'But what if they *had*? What if the blood got elsewhere?'

'He couldn't leave the jumper at our house and it was too much of a risk to put it in a bin. What if it was found? He wore it and washed it later at Natalie's.'

'Natalie knew?'

'Not at first.' Lily's throat worked in silence. 'But then he began to hit her.'

Safa remembered all those times she had asked after Natalie, and Harry had made excuses – at work, out shopping, in bed with a migraine. Really, she had been nursing bruises.

'There was a reason I didn't ask for bail, Safa. I needed time away from him. I needed to steady my nerves so I could keep on going.' Lily hunched with guilt. 'Instead, I saddled my sister with him.' A rash of colour laced up her neck. 'I hoped that the shock of what happened would fix him, but it's *in* him, Safa. Whatever it is, it's in him.' Lily squeezed the cuff of her sleeve. 'The first time he hit Natalie, she came to see me. I begged her to keep his secret. I told her that I had given up my freedom and smeared my husband's name to save Harry. I begged her to wait for the verdict. I told her I'd be set free and she would no longer have to deal with him.'

Lily's face was blotchy with emotion. '*Just a few months, Natalie. It's just a few months.* I recited it like a mantra as if a few months of being punched and slapped was nothing.' Lily's voice trembled. 'I put my own sister in danger and then I emotionally blackmailed her.' She took a sharp breath. 'And I knew what I was doing, Safa. I know how tough she is. I saw what she went through with Mum. I know her capacity for pain. So I used it.' Lily's voice cracked. 'I just let her take it.'

Safa reached out, but Lily pulled away, not needing – or deserving – comfort.

Lily spoke faster now, keen to confess it all. 'I didn't realise that they would use the affair with Talia as a motive. And then Harry stood up and said that he'd never seen Richard hit me. Part of me was furious with him, but part of me was glad he said it. I'm glad he told the truth because Richard didn't fucking deserve all the lies I told.'

Safa felt a tang of guilt, like metal on her tongue. She was the one who'd told Harry to tell the truth in court – and he *had*. Her advice had unwittingly sealed a guilty verdict. 'Lily, you can't take the blame for this.'

'I already have.'

'Harry needs help. Not a cover-up.' She remembered the young boy who had wept over penguin chicks dying on TV. The thought of him battling a rage he couldn't control made Safa ache. She understood Lily's compulsion to protect him, but whatever darkness had got inside him would only fester in Withy House.

Lily, however, disagreed. 'I'll get him help as soon as all this dies down.'

'That could be *years*, Lily. Can you really live with him hurting Natalie? She doesn't have anyone to defend her.'

'That's the thing, isn't it?' Lily's voice took on a bitter note. 'We cry feminism but when it comes down to it, we are cowed by the violence of men, lost without their protection.' She swallowed. 'I read that 90 per cent of CPA cases are sons being violent towards their mothers – and that it affects one in ten families. Can you believe that? Is it the corrosive hose of social media, or is there something in their genetic makeup that tells them to hurt the women in their lives?'

Safa gripped the edge of the table. 'Lily, you have to do something. You can't just sit in prison passively. You can raise awareness of this issue. Harry is a minor. He clearly has a problem. We can get him help.'

'No.'

'I can't let you take the fall, Lily.'

'You have to.'

'I won't.'

'What can you do?'

'I'll write about it.'

Lily wasn't spooked. 'I'll deny it all.'

'I'll get Natalie on record. I won't let you rot in prison, Lily. Don't you see? This is just another form of control. You're not helping Harry. You're enabling him.'

Lily's jaw hardened. 'All of this was off the record.'

'No, it wasn't.'

Lily fixed her statue gaze on her. 'You wouldn't dare.'

'I have to.'

'If you do, I'll sue the fuck out of you.'

'Fine, but at least you'll be free – and Natalie will be safe.' Safa reached for her notebook, but Lily snatched it off the table.

'I don't need rescuing, Safa. Not this time.'

'I won't argue with you, Lily.' Safa stood up to signal her resolve. She held out a palm for her notebook, but Lily smacked the hand away. A guard looked up sharply. His body tensed, alert to trouble.

Lily's voice was low and menacing. 'Safa, if you do this, I will spend the rest of my life ruining yours.'

Safa gave her a doleful smile. 'I believe it too.'

'Safa, please.' There was panic in her voice now. 'Think about Harry.'

It made Safa ache that even after all she had suffered, Lily's instinct was to save her son. Did he choose to hurt her so much because a mother's threshold of pain was so high?

Lily dropped the notebook and grabbed Safa's lapel. 'Safa, don't do it.' The guard was there in a flash, pulling Lily back. She tried to wrench away from him but he held her fast. 'I'll make you pay for this, Safa. I swear to god.' She kicked out in an effort to shake off the guard. He closed an arm around her neck and began to wrestle her backwards. 'Safa, I beg you! Don't do it. Please!'

Safa felt a bleating sorrow as she watched them go. She knew that this would destroy their friendship for good, but she had to tell the truth. This she knew with a sure and merciful clarity. There would be no dark night of the soul, sorting right from wrong. Her only option was to tell the truth. Wearily, she retrieved her notebook and headed to the newsroom.

Chapter 26

Safa was exhausted. She had begged an extension from Kevin and stayed up late every night this week to rework her piece on Lily. She had changed the angle to an intimate portrait of CPA, the last taboo in domestic abuse. She had been shocked by its prevalence but also its obscurity. Women had ways to talk about domestic abuse but this specific variety was largely hidden from view, shrouded by shame and maternal instinct. Safa knew that this was a ground-breaking piece; one that would change the narrative – maybe even win a Whitney.

As dawn filtered through her blinds, she added the finishing touches and felt an immense pride. This was the sort of work that she wanted to be known for: deeply researched, sensitive, nuanced. She imagined all the women who would see themselves in the piece; who could use it as a way to start a difficult conversation. *You know that viral article in* The Echo? *That may be what's happening to me.* With this piece, Safa could change the vocabulary of domestic abuse.

Jittery with nerves, she read it one final time, tweaking words here and there until it was perfect. She knew that Kevin would be proud of it. This, to him, was the true purpose of journalism: to journey into darkness and try to find light.

Who needs killer instinct? she thought as she prepared a preview link for him. This piece would finally establish her as a reporter worth investing in. She was about to send the email when her phone began to ring. She snatched it up and saw that it was Imran.

'Hey, it's a bit early for you,' she said.

Imran sounded breathless. 'Safa, there's been another one.'

She blinked. 'When?'

'Last night. Another widow.'

Dread lined her stomach. 'He's speeding up. That's two in two months.' She flexed her fingers wide. 'What happened with Haughton House?'

'I searched it myself, Safa. I knocked on every door, but no one knew who he was.'

'What about the flats where no one was home?'

'I went back to those. I've been to every single flat in the building. No one knows a man fitting the description.'

'Fuck.' Safa felt her frustration build. 'Listen, Imran. I need to think. I'll call you later, okay?' She hung up and sprang to her feet. She grabbed her keys and left her flat, desperate for some air. Instinctively, she headed to Regent's Canal. Water always helped her think. She sat outside the Ragged School Museum and tried to think of a plan. The Glassman had attacked at least three more women since Safa had lost her research. She had threatened, then begged, then guilted Oliver Witherow, but he remained unmoved. Safa considered approaching him about a joint investigation, but a paper like *The Clarion* didn't need *The Echo*. Besides, Oliver would almost certainly do none of the work but gladly take the credit. She imagined him on social media, *humbled* by the praise, *grateful* to be able to do this work, *indebted* to his colleague Safa Saleem for her assistance and support. A man like Oliver would have no qualms about passing off her work as his own.

A thought occurred to Safa, but she pulled away from it, her entire body tense in protest. *No.*

But it was too late. The thought had taken hold. Safa understood that she had been wrong. She *did* have something to trade after all.

*

It was a freezing November day, but the door to The Green Cab Café was open, airing out the grease. Safa drained her second cup of coffee and checked her watch again. Oliver was half an hour late. If she didn't know him better, she would think it a power play, but knew it was more likely sloppiness. When he finally did turn up, he didn't apologise; simply slid into the booth and looked around with patrician distaste.

'Interesting choice,' he remarked.

Safa had a flashback to her time at *The Clarion* where polish was on people like a birthmark. Back then, she had been keen to impress him, but now she didn't care what he thought of her, or her tacky little café.

'I want to tell you a story,' she said as Oliver sipped his tea.

He tilted his head in amusement. 'Is it a comedy, tragedy or history?'

'Do you think you can be serious for ten minutes?' Before he could muster a quip, she added, 'Set a timer if you want. Ten minutes is all I'm asking for.'

He leaned back in his chair, showily nonchalant. 'Okay. Go.'

Safa held his gaze. 'When I was eight years old, I caused my mother's death.'

Oliver blinked. 'Oh-kay,' he said slowly.

'Believe it or not, I was a funny kid. I was loud and curious and cheeky – but one night changed everything.' Safa gritted her teeth because damn her if she was going to show weakness in front of Oliver Witherow. She dug her fingernails into her thighs underneath the table. Then, she began the story of what happened at the hospital. She told Oliver about the missing translator and how she misunderstood the meaning of the word *allergic*. Calmly, she took him through the worst hours of her life: her mother's death, the hushed conversation between her dad and the interpreter, the gut-wrenching realisation that she had got it wrong.

'My mother died because she couldn't speak for herself. I had to do it and I failed. There are other women like her; women who don't speak the language of this country, who aren't au fait with its mores, who are treated as "other" by every authority they have to deal with. These are the women that the Glassman targets. He knows they are silenced by their lack of language but also misogyny and cultural taboos. But *I'm* here. *I'm* a voice. I can be *their* voice, but you – and *The Clarion* – have taken that from them, from me.'

Oliver's expression was unreadable.

'And I know that doesn't mean a lot to you, so here's what I'm going to do. I'm going to give you the biggest scoop of my career in exchange for your – or rather *my* – Glassman materials.' She placed a memory key on the table between them.

Oliver eyed it with suspicion. 'What is it?'

'It is a ready-made belter of a story. You don't have to do any footwork, chase any sources, check any facts. You won't need to do any work at all. It's all there for you.'

'What is it?' he repeated.

Safa exhaled slowly and slid the key across the table. 'Lily Astor didn't kill her husband. Harry Astor did it.'

Oliver let out a snatch of laughter. 'Bullshit.'

'It's true. Her sister, Natalie Baker, is on the record. It's all there.'

He reached for the memory key, but Safa closed her hand on top of it. 'But, first, you walk me to your office, you buzz me in as a visitor, you take me upstairs and you hand over my materials.'

'Not until I see what's on here.'

'I've told you what's on there. It's an award winning story, Oliver. Maybe *the* award winning story – and it's yours. You don't even have the change the words. Take it. Use it. Put your byline on it.'

He assessed her carefully. 'This is a trap.'

'I won't tell a soul.'

'You really want the Glassman that badly?'

'Yes. I told you why.'

He stared at her hand that covered the key. 'If that really is what you say it is, this is going to be the biggest story in the country.'

'I know that.'

'You'll get fired from *The Echo*.'

'Maybe. Or maybe Kevin knows I can do it again and he'll trust that.'

Oliver considered this. He was either too smart or too greedy to question her further. 'Fine.'

Safa withdrew the key and dropped it in her bag. 'Let's go,' she said, tossing a ten-pound note on the table. Outside, she headed towards the tube but Oliver gestured in the opposite direction and led her to his silver Jaguar. She rolled her eyes but got in. In silence, they drove to *The Clarion* offices. At reception, he told her to wait.

'If people see us together, it will look weird.'

'No way,' said Safa. She didn't trust him to give her everything. She waited for her visitor pass and followed him to the lift.

Inside, Oliver asked, 'Did Harry really kill his father?'

'Yes.'

He bounced on his feet, unable to hide his glee. The lift pinged open and she followed him onto the floor. The smell – newspaper print and coffee – raised a lurch of nostalgia. Safa had loved her time here; was devastated when told to leave. She felt eyes on her as she followed Oliver to his desk, opposite the one that used to be hers. In her place sat a young white woman with delicate features and thick blonde hair, dressed far too well for newspaper wages. Safa averted her gaze and hovered awkwardly by Oliver's shoulder. She watched as he compressed her files and sent them to her. He hovered over 'Send' and held out his other hand.

Safa took a deep breath, then planted the biggest story of her career into Oliver's palm.

*

Harry opened the door and beamed with surprise.

'Aunt Saffie, you didn't say you were coming today.'

'Hi, Harry. Is Natalie home?' Safa had spoken to Natalie earlier and arranged for her to be out when this happened.

'No. She had a doctor's appointment.' He held the door open and Safa walked in. She glanced at her watch. It was 8.30 a.m. By the time she finished talking to him, the story would have broken.

'Do you mind if I make myself a cup of tea?'

'Sure.' Harry followed her to the kitchen.

'I'm sorry to just drop in like this. Do you want a sec to run up and get changed?'

He looked down at his pyjama bottoms and his T-shirt with its baked bean-coloured stain. His mouth curled sheepishly. 'Yeah, sorry. I just ate. Give me five minutes.'

Safa didn't want him to be photographed like this. He was Lily's son and deserved some dignity. She took her tea to the table and waited. Harry returned a few minutes later. His hair was freshly brushed and he wore clean jeans and a cream-coloured jumper. Safa gestured at the chair next to her and waited for him to sit.

'Harry. Something is happening that I need to talk to you about.'

He propped his elbows on the table and it struck Safa how impossibly young he looked. She wasn't trained for this in any way, but she couldn't let the first person to tell him be a faceless authority. She couldn't ask Natalie to do it, so had to be here herself.

'Some things have come to light about the night your dad died.' Safa monitored his reaction. She was acutely aware that she had to do this gently. 'Harry, they know that your mum didn't hurt your dad.'

He didn't startle or flinch. There was no shock or angst; just a quiet calm.

'Do you understand what I'm saying?' She waited. 'Harry, they know what happened and we're going to get you some help, okay?'

For a moment, he didn't move. Then, he got to his feet – slowly, deliberately, with clear intent to leave.

Safa reached out and gripped his arm. She felt the tension in it, firmly coiled to strike. For the first time, she saw how Lily and Natalie were right. 'Harry, you don't need to talk to me, but please sit down.' The muscle in his arm was rigid and Safa held her breath. 'Please.'

His features grew dark and different and the veins in his neck stood out. He clenched and unclenched his fingers, on the cusp of rage. The air crackled with warning and Safa felt a bolt of alarm. She pushed her own chair backwards, slowly like prey. 'Harry.' She brought herself up to his level. 'Please sit down.'

His face twisted like he'd tasted something rancid. He bared his teeth and pressed his fists to his temple. Then, he let out a howl of black, necrotic rage. It was so loud and sudden, it made Safa flinch. Harry grabbed fistfuls of his own hair.

'I told her not to do it. She didn't have to do it! I would have taken the blame.' His voice was shrill with panic.

Safa didn't speak, letting his anger flare.

'It was her idea! *She* told me to go to Stephen's.'

'She wanted to protect you,' ventured Safa.

Harry struck the table. 'I didn't need her to! I never asked for it.'

'She's your mother. She was always going to protect you.'

'Then why did she try to get rid of me?' Harry's voice cracked with need.

Safa wanted to go to him but the fumes of his rage were too thick. 'She was practically a child herself, Harry. She was under incredible amounts of pressure, but she always loved you.' Tentatively, she added, 'And I know you love her too.'

'I don't love her.' Harry's neck flushed red. 'I hurt her.'

'That wasn't you, Harry. I knew you before the toxic bile you picked up from *Bobby*.'

Harry looked up in surprise. 'This isn't Bobby's fault. He helps me.'

'No he doesn't, Harry.'

'He *does*.' Harry's features were hard. 'You all say he's toxic but you don't understand him.'

'Then help me understand. Tell me what he has done for you.'

'Bobby gets what life is like and he tells us the truth.'

'What truth?'

Harry snatched in a breath, still so close to rage. 'Bobby says that life is like a chessboard. If you're a woman – a queen – you get to move straight across it, but if you're a man, you can only move square by square.' Harry unclenched his fist, but the veins in his hand were rigid. 'Imagine a party on a yacht, he says. If you're a woman, you can get lip filler and a boob job and you get straight on. But if you're a man, you need to move through all these squares. Looks is one. Money is one. Your job. Your car. He teaches us the truth about life – so why is that toxic?'

Safa could understand why this thinking was seductive. It taught young men that they were in charge of their destiny, immune to the vagaries of fate. If they were bold, forceful, *aggressive* enough, then they too could get on the yacht.

'Can I ask you a question, Harry? Why did you only hit your mother? Never your father?'

There was a cold glaze in his eyes. 'Because she wouldn't hit back.'

Sadness closed over Safa. *It's as simple as that*, she thought. *Because she wouldn't hit back.* She waited for more. She wanted him to break down and cry; to show the humanity she knew he had. Instead, he stared at the table, his skin slowly pinking. Safa reached past her own anger and spoke to the boy she loved.

'There are two things I want you to know, Harry. The first is that your mother loves you. She has always loved you and she always will. She would have spent the rest of her life in prison for you. Do you understand that?'

He didn't respond; only hunched inward.

'You are loved, Harry, and I want you to remember that. The second thing is that they're going to come.' A pause. 'Reporters, photographers, spectators . . . The police.'

Fear leapt in his eyes, boyish and wild. 'What will they do?' he asked.

'They're going to want to talk to you.'

An alarming heat rose in his cheeks. 'Are they going to lock me up?'

Safa couldn't lie to him. 'For now, that's likely.'

Harry stood erect, but his courage gave way. His hands began to shake and his body took on a chemical smell: muggy and hormonal. Sweat stained his collar and his skin was slick and ruddy. To Safa's immense relief, she saw the tears come. It was clear to her then that beyond the man he was so desperately trying to be, Harry was still very much a child.

'I'm going to come with you, Harry,' she assured him. 'I'll be there through everything. For now, I'll tell you the same thing I told you the day you went to court. Just tell the truth. If you feel lost or nervous or confused, just tell the truth. Do you understand?'

Harry's tears spilled over, but he made no move to wipe them.

Safa spoke more urgently. 'Harry, do you understand?'

'Yes,' he replied with a thick sob.

Safa reached for him but before she could make contact, the doorbell rang, followed quickly by three loud knocks.

'They're here,' said Safa. She saw the terror on Harry's face. His body was tense and ready to bolt. She held out her hand. 'I've got you,' she said gently.

His gaze darted wildly to the corridor. 'I'm scared, Saffie.'

'I know,' she said, hearing the choke in her voice. 'It's okay to be scared.'

His hand quivered as he took hers and together they walked to the door, shoulder to shoulder into the storm.

Chapter 27

Safa left courtroom eight and ducked into a bathroom, wanting to wait until the chaos died down before she ventured out. In the month since Oliver Witherow had gone public with the story, anything surrounding Harry's case had been besieged by media interest. Today was his first appearance at the crown court and the press had swarmed the building. He had been remanded in a Young Offender Institution and was facing twelve years in prison if found guilty of murder. Lily, meanwhile, had been exonerated. Safa had tried several times to see her, but Lily understandably ignored her. On quiet nights, Safa *did* question if she had done the right thing, but in those times of doubt, she turned to her north star: the truth. She knew that truth was only one virtue. There were others – loyalty, discretion, sacrifice – that would have better served her friendship with Lily, but Safa had done what she felt was right.

Outside the court, the reporters had dispersed and Safa headed towards the car park. There, she saw that some comedian had scrawled 'Clean me' into the windshield of her battered Clio. Sheepishly, she shrugged. They had a point. Perhaps she would stop by a carwash on her way back east. She unlocked the car and heard footsteps behind her.

'Safa.'

She turned and balked in surprise. 'Lily?'

'Can we talk?' Lily still looked too skinny, but her hair was a little brighter and her skin a little less sallow than the last time they had seen each other.

'Of course,' said Safa. 'Do you want to get a coffee?'

'No. This won't take long.' The wind swept through the car park, making Lily shiver. 'Maybe we could talk in your car?'

'Sure.' Safa let her inside. Her car was neat enough, but it was worn and poky, many miles away from Lily's luxury SUV. Safa wound down the window, then wound it back up again, the chill too aggressive.

Lily neatly lay her palms on her lap. 'I want to thank you,' she said.

Safa waited for more, sure that this was a confrontation.

'For doing what I wasn't strong enough to.' Lily smoothed a crease in her skirt. 'To be brutally honest, I'm relieved, Safa.' She made a throaty sound. 'We convince ourselves that motherhood is martyrdom. We are told that bearing children fills a void. Perhaps it's no coincidence that, initially, it's literally true. This new being fills a literal void in your body. But, really, it's a form of erasure. From the very first doctor's appointment, I was no longer "Lily" but "mum". That is literally what they called me throughout the whole nine months. Richard and I laughed about it once. He said, "Well, maybe there are just too many pregnant women to remember," and I said, "Imagine going to the doctor's and the staff just calling you 'human' because there were too many patients that day. It wouldn't happen."

'But I bought into it, Safa. I bought into the fact that he was meant to be everything; that I should give my life for him. And I would have. You *know* that, Safa, but the truth? The honest, unpalatable truth?' Lily exhaled. 'I'm glad you did it. I'm glad you did what I couldn't do. I would never have exposed him, but I don't know if I would have coped in prison. I hated every second of it. The thought of being inside for the rest of my life . . .' Lily shook her head. 'You saved me, Safa.'

Both of them fell quiet. Safa felt a clash of emotion: the airy lightness of absolution mixed with vinegar guilt for condemning Harry. Beneath them both was the certainty that she had found her place in the world: as one who sought the truth.

'I have two things to ask of you, Safa. First: please don't ever tell Harry that it was you who gave his secret away. Let him think it was *The Clarion*. There are so few people he trusts. I want you to stay in his life.'

Safa nodded. This was one truth she was willing to keep. 'And you? Will you stay in his life?'

'I want to, but he refuses to see me. I don't know if he'll ever stop hating me.'

'It's *shame* he feels, Lily. Not hate. He's ashamed of what he did to you.'

Lily kneaded the cuff of her sleeve. 'But I don't know if *I'll* stop hating *him*.'

Safa reached for platitudes – *don't say that, you don't mean that, it's just the anger talking* – but this was another form of erasure of what she really felt. Instead, she said, 'I think you will, Lily. In time, you will stop hating him.'

Lily gave her a sad, wistful smile. 'The second thing I need from you,' she paused to steady her voice, 'is Patrick Meaden's number, if he's willing. I need to go and see him and tell him that I'm sorry.'

'I can do that,' said Safa. She noted the sharpness of Lily's cheekbones, the gauntness in her wrists. 'Will you be okay?'

'Financially? Yes. Emotionally? Who knows.'

'Are you going to go back to work?'

'I don't think so. Maybe I'll take some time off.' She gestured vaguely. 'I'd like to stop pretending.'

'I think that's a good idea.' Safa traced the ridge of her key. 'Are we going to Narrow Street?'

'No. There's someone else I owe an apology.' Lily clicked in her seatbelt. 'I'd like to go to Richard's grave. I need to tell him how much I loved him. And I need to say sorry for what I did to his name.'

'Okay.' Safa put her Clio in gear and took Lily where she needed to go.

*

Safa knocked on Kevin's door and stuck her head in, but he ignored her studiously.

'Kevin.' When he didn't look up, she dangled a box from Paul bakery at him. 'Ke-vin,' she repeated in a singsong tone. 'It's an Éclair Paris Brest. Two in fact.'

He closed the lid of his laptop. 'If you think you can worm your way into my good graces with sugar, then you have another think coming.'

Safa walked into the office and placed the open box on his desk. His gaze flickered to the praline éclairs and Safa knew that she had him. Their relationship over the past three weeks had been distinctly uneasy. After an initial bollocking for giving away *A Killing on Narrow Street,* Kevin had swapped to a terse surliness that wasn't wholly tongue in cheek. He saw it as a personal failure that Safa had given the story away. What was the point in mentoring reporters if they were so patently soft?

'There'll be other chances, Kevin.'

'Yes, but this one was in the bag.'

Safa dropped into the chair opposite. 'You don't know that.'

Kevin looked at her from across the top of his glasses. 'I take it you haven't heard.'

'Heard what?'

'I have the embargoed list of winners for this year's Whitneys.'

Safa saw the look on Kevin's face and her stomach gave a single churn.

'Oliver Witherow of *The Clarion* won Feature of the Year for *A Killing on Narrow Street*. He didn't even change the fucking title.'

Safa swallowed hard. 'No, I hadn't heard,' she said, trying for nonchalance.

Kevin sighed. 'You're a fool, Safa. This would have changed the trajectory of your entire career.'

Safa forced a smile. 'Maybe I like it here.'

'Fuck off with that bullshit.'

Safa made a face, but knew that Kevin was right. Oliver had got her job and now he had her prize. She thought of her dark green binder, now filled with her original materials, including the crucial email address of the victim's daughter whom she hoped to meet. It had brought her one step closer to the Glassman and, for Safa, that was worth it.

'Where's your killer instinct?' asked Kevin. 'You'll never be a great reporter without it.'

'Maybe,' said Safa mildly. 'Or maybe my other traits make up for it.' She had courage and conviction, persistence and humility, and those things were worth something. She smiled at Kevin dolefully. 'There'll be other chances.'

'Safa, I've been in this game for forty-two years and I've never seen a working-class kid win a Whitney. You were so close.'

'Some things are worth more than a prize.'

'Jesus Christ. I've taught you better than to be so clichéd.'

Safa grimaced and stood. 'I can see that I'm skating on thin ice here.'

'Fuck off out of here!'

Safa laughed and headed out. She heard Kevin chuckle behind her and knew that their relationship would be okay. Back at her desk, she found an enormous bouquet of flowers next to her laptop. She looked over to Tim. 'Hey, who brought these?'

'I don't know. They were there when I got here.'

Safa traced the delicate petals of the blood-red roses. She searched for the envelope and plucked out the card inside. The note was handwritten and just two words long.

Let's play.

She frowned, then realised that there was something else in the envelope. She emptied it on her desk and it glinted in the morning sun. Safa felt a white-hot alarm when she registered what it was: a neat little square of glass with frosting that she recognised. This was the glass that had been cut from her bathroom window. Wildly, she scanned the newsroom, then darted to the window with its view of Mile End Road. She searched the weathered shopfronts of chicken shops and takeaways for a figure hidden inside. There was no one. She watched for a long while, but saw nothing untoward. When her breathing finally slowed, she went back to her desk and studied the piece of glass. The sensation in her gut almost felt like butterflies. The Glassman had thrown down the gauntlet and invited her to pick it up. The panic of finding that hole in her window was seared into her memory: the whistle in her ears, the strobe of her heart going too fast. Safa had brought herself to the Glassman's attention and wouldn't easily escape it. It filled her with a bristling dread, but she thought of the look on Rukshana's face – the sickly horror and unspeakable shame – and knew that she had to face him.

'Don't be scared,' she said out loud. She said it to Rukshana and she said it to herself. She smelled a blood-red rose, then leaned back in her chair. For better or worse, Safa Saleem was ready to duel.

* * *

Acknowledgements

Thank you to my agent, Jessica Faust. Your phone call all the way back in 2017 was one of the best moments of my life. I will never take that 'yes' for granted. Thank you for everything you have done.

Thank you to my editor, Manpreet Grewal, for making me a better writer – and making space for so many of us.

Thank you to Lisa Milton and the brilliant team at HQ: Halema Begum, Dawn Burnett, Angie Dobbs, Rebecca Fortuin, Brogan Furey, Stephanie Heathcote, Amal Ibrahim, Hannah Lismore, Komal Patel, Joanna Rose, Emily Scorer, Lauren Trabucchi and Isabel Williams.

Thank you to Peter Borcsok and the team at HarperCollins Canada, and to Lucy Stille and BookEnds Literary Agency for bringing my books across the pond.

Thank you to Gaby Lee and all the booksellers, librarians, bloggers, readers and reviewers who have championed my work. Reading changed my life and I am grateful for the work you do in bringing books and stories to others.

Thank you to those who so patiently helped with my research: Graham Bartlett, Helen Bonnick, Matthew Butt KC, Beth Duffell, Michelle John, Nadine Matheson, Carri-Ann Taylor and Penny Willis. As ever, I hope you will forgive me for any errors I've made or creative license I've taken with your meticulous advice. Thank you, also, to Mickey Cunningham. I'm so grateful that Safa Saleem brought me to Mickey's Boxing Gym.

A special thank you to all my fellow authors who have read, shared and celebrated my work. I dare not try and name you all but I hope you know how grateful I am for your generosity.

Thank you to my friends Rabika Sultana, Serena Wong and Priya Patel for getting me through a bruising year. And to Peter Watson for the many good years before it.

Finally, thank you to my sisters, Reena, Jay, Shopna, Forida and Shafia. It's sad that 'the sisters' are now known as 'the aunts', but I'm grateful that we get to grow older together.

Turn the page for an exclusive extract from the page-turning courtroom drama and gripping legal thriller from Kia Abdullah

Chapter 1

Salma had always sworn that she would never end up in a place like this. 'It's a bit like purgatory,' she had joked when they first came to see the house in a harried half-hour before work one morning. The estate agent, a hawkish woman with a watchful gaze, had herded them from room to room and Salma had murmured politely, even commenting on this or that 'lovely feature' as she and Bilal locked eyes, amusement passing between them.

They had agreed to view it only because there was a gap between their other bookings and the agent had pushed this property. It was in a neat cul-de-sac on the eastern reaches of the Central line. It was built seven years ago, said the agent, and still had the bright, bland feel of a new development. There was a dizzying amount of brickwork and even its name, the mononymous 'Blenheim', felt like an artless attempt at class, like petrol stop perfume or 'Guccci' shades. Upstairs, out of the agent's earshot, they had giggled about the perfect lawn.

'Do you think Neighbourhood Watch will knock down your door if it grows above two inches?' said Bilal.

Salma fought a smile. 'We're being snobby,' she said but with laughter in her voice.

The agent walked in and the two of them sprang apart like children caught red-handed. She nodded at the window, her silver-brown bob swaying with the motion. 'It's lovely, isn't it?'

'Lovely,' Salma agreed.

That was six months ago and after close to forty viewings, they had both grown weary. Nothing else matched Blenheim for price, condition, space and safety and so they talked each other into it. *Four double bedrooms*, said Bilal. *And it's still on the Central line*, said Salma. *The neat streets and quiet neighbours.* If they could set aside their vanity, they could be happy at Blenheim and so they had put in an offer – and here they were, their first week in their new home.

They hadn't yet met their neighbours but, yesterday, a square of white card appeared on their doormat inviting them to a May Bank Holiday Barbecue. *No need to RSVP. Just turn up!* it said in jaunty letters. Salma had read it uneasily. She wasn't an introvert by any means but did find parties tiring. She far preferred to meet new people on a one-to-one basis. Still, they were new here and had to make an effort. Salma had prepared some potato salad and told her son, Zain, that he had no choice but to join them. They approached 13 Blenheim like a trio of soldiers heading into battle. Outside, Salma paused and assessed her husband and son. As she straightened Bilal's crooked collar, he caught her hand and kissed it.

'Here goes,' she said. She rang the bell but no one answered. Music bled from the garden and Salma counted to twenty before she rang again. Zain ventured to the side of the house and pointed at the open side gate. They walked through in single file and hovered at the edge of the gathering. There were about thirty people of varying ages, laughing and milling around. Two men were tending the barbecue, both of them wearing white polo shirts paired with khaki shorts. At first, Salma thought that they were hired staff but realised they were guests. Cheers went up around them as they dished up the first tranche of meat, filling the air with a pleasantly smoky smell.

A woman spotted them and her eyes lit up. 'You must be the new arrivals!' she called. She detached herself from the group and pulled Salma into a matronly hug. 'I'm Linda Turner, the hostess.'

'Oh hello! I'm Salma. Thank you so much for inviting us.'

'Bilal,' her husband introduced himself. He saw the crease of Linda's brow and promptly added, 'Call me Bil.'

She brightened. 'Bill! How wonderful to meet our new neighbours.' She turned to Zain. 'And this must be your son. My, what a handsome boy!'

Zain smiled politely. 'How do you do?'

She whooped with delight. 'And such manners too!' She saw the glass bowl in his hands. 'You didn't have to bring anything! But thank you.' She took the bowl and ushered them into the party. 'What can I get you to drink? We have wine, beer, cider.' She paused. 'Or we have fresh lemonade and fruit juice.'

Bil smiled. 'A lemonade would be lovely – thank you.'

'Make that three,' said Salma.

She beamed. 'Wonderful!' She smoothly introduced them to their next-door neighbour. 'This is Tom Hutton. He can give you the lowdown on everyone here.'

Tom greeted them warmly. He was in his mid-forties, muscular beneath a navy polo shirt, and with thick dark hair splayed beneath an orange cap. As he spoke, a young bull terrier bounded up to him. 'Her name is Lola,' he said, bending down to pet her. He looked up at Salma. 'She was a showgirl,' he deadpanned.

Salma broke into laughter. Tom nodded in approval as if she had passed a test. Lola snuffed at Salma's feet.

'You don't mind, do you?' said Tom.

'No, not at all. We have a dog too, a lab called Molly.'

'Oh, that's great. This is such a dog-friendly neighbourhood. You're going to love it.'

Linda cut in to hand out drinks. Bil volunteered to help with the barbecue and she happily whisked him away. Zain took his drink to a corner of the garden and busied himself on his phone.

'So what do you do?' asked Tom.

'I'm a teacher,' said Salma. 'Geography at a secondary school,' she added, pre-empting his follow-up question. 'What about you?'

'I work in advertising. At Sartre & Sartre.'

'Oh wow. That must be glamorous.'

'It can be,' he said with a grin, enjoying the compliment. 'And what about Bil?'

Salma felt herself tense. 'He's a restaurateur,' she said, despite the fact that his restaurant, Jakoni's, had shut down earlier that year.

'Restaurateur?' Tom puckered his lips in a show of approval. 'You must be doing all right then, no?'

Salma looked bemused. 'I mean, we're doing okay.'

'Sorry if that's rude. I was just wondering how come you got this place then?' He nodded in the direction of their house.

Salma relaxed, relieved to find that he too was sceptical of Blenheim. She smiled playfully. 'It's not so bad, is it? Where else would I find such a pristine collection of lawns?'

Tom frowned. 'It's just that I would've thought you were above the threshold.'

'Threshold?' Salma was confused.

'For social housing,' he said.

It dawned on Salma what Tom had really meant: not *you're wealthy so why would you choose to live here* but *you're wealthy so why did you get social housing?* She shifted awkwardly. 'We actually bought it privately.'

'Oh!' Tom looked mortified. 'I'm so sorry. I didn't mean to assume. In fact, I *wasn't* assuming. I was certain that the house next to us was part of the social housing.' He cringed visibly. 'I must have been mistaken.'

Salma waved in a show of nonchalance. 'Ah, if only! It might have saved us a pretty penny.' Her voice laboured with the effort to put him at ease. She groped for another topic.

'So what school do you teach at?' asked Tom.

'Ilford Academy in Seven Kings.'

'I see. Do you enjoy it?'

Salma could feel the conversation slipping away, but was keen to keep the momentum going. If they parted now, it would surely make things more awkward the next time they met. 'Yes,' she replied. 'It's especially nice in August.' She laughed at her joke but it came out forced and hollow. She didn't understand why she was being this way. She was normally poised and confident, perfectly versed in small talk. She reached for a question but was interrupted by a woman who slid up next to Tom. Salma stared for a second. She was tall and willowy with white-blonde hair, delicate cheekbones and a tiny gap between her front teeth that seemed to only add to her charm. She held out an elegant hand.

'Willa,' she said. 'Like the writer.'

Salma shook it and pretended to know which writer she meant.

'Although pictures are more my trade,' said Willa.

'Oh. Are you a model?'

Willa made a snap of laughter. 'You're sweet but no. I paint sometimes. Mainly, I run our home.'

'Oh, sorry. You look like you could be,' said Salma. 'You must get that all the time.'

Willa rolled her eyes. 'Thank you, but it's fucking embarrassing. I'm like an Aryan wet dream.'

Salma nearly spat out her lemonade. She couldn't tell if Willa was simply outspoken or if she actually rather enjoyed Salma's display of shock. She looked across at Tom, who didn't react, only slid an arm around Willa's waist. Salma cleared her throat. 'How did you both meet?' she asked, steering them into safer territory.

'I know what you're thinking,' said Tom. 'How did a brute like me end up with a girl like her?'

'Tom used to be a firefighter,' Willa cut in. 'Believe it or not, he ran into a burning building and saved me. I was twenty-one. He was twenty-seven and that was that.'

Salma looked from one to the other. 'That can't be true!'

Willa gazed at Tom adoringly. 'One hundred per cent.'

'Oh my god. That's incredible.'

Willa burst out laughing. 'I'm just fucking with you!'

Salma grew still. Then, she smiled and pretended to be in on the joke.

'Of course that's not what happened,' said Willa, 'but the real story is almost as cute.'

Salma waited but Willa was speaking to Tom now.

'Do you remember how you chased me for months? Sending me flowers and chocolates. God, wasn't there even that H. Samuel bracelet?'

Tom looked at Salma sheepishly. 'Willa's family are rich,' he explained. 'So here I am sending her Milk Tray and a five quid bunch of flowers while she's used to' – he looked over at her – 'what's that poncey brand you like?'

'Charbonnel et Walker,' she said smoothly, then turned back to Salma. 'He wasn't a firefighter but . . .' She winked. 'He did let me ride his pole.'

Salma chuckled politely. She, like most people, did a subconscious thing when she met someone new. She assessed whether they were part of her 'tribe'. Tom and Willa with their strange, abrasive humour were far too different to her. Normally, Salma wouldn't mind and simply get on with her day, but this was a new neighbourhood and she had to make an effort. 'You mentioned that you run the home,' she said to Willa. 'Do you have kids?'

'Yes. A son, Jamie. He's sixteen.' She must have caught Salma's surprise because she added, 'I had him young; at twenty-two.'

Salma calculated that Willa was thirty-eight, five years younger than her. 'That works out well for me,' she said. 'My son, Zain, is eighteen and I'm sure he'd love to meet Jamie.'

'That would be lovely,' said Willa. 'Jamie needs to make a few friends.'

They talked for a while longer and Salma scanned the crowd for Bil. She saw that he was cornered by Linda and excused herself to join them.

'What is that delicious nutty flavour in the potato salad?' Linda was asking.

'Fried pine nuts,' said Salma.

'Ah, well, thank you for indulging us. For reference, I can handle my spice so if you ever want to bring something with a bit more zing, you'd be more than welcome to.'

Salma smiled. 'Of course. I'll bear that in mind.'

Linda clapped her hands, twice like an excited child. 'I look forward to it.' She glanced over Salma's shoulder. 'Well, I should mingle. Please help yourself to the food and drink. There's so much to get through.' She beamed and then left in a cloud of activity.

Bil looked at Salma. 'How long do you reckon before we can leave?'

'Stop it,' she chided. 'We have to make an effort.' She fixed on a fresh smile and led him back to the fray.

*

Salma felt herself uncoil, the tension leaving her muscles as soon as they left the barbecue. Blenheim looked uncanny without any streetlamps. The council insisted that lights would spoil the character of the local area, leaving it eerily dark. Bil caught her hand in his and they headed home in silence, needing total privacy before they could fully relax. Zain walked on ahead and left their front door open for them. Salma crossed the blue-black lawn, which was still a consistent one-inch tall. Their neighbour Tom had mowed it while the house was being sold. Salma kicked a few pebbles back onto the path and retrieved a palm-sized banner from the ground that Zain had stuck in a plant pot. She dug it back in place and followed Bil inside. She closed the door and sagged against it.

Bil laughed. 'You okay?'

'Do you think I should take Linda some *naga* next time?' she asked archly.

'Well, she *did* say she can handle her spice.'

Salma covered her face and groaned.

'It's okay,' said Bil more seriously. 'It was just a lot in one go.'

She nodded vigorously but didn't uncover her face.

Bil pulled at her wrist playfully. 'Come on, it wasn't that bad.'

She looked at him. 'Bil, did you hear what they call people who haven't lived here from the beginning? "Offcomers." Not newcomers. Offcomers. It sounds like a bloody horror movie.'

A smile tugged at his lips. 'They were being tongue in cheek.'

'And that guy – Tom.' She gestured next door. 'God, it was *so* awkward.' She explained how Tom had assumed that they were in social housing.

Bil winced with sympathy. 'Stuff like that's going to happen,' he said. 'But they'll get to know us soon enough.'

'Oh!' Salma cut in. 'And you should have heard his wife!' She shared some of Willa's choice remarks.

Bil laughed. 'She was probably just trying to impress you. People can be like that at parties.'

Salma raised a brow but didn't disagree. She was more cynical than Bil and though they shared a sense of humour – dry and sarcastic – his natural temperament was optimistic and she didn't want to spoil their evening. Salma had tried hard to stay upbeat ever since Jakoni's shut down in January following a horrendous year for the industry. It was her job to keep Bil's spirits high, just as he always did with hers.

'You're right,' she said as she fit herself against his chest. 'They'll get to know us soon.'

He rubbed the small of her back. 'You okay?'

She nodded.

'You don't think we've made a mistake?'

There was the tiniest pause before she answered, 'No, I don't. I think we can be happy here.'

'I think so too,' said Bil.

She tipped back her head and kissed him. 'Right. I'm going to take a shower.' She detached herself and headed upstairs. She paused briefly on the landing to listen to the click of Zain's keyboard in the attic.

In the bathroom, she peeled off her clothes, which smelled of smoky meat, and tossed them in the laundry bin. In the shower, she realised that she could hear voices on the other side: the deep murmur of Tom's voice and the lighter pitch of Willa's. She pressed her ear to the wall, but couldn't make out any words. She listened to see if their conversation had the tightness of an argument or the lightness of a joke. Were they discussing her family, just as she had discussed theirs?

Tom's words returned to her and she flushed with embarrassment. *I would've thought you were above the threshold.* Despite what she had just told Bil, she *did* worry that they had made a mistake. If they had known that they would lose the restaurant, they would almost certainly have stayed in Seven Kings, on their estate off the high street. By the time the restaurant closed, however, they had already started the process of buying their house in Blenheim and convinced themselves to take the leap. Five months later, they still hadn't sold the restaurant premises and things were getting tight. The thought brought a familiar unease and Salma had to remind herself that they barely had a choice. Not after what happened with Zain. This was the safest place that they could afford and they would make the most of it. It was true that she missed her old neighbourhood – the big, messy families and rows of crowded houses – but Zain had room to breathe here: a large bedroom, his own bathroom, a balcony and a garden too. There would be a period of adjustment of course, but they were sure to fit in before long. They had to. They had nowhere else to go.

*

Zain blew out a lungful of smoke, fanning it as he did so. If his mum found out that he smoked, well, then there'd be hell to pay. Her father had died from lung cancer and she was a full-on fundamentalist when it came to smoking. It was annoying, but Zain knew it could be a lot worse. Some of his friends were basically double agents: respectful, obedient, *seedha saadha* with their parents, then practically feral behind the scenes. At least his mum knew what was what and allowed him certain liberties if he didn't take the piss.

He took another draw, felt it burn in his chest and exhaled slowly. His thoughts went to the barbecue and the repetition of that dreaded question: *what do you do?*

I'm a student, he had told them, hating himself for the lie. In truth, he'd been kicked out of college last year, which meant he couldn't sit his A-Levels, couldn't go to uni, couldn't get a decent job and was living with his parents like a deadbeat, spending his Friday nights on Twitch, live-streaming his coding. That's one thing he could do, but most tech jobs asked for degrees. The startups that claimed to overlook formal education relied on other cues – accents and expensive accessories – that Zain lacked too. Trying too hard felt worse than not trying at all and so he gave up looking.

He leaned over the balcony wall and took another drag of his cigarette. A knock on his door made him startle and he hurriedly stubbed it out.

'Hey, kid.' His dad poked his head in the bedroom. 'I wanted to—' He trailed off as he caught a residual whiff of smoke. He gave Zain a stern look. 'If your mum finds out, she'll kill you first and kill me second.'

'She won't find out.'

'Kid, she finds out *everything*.' He stepped inside but hovered by the threshold. 'How are you getting on?'

Zain leaned against the balcony. 'Okay.' There was a time when he would laugh at his dad's late-night pep talks, filled with ironic vim. *There's nothing that can't be solved with a list*, he'd say, taking a sheet of paper from the printer to note down practical steps. Now, these talks felt medicinal: delivered at regular intervals, designed to prevent or cure.

'What did you make of our new neighbours?'

'They're all right if a bit "Borg Collective",' said Zain.

His dad fixed him with a blank stare. 'Resistance is futile,' he said in a robotic monotone.

Zain smiled, briefly lifted, remembering their old camaraderie. He reached for another quip but his dad was serious again.

'I know it's been a weird time but your mum and I are feeling good about this move.'

Zain raised a brow in doubt.

Usually, his dad would break ranks and admit this wasn't true. Instead, he fixed Zain with a sincere look. 'Trust me,' he said.

Zain nodded but looked away.

'You'll find your way, kid.' He gripped the doorknob: a sure-fire sign he was almost done.

'Yeah, I know,' Zain lied.

'Okay.' He nodded firmly as if the matter was settled. 'I'll see you in the morning.'

'Yep,' said Zain. He waited until he was gone, then reached for another cigarette. He was about to light it when he heard a cough next door. A boy leaned out from the next balcony, past the thick column of brick separating their two houses.

'Shit. Sorry, mate,' said Zain, clicking off the lighter.

'Oh, I wasn't dropping a hint,' said the boy. He was close to Zain's age, white, and looked like he belonged in a boy band: thick brown hair styled stiff with gel, a touch of K-pop in his delicate chin.

'Nah, it's all right,' said Zain. 'I'm done anyway.'

'It's nice having the top room, huh?' said the boy.

Zain noticed a quirk in his speech: the s dropped from 'it's'. *It nice having the top room, huh?* 'Yeah, it is,' he replied.

The boy stretched across the column – so far that Zain worried he might fall. 'I'm Jamie.'

'Zain.' He shook Jamie's hand and was surprised by his firm grip. There was nothing he hated more than a limp handshake.

'So—' Jamie lifted his chin at the garden. 'What brought you to paradise?'

'The search for a better life,' said Zain, matching Jamie's tone.

'Ha! Prepare to be disappointed.'

Zain smiled. 'How long have you lived here?'

'Um, we moved here when I was nine, so seven years now.'

'What's it like?'

'It's all right.'

Zain noticed that he dropped his s again – *it all right* – and wondered if he had a speech impediment. He felt a drop of affection and wondered if this is what it felt like to have a younger sibling. Relatives often joked that Zain was an old soul. They didn't understand that as an only child you ate most of your meals with adults. You listened to adult conversation, adult concerns, and it was natural to inherit them. He remembered using the word 'inquisition' soon after starting secondary school and being teased no end. After that, he deliberately dumbed down his vocabulary. Sometimes, he stammered not because he couldn't find a word but because he was trying to swap it for a shorter one. That was the thing about Selborne Estate. It gave you a sense of community, but it also held you back. Zain had seen this play out with his friend Amin. He had secured a good job straight after school: IT support for a medical research centre in the city. Every day, his old school friends would see him leave in the frayed brown suit he'd inherited, a satchel slung over his shoulder, and tease him for being a *boroh saab*. A big man. *He's too important for us now*, they'd say. *Rah, look how he's ignoring us.*

One day, Amin turned up in a grey hoodie and jeans.

'Ey yo, what's going on, man?' asked Zain.

'You won't believe it, mate. They fired me.'

'Wait, what?'

'They said I stole from the petty cash.'

Zain narrowed his gaze on him. 'And did you?'

'Nah, course I didn't.'

'Then they can't do that!' Zain got so riled up but mid-rant he registered Amin's nonchalance. He was hit with a cold suspicion that Amin had done it on purpose; had got himself fired because he was tired of being othered, not by his colleagues at his fancy office but by his friends right here at home. Selborne Estate was a safety net but one with a ceiling you couldn't escape.

It's partly why when Zain's parents suggested the move, beneath his initial resistance, he felt a seed of relief. He hadn't known then that they'd end up in this wasteland of a street.

'Seriously though, I can't wait to leave,' Jamie cut in.

'Where would you go? Uni?'

Jamie shrugged. 'Start my own company maybe.'

Zain laughed but then caught his look of hurt. 'Sorry, I just— It's not that easy, is it?'

Jamie ducked a little, embarrassed. 'No, you're right. It's stupid.'

'Nah, man,' Zain backtracked guiltily. 'It's not stupid. It's better than working for someone else.'

'I've applied for some funding from Google's startup fund.'

This piqued Zain's interest. 'Oh, yeah? So you have an idea?'

'Kind of.' Jamie hesitated. 'Well, yeah.'

Zain raised his brows to show the younger boy that he was impressed. 'What is it?'

Jamie withdrew, suddenly shy. 'Well . . . Hang on.' He

retreated into his room and returned a few seconds later. He handed Zain a stack of designs with mock-ups of an iPhone screen. 'It's an app,' he said. 'To help deaf people communicate with hearing people.'

Zain looked through the designs. 'How does it work?'

Jamie explained the app's purpose – a real-time sign-to-speech translator – and talked him through the designs.

'How come you're interested in this?' Zain asked.

Jamie set down the stack on the wall. 'Well, I don't know if you can tell, but I'm partially deaf. I was born three months premature but they didn't realise there was anything different until I was about four. By then, certain sounds had escaped me. I've seen a speech therapist but even now, I sometimes miss letters. It's kind of like talking in a different accent, you know? You always have to be concentrating so eventually I decided, so what? What's normal anyway?'

'Good on you, man,' said Zain.

Jamie flushed. 'Thanks. I just need to find someone who can build the damn thing now.'

Zain fixed his gaze on him. 'You know I code, right?'

Jamie did a double take. 'Really? Would you be interested?'

Zain considered this. 'I mean, *maybe*.' He studied the designs again and quizzed Jamie in more depth. 'Okay,' he said finally. 'Why the hell not?'

'Seriously?'

'Yeah, seriously.'

Jamie beamed. 'Fuck, man. That would be fantastic.' He reached out his hand again.

Zain shook it and something warm pitched inside him: a sense of purpose and comradeship.

There was a call from inside Jamie's house. 'Shit, that's Mum. I better go. Here, take my number.'

Zain keyed it into his phone and listened to Jamie scurrying inside. He looked out over the inky grass and felt a new thrill of hope. Maybe he *would* be all right here. Maybe, retrospectively, he hadn't lied to his dad at all.

*

Salma turned sideways in the sunlit mirror. She groaned, noting the paunch around her midriff.

'No one tells you that, after forty, you basically can't eat bread,' she said.

Bil leaned in and nuzzled her neck. 'You don't look a day over twenty-five.'

'Get orf,' she said, mimicking the boys from the Eighties Accrington Stanley milk advert.

'Oh my god, are you trying to do a Scouse accent?'

She frowned. 'Were they Scouse? I thought they were Geordie.'

'God, you Londoners.' He threw up his hands in surrender. 'You're all hopeless.'

She laughed, warmed by the playful push and pull of their marriage.

Bil threw on a T-shirt. 'Will you have time for breakfast?' he asked.

'Sorry. Not today.' She felt a thread of guilt as she kissed him goodbye. When his restaurant shut down, Bil went straight back into work, taking a job beneath his skill level at a curry house in Newbury Park. He was on gruelling split shifts, but still woke up every morning to make her breakfast. It was through sheer luck that she had married into kindness. It had never appeared on her wish list for a husband. Hardworking, yes. Ambitious, confident and successful – but kindness felt somehow twee; old fashioned like grandfather clocks and shoe polish. It didn't quite say 'sexy'. The first time she saw Bil, he was fully in work mode: charming but in the studied, patient manner of someone with pressing things to do. A diner at the next table had insisted on meeting the chef and Salma had been surprised by his age: late twenties at the oldest. As the diner droned on, intent on impressing his date, Bil caught Salma's eye with just enough of an eyebrow raise to signal his amusement. Salma had laughed out loud and watched Bil struggle to keep a straight face. For months afterwards, she had repeatedly visited that same restaurant until Bil finally got the hint and asked her out. She had a picture of what he would be – a young, brash culinary prodigy – but the man she got to know was fun, playful and, most of all, kind. Nearly two decades on, he was still cooking her breakfast in the mornings. The thought made her smile even as she grabbed an apple from the kitchen and hurried out the door.

Outside, she noticed that Zain's banner was on the ground again. She picked it up and traced the flimsy fabric. *Black Lives Matter*, it said, printed black on pink. She had demurred when Zain first displayed it.

'I think we should meet the neighbours first before we put up something like that,' she'd said.

Zain had looked at her scornfully. 'Because *that* will inform whether Black lives matter?' he'd asked.

She'd sighed. 'Just put it somewhere not too in-your-face.'

Now, she stuck it back in the plant pot. As she headed to the bus stop, she heard a beep to her left. Her neighbour, Tom, was in his car and she raised a hand to wave. He rolled down his window and beckoned her closer.

'Morning, Salma.'

'Hi, Tom. How are you?'

'Good good.' He took off his sunglasses. 'Listen, can I ask you a favour?'

'Of course.'

He grimaced as if this pained him. 'Can you guys try to park in front of your house?'

Salma looked at her car, which overshot her house by a foot. 'Oh, sorry! I didn't realise there was designated parking.'

'No, no. There isn't. It's just we have two cars so if you overshoot, we can't get both of ours in.'

'Oh, right.' Salma frowned. 'Well, sometimes people park outside ours, so we roll forward a bit so our car will fit.'

'Ah. Maybe you could find out who's doing it and have a word?'

'Um, I mean, sometimes it's different cars.'

'Okay, well . . .' He tapped the steering wheel as if trying to find a solution. 'If you can't figure out who it is, then that's fine obviously, but it *is* a bit of a pain for us to park around the corner.'

'Of course,' said Salma evenly. 'I'm sure it is. We'll try our best.'

'Thank you,' he said apologetically.

Salma readied to go, but Tom stopped her.

'Sorry. While I'm being annoying, I should say that the fence between our gardens has a loose board. We fixed it last time, and then again when the house was empty, so maybe you guys could have a look at it?'

Salma smiled. 'Of course.'

'Great.' He beamed. 'Thank you for understanding. Have a good morning.'

'You too,' she said, her cheeks burning hot. Surely, it wasn't reasonable to claim a section of the road just because it passed your home? She wished she hadn't agreed so easily. Or that she'd at least made a pointed joke to show him this wasn't okay. She found herself preoccupied all the way to work. Next time, she would speak her mind.

She approached her school, a flat, grey building in a godless corner of Ilford. She passed through the security gates and headed up to her classroom. There, she felt at ease. Unlike some teachers she knew, Salma loved her job. She enjoyed the constant hum and activity, and thrived on being busy. It didn't even bother her when people made snarky comments about *all that time off*. Very few people could do what she did effectively and that fact made her proud. She settled into the room, a small rectangular space dripping with maps and trinkets. Salma took comfort in crowded places. Perhaps that's why she struggled with Blenheim: all clean lines and large, wide spaces. She stowed her bag and prepared for her tutor group, but a knock on the door interrupted her.

'Miss, can you help me?' It was Haroon, a shy, rake-thin boy in her class. He hovered at the threshold.

'Yes.'

He came in and sat by her desk. 'Miss, I've been trying to fill this in, but I can't work it out.' He held out an A4 form.

She glanced over the first page and saw that it was a housing benefit application. 'Can it wait until clinic tomorrow?' she asked.

'If I don't send it today, there'll be a gap in our payments.'

Salma nodded. 'Right, okay, well, the class is coming in, but can you drop by here at break? We can go through it then.'

'Can we finish it in twenty minutes though?' he fretted.

'Should do. If not, I'll call them and ask for an extension.'

This relaxed him a little. 'Thanks, miss.' He headed to his desk at the back of the classroom.

The 'clinic' Salma referred to was her labour of love. She had pitched it as 'a Citizens Advice Bureau for pupils', but met resistance from the head.

'It plays into stereotypes,' George had said, 'that B-A-M-E people can't help themselves.'

'But what if they *can't*?' she'd asked, frustrated.

'Then it's not our place to help them.'

Salma couldn't bite her tongue. 'This is where your leftie sensibilities actually interfere, George,' she'd told her.

After a protracted battle, George had acquiesced. 'Fine. But if the press get wind of this, they'll make a meal of it.'

'It's volunteer-run!'

'On school premises.'

'Are you in or out?'

'Fine,' she'd relented. 'I'm in.'

And of course there *was* a need for it because despite what George had said, there were plenty of pupils who needed help. Children like Haroon, with parents who couldn't speak English, had to navigate labyrinthine systems like HMRC, the NHS and DWP. Last week, a pupil came by the clinic and asked her to explain a bowel cancer home test kit so that he could translate it for his mother. Salma watched the young boy redden as she explained it step by step. Eventually, she asked if he would prefer one of the Urdu-speaking female teachers to call his mum and explain. The boy had agreed with great relief.

Haroon took his seat and the rest of the pupils filtered in. They were a lively group, but after four years in Salma's form class, easy to control. She had enjoyed watching them mature: Patrick who had started off a nightmare but was now a fine young man; Ritesh who was far too serious but bloomed into a comedian. Some kids, like Haroon, stayed the same and others went the opposite way. Tara, a studious, gawky kid, had discovered boys and make-up, and let her grades plummet.

Salma hoped that she had got the balance right. When she first became a teacher, to her, 'making a difference' meant creating doctors and lawyers, fulfilling parents' dreams and funnelling pupils to top-tier unis. She slowly accepted that this wasn't possible – not with the budget and restrictions they had. Then, she realised that 'making a difference' didn't have to be so grand. It could be as simple as helping Haroon with paperwork so that he could rest easy today, or telling Faisal that he needn't explain to his mum an embarrassing medical test. It was taking the web of a million worries that made up adolescence and unpicking a little corner of it.

The bell rang to signal the start of teaching hours. 'All right, settle down please,' she called. She opened SIMS to take the register and start a new school day.

*

Willa beeped the car horn once, then again, this time more prolonged to make sure that Jamie heard. He came hurtling out the door and hurried into the car.

'I haven't got all day, mate,' she said.

'Oh, really? Women's bake sale pressing, is it?'

She tapped his arm in a light rebuke. 'Hey, remember what I told you?' she asked.

'I won't tell Dad,' he promised.

'Good.' She gestured towards their new neighbours' house. 'You should have come yesterday. You could have met their son, Zain.'

'What were they like?'

Willa scrunched her nose. 'Hard to say. They kind of seemed to be putting on an act.'

'Yeah, but everyone does that at first.'

'*I* don't,' said Willa.

Jamie made a face.

'Do I?'

'No, but you go the opposite way.'

'How so?'

He shrugged. 'I don't know, Mum.' He reached for his phone, but she stopped him.

'How so?' she pressed.

'I don't know. I can't explain it.' He freed his hand and took out his phone.

Willa felt embarrassed by the implication. If her sixteen-year-old son thought she acted fake, did others think the same? She resisted the urge to grill him further. God forbid she become *that* sort of mother.

She manoeuvred out of the cul-de-sac and drove three miles

to South Woodford. She parked outside what looked like a large house. She led Jamie inside and through to the waiting room, all hushed tones and plush upholstery.

Jamie's audiologist, Tania, greeted them and led them to an oblong room. At the end stood an audiometric booth – a small enclosure almost like a photo booth – which was used to test his hearing. Willa had noticed lately that more and more sounds were evading him. His condition wasn't degenerative, but she worried that the amount of time he spent indoors was making him less fluent.

Tania took him through his standard raft of tests, usually done once a year. This session was additional. Jamie sat inside the booth and Tania ran through the usual spiel: if you feel anxious, then just say and we'll let you out. Jamie was asked to press a button every time he heard a sound. In another test, he was asked to repeat what he heard in his ear. Willa hated this test. It was always the one that made him lose heart.

Tania always told him, 'Even if it's a fraction of a word, try to say it. Even if it's an approximation, say it. Just say whatever you think you heard.' And Jamie would always start by trying – *oof*, *lek*, *sen* – but then dwindle into silence, embarrassed by how hard he found it. Willa tried to catch his gaze, but he studiously ignored her.

Eventually, Tania released him from the booth. 'Are you keeping up with your verbal exercises?'

He gave her a guilty look. 'When I can.'

'Jamie.' She angled her head in disapproval. 'It's really important that you keep up with this. I promise you'll see an improvement.'

Willa stepped forward hesitantly. 'Tania, could we try the

Opn hearing aids again? I know we said we'd leave them, but I want to give them another try.'

Jamie frowned. 'Why?' he asked her.

'Because they help you.'

'But I don't need them.' Last time, he had said the same, but she'd seen the way his eyes had lit up when he put them in. He was only saying no because he knew they couldn't afford them.

'Just try them, Jamie.'

Tania rolled over to her desk and took out a pair of the premium aids. She helped Jamie try them and encouraged him to take a walk around the building. As he stepped out, Willa's voice dropped low.

'We'll take them, Tania, but can I change our billing address?'

'Of course.'

Willa read out the new details and hurried to explain why the name and address were different to hers. 'They're my dad's details,' she said. 'Do you need to speak to him?'

Tania waved away the question. 'I'm sure you're not out there stealing credit card details,' she said with a laugh.

Jamie reappeared in the doorway.

'They're yours,' said Willa.

He looked from her to Tania. 'How?'

'Grandad,' she answered. 'But don't tell your dad, okay?'

Jamie exhaled, clearly ill at ease. For a second, it seemed he would refuse but then he nodded hesitantly. 'Okay,' he agreed. They settled up with Tania and returned to Willa's car. Jamie braced himself against the dashboard.

'Are you okay?' asked Willa.

He nodded. 'It's . . . weird. I can hear you breathing.'

Willa grew still, quieted by emotion. She turned her gaze to the road so that Jamie wouldn't notice. She felt angry with herself for heeding Tom for so many years. He was a proud man and refused to take money from Willa's family, so Jamie had suffered substandard care. After seeing his reaction to the Opn aids, she'd secretly asked her father for help.

'I'm proud of you,' she said.

He shifted awkwardly. 'Whatevs.'

'No, hey, I *am*.'

'Thanks,' he said, looking sheepish. She and Jamie had always been more like friends and these bouts of earnestness often embarrassed him.

She reached out and ruffled his hair. 'Come on, let's go.' She put the car in gear and headed to his school. She waved him off at the gates before returning home.

There, she flopped on the sofa, a seaweed-coloured Chesterfield gifted by her mother. It wasn't *leisure* that Willa had a problem with – working did not appeal to her – but that *this* wasn't leisure at all. She had imagined floating from room to room in a central London townhouse, working on her art perhaps – but then she'd met Tom.

At first, she was charmed by his insistence that he pay their way. She was thrilled by his old-fashioned gallantry but, equally, she assumed he would change his mind after they were married. They would need a nice house, good furniture, a quality education for Jamie, but Tom refused to take her family's money. He clashed with Willa's father and did not want to owe him a thing. Initially, Willa didn't care. When you'd never worried about money, you assumed you never *would*. In fact, her new low status felt desirable: a contrarian 'fuck you'.

Money issues, she would say with a tinkle of a laugh as if it were a rare piece of furniture, but then she realised that most people lived on forty thousand pounds a year and really, that was nothing at all. When her friends realised that her money issues weren't of the *crumbling estate, old money* variety, some began to distance themselves as if poverty might be catching. Tom remained adamant that he wouldn't take her father's money and Willa had relented, but damn him for letting it affect their son.

She sat cross-legged on the sofa and rubbed her belly with a palm. It would be different this time, she decided. This time, her child would get everything that Jamie had lacked; everything that she, at twenty-two, hadn't been equipped to give.

For years, she and Tom had tried for a second child. Eventually, they accepted that it wasn't on the cards, so when she realised she might be pregnant, she wanted to be certain before telling Tom. This time, things would be different. Willa would be the mother she had failed to be at twenty-two.

*

Salma loved this time of day when the students had left the building and the heat of recent bodies cooled, the hum in the air now quiet. When Zain was younger, she would rush from her school to his, pedalling furiously on the relentless circuit that made up working parenthood. Now, she basked in this time: the lull between her professional and personal lives.

If pushed, she might even admit that this was her favourite room in the world. Her antique compass and the Mercator map on the far wall were more powerful than art to her. She taught geography, but her subject was irrevocably twined with history: the straight lines of Africa, Britain's place in the centre, the international date line, Greenwich Mean Time. Was there any other image that spoke of so much?

When Salma was eleven, she made a list of four places she wanted to visit: Easter Island off the west coast of South America, Tristan da Cunha off the west coast of Africa, Baffin Island in Canada and continental Antarctica. These, to her, were the four corners of the earth and it saddened her now to realise that she hadn't got anywhere near them. Maybe next year if their finances were in better shape and Zain had sorted himself out, she and Bil could make some plans. *If.* A tiny word that puts entire lives on hold.

She sighed, wistful, and packed up for the day. On her way home, she popped into her local Tesco, adding up what she needed to make it to the weekend. In the end, she bought more than she intended and on leaving the supermarket, felt her left knee grind – an old cycling injury. Annoyed, she ordered an Uber. She hated to waste the money, but knew that she shouldn't strain it. The car arrived within minutes and she bundled inside with her shopping. It was a short drive along Horns Road and they soon turned onto Blenheim. The driver parked across from her house and Salma got out and thanked him. As she dragged the first bag towards her, a tin of beans spilled out and rolled beyond her reach.

'Sorry!' she called to the driver. 'Can you give me a minute?'

'Of course, love.' He cut the engine. 'Take your time.'

Salma bent down to retrieve the tin. Across the street, a flicker of movement caught her eye. Tom Hutton was in his front garden, throwing a yellow tennis ball from one hand to another. Casually, he approached the fence that divided his garden from hers. He paused there and glanced up and down the street, his gaze skimming right past the Uber. He whistled nonchalantly, then raised the ball and threw it into her garden. It knocked the banner from her plant pot and went skittering across the lawn. The whole thing was so quick that Salma nearly missed it. She blinked, not quite able to decode what she'd seen. Tom glanced up and down the street again. He tugged the hem of his blazer, then turned and disappeared into his house.

'You all right, love?' called the driver. 'Need some help?'

'No,' said Salma quickly. She snatched up the tin and stuffed it in her bag. 'No, thank you.' She retrieved her second bag, stalling until Tom's door was closed. Finally, she stepped back and the car moved off. There, alone in the open street, she felt uncomfortably exposed.

Almost immediately, she started to doubt what she'd seen. She had been crouched in an awkward position and flustered by the delay. Could she have misread his actions? But no. There had been something very deliberate in the way he had glanced around and carefully taken aim. A singe of fear arrived with a question. *Where the hell have we moved?*

Gripped by *What Happens in the Dark*? Don't miss the explosive and thrilling debut from Kia Abdullah

IT'S TIME TO TAKE YOUR PLACE ON THE JURY.

The victim: A sixteen-year-old girl with facial deformities, neglected by an alcoholic mother. Who accuses the boys of something unthinkable.

The defendants: Four handsome teenage boys from hardworking immigrant families. All with corroborating stories.

WHOSE SIDE WOULD YOU TAKE?

Make sure you've read the shocking and jaw-dropping courtroom drama from Kia Abdullah

ARE YOU READY TO START THIS CONVERSATION?

Kamran Hadid feels invincible. He attends Hampton school, an elite all-boys boarding school in London, he comes from a wealthy family, and he has a place at Oxford next year. The world is at his feet. And then a night of revelry leads to a drunken encounter and he must ask himself a horrific question.

With the help of assault counsellor, Zara Kaleel, Kamran reports the incident in the hopes that will be the end of it. But it's only the beginning . . .

Don't miss another gripping psychological legal crime thriller from Kia Abdullah!

ON AN ORDINARY WORKING DAY . . .
Leila Syed receives a call that cleaves her life in two.
Her brother-in-law's voice is filled with panic.
His son's nursery has called to ask where little Max is.

YOUR WORST NIGHTMARE . . .
Leila was supposed to drop Max off that morning. But she forgot.
Racing to the carpark, she grasps the horror of what she has done.

IS ABOUT TO COME TRUE . . .
What follows is an explosive, high-profile trial that will tear the family apart. But as the case progresses it becomes clear there's more to this incident than meets the eye . . .

ONE PLACE. MANY STORIES

Bold, innovative and empowering publishing.

FOLLOW US ON:

@HQStories